GOODMAN 2020

FRED PFEIL

Indiana University Press

BLOOMINGTON

Camerado, I give you my hand!
I give you my love more precious than money,
I give you myself before preaching or law;
Will you give me yourself? will you come travel with me?
Shall we stick by each other as long as we live?
—*Walt Whitman, 19th-century poet*

I never met a man I didn't like.
—*Will Rogers, 20th-century humorist*

GOODMAN
2020

Foggy Bottom, the setting of this story's first scene, is an area of central Washington where political power is presumably held: in the White House, the Executive Office Building, FBI Headquarters, etc. The Lincoln Memorial is within its environs; and at night, with the correct outdoor nocturnal pass, one can stand by the Potomac River which bounds this area to the south and west, look across, and see the natural gas burning in John Kennedy's memorial, like some barbaric tribal campfire from another age.

It is an odd zone, almost contradictory in some ways. Seat of the government and the national police, yet also a residential section, perhaps primarily so; and it is not entirely safe. Expensive gabled houses from the early nineteenth century, heavily guarded by surveillance systems, guns, electrified barbed wire, cast uneasy eyes upon their neighbors, ugly apartment buildings gone to seed, packed with shifting, volatile groups who can be heard out on the sidewalk at night plotting and laughing long after curfew hour. Yet there is a certain glamour for Washington's truly well-to-do, especially if they are young, in living adventurously for a time in one of the expensive homes—even, sometimes, making piquant, discreetly functional contact with the folks next door.

A zone of ambiguous residence, then, equivocal purpose—and misnamed. No great fogs smear its outlines into consistency at night, and it is not appreciably lower than anywhere else in the Capitol zone. So, in a funny way, it is only right that the story begin here, in an expensive Foggy Bottom duplex, with a sudden inconsistency: with Ernest Goodman, professional friend, hitting his closed fist against the face of Claudell Westerbrook, a young black man, the son of a powerful senator, and Ernest's client, the man he is paid to befriend, on this un-foggy night of May 21, 2020.

Ridiculous to him, his hand is still raised in the air. On the parqueted wood floor, Claudell has propped himself on one elbow, and regards Ernest with some fear yet, together with a nascent sardonic smile pulling at his bruised lip. The two of them are ringed by the rest of the party, perhaps thirty of them, all young and cynical. Some are giggling aloud; many smile. Many, both women and men, wear the newest accessories to clothing, ornaments made from taxidermised animal parts: fish fins like tiaras glinting silver atop hairdos, bracelets of rabbits' feet, necklaces of various kinds of eyes. Mounted on loose shapeless bodies in well-cut draping clothes, their heads press forward, eyes narrowed, assessing the fun in the scene.

One woman, wearing the older style of stone jewelry, turns away at the back of the crowd: Charlotte Partlow, Ernest Goodman's lover. She is biting down on her lower lip to keep herself from crying, lowering her head to keep anyone from seeing her expression and amusing himself by asking her what is wrong.

Ernest is aware of all this; and of the fact that his career as a professional friend, so bright just a few months, a few minutes ago, is quite probably over. His utter loss is Claudell's complete satisfaction. His hand begins to quiver in the air. A low dull pain, like the vibration of an air conditioner, thrums stupidly in his head. Yet still, instinctively, he wonders all through this long second what look is on his face.

From the next room float the sounds of a musictape, post-tonal improvs, computer generated. A few people slowly resume their dance. Ernest drops his hand. Claudell's smile appears full blown, widens as he springs to his feet.

Very sorry, he says, tapping Ernest's shoulder, speaking in a shrill mock-British voice. I take it all back. Please forgive me, won't you? Have a dance?

Ernest takes his arm. Off they whirl to all four corners of the room, in which authentic lava lights, relics of the antique '60s, bubble and glow. The rest of the party claps, laughs, turns away. Someone, a young man with small paws dangling from his ears, spots Charlotte.

Hey hey! he calls brightly to the rest of them, to anyone: Will you take a look at *this*!

But then you danced together, Charlotte says afterwards, in the trans on the way home. Doesn't that mean anything?

Ernest sighs, leans his head against hers. Their position is somewhat awkward in the hard plastic seat, but there are only five or six others on this run past curfew, and no one is watching them.

Not really, he says. It was just a way of closing out the scene. That was the hit I got off it, anyway.

This last, she knows, is added for her benefit. It is his profession. He knows what he is doing, after all.

But can't you just go by tomorrow morning and try to pick up where you left off? Try to pretend it didn't happen? she says, stroking his arm.

No, he says, gently. It doesn't work that way. The other person doesn't have to forget.

He kisses her brown hair, squeezes her hand: the signal he will not explain it, will not talk about it any more. Don't worry honey, he says. Everything'll be all right.

In another moment he has snuggled down further in the seat, leaned himself more against her, his head against her arm. She stares out the tinted trans window at the few people outside, the guards, buildings, lights smearing by. His weight makes her wonder: could he be asleep?

He could be but he is not. Already he is trying to feel calmly, rationally through what has happened, what it will mean. Starting not with what Claudell said—for that must be forgotten, instantly—but with that first frozen second afterwards, his mind returns to stem the alarm in silence, hidden from her, to stand over the disappearing possibilities. That they could have stayed in Washington, made a home here, that he could have moved up in the firm, that Billy could be proud of his new father someday, that Charlotte might be free from fear, that he could have work, that they could be safe. It is important, he knows by both instinct and training, to recognize such disappearances early, before they happen if possible. Only in that way can their effects be minimized.

34805 Maryland, says the trans, stopping noiselessly at their address.

The last guest is gone. Claudell sits in the music room, across from the sound system banked up the length of the wall; sits staring blankly down at his hands cupped around the snifter of Hennessey. How stupid, he is thinking, how pathetically typical. As if you were the hired one, the one who fucked up. As if there were any reason for you to be ashamed of your own needs. Without looking up, he fumbles a hand over for the phone beside him, on the leather stand. Utters a number which rings three times.

Westuhbruk residence, comes the drowsy yet still golden voice. Senahtah Westuhbruk hyuh.

Daddy, he says. Claudell.

Rumpled noises: his father sitting up. The click of an oldfashioned bedside lamp. He can picture the map of steep wrinkles composing itself on his father's face. Whut is it, boy, whut's wrong?

A slight altercation with my friend Ernest, Papa, says Claudell, still caught between his pain and blithe indifference, pronouncing *Papa* in the French style. He lost his head, I'm afraid. It came to blows.

Tuhn on yuh screen, says the Senator. Lemme see.

Claudell presses a pink button at the base of his own viewscreen, points at his bruised lips, giggling. Right in the kisser, he says, smack in the puss, square in the mug—

Aw raht, awl raht, says his father. Thass enuff, boy, ahm tahd. You know whut tahm it is? Gawd damn neah fuh thuhty!

Claudell's sore cracked mouth twists into something even uglier. I *had* thought, he sniffs, you'd want to know right away.

Sound of the Senator's bulk shifting; sound of the Senator heaving a solemn gust of air. Suhtenly suhtenly, he says. Yuh uhlahcruhty gladdens mah haht. Ah'll jes cahl up that awgahnahzashun fust thing tumorruh.

And that's the end of Ernest, right Daddy?

As fah as we ah concerned at any rate, that is thuh end, boy, thas raht.

Thanks, Daddy, Claudell says, jabbing the screen button out.

Naht, deyuh chile, says his chuckling father, laying on thick as ever the white southern accent, the plantation owner shtick that has amused his constituents on- and off-screen for fifteen years; against which Claudell has developed his own accents, primarily British and French.

Now, still smiling, snifter light in his hand, Claudell walks over to the high french windows, throws one open. On the lawn below the guard wheels and looks up, raises his machine gun halfway to his shoulder. Claudell raises his glass, laughs down at the white face but then looks quickly away before the voice within him grows any louder or more distinct. *I did not mean to do this*, saying it to his friend, purchased or not. *I did not mean to do this to you.*

Across the street, lit bluegrey with the reflection from the spotlights on his house, the buildings seem to hang limp, disembodied, in the windless air. He looks on at the sight until the voice has died away and he has started to hum, then softly sing along with the sound system continuing behind him:

> *Mick-key Mouse . . .*
> *Mick-key Mouse . . .*

Now he feels better; feels okay again, in fact.

His father and mother both are bald, but their skin is unblemished, unwrinkled, translucent, as they direct him around the house and farm-buildings, glowing iridescently. They are telling him something though their mouths do not move; they are telling him where he lived, what he did, but not the way he remembers it happening, another way so that none of what he thought happened was real, was true. But even in the dream he does not know, cannot hear what they say.

Beside him the bed lies open, empty. Charlotte sits in a vinyl armchair across the room. One hand carries a joint rather clumsily back and forth from her mouth, one circles the nipple of a breast; her eyes are on his sleeping figure with an expression she would not recognize as hers, the same as a workingclass wife's or mother's a century or more ago: the same assessment and anxiety, the same helpless endless calculation with no hope of a final sum.

In the next room, on a clever transparent trapezoidal bed folded out from a piece of Japanese origamiesque sculpture which adorns the front room during the day, sleeps her four-year-old son, Billy Partlow. He is sweating in his sleep, a strand of carrot hair stuck to his brow. His arms curl up before his face like paws or fronds. He makes a soft unknowable dreaming noise. He dreams he is rolling down, falling down a wonderful frightening giant green hill.

Meanwhile the plan grows, messages move, on paper, through satellite, over laserbeams, on tape. The Senator's call to the Washington office of the National Acquaintance Services of America (NASA) engenders a host of other messages traveling within that system, between that system and other systems (e.g. GuardAll Inc.), and between those systems and the system of management which presides over all of them, OMNICO Inc., a trans- or multinational conglomerate. These messages, and the actions that proceed from them, both so various that it would be impossible to follow them all out completely, are in effect themselves responses to the intention around which they are grouped, i.e. the stated desire of the head executive officer of OMNICO to acquire a reliable trustworthy friend, a known and tested quantity. It is that desire they are primarily intended to satisfy. Yet, like all messages and human actions, like any dream, they begin before and go beyond it too.

A clumsy arrangement: few people have jobs, most work has been automated and/or sent overseas. Yet multinationals still need many if not most of us as part of the huge market they must keep hold of to survive and expand. They cannot make enough by selling their products from one subsidiary to another, or from corporation to corporation, or by getting in on the little non-nuclear wars that flare up here and there from time to time.

So corporate profits and the incomes of those with jobs are heavily taxed by the U.S. government, and the tax money flows through an administrative strainer to the people at Claudell's party, and to the folks on the streets beyond his house, and to the people in the apartment building in which Charlotte sits staring at Ernest's face. So that they can buy Italian shoes; Japanese couches; full-wall videophones; imitation taxidermised animal parts manufactured in Hong Kong.

But in such neighborhoods it sometimes happens that a fine old brownstone caves in suddenly like a sick old person's face; or the people in the upstairs apartment set fire to their own rooms and take off. People—good people, people who've always had enough—suddenly start shooting junk, or taking other newer chemicals (e.g. "hotzie") that bring immediate ecstasy at the cost of severe long-term damage. Someone finds a stain on a blouse bought in a Bloomingdale's, and the whole mall gets pulled apart, guards come, people get torched down.

Appropriate measures have been taken to keep the lid on this queasiness, these random outbursts: new security regulations, pass restrictions and curfews, more police far better equipped. But it is a new, odd poverty and hard to control, this pointlessness; famine of purpose; drought of need.

Next morning, following the phonecall he knew would come, Ernest chooses a muted brown robe to wear to lunch with T.D., his old trainer, whom the company has chosen to deal with him, and arrives fifteen minutes early for the appointment. But T.D., in a red tunic, is already there and seated, waiting for him, his hairy fingers twiddling the stick in his manhattan glass.

I still can't believe it, he says. Spent the whole morning feeding it back to myself and still can't make it compute. What the hell did you think you were doing?

I didn't think at all, says Ernest, carefully expunging the dread from his face and voice, closely watching T.D. I wasn't up to anything, he says. I can't believe it either, quite.

T.D. narrows his eyes furiously on him, then sighs. Well, the Senator's called all the way to the top, so that's where the shit's coming from. Then suddenly, obscenely, his dark face twists in rage and lunges forward: And you know what *that* means, baby? That makes you the first blot on the whole enterprise, the first official black sheep—eyes flashing fingers waving in the air—and *me* your trainer. And that is just fucking great.

But already Ernest can smell the act. The speech has gone on too long, T.D.'s last sentence reeling out within easy hearing range of the approaching waitress. The T.D. who trained him would never lose control like this, never says a *fuck* without knowing exactly how it will be heard and by whom. He has said it now in front of the waitress to show Ernest he is Distraught, Out of Control. Why, Ernest asks himself, pretending to range his eye once more down the list of luncheon entrees, does T.D. want me to think that?

Because he wants you to feel sorry for him, give him something? Make some statement to the effect that he is blameless, not responsible, save his ass?

BLT on toasted rye, iced tea, he says, raising his head to the waitress and smiling: Is the bacon real?

No sir, she smiles in return. Textured vegetable protein, low cholesterol—

Hmm, Ernest says, still mulling: Well, skip it. Bring me the fruit and cheese plate.

Only when the waitress turns does he look back at T.D.'s stormy face. So, he says levelly. Anything I can do to keep the shit from coming down on you?

He uses the word *shit* deliberately, to match T.D.'s diction: a professional habit almost reflex by now, even when the motivation for the model behavior is unknown. Could T.D. be doing Out-of-Control to show how upset he actually is? He is getting older, after all. He is Jewish. And an old Jew is not going to last forever in an organization as innately and properly conservative as NASA, given the fact that even Jews themselves and the most vociferous blacks want young caucasians for their friends, for reasons far deeper than spite. So is that it? Is it real fear?

But now T.D. is leaning his face forward again, twisting his brow and eyes into a grimace of incipient hysteria. *Goodman*, he says, you don't seem to realize the situation you're in. Nobody, at least officially, has ever struck a client before in the history of this business. You know what I mean? He shakes his head, makes a little incredulous laugh: I mean, you're the worst thing that ever happened, *ever*, to the National Acquaintance Services. I mean right now you could cut your throat for me and it wouldn't make a goddamn bit of difference to the folks upstairs. You're already a dead man as far as they're concerned. They wish to hell you'd never been born.

Still, why this excess, this run-on? Ernest wonders. What the hell does he want?

The waitress arrives with T.D.'s caesar salad, Ernest's fruit and cheese plate. T.D. holds his wild smile and continues to talk through her arms setting down the plates. And the thing is, he splutters, the *really* incredible thing is, you've fucked up *so* much I think my job's *safe*. I mean, I don't believe anybody will *dream* of blaming me, it'd be like—

So okay, T.D., Ernest says, calmvoiced. What do they want me to do?

T.D. lets his fork drop holding half a boiled egg, and begins to talk in a whisper. They're worried about company rep, he says. Apparently this hasn't leaked out yet, and they think they can keep the Senator and his kid shut up. But that leaves you the hot one, the one unknown quantity. So you've got to go. All we want you to do is disappear, get out of Washington, keep your mouth shut. In exchange, we'll let you set up so you can be a Friend on your own hook. We'll get you your own office in another place—say San Francisco—send you referrals—

So I still need NASA even when I don't work for them any more, says Ernest blandly. So I have to keep the deal. Very nice.

Listen, T.D. says, you want to work? You want a job, or you want to go live with the slugs?

A three-beat pause; Ernest makes his face stay blank.

Listen Ernie, T.D. says in a softened, wheedling tone, it's a good deal, the best you can get. What else you know how to do, huh? I'll make sure you get enough business, I promise you Ernie. Ernie, you gotta do what I'm telling you. I'm in trouble Ernie, my job depends—

Charlotte and Billy, Ernest says. They come too.

You'll fly out together! T.D. says, wildeyed, waving his fork. Relocate in San Fran, in a beautiful place by the end of the week! Save my job, Ernie, he says, beginning to cry, his face darkening to a tomato shade: I'm pleading with you. You won't get a better deal!

For something to do, a gesture, Ernest puts another chunk of apple in his mouth, makes himself chew it though it tastes like plastic foam, like nothing. This much, this far, and still you can't tell what the act is, what's behind it. But what other choice do you have? At least this way, like T.D. says, you still have a job; whatever the real reason behind it is. What other choice do you have?

All right, he says. I'll go.

T.D. draws a long shaky breath and stops crying. You won't regret it, Ernie, he says, I promise you. I'll get the tickets to you this afternoon, for tonight. Can you be ready?

Don't waste any time, do you? says Ernest, smiling.

No, says T.D., smiling back. Not when it's a matter of the rep.

We'll be ready, he says.

T.D. nods, gives him a short firm chin-up smile which suddenly checks itself, turns into nervous wetting of his lips.

Ernie, he says. I can't help myself, I have to ask. Ernie, you were one of the best I ever supervised, you can befriend like nobody else I've ever seen just coming in, *nothing* can stop you. Ernie, what did the son of a bitch *say?*

Seems to me that's what I'm never supposed to tell, Ernest says. Isn't that what you guys just bought?

T.D.'s brown eyes sparkle brightly as he laughs out loud, heartily, and bends back down over his plate, shaking his head as he jabs into his salad again, stuffs a green wad in his mouth.

I always said, I always will say you were one of the best, he says to Ernest who is even now instinctively panning his eyes over the features of the other diners in this select metallic restaurant by the river, the classic old Watergate.

One month later, in his new office on the edge of San Francisco's financial district, next to the famous TransAm pyramid, Ernest is sitting at his desk, staring without focus at the recessed light fixtures above him and forward a little—the ones that would illumine the first person to whom he could offer his services, his hand. He is thinking about what T.D. said the last time they saw each other, at lunch at the Watergate. He is thinking about the word *slugs*.

2

By now there is no name for the huge oppressed class whose only task is to consume; almost no one thinks of social class at all. So *slug* keeps reappearing, drifting into his mind as he sits at his desk killing time. Slugs. Somehow he never thought about it just that way before. Slug.

The taps come so soft he first thinks he has imagined them; but they repeat. His heart flies around in his chest as he calls forth his voice.

The person who whips through the doorway seems to be not more than four and a half feet tall from his battered black boots to the Budweiser hat that flips off his wavy black hair into his hand, fast and smooth as jujitsu.

You Goodman, right? Acquaintance man? Thees the right place, hah?

Ernest's eyes sweep the man's round olive face—narrowed eyes, drooping moustache, wide frowning mouth—and squint tensely back.

Right place? Maybe. Name's Goodman, anyway. Acquaintance man. You?

The chicano's arms hang action-ready at his sides. Paco Ramos ees what I am called.

Ernest leans back in his chair, throws out his legs, plops his feet on the desk Henry Fonda style, imperturbable. Beckons toward the padded chair across the desk: Well, Mr. Paco Ramos, what can I do for you?

Paco approaches; sits staring a long time into his steeled face. Then kicks his boot against the desk's imitation wood front, hard.

What ees thees sheet weeth the desk? You want to make me feel like I comeeng to you for a job or what?

It is nothing, he says through flattened lips. Almost says *eet* for *it* and *ees* for *is*. It's just the way it came.

You ought to change eet then. Slowly his round head turns, glaring at the entire room. When he looks back again at Ernest, his smile is a swift flash of teeth: You won to smoke a number?

Why not, he says, turning his hands palm up, curling a corner of a lip.

Paco bends over, reaches into a black boot, pulls up a bag. Soon they are passing a fat joint, some sort of strong homegrown, back and forth across the desk. Wisps of blue smoke curl past the expressionist prints you and Charlotte picked to warm the room. San Francisco sunlight spills onto the carpeted floor like some light cooking oil . . . safflower? Can NASA, T.D., have referred this guy to you?

So, he says, smiling brilliantly, hitting the record button under the desk with his knee: What brings you here?

Paco exhales; his brown eyes stay opaque. I get around. I hear thengs. Somebody tell me you was new in town, what you do. You make frens for money, right?

Ernest flips him the grin again. You could put it like that.

The wide mouth moves into something close to a snarl. You theenk you could be my fren?

He leaves a pause, then shrugs. Who knows? I don't know anything about you yet. Like who referred you, for starters.

Paco laughs mirthlessly, slaps his hat against his hand. Referred? he says. What ees referred? I know thees city like vens ronneeng blood through me. Understan? I am een a certain place at a certain time and somebody tell me, Hey, new hustle from the east office off Montgomery, do thees fren theng. I don't remember who, where. Thass how I stay alive and well, understan?

Okay, he says. So what is your hustle then?

Oh, Paco says, smiling lightly, widely at last, I don specialize. I do all deeferent thengs.

He fades his own grin. You get me in any trouble with the law and I'm all through, you know that.

The short man's face, voice, chill with pride as he stands and redons his beerhat: I keep you out of trouble like I keep myself. And I can pay what you ask, eef you can be a true fren. You come to my house tonight at eight, 2738 Noe Street in Noe Valley. We talk more then.

All right, says Ernest, standing too. Thanks for the joint, he says as they shake hands over the desk. Went down real nice.

Paco scans Ernest's face, nods, wheels and heads for the door, a little round stub. A little round stub of a chicano crook, with strong home-grown in his boot.

So how come you want me to be your friend?

Paco pivots, small hands still ready at his sides. I come een to see the hustle. I stay because I like your style. I weel see you tonight, at eight.

Paco Ramos walks out of the building into the light crisp breeziness of the sunny street; turns right into a skyscraper's shroud of shade on Sansom where for two blocks he struts bandylegged in his loose trousers, throwing superior leering glances left and right at the corporate buildings around. A long black limousine rotocar pulls suddenly out of the traffic choking the street (cars are permitted in the financial district). Paco steps into the back seat. The car pulls back out, horn blaring, and glides away.

Ernest stares at the TransAm white tower against the blue enamel sky with its first smoke of fog; stares and listens to the tape play back the scene. This one too will want to get his digs in at first. Demeaning, demeaned; the classic first reaction to get past. Only more so in this case because of the whole racial-cultural thing, which is probably what that laid-on accent is about. Only thing to do is hang loose, wait and see what abuse he hands out—that, and hope the guy can actually pay. Playback over, the tape's hiss barely audible; a few office lights glow on in the TransAm. So, he wonders, quietly waiting—that all for now?

Billy and Roger, the other kid in the neighborhood, have been having races halfway the length of the sidewalk, as far as the house of the mean rednosed man; and Billy will stop while the other boy runs on; will look up at those same fog plumes, startled as if by something he knew but forgot. When were they before: in a dream, in Washington, D.C., here in this new place? Where do they make you think of? He does not, will not know; the questions splash down over him, he rears forward down the known safe street after his friend.

Charlotte comes out on the old wooden landing of the shabby refurbished apartment house and looks down the street to see where Billy is, if everything is all right. The clean fading light illumines childlike freckles on her own face and neck, until she leaves the mottled sunlight and crisp air, goes back inside.

Imagine the movements of any four people through the city. Imagine the lines formed by their movements, the shapes that result when those lines are linked up. If it is true that really, strictly speaking, relations stop nowhere, our alternatives are paranoia or a terribly demanding love.

She was born and raised in one of the last pockets of what, before the rapid industrial and urban shifts of the '60s, '70s and '80s, had been called the Deep South, her family among the oldest and most patrician in Mississippi, part of a class which despite its corruption and cruelty was too unproductive and inefficient to survive. Yet its residual hold over the land and the minds of the land's inhabitants was still such that even at the time of her birth, in 1994, her father was still a young aristocratically handsome state senator, a man widely respected, even beloved by his backwater redneck constituents and their local pols, hated and despised only by his lovely alcoholic wife. Entertaining no specific memories of this earliest time, Charlotte can nonetheless close her eyes and feel the excitement drifting smokelike along the shining endless corridors, the sweet-sour tangy odor of her father's eau de cologne impossibly melding with the gilt curlicues of the Senate Chamber itself. But her father, that strong sunny smiling man, refused to make his peace with the new order; he spoke against rampant unchecked development as his father had against civil rights, in the name of a tarnished pastoralism which itself had never been more than a grotesque mockery at best in the dead sunstruck towns and stunted woods of the upstate counties he served. Such intransigence—so ridiculous, so hopelessly self-deceived—virtually guaranteed he would be struck down himself in the last purging wave of scandals to sweep the state clean of the old peckerwood politics of the gladhand and open bribe, making way for the multinationals and their lobbyists. Publicly censured in the Senate one spring, he was defeated for re-election in the fall; and Charlotte grew up watching his face grow puffy and pallid with alcohol (although his drinking was never like her mother's: never furiously silent, patient, exhaustive, methodical as injections) and ever more frenzied deals. He bartered his good name for pitiful messes of cash, lent it in support of quixotic corrupt schemes to sustain tiny statewide monopolies on lumber and sugar and cotton, to keep them from the conglomerates. He died in a senseless small-plane crash outside Biloxi in her senior year at Randolph Macon, and

Charlotte thought she would go out of her mind with grief. Yet it was her mother who, one week after the funeral, had to be restrained, then institutionalized. The family fortune was gone by the time she finally succeeded, four years later, and was found hanging in her room from her husband's wide black leather belt.

He leaves the viewscreen off; that way they will both be more comfortable.

Hey T.D., he says. It's Ernie.

Ernie—T.D. says. Oh, Ernie, right. Well hey kid, what's up?

You run a call through NASA to the FBI for me still?

I guess so. Sure. What's the name?

Ramos, Paco. That's last name first.

You don't have a government i.d. number on him?

Nope. Sorry.

Okay. I'll get back to you.

And does in fifteen minutes, sounding more jovial. Paco Ramos has been convicted on two counts of car theft (back when there were cars), three of assault and battery, has served a total of five years in a behaviorist prison in the South Bay. Arrested but not tried on two counts of grand larceny, one of pushing hotzie. Has a black belt in karate and is considered armed and dangerous whenever the police want him to be. His rights to all passes beyond daytime work have been revoked for a four-year period which is not yet half up. He is married, with children. He is thirty-six years old.

Jesus Christ, T.D. says when he is finished running it down. Where'd you pick up this one?

Don't laugh, T.D., Ernest says. Thanks to all that nice business you been bouncing my way, I think this guy's gonna be my first client.

Three months after her mother's death she marries the young man she has dated stormily for three years, a Kentuckian from the companion college of Washington and Lee with her father's good manners and looks. She wants to have children, a home and family—an increasingly eccentric and difficult task. But less than a year after Billy is born, her husband Randall begins to disintegrate. He has no power, he cannot work, there is no place for him or his mythology of magnolia arête in the consumer world. So despite Freudian, Jungian, Gestalt, Skinnerian, TA, scientology, and all the other methods of personality retrieval finally he too is sent away to an institution, one of the new Regroove Centers springing up every-where. When he returns six months later, his face is riven with fresh lines, his charm is lost. He wants and gets a quick divorce, then suddenly takes off for Chile and a job with ITT, leaving her in Washington with Billy, not knowing who she is or what she wants or where she belongs. But she still knows superficially a few people there through the shredded grandeur of her father's name—the Estovers, the faded Longs and Byrds—and is occasionally invited to fill out the edges of the company at a small-scale political fete. So it is that on a given drizzly November night she meets Ernest Goodman at a diplomatic dinner, accompanying a young attache. They sit across from each other during the meal; she makes polite con-versation, tells him stories of the Old South he seems to enjoy. Afterwards she finds herself thinking of him out of all proportion to the little that passed between them, growing unaccountably excited at the memory of his bland good looks. Two weeks later, through her connections, she hunts down his address and calls him up, amazed at her temerity. This time they go to bed and become lovers. He is gentle in ways that remind her of her father but without her father's violence and ambition; in bed he is tender, even clinging at times. Both of them are dazed, at times embarrassed at the intensity of this love, of their desire to go on and on, be a family, husband wife son. Neither thinks of the relationship between this desire and the dead sweetstinking past behind her, or between their life together and his work. For her there is only this love, only Ernest and Billy, lover and son, out there between her and the pillow coming down over her face.

Late afternoon, Ernest back home. As he talks Billy keeps running in and out, throwing himself at them, being a pest. He is standing by her chair now, picking and pulling at the short wavy hair above her ears.

That's great! she says to Ernest. That's really—Billy, what in the world are you doing?

The boy stares down at the chair's chromium arm. Bothering you.

She lowers to his pouting face. Why?

His head droops lower yet, disconsolate. Because I don't have anybody to play with. And you won't let me go outside.

I'm sorry, she says. She sets down the stinger she has been sipping from, and touches his arm. You know you need a pass to be outside by yourself now, honey, and you're still too little to get one, and Ernest and I are talking about important things. Can't you amuse yourself for a minute? What about your tapes?

The enormous boredom of a child in a world of dead things. I *heard* the tapes, he says, his mouth trembling. I can't a-muse myself.

Both of them smile at the careful new way Billy has to say the word. Billy, Ernest says softly, I'll tell you what. You go on and watch the screen or listen to your tapes for just a little while more and then I'll be in and we'll make a painting or something before dinner, all right?

Already he is coming to understand that his relationships are founded, composed of a series of deals: this the best you can get?

All right, he says, still snuffling for form's sake; and prances away.

Do you really think it's great? Ernest says, looking back at her. You don't like it, do you.

She pauses, smiling, in the act of picking up her glass again. In the world she knows, it is not a good sign when men talk much about their work; nor does he, usually.

Paco Ramos is married to a small dark Mexican woman who has borne him seven children and kept the house and fixed the meals and lied for him to the police innumerable times. I could tell you her name but it would not matter; it is so immaterial to what she has to be that it is very rarely used, even by Paco, even by herself.

She has dished up the spicy stew in bowls for Paco, the other men, and the women the men brought with them. She herself will eat later when she clears the food away, picking from the dishes and the pot. When she has served them, she sits at the table and watches them eat and listens to everything she can catch of the English Paco and the men are saying to each other, all their plans, and the few comments of the one woman in the bright whore's clothes with her mouth painted in a red gash who says something in English once that makes Paco's eyes crinkle, makes him shout his largest laugh, while she keeps her own face blank as a dog's and does not look at anyone except secretly, from the corners of her eyes, and does not speak herself until the children swarm in, shouting, laughing, wanting something, and she chases them out with a harsh short burst of threats.

This is Paco's wife.

The thing is, Ernest says, rubbing his forehead, NASA's not lifting a finger for me, nothing's coming in, you know? And I think it might be a real growth assignment for me. He's a new type for sure, you know?

He is talking to himself, they both know it. Just as they both know the guy as a chicano has neither power nor prestige. If it makes Ernest happy, working again, fine with her. Besides, what would happen if she ever really disagreed, if she ever had to ask him to do something against his will?

So her smile softens into a self-effacing grin, confession of sweet ignorance accompanied with a small shrug. Sounds interesting to me, she says. Very interesting.

Well it is, says Ernest smiling back just as strong and relieved as she wants him to; and continues to speak as she stands, crosses to switch on the egg-shaped lamp beside the couch, nestles down at his side.

And don't forget the money, he is saying, laughing, shaking his head: For a while there I was beginning to think pretty soon we'd have to go live with the slugs.

She looks up into his brown eyes. Slugs? she says. Well, I guess you better do it then, huh?

Again he laughs that same easy laugh; and then they kiss.

Because of the people who are here tonight Paco's wife has served a paella, a rich stew of saffron-spiced seafood and vegetables on rice that must be started a day in advance. It is good, but certainly no better than the frozen stuff you can buy off the screen. Industrial cooking and freezing techniques have so advanced in this country, the cuisines of the world have been so impeccably studied and removed from their locales, that it is possible to buy a frozen dinner which, when subjected to a few seconds worth of radarwaves, becomes an easy exotic treat.

So Charlotte "cooks" coq au vin and selected French vegetables for Ernest, a small bland cheese enchilada and some refried beans for Billy, an Indonesian rijsttafel for herself, as Billy slaps a drawing on the kitchen table and looks triumphantly up. What do you think this is of?

Ernest sets their glasses at their places on the table and peers down. On the right border a bank or cliff of green, black, swarming with dirty yellow worms; tangle of blobby shapes, all colors in the middle, lines streaming out of them; on the left a large patch of blue. Sometimes he wonders if he isn't being tested, or worse—baited, trapped. But not when he looks back at the pure gaze coming up at him, arms held in tight as wings against the ribs; then he only wishes that the picture looked like something, anything, he could make out.

He pokes a finger at the blue; if it were sky it'd be on top. Is that water?

Billy nods. A pond, he says, and points: And all of them are running in it to get wet.

Charlotte crosses to the table with their dinners, fresh-hot from the radar: Put your colors up now, time to eat.

Why do they want to get wet? Ernest says. Who are they?

Billy purses his lips; his fingers trace the blobby shapes. There's a lion— mother wolf—elephant—

Charlotte stops beside Ernest and looks down, one smoking meal still in hand. The puzzlement on her face, too, makes him feel somewhat relieved.

And what's the green and yellow, she says, this over here?

That's the jungle, Billy says, watching them both closely, eyebrows raised. It's on fire, see. So the animals all have to run in the water and stay cool and get away.

And he looks up often as he eats, at the two of them talking. He watches them closely, without listening to what they say, or their expressions. He does not think of them having expressions. Their faces are who they are. His own face stays hooded, watching them, waiting to see who Ernest is to his mother, who she is to him, who that means they both are to him. He has been watching them this way ever since Ernest came, watching and waiting to know, to be who he is too. He watches them across the table, him and her. He sees the way their faces change.

When the phone rings Paco starts to rise from his chair, but is abruptly motioned down by one of the others, a tall lean young man with a deeply lined face.

That'll be for me, he says.

Paco's hauteur collapses; pouting, he turns to his wife. Get up and make sure the children are out of the room so this man will not be disturbed, he says in Spanish to his wife.

So she scuffles ahead of the man down the hall, though she knows all the children are outside.

The man pays no attention to her, picks up the receiver on the third ring. Old model, screenless; just as well.

Yeah?

Control Three, says the man at the GuardAll substation. Danny, how are you? Everything set?

Sure. Fine.

Okay. A little nervous, scared of messing up. The man at Paco's laughs. But the poor shit likes it too—you know, the whole Zorro routine.

The other end chuckles back. Well, it won't do any harm for him to think he's the one in danger. And keep hitting him with what a big step he's taking, and how much we all appreciate it, all that shit—

The man's mouth stretches toward the back of his head as though jerked by wires. Yeah, he says, okay, great.

All right. Talk to you later.

Later.

Their voices have no tone, their faces no expressions; their conversation can be recorded but not described. When the man returns to the table, Paco is telling a loud filthy joke in Spanish to disguise his fear, and laughing throughout the telling, drawing his lips back over brown gums, ruined teeth. When the man enters Paco stops, frightened at the way the man looks through him.

Well, the man says, it's about time. We'll go over it once more and then take positions, all right? But it is not really a question.

When the dishes are cleared away she comes out too, and stands on the porch with the door ajar behind her, letting out a golden pool of light. The short fat guard on their corner looks up from Ernest's pass and waves to her. She waves back and smiles as Ernest and Billy turn too.

Ready? Ernest says as they crouch down.

Billy nods, his face furiously set.

Go!

The fog is so thick that halfway down the block they disappear into the grey, except for Billy's laughter floating back. While they are gone she rubs her arms against the chill. Nice going! she yells when they return. Boy, you two sure can run fast!

Okay son, Ernest says after four times up and down the block, pacing it so the boy wins by a step or two. It's time for me to go.

Billy's laughter stops. I don't want to go in, he says, almost crying. I'm not your son.

Billy, she calls. It's time now, honey, come on.

He cries a little but lets himself be led up to the door. They wait until he has gone inside before embracing.

I might be late, Ernest says. Don't wait up.

She goes inside but stays in the front room where Billy sleeps, where she can see him standing on the corner next to the guard, hear the guard's jovial laugh, until the white oscillating translight bores a hole through the fog and the guard beams the cornerbox open with his laserkey and trips the passengerstop, and Ernest, waving, gets on. Then she goes back in to the apartment to the screenroom, where Billy is watching a cop show.

There is a moment when the change happens, the change he knows and does not know whenever he goes to work. Before it happens he is— who? Himself. Ernest. Me. After it happens he is a man at work, a professional friend. When does it happen? When he releases her, when he makes the fat guard laugh, watches the trans approach, as the doors open and he steps up into it, as he waves automatically, without seeing her in the window, without knowing or wondering whether she is still there? When does the change happen? How is it faces change in this way?

The trans heads south, past neighborhoods and malls, down the west edge of the Mission District with its restored Eastlake row houses, enclaves for young corporates; sudden increase in street lighting, number of guards. Then, as the trans rolls into Noe Valley, a decline in both. Here and there some lighted signs adorn the fronts of seedy buildings: stores, bars, night-clubs, old stuff with small groups of people, chicanos mostly, clustered on the street. If T.D. and the rest of them at NASA could see you now, somewhere in a neighborhood like this . . . But at least you're working again.

The trans stops at a dark empty corner. Electric voice intones: Twenty seven thirty eight Noe to your right as you step off, this vehicle is on cross street Church, if you need assistance call—

He is not listening and, once out on the street, has to check the house numbers flaking away with the paint. Which way? Up the bluestruck hill to the right, houses pressed together like snaggled teeth, streetlight again quite clear on top? When did the trans cross over out of the fog?

Loud raucous laughter hurtling hooplike down the street as he starts to walk up, loud spicy music from somewhere, thick rhythms of drums. Always the hardest moment to hold, just before the time, your heart races, tries to pull your mind along, make you construct identity presume behavior of the other, sure to be wrong because premature. Remember the greats, Krishnamurti and the others from back in school. Stay in the present, let the present equal all time. Look downhill to past, uphill to future, and in your incompleteness and desire you will manufacture a self, deluded self; stay fully in the present and have none. Experience only the music, footfalls, quickened vigor of your breath.

Two seven three eight Noe, many-gabled double apartment house jagging out from the side of the hill, Paco's on the left the site of the noise. People sitting on windowsills, crammed in doorways, wriggling shapes inside all cast in red light, all chicanos sleek in bright cheap clothes, eyes flitting over him without interest or recognition letting him go again.

Head lowered slightly, he smiles, starts moving toward the door: then, miraculously, Paco has popped through the crowd in flowered shirt and shorts, beaming, slapping his arm: Hey mi amigo, I ask some people over to take a look at you themself tonight, hah, whole lot of my people like one beeg family hah? he laughs and a huge mustachioed hooknosed man in the doorway looks up from the face of the woman crushed against him in the red light and laughs too.

So they all here to see you, Paco says, come on eenside.

He pushes his way past the hooknosed man after Paco into the room at the end of the hallway, yellow scuffed walls with people standing sitting butted up against the heavy scarred table in the center, under layers of smoke from all the joints. From the next room the roar of Mexican moog stuff is so great he has to tip his head to catch what the orangefaced pockmarked woman mumbles from where she leans against the yellow wall as Paco shouts with glee plucking his robe *Hey what you leesten for anyway you can't tell what you heer—*

He raises his eyebrows, shakes his head, closemouthed grin. The smoke litters his mind, stings his eyes, makes molecules swim from the walls, bottles, joints, cigarettes, syringes on the tabletop. Paco reaches up and out, grabs another woman with wide tracks of lipstick across her mouth, shouts something leering at him, plunges into the crowd leading into the next room where the tinny moog music and the red light seem to be coming from. He follows, and finds a place along the cracked plaster back in the red crush and smiles the one he knows now Paco wants, the tough whipped smile of one too hip not to know he's second best, turning the smile up more whenever Paco's shining eyes appear out of the lurching crowd, keeping his mind relaxed and empty until Paco works his way through the hunched sweating bodies to him again.

Haveeng fun, amigo?

Twitch eyebrows. Keep the beaten smile on; soon it will be habituated, reflex.

I'm just fine, he says.

Paco searches his face, looks satisfied. Okay, let me go take thees heavy pees I got. Then we talk een the back.

In the next room a couple lies sprawled out on the table, half their clothes off; a few men whisper in the hall. Away from the music and the red light everything seems quiet, distant. He and Paco move like moonwalkers back through the kitchen scattered round with crusted pots and pans. Off to the right is a large room with little heaps in blankets—Paco's kids, sleeping?—on the floor. Straight ahead, through the open door, is the bathroom with a gaunt cleanshaven young chicano rocking on the john, flannel shirt rolled up the left arm, spike still dangling from the hanging right hand.

Hey man, says Paco, get the fuck out of here.

When the junkie's eyes find them, he totters up and wobbles past, mumbling: Hey sorry man.

Ernest follows him out with cold eyes, figuring that is what Paco wants. When the junkie gets out to the hall someone pushes him and laughs. Nobody likes junkies here. Nobody guesses heroin will soon be legalized.

Paco buttons up, hitches his pants, grunts, looks at Ernest with curiously veiled eyes: Okay. Now we go een here, get the money feeger out and talk hah?

Ernest nods silently briskly back; and is still considering the meaning of that last mysterious look as he follows him one last time into a room, the bedroom, where the children lie in heaps on the floor, the woman—Paco's wife—lies in a bed, and his eyes at last begin to take in the blood pooling out from the net of cuts on her face, from the skulls of the children in heaps on the floor, and Paco ahead of him begins to scream.

Then the music from the next room stops; a siren matches Paco's cry. The siren is quite near—perhaps outside? Has this really happened? Are they all dead? From the place he occupies in the room he feels he can see everything, the dancers in the kitchen rammed together mambo line jamming out the back, men in grey uniforms, no doubt police? crashing windows in, Paco s large yellow teeth screaming wide still, the blood spreading over the bedroom floor across the woman's face.

He holds out his hand to Paco. For support or to get him to move? In character or out? When the uniformed men come, they have to pick the hands apart to take Paco away, along with the bodies. Leaving Ernest in the middle of the bloody empty room with the look he chose for Paco still stuck on his face.

This particular OMNICO building is modeled after Le Corbusier's brutalist constructions: blank mammoth concrete facing, slits for windows, four short thick outraged pilotis for its support. Deliberate violation of the land it stands on, the city around it.

Inside, high up, the room is a rectangle, its sides twice as long as its ends. On the long wall facing out four slits admit four strips of light, whose effect on the room is canceled by the even intense white issuing from the ceiling. The floor and the four walls are solid puce, and enclose a rectangular table cut from black rock and chairs of black plastic and steel, each set with sharpened pencil, yellow pad, and man.

Not all the men are white; one is black, one Chinese, one Spanish or South American. But they are all still dressed in dark conservative suits; and one of them is speaking, slowly, clearly, using the same dull words. The receptivity of those in Congress in a position to lend force and momentum to the passage of the proposed legislation gives us reasonable reassurance that we can move decisively ahead . . .

He goes on; it is useless to follow him. Not just because his words are so deadening but because you already know the sound of it, the language that moves us on the grid; just as all of them at the table know what is being said, what will be said. Except for the man at the head of the table: what he knows, what he will say.

Okay, all right, he says evenly, suddenly. How fast can Westerbrook and Sampson get it through? When can we actually go into production on this thing?

His hand presses her sternum. She is above him, astride, her knees grinding the bed. Their chests are wet, slick. Here you must imagine, we cannot remember this, bring it back. His penis in her vagina. As if they were both laughing, though her mouth is open shocking as a fresh wound, his face as if burnt. You would know they were not hurt, are in that place where only their desire has ever happened to them and always is growing and always met with this one answer, asks itself again. What I want to do is twist the words break the pattern reach through break the pattern to find fucking: fucking. Here; now; you; you; in. It is the inadequacy of the words inapplicability of sentences noun verb object coalesce makes me want to use violent she explodes he is driven in spiked. A cry from one of them. He comes. She comes. You can imagine this.

The man who was speaking blinks and starts again. I think, he says, passage time will be considerably expedited by the sponsorship of Senator Westerbrook, given his—uh—ethnic origins and the traditional association of the, ahm, substance with black communities and cultures.
  Richard, says the man at the head of the table, weighting the words: Just tell us how long.
  Richard's eyes fly up as if looking at his brain. Maybe six months, maybe a year, he says. Westerbrook says he can't say for sure.
  We can get it faster than that, the man says softly. He taps his fingers twice on the stone tabletop. We can get that thing through the Senate in a week, Westerbrook's a fool. Get his name off it, start cutting him out, get somebody else on it.

Charlotte slides falls down and Ernest's face hangs blank beside hers, her shadows of hair. She stirs against him, nestles her head against his smooth neck, rolls her legs together to keep his sliding sperm in; it and the warm waves that fan up her back. She shuts her eyes.
  Another peace edged with a slight alarm, faint acridness of burning leaves on a gold day. On the front lawn of the old house in Tuscaloosa yardmen stroke them into heaps and light them up. Both young and tall and very black, they stand while she watches from behind the oak; they place their hands on top of their rakes and lean on them, in their white cotton shirts, with their hooded eyes. Do they know she is watching them, will they see her? Smoke drifts, air is crisp, they are talking, she cannot move. Into a corner comes her father in brown riding pants, his high brown boots. He strides out onto the porch, stops in the center of the colonnade

with his hands on his hips. His face looks out on all she sees, the green yard, black men, fire, and the black men start moving again, the picture moves all around him.

Where is Paco?

The picture slides away. She lifts her head, sees his eyes staring wide at the ceiling: thinking, worrying. She hitches up on an elbow, looks through the bedrailing to the window where the filmy light blows in with the breeze. Whoever's in the apartment overhead has the screen on all the time, some of its words drift down: *new, flavorful . . . some sense out of your life.* Billy will be waking soon. She shifts her hips forward and rolls off. Ernest sighs but does not move. She plants kisses below his blue eyes without looking at them again. Time to get up, sweet, she says. We're running late.

He grunts and sits up heavily on his side of the bed, running his fingers through his hair.

She hurries to the bathroom, uses the bidet, washes up; then off to the kitchen, triggering the screenroom on her way through: *Good morning,* as the image pulses to focus, bay and sky, *this is your network welcome to June 22, 2020 another day of your life on a cool grey morning here in San Francisco you have a temperature of sixty-one pollution index average radiation level nine point . . .* How can it be on all the time upstairs? Whoever's up there, someone must be sitting in front of it, in that room all day.

Frowning, she reaches up in the cupboard for the WakeUp, spoons it into two mugs. As it fumes, heating itself, the kitchen's cold creeps into her, through the thin plastic of her robe until she is hugging herself. When she looks up he is framed in the doorway, smiling face flushed from the day's depilatory, flesh tucked away in the green unisuit.

Your WakeUp's ready, she says, smiling back. You want anything else?

Naw, he says. I'd better get down there. I sure wouldn't want to keep anybody waiting, you know.

They drink the WakeUp standing against the counter, his arm rubbing her back. She feels the tension in him; feels afraid, watery weak from the lovemaking. He kisses the side of her head and puts the cup down, he is already moving away. She cannot look at his anxious face.

Bye sweetheart, she calls after him. Have a good day.

As she walks through the screenroom again a cartoon flashes, loud music, two large women beating each other with clubs. In the front room

Billy still barely sleeps, his feet kicking the foldup bed, mouth whispering words. She lies down beside him, curls her body on the little mattress carefully. She can hear his breathing, smell his skin's dry milkiness.

Then his arm flops backward, taps her face. When she tries to hold him he wriggles away, staring off.

Good morning honey, she says. How are you today?

I'm *really* hungry, Billy says, his brown eyes still fixed on the ceiling. Can I have something really really good?

He raises his head and looks sightlessly off, as though consulting something, somewhere else; then back down at them. Who's equipped to do some more market studies, try sample areas?

The olive-skinned latino leans forward and places his forearms on the table. We could take it, he says. Do it out of the Managua or Bogotá works. No possibility of any legal problems there, and probably considerably less expense. Try it out on assimilated natives, those in low-echelon management—

No good, says the man at the head of the table. For Christ's sake, Jaime. There's no correlation between your people and our population. Besides, I don't care what we got the AMA to say. I don't want to hear of a single OMNICO employee anywhere at any level shooting junk, is that clear?

They mumble, nod.

Now, he says, who else has got some ideas?

But the table is still silent, their faces nervous and downcast.

He lifts his brows and sighs. Come on, he says, patiently, as if reciting to children: Who's got a way to run a goddamn market survey on this goddamn thing?

Past eleven by the time he steps off the elevator. But nothing else has come in since Paco, NASA is obviously not lifting a finger, what difference does it make?

Hello? says the soft voice behind him as he leans over, unlocking the door. Are you Mr. Goodman?

Ernest Goodman, that's right, he says straightening in the open doorway with a slight smile, beckoning with an outstretched hand.

The man who pads up to him is tall and fleshy pink, wrapped in a conservative grey one-piece, his only hair a rim of fleecy blond running to white above his ears.

Oh good, he says, wrapping Ernest's hand in his large doughlike mitt: I'm Oliver Sampson.

Won't you have a seat? says Ernest, opening his smile up.

The oval body passes his and sinks, smiling nervously, into the chair across from the desk. My, he says, this is really a lovely office you have here. It's so *austere*, he says then looks quickly away. In a good way, I mean.

I'm glad you like it, Ernest says.

Oh I do, says Sampson. It's so nice, you know, that you've preserved the clarity of the space here instead of trying to smudge it up—he lifts his sparse eyebrows, purses his lips—the way so many people do with this horrible new furniture, all those curved electrical things.

Yes, I know, Ernest says. The way people do these things sometimes, it's terrible.

Oh, and you've picked such wonderful classic old Abstract Expressionists for the *walls*, too, Sampson says turning in his seat: That's Rothko, isn't it?

Yes, Ernest says, and cocks his head: I'm flattered that you recognize it.

Oh, Sampson says, trembling in modesty. Oh, well, I used to follow it. And I still go to shows of the old stuff; the things that, you know, *mean* something. But what they're into now doesn't hold me very well, I'm afraid. Those giant machines, blocks of metal with the voices inside. It all just seems so—

Pointless? Ernest offers. Artificial?

Sampson's head nods hard, his eyes shut. Exactly, he breathes out. But when his brown eyes open again they seem slightly glazed, as though with irony or pain.

Is something wrong? Ernest says, knitting his brows.

No, says Sampson in a trailing voice. It's just a sad world, is all. The moon face is turned away now, down toward his shoes. It's a sad world where a person has to—I mean, meaning no disrespect—

Oh, he says, rising off the front edge of his desk: Mr. Sampson—

Oliver, groans Sampson: Please.

And you must call me Ernest, he says, squatting so they are on the same level, looking into each other's eyes. You know, Oliver—we both do—what modern life is. Atomized, fragmented: the webs of kinship shattered by technology, family ties loosened or smashed, our cities sprawling jungles full of crazies and creeps—

Oh, that's so true, Oliver says, his lips parted wide. Do you know every time I go out any more I see the streets just packed with homosexuals, staring at me, saying things? And the *blacks*, he says, the *blacks* . . .

Yes, he murmurs. So you see? There's every reason why you should come here.

The brown eyes search his face imploringly. You really think so? Oliver says.

If I didn't, Ernest says, I couldn't be here. I couldn't go on myself.

A soft pause, then Oliver's face goes vermilion: Still, he says, fumbling in a pocket, aren't you—I mean, don't you—

Now, now, Ernest says, gently laughing, patting Oliver's hand. There's plenty of time for us to talk contracts when and if we see each other again. You just leave that to me, all right?

All right, says Oliver, beaming. Then lurches forward in the chair, his voice high with excitement: Say. How would you like to come by my little place sometime? Perhaps for dinner? I *am* a very good cook.

Love it, says Ernest, sparkling his eyes. Where and what time?

Out in the Sunset district? Oliver says. 4615 Cabrillo? Around four-thirty, five o'clock tonight?

Fine, Ernest says, smiling with great open warmth.

Now no longer do most men need to seize, produce, exploit; now they may yearn and acquire like their women, become "feminized." But for a time in the dawn of the new century even advertising agencies were confused by this transformation, as consumption levels sagged among white males. It was even discovered that the blonde whose cleavage framed a bottle of scotch, the svelte lovers strolling cigarettes, the outlines of the fucking couples in the cocktail glass actually seemed to have a deterrent effect on sales. Heterosexual imagery had begun to fail.

Ad agencies all over the country flailed for an explanation of their sudden impotence. J. Walter Thompson, Inc., hypothesized a temporary mass neurosis brought on by a mixture of the surges in unemployment and the depressant effects of the twin reactor disasters in Seattle and Kansas City in 2008–09. "As a result of these short-term phenomena," reads a Thompson whitepaper of the time, "the popular mindset seems opposed to creating anything—or even just having 'fun.' "

Yet deeper research during this time unearthed even more ominous findings. Studies showed that the average American couple, married and unmarried, between 18 and 35 fucked less than once a month; for older couples the figure was correspondingly lower. And the most comprehensive statistical analyses suggested the disinterest and/or incapacity was chronic; Americans had not been straightfucking much for a long time, and were unlikely to do so in the foreseeable future. And so, while Oliver was divorcing his wife, trying hopelessly to meet and make other women, dabbling shamefully, clandestinely, with his first men, losing his pretty curly hair, advertisers too confronted their worst fear: that straight sex, at least, had been consumed along with its containers, that we had eaten it, shit it out, and gone to some other place to which a new passage would have to be forged, somewhere new metaphors would have to locate, and fast.

The names of the first research team to find the way are unknown and insignificant; the discovery was practically simultaneous across the advertising world. In fact, from the mid-'70s on in the preceding century clues had been there all the time: the advertising that brought in the highest and most constant level of consumption, beginning with Coca-Cola's "It's the real thing" campaign, the ur-prototype, wrapped its client commodity in an authentic but ordered—in current advertising jargon, "sincere'—package, stirred our desire with the promise of reality itself.

Settings and backgrounds for these ads are likely to be quite stark: white walls, a table, a chair. A very few elements whose reality is indisputable, luminous; perhaps just a flat geometrical design. And on the table (say) a single pair of platinum earrings, a box of cryogenic corn, a pack of cigarettes, accompanied by a quiet voice or slender typeface. "It fits in." "True Food is clear food." "The Fact."

By now, in 2020, though the advertising firms have discovered and duly noted the change from straight to gay that makes Oliver Sampson frightened and ridiculous, few screenads or billboards use any kind of sex any more. Alongside the need to be assured that the world we exist in is real, sexuality is a relatively ephemeral ploy.

At the back of their apartment is a set of worn wooden steps leading down to a small yard of dank packed earth. A gloomy place, blocked from what little sun there is by aging '60s highrises all around. It makes her think of some prisonyard she saw somewhere once, in an old movie, a place where men walk around in chains. But Billy, for some reason, likes to play back here.

On the bare ground beyond her he lines his plastic spacemen up. All right, he mutters, I put you guys over here, you have the laserguns so you can kill anybody. He picks up two, faces them in his hands, walks one over the dirt. You just got off the rocket, he just got off the rocket and he walks on the planet, sees this guy, he says Hey you an Earthman too? and the other, blam! And throws one spaceman, blasted by lasers, a few feet away, as faintly from inside she hears the shrill of the phone.

Honey, she calls: I'm going to get the phone. He does not look up.

She walks back in the kitchen, answers it on the third ring.

Hi, sweetheart.   Oh that's wonderful, honey. I knew it had to break. What's he like?   Yes . . . yes . . .   I'm sure you can.   Oh, that's wonderful . . .

All the while she talks and listens she is smoothing the hair back off one temple, fingering wrinkles out of her suit, her eyes on the aqua butterflies of its design, her mouth smiling only when she speaks. She has not turned her phonescreen on, nor has Ernest. She does not like to be seen from somewhere else, she does not want to see him as an image on the screen.

All right, she says, I just won't look for you until I see you then. Yes, congratulations, sweetheart.   I love you. Goodbye.

She hangs up, looks out the kitchen window onto the dark back yard. Billy is still moving his spacemen around, pointing their laserguns, little words falling from his mouth. Ernest has a client, there is nothing to worry about, everything is all right. Why not try a little reading today?

Her life is surrounded and constructed by men.

A faded decal on the door reads This Home Protected by GuardAll Security Systems; so he blanks his face before ringing the bell and triggering the screen inside.

GuardAll Systems, Inc., is a unit of Imago Rand, a holding company acquired in 1992 by OMNICO for 125.3 million. GuardAll produces security systems, including home systems like this one, with its electric-eye self-locking mechanisms and alarms, and constant video surveillance of the immediate surroundings of the client premises. Thus not only does Ernest's image flash on Oliver's GuardAll screen (not to be confused with a phone or media screen), but it is transmitted to a special computer-monitored station which records it and which, in the event of danger or violence, can trigger and direct lethal streams from inbuilt lasers set in the doors and under the eaves of Oliver's house. Each system, moreover, is open to human inspection and control: a technician at the monitor station need merely modify slightly the system's programming to have the images thrown up on small video, and to leave the decision to act or not, should the issue arise, in human hands. Of course, along with this human safe-guard comes the possibility of human abuse, since all screens are reversible; they can transmit as well as receive. Thus—again, with a few simple pro-gram modifications—an individual security system can be converted into a surveillance system whose object of attention is the homeowner himself.

Well, my goodness! flutters Oliver with a high laugh. Come in, come in.

The men around the table still seize and exploit, of course; most of them, accordingly, are expected to be straight and take wives. The man speaking now, for example, in his mid-fifties like Oliver, is twice married with two children, one of whom killed herself with a brisk shot of hotzie in La Jolla a few years ago. But the irony of this in his present effort does not occur to him.

I've been thinking about this, uh, matter, he is saying. And it seems to me that if what we want is the standard consumer sample, we will be getting into an area which is going to be pretty costly. What we would, unh, be getting into here is some pretty, uh, sizable outlays of goods and services and capital to the appropriate officials and agencies for their co-operation in this sort of thing. Otherwise we might find the, uh, legal— complications, *im*-plications getting a little—thick, so to speak.

And the man at the head of the table is looking at him sideways, his own face blank, his chin resting in the palm of his hand. Yes, Harry, he says: Go on.

The low-ceilinged musty room is crammed with furniture: tall Ed-wardian desk with Louise Quatorze chair drawn up to it, leaded glass bookshelves overhead; Danish modern wingbacks; beanbag chair; an Early American coffee table with a formica top between him, in the overstuffed couch with its swooping maple arms, and Oliver, leaning back in a black Fat Boy.

He runs his hand along the coffee table's edge. Oliver, he says, could this be real Ethan Allen?

Why, yes it is. Oliver sits up snapping his lounger abruptly upright, his face aglow: You know everyone who comes here and knows anything about this sort of thing—and there aren't many any more, believe me, who do—asks me about that piece and this black recliner.

Indeed, says Ernest. Also a handsome piece.

And you know, says Oliver, slapping a squat black vinyl arm, you could get these things for a song ten, twenty years ago, back at the turn. People were practically throwing them away to get this new objectified stuff. But I wouldn't let mine go. That new stuff is simply inhuman, that's what I used to say to Eleanor, my ex-wife. And here now it's practically antique.

Yes, Ernest says, waving his hand in languid emphasis: People are finally beginning to value these things again. The sense of individual comfort and dignity that arises naturally from one of those recliners. Even, perhaps, that continuity with the past, and sense of it as a solid, living tradition that that marvelous desk and chair of yours imply.

My great-great-grandparents', Oliver says quietly.

For a few seconds the room is filled with a solemn hush. Then Oliver leans back in the Fat Boy, his feet in pointed Turkish slippers on the black rest, his face soaked in placidity. It's rare to find a young man with your sense of values today, he says. I can't help wondering where you got it. Do you mind if I ask? Is that within the rules?

We're friends, Ernest says gently, seriously. Everything's within the rules. Then his face breaks into an easy grin: Well, I grew up in Kansas. Daddy was a farmer. Our farm was about a hundred years old, I guess. So I grew up—you know—close to the land and around old things. You learn to care about old things and keeping things up on a farm like that.

Oliver's face regards his with a soft, lambent glow: It *sounds* wonderful. Why in the world did you ever leave?

That's the way Daddy wanted it, Ernest says: He couldn't see any future in it any more. He looks down, off the shiny enameled tops of his Italian shoes. And maybe he was right.

Slowly, grandly, Oliver heaves forward, up and out of the Fat Boy and down again beside Ernest on the couch, so close Ernest tips toward him.

There's a process in history, he says, his eyes wet, his mouth quivering, known as the Pendulum Swing. And someday—in my lifetime, I hope— it will swing back. The niggers and women in this country—those things that call themselves women anyway— aren't going to rule forever.

Ernest looks back at him; their eyes, their faces very close, the huge hand rubbing his knee. I hope so, Ernest says. I really do.

Oliver breathes heavily; slowly his face fills with blood. His hand releases Ernest's knee, his gaze drops away: Forgive me, he says. It's just when I get on certain subjects, I—

Suddenly, awkwardly he rises, his eyes blurred with tears. But really, he says, smiling shakily: This is so self-indulgent. I should get our dinners on, you know? We're eating French tonight, coq au vin, and I want you to know that there isn't a single cryogenic ingredient in it, everything's either frozen or perfectly fresh, and I did all the cooking myself. I'm very proud of that, you know.

Oliver, Ernest says, his face gently stern, his voice firm: You must never mind being self-indulgent with me, not ever. That's what I'm here for you know, he says, touching the robe, peering gently at the swollen moon face. So that for once in your life your self can be cleanly, purely indulged, n'est ce pas?

Mais oui, says Oliver, somewhat hoarsely.

Niggers and women, the younger of the two greenclad technicians is still laughing. Where the hell you suppose he got that?

A lot of people used to think shit like that, responds his partner, whose eyes stay fixed on the screen: blacks and shit like that. I'll tell you though, George, you should listen to this guy, he's pretty good.

On the screen before them Ernest is reaching for the robe: . . *you must never mind being self-indulgent with me, not ever* . . .

Oh yeah, says George, he's all right I guess. But you sure wouldn't take his job. How'd you like to have to cozy up to that fucking whale? He starts to laugh loudly again, his thin face reddening: Niggers and women, I can't believe it . . .

Glad you're getting off on it anyway, says the older man. Bores the shit out of me. I don't see why we couldn't have just programmed for this.

What Johnson told me, says George. He said Hamilton upstairs told him whoever wants it done, he doesn't trust the machines. Said he wants human beings on the controls, not circuits.

I think that's a crock, says the older man. You know what I think?
What?

I think maybe we're getting tested too.

George's head jerks around. What for? he whispers.

Who knows? says the older man, still intent on the screen. Maybe to move us somewhere else. Maybe just so there'll be somebody to blame it on if something fucks up.

George turns his pockmarked face, now bloodlessly white, toward his partner. Sam? he says. You don't think—

Don't worry, kid, Sam says. It's easy. Nothing's gonna go wrong.

At the end of the meal two bottles of Johannesburg Reisling, '03, are gone and Ollie's face across the table looks like a smogswollen sunset. I don't like to say things, you know, water over the bridge, he is saying, round indignant eyes afloat: But that dirty bitch Eleanor ruined my chances for a decent life. You know what she used to call me?

He leans across the table, purple lips trembling: Said I was only half a man, he hisses. Her, big woman's liberationist, end patriarchy and the rest of that pathetic drivel. And she calls me queer. Fag. Cocksucker. When I had never, not once laid a single finger on—

Disgusting, Ernest says, setting down his cup of jasmine tea. What a nightmare it must have been for you. A woman like that with no tenderness, no softness, no sympathy. Are these decomposable?

What? Oh yes, Oliver says, smiling loosely, trying to get up. But you're my guest, you mustn't do that.

I'm your friend, Ernest says wide-eyed, hands full of plates. At least I hope so. Now where's your chute?

Cabinet under the sink, Oliver says.

He can feel Oliver's happy eyes on him as he crosses the kitchen, stoops and pitches the dishes away. There seems to be only one good thing about it, he says, wiping his fingers on the linen dishtowel: That it's over and she's out of your life.

Yes, Oliver says, leering: Out of life altogether, matter of fact.

The hands stop moving in the towel. Ernest cocks an eyebrow ironically, half-smiles. Yes? And how did that happen?

Oliver's head drops back against the chair. It was all very exciting and mysterious, really. After the divorce—oh, maybe two or three years after—she and some of those other women, feminist bitches, you know—and some of them very big names back then too—well, the government, Congress or somebody cooked up this notion of sending them to China to see how women were being treated there, what jobs they had, etcetera, etcetera. One of these government goodwill things they were still always having back then. My brother, Brother Tom was I think perhaps the one in charge of selecting who would go.

His eyes are half shut. Like a tortoise's, one heavy hand flaps in the air: And do you know about two weeks into their little journey *every single one of those women*, including Eleanor, was *killed* in a Chinese train wreck outside Shanghai.

Good god, Ernest says, moving back to the table: Every one of them?

There was some talk of hankypanky, of course, Oliver says. Brother Tom even had to put an investigation team on it, and they had more congressional hearings. But—he spreads his hands, framing the melon head, the wide smile—there was nothing to it, I guess.

He reaches for the teapot, chuckling: Still and all, you know, it was enough to give one faith in divine justice, if not providence. More tea?

"Her glistening skin gazed. Wounded by winning, he bowed his head and with suppliant lips took a nipple, faintly salt and sour, in." A shriek from the screen brings her eyes up from the page to the giant head of a woman screaming in extreme close-up. Billy! she says frightened: For goodness sake now, turn that down!

The boy's face flashes to hers, frightened too. For him it is as if the images had coalesced, his mother and the bad woman on the screen, screaming because the police have caught her and are going to kill her now.

But already, at the sight of his eyes scared and crazy, his jump up to turn down the screen, regret and shame replace her fear:

I'm sorry, Billy, she says. Come here, baby.

Curiously he comes over, his face sullen, curled in on itself. She kisses his cheeks, his soft red hair: Honey, I'm sorry, she says. I was trying to read and that was just too loud. What is that program anyway? She looks up to see bright blue rays slicing the woman into strips; looks away quickly, forces calmness into her voice: What did she do?

Oh, the boy says, she wrecked a bunch of things and stuff.

She glances up once more. Now the men are walking away from the body. Now the trefoil badge of nuclear security looms on the screen. So, sabotage, that was it.

Once the contract is out on the table between them, Ernest lets his eyes drift off and up to the nouveau-expressionist relic of the early '80s, on the opposite wall: marauding cats leaping over sofas, luridly foreshortened perspective, smudged magenta shades. A standard contract, ten G's a month, automatic deposit, drawn up more or less along straight NASA lines except with the clause struck relating to physical intimacy so as not to freak this particular client out. Yet, as it happens, Oliver barely pretends even to scan the document; from the corner of his eye Ernest watches his lips move, half-reading, half-trembling, holding the hand clasping the pen in the air above the signatory line on page two for all of thirty, forty seconds before scrawling out the squat looping letters of his name.

Then, as the beaming head looks up from the page, Ernest holds up one staying hand, palm decorously out, as if to say Don't mention it please. Do you mind if I ask you, he says, a personal question?

Oliver titters, pinkfaced. Oh Ernest. Now it's I who must insist—

Ernest laughs with easy grace; then his face quickens again. Your brother, Congressman Thomas Sampson, representative from Connecticut—was it by any chance he who mentioned me to you?

Why as a matter of fact it *was*, Oliver says, his mouth agape in pleasant surprise. Tom and I have always been close, really;, and I was talking to him on the phone just a few days ago about the kind of thing I have to put up with around here—you know, not knowing anybody, with all these *truly* queer men around, he suggested I call you. Had your address and everything, actually.

He leans across the table, whispers through a round O, as if someone else were in the room: Actually he's even going to pay for it. From what I understand, my little, uh, stipend, would never—I mean—he wriggles, sighs, stares past Ernest at the Warhol silkscreen of Marilyn on the wall beside the china closet—One simply cannot find employment any more . . .

Ernest stands, rounds the table, until he is in back of Oliver, who still stares miserably off. Expertly his fingers knead and work the flaccid shoulders beneath the robe. Of course in this world there is no suitable job, he coos. But you mustn't take that as an indictment against *yourself*— —

The hands move in broad circles; he can feel Oliver's deepening breathing, see the round bald head relax. I merely asked about your brother, dear, he says, because I thought that must be how you heard of me, that's all. You see, I'm from Washington, and though I never, unfortunately, knew your brother, I did know some people who knew him. So that's how he must have known about me.

You see, he says, leaning close to one fuzzy red ear, whispering too now, I don't advertise openly. You never know who could just walk in off the street.

The large head rises slightly, bald crown gleaming in the light: Women and niggers . . . I can't tell you how happy I am you don't take *them*. A fat finger rises in the air, Ernest goes on rubbing: They're the ones that want to ruin us men, make us all fairies and queers. So they can take over. Well I'll tell you—

Shhhh, soothes Ernest. There, Ollie, there. And in the long silence, he smooths his hands down pads and ripples of flesh on the back, neck, and sides until Oliver groans: Oh that's so nice . . .

When Ernest stops rubbing he lets his hands rest on the older man's shoulders; another silent moment like that.

Oliver, he breathes at last.

The huge head lolls, eyes rolling backward: What, dear boy?

I think perhaps I should leave now. It's getting rather late.

Oh *yes*, Oliver says loudly, frantically, heaving to his feet. Dear me, how selfish I am, he says, waving Ernest to the living room again, back through the sea of furniture. It's just that I—he says, halting, turning wide frog's eyes, crimson face in the hallway—well, I haven't had such a wonderful fellowship with another man in years, just years—

They stand quite close together out in the front landing, looking at each other, smiling. A faint sweat dots Oliver's brow. I hope you won't have any trans problem, he says. It still runs quite regularly even this late. You do have some sort of curfew pass, don't you?

Yes, I'm sure I'll be fine, Ollie, Ernest says and grips the older man's arm above the elbow, the loose flesh wobbly in his hand. 'Night, dear friend, says Ernest in a low, seriously moved voice—and then looks up: You do have laserlights installed up there, haven't you?

Yes says Ollie, hardly glancing up himself, far too happy to alter his giant pink grin: They do seem to be out, though, isn't that odd?

You have to go to sleep soon, honey, she says.

I'm not tired, he pouts, though already, helplessly, his body sags against hers. I *need* to watch some more.

She lets him be, tries to go back to the book: *Couples*, the classic college edition Ernest must have had to read sometime at Yale. Unpacking two months ago, she'd found it stuffed in one of his boxes; and its cover had attracted her, the Blake watercolor of Adam and Eve asleep in their pure knowledge on their strange flowered bed.

But the book is not like that at all; she has a hard time with it, finds herself repelled by the glossy strings of words whose meanings keep eluding her. "Birds chirped beyond the rainbow rim of the circular wet tangency," she reads now. There is no place for her here. If she could read this book she could go shopping too each day like the others, like most people, for things as beautiful as these words. But instead she has to sit and wait for the tingle, the low electric hum of her anxiety once again to take some shape, form some specific worry in her mind.

What was the radiation count today, should I have kept him in after all? People talk all the time about it, rays piercing genes, defects that won't show up until he's twenty, fifty . . .

As she thinks her hand reaches for the boy, gripping his shoulder for the sureness of his flesh, his bones, hers; and the pages of *Couples*, chronicle of the adultering middle class and their search for salvation in the long-gone godless '60s, a classic, turn unseen in her lap.

They are the last words that pass between them. In the next second the two of them can hear the laughter, the steps. Then, while they watch from the landing, up the street comes the crowd of boys, six of them, all young, around thirteen, all black. Clearly in a foreign neighborhood, far past curfew, stepping carefully, muttering to themselves, searching something out—until their eyes, round and white under the mercury lamps, light on the two of them, and they turn virtually in unison, as one.

Then, in the stillness that wraps the misty neighborhood, the silent city all around, the rest is like a pantomime, a slow nightmare: the way they run up the sidewalk, the concrete porchsteps, shove him aside, and while the lasers fail to stream down and alarm fails to sound and Oliver whimpers Please now dear boys now don't touch me please please no stay and bright knives come out aglint as if with their own light, Oliver holding out fat sweaty hands, penetration of the knives through groin and Oliver's last cry soaring up, straight up, until one of them turns his young ageless eye moonbright straight into his, Ernest's, saying Don't you think you best be gone?

And Ernest Goodman looks back into those eyes and is already running, pushing off the steps and down the sidewalk, slowing down slightly as, first, he begins to move towards someplace definite, the nearest trans corner stop where there is a guard for there are no guards around here, then more, down to a forced walk, when two blocks ahead at last he sees a grey uniform standing under a streetlight.

By the time he reaches it the swirling in his head has subsided to something like a low constant controllable buzzing and his face is carefully smoothed out. Got a late pass? says the guard, a frowning, shortbrowed stocky white man. Sure thing, he replies. Only perhaps ten minutes later,

halfway or more back home again on the trans, does his body allow itself
to shake uncontrollably. Whatever is happening has happened again.

You can go ahead and reactivate that system now, I guess, Sam says
when the pack is offscreen.

George's hand reaches for a switch but hovers, shaking. At the edge of
his scalp, along his black hair, he is sweating thick rolling drops, and he
is still watching the monitors.

Niggers and women, he says, his mouth twisting. Boy, they sure called
his number, didn't they? They really got him, didn't they now.

Come on, George, says the older man. It's late. I want to get home.

Come on my ass. The younger man's voice is rising, eyes squinching
in his scarred red face. Did you see that just now, man? I mean, what the
hell was that anyway? What the hell we doing here? What the hell is this
shit about?

Hey George, says the older man gently, leaning back in his chair: come
on. You don't know jackshit about it and neither do I. It's just a job, okay?
And now it's over.

You're telling me *that's* a job? George says, pointing stiffly, furiously
at the screens. You think that's *business*?

Sam stands, steps over to his panel, and flicks a switch. The monitors
darken on the image of the fleshy body, tattered robe, blood dribbling down
porchsteps. That's right, he says. That's what I'm telling you. And you
and I don't know Sampson, we don't know Goodman, we don't know a
goddamn thing, all right?

For a second George stares back at him; then at the blank monitors.

Shit, he says, standing slowly, his voice lowering almost to a murmur:
It was his own brother, wasn't it? His own fucking brother set him right
the fuck up.

The old man runs a slow, tired hand back through his shoulder-length
grey hair, then claps it on the boy's back. *You don't know*, he says. That's
the thing. Now come on, let's get out of here, let's go home.

And you know, he says, how much consumption that pulls in.

Good point, Harry, says the man at the head of the table, tapping his
pen. All right. So we do the research in-house. We can keep it quiet enough
that way, can't we?

Sure, right, why not, of course, comes the chorus of the rest of the men. Yes, whispers Harry himself, flushing in his triumph, the backs of his knees wet inside the grey suit. He has cut through, thought well, told a part of the truth. The rest of him—his present wife, his dead and living children, what he thinks of as his life—is far beyond him now. Something thrums, something pulses deep in his loins, like a cobra beginning to rear.

I'm telling you, Ernie, T.D. is saying. I had Central Data put out tracers on Sampson three times to make sure. Nobody here put Sampson on you. His brother the Congressman has never been a NASA client.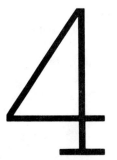

In the screen Ernest's hair, tousled from the passage of his hands, makes him look shabby, and a little nuts; that and the way he is not keeping his eyes in any one place.

Well *somebody* set him up, Ernest says. Those kids, they were out of their neighborhood, after curfew. And they spotted him. They pointed and said like, Look there he is. And another thing, the guy hated blacks. Somebody *knew* he hated them, somebody used it—

T.D. stops rubbing the stubble on his chin, bridges his hairy hands at the fingertips, tips them toward the screen: Do you mind if I suggest something here?

That his brother set him up? Ernest says. It looks like he set up the guy's wife years ago. But why Ollie himself, in front of me?

T.D. rises and turns, half-hiding his display of growing anger from the screenlens following him about the room. I was going to suggest something simpler, he says, a little more direct. The guy had a thing about blacks, right? So maybe some of them knew about it. Maybe he said something out loud on a trans, and they came after him. I mean, that'd make sense, wouldn't it?

Ernest looks down at his desk, his mouth twisting; still at his office this late, T.D. thinks, must not want what's-her-name to know; good.

Okay then, he is saying, what about the other guy, Paco? Just before the contract's signed there, bam, same thing. I'm telling you, T.D., something's going on.

Crap, says T.D. He stops pacing, looks directly at the screen. It wasn't the same thing, Ernie. It was the guy's wife and you were in a rough neighborhood anyway. Look, he says, it's a crazy world out there. Crazy things happen. You're not dealing with our clientele any more.

Shit, Ernest says. I'm not dealing with any clientele. Things go on like this much longer and we're going to have to get on Welfare. He lifts his head and smiles: I sure could use one of those referrals you promised me.

You might get one soon, says T.D. I happen to know your name was put up to somebody the other day. Then his large brown eyes soften sad as a dog's: Anyway, you think you got troubles. Word's getting passed along here that all instructors are going to have to go out in the field for evaluations. Know what that means for yours truly?

Ernest's look on the screen is concerned, sympathetic: Ever think of getting a nose job?

Wouldn't do any good, T.D. says. It'd get out to the client somehow anyway. Or he'd just know. He gives a short bitter laugh: You know what they used to say? Some of my best friends are Jews.

Well, Ernest says, one of my best friends is. And one of the best in the business.

T.D. smiles. Yeah, yeah. What more do you want?

Who'd you refer me to? Ernest says.

C'mon Ernie, T.D. says. I'm in enough trouble with the company as it is.

Fuck the company, Ernest says, grinning: They're never going to know. Who is it?

Listen, T.D. says, it's my ass, not yours. And it wouldn't do you a damn bit of good to know, now would it?

Ernest keeps the grin on. That your best schoolmarm voice?

T.D. smiles back. Get off the phone, Ernie, he says.

Thanks for checking, T.D., Ernest says. Thanks for everything. Goodnight.

Goodnight, T.D. says.

Standing in place, T.D. adjusts his choker, centering its chief garnet on his throat, smooths his hands down his hips, sighs. Then the screen fills again, this time with a lean ruddy man standing before a background of flat grey in a Romanesque robe, his hair a tangle of prematurely silver curls.

That was very well done, Mr. Duberman, the man says, briskly and without smiling.

Thank you Mr. Merrill, says T.D., mirroring the man's expressionlessness. I think I put him off our scent.

You reassured him very well, Merrill says. Though of course we don't want him to relax *completely*.

T.D. feels light sweat breaking out on his palms. Mr. Merrill, he says, I know this boy, I trained him. He's putting up a good front but he's not relaxed. He's worried sick.

As well he might be, Merrill says slightly bowing his head. And of course I appreciate your concern. But obviously we must be able to assure our client that there are no other weaknesses in our friend but the known one, especially insofar as our client's particular—uh—interests are concerned. The tests are shaped specifically with these considerations in mind. You do understand this, don't you, Mr. Duberman?

Yes sir, says T.D., serious, brighteyed. Of course.

Very good then, says Merrill, and pauses. T.D. watches him stroke his chin, looking off, a five-beat reverie. Be a lucky fellow if he makes it through, Merrill says at last.

I'm sure he will, sir, says T.D. nodding. If I may say so, sir, as his trainer, he's the best—

Sorry to bother you at home, Mr. Duberman, says Merrill.

Oh, says T.D., listen, that's quite all right sir, I—

But the screen is already blank.

The man at the head of the table leans back in his chair and regards them all: So who can keep the right low profile on this one?

Beneath the halfbald hairpiece his scalp has started to itch like crazy from its close contact with his real hair. He looks up; concentrates on the ooze of even light from the ceiling, senses pressureless sterile air. Lets his attention go, gliding upward as to some vast blue emptiness, waste of sky . . .

What about NASA? someone says.

He looks back down at them. Another man jerks forward in his chair as if pushed from behind.

I don't think that's a good idea, Mel, the someone—Joe—says, shaking his head vigorously. That could get us into a lot of problems if we start infringing on the nature of the acquaintance bond, you know. I mean, we've got some pretty important people involved as clients here—

The first man, Mel, draws his shoulders up under his coat, preparing to reply. The man at the head of the table watches, slightly bored, as if it were a ballet, and smooths the back of his head as if the greying hair there were real. Part of his mind imagines the passage of time elsewhere, outside the room.

Standing by the window the following day, back to zero. Standing looking back out at the TransAm—for so long in a trance of sight and thought what he sees becomes who he is, the pyramidal building opposite both a map of his desire to be enclosed, strong, safe, large, and his dread of being left out, small, outside.

The phone rings on his desk; the screen stays off. Must be Charlotte then. He picks it up and says, Hi honey.

Shit, comes a strange voice: That your standard opener?

Not always, he says. Sometimes I use Sweetheart or Light of my life.

A burst of sharp laughter, clipped short: Well, maybe we can work out something a little different for you and me, okay? Her voice is curt, nervy low: Some of us have a little problem dealing with frontal affection.

I'll tell you what, he says, slouching against the edge of the desk: I'll make my affection for you very, very latent. You won't even know it's there. Where do I meet you?

She laughs again, a little softer: Bertolino's pipebar at Fillmore and Union in the Union Street district. I'm in an orange caftan.

And your name? Ernest says. I have a thing about names.

How regressive of you, she says. In the society of the future we all get numbers, didn't you know? Then, quickly: Helena Fort; see you soon. And the phone is dead.

It is midafternoon, primetime buying hours, and a rare bright balminess in the air. The trans he boards, accordingly, is crammed with the sveltes. Almondfaced men in tight lizardskins, with high sparkling mounds of hair; women with borzoi heads, coiffures raked back in swirling cones. Their indifferent murmurs merge throughout the ride like a smooth current broken only when he gets off and, in the crowd that shoves out with him, yelps as something pierces his side.

Oh, says the pretty young man pressed next to him: So sorry.

As the others watch with narrow smiles, half-closed eyes, he raises a silver ring on which is mounted a silver thorn perhaps one inch long, tipped in crimson now. Didn't hurt you too much? he says.

Ernest shakes his head No.

Do forgive me, the young man chortles, curling one strand of hair back over a small white ear. Then puts the thorn in his mouth and licks it off, to the delighted laughter of the crowd.

The air under the Union geodesic is fresh; the combination sunlight, both amplified and artificial, dazzling. Shoppers all as soignée as his trans-load strew the streets, surge in and out of the oval entrances of the high dark cubelike stores. They fill every table at Bertolino's where, between the hash smoke and the crush, it takes him a long moment to discover the orange-caftaned woman seated at a table quite close by, staring back from the strange pink pupils of her eyes; anchovy pink, contacts no doubt.

Helena Fort, he says and reaches out a hand.

She touches it briefly, motions him beside her on the aqua triclinium. I bet you always show up for your first encounter in something six months out of date, with a little blood on it, she says. Reverse strategy, right?

You've already used that kind of line once, Ernest says. I wouldn't trade that heavily on it if I were you.

A trace of a smile glides by her lips, her long jewelled hand indicates the table: Thanks for the tip. Try some hash? House specialty.

I'll pass, he says. You go ahead.

She raises up on an elbow, leans over the table's rough stone surface, to the hole in its center where the hashcube glows. Its orange light flares her features as she breathes: wide thinlipped mouth, long nose with nostrils flared to draw the smoke in, high, prominent cheekbones. A shudder rustles her robe. Ah, she says—ah, yes, with her ironic smile, eases back on the couch.

You come here often? he says, smiling too.

When there's nothing else to do. Her strange eyes, glassy now, seem focused on a point behind his head: When I'm bored. About once a day.

Sounds like a rich full life, he says, shrugging. What do you need me for?

Wrong verb, she says, almost dreamily. I don't need you at all. She strokes the velvet of the couch, a slow, full smile growing. Let's just say you're my obligatory purchase for today, all right? How does that suit you?

Fine, he says easily. If that's what you need.

She aims her index finger at his eyes: I warned you about that word. Then settles back, her lips curled: Go ahead though, you're the expert. Tell me why I'm buying you.

Ernest takes a pause. Maintains sidelong eye contact with Helena; listens a second or so more to the man telling someone else a story at the next table over, on his right: So after a month I called up. Listen, I said, I got this *rag* a month ago and don't know *how*, I mean I bought something there that day but it wasn't *this* thing, but I wasn't sure, you know, and it just took me *forever* to realize that what must have happened is on the way *home*, on the *trans*—

All right, Ernest says. You'd like me to think that you're bored but it's not that. The world's full of things for bored people. And you're too smart not to have something that interests you. None of this, maybe—his hand sweeps the bar—but something else, I don't know what. Anyway, he says, that's not why you called me. You called me because you want somebody to trust.

Cool amusement in her answering glance: What makes you think I can trust you?

For one thing, there's money involved, Ernest says. A contract. I'm a professional. For another, I tell you the truth.

The man at the next table is still talking: . . . those norotane leggings with the inset eyes . . . I know, can you *believe* it?

Helena Fort slides her tall body upright. I don't care how good you are, she says. I won't hang around with anybody in bloody clothes. Let's get out of this shithole and I'll buy you something I won't have to wince at.

They weave their way through crowded tables, pay their cover at the steel front counter, pass through the turnstile into sunlight. Her red hair, pulled atop her head and pinned with an aluminum star, flashes and spangles in the light as she stands, arms akimbo, beside a urethane tree on the street, looking at the tall blank buildings, the busy oval entranceways stretching off.

Then her eyes, showing crow's feet at the edges, narrow on him: Bring the contract with you?

Uh-uh, he says. You wouldn't sign anyway. You don't know whether you trust me yet.

She grins, radiant. I just wondered how hungry you were for the sale.

Then she lifts his arm, examines the bloodstain, her smile closes: Shit. You aren't really hurt, are you?

Small mishap on the trans, he says. I'm all right.

Let's go then, she says, and strides ahead.

Their passage through the oval opening breaks a directed lightbeam like that of an electric-eye door; this "knowledge" is transferred to a simple computer-scan system that tracks them through the store.

From the entranceway they can look upward through a longitudinal slice of air, the building's open center, on either side of which, on every level, are the same blank walls of dark plastic or steel the building's exterior displays; only the presence of hundreds of small oval openings suggests the honeycomb of rooms on every level of each side.

This open space itself is lined and crisscrossed by a maze of slow belts like those in today's larger air terminals. Rising, falling, full of consumers crossing diagonally and side to side, this black and silver tangle rears toward the open bright white of the mall's enclosing dome high overhead. In all directions the consumers glide, with easy step-on, step-off access from one slow belt to another, or from belt to room.

There is something disturbing, though, about the sight of the mass of belts like some giant black liana, its vines infested with those swarms in gorgeous dress; something troubling about the way their murmurs and cries merge to form a muddled clamor rising to the covered sky like prayer; something disorienting about rising, falling, crossing belts with other well-dressed white bodies (they are of course, mainly white) in a random relationship to yourself.

As Helena and Ernest move up, down, and over on the belts, through their soft roar of talk, then, they feel more and more desire for safe, sure reality, a deepening urge to go into the rooms they pass. When they do step off the belt into one, they find themselves in a small square enclosure whose walls carry the sheen of rolled steel, or dull solidity of concrete, with no adornments or furnishings.

No sound enters from the belt outside; in silence the two of them confront a single object, usually placed in the center of the room. A robe, piece of jewelry, appliance, objet d'art, wrapped in its aura of irrefutable certainty, reality, thereness. After the confusion outside the room, what they feel now in the presence of the object, whatever it is, is not unlike the sense of pure, solid being we are said to feel in the direct presence of a great work of art.

For all that, though, they may not want it; if it is a piece of clothing, it may not fit. Then they must get back on the belts. They must move to another room, and another, and another—there is time for those without work—until their quest ends in the right real thing, truth and stasis in a small solid space.

So strong is this pull toward reality and definable space that even Ernest, whose lack of definition is his trade, who is on the job besides, is drawn in by this titillating, primal rite; and, with the assistance and advice of Helena Fort, exchanges his stained drab unisuit for a scarlet robe with a high stiff collar and a pair of pink plastic leggings with inset rabbits' eyes.

Then back down the bewildering maze of black moving vines, through the tower of noise, to where the central computer, a machine about the size and shape of those that issued time tickets in latterday parking lots— the same computer that has tracked them through the store—records the items she holds out to it, accepts her U.S. i.d. for billing, issues a receipt stub. And through a turnstile, back out the large oval door to the street.

Thought you didn't care for beastery, Charlotte says late that night in the bedroom. You laugh at it on other people.

You're right, he says. He keeps his eyes on her, away from where the leggings rest against the wall, rabbit-eyes gleaming: It's silly stuff. I wouldn't wear it if I didn't have to look the way she wants me to.

She looks away from him, palelipped: You wouldn't want me to buy clothes like that. You'd think I looked terrible in them.

I think they look terrible on *me*, he says. They look stupid. He comes off the bed, squats on his haunches before her: I *had* to buy them. Can't you see that?

You bought them because you liked them, she says. And you liked them because you were with her.

Ohhhh, he sighs. That's it, isn't it? That she's a woman. Isn't it? That she's my first woman client.

And you like her, she says, turning suddenly her hot blind eyes into his. You liked her today. You had a good time.

I'm *supposed* to like them, he says, feeling the blood rise to his head. It's what they pay me for, for Christ's sake. You don't object to it when it's a man, doing the same damn—

But Charlotte has turned away and risen, is moving over the floor to the doorway where Billy stands in his blue sleepers, his eyes dazed and abject.

I can't sleep, Mommy, he is saying. I need a drink.

As Ernest walks behind them through the screenroom, it flashes the image of two ragged women wading waistdeep through a verdigris jungle swamp, with the sound mercifully down. Ahead, she does not speak to the boy, but cups the back of his head against her hip so his body brushes against hers.

She will always love the boy that way, unquestioning, no need for proof: for him she does not have that kind of love.

He stands and watches while she draws the glass of water, drops the purifier in, watches the child drink. He trails behind them as they walk back through the screenroom where the jungle flares again, followed by a blank grey room with something Italian—manicotti—shimmering in the center. Past their bedroom and into the front room, where she strokes and kisses the boy's round cheeks, smooths his hair, draws the blankets up: Now go to sleep, sweetheart. It's way too late. Mommy will see you in the morning.

Ernest looks at the boy; the little eyes, restive, opaque as a squirrel's, watching him leave. Goodnight pal, he says; but the boy does not reply.

Back in their bedroom they have nothing to say; the space between them aches like a bruise. Charlotte programs the bedside console for music (Baroque oboe concerto), alarm (7:30 a.m.), and rolls heavily into bed. He reaches for the lightbutton on the wall.

At first none of their limbs touch. He can only hear her breath; then makes out her still face, eyes open, poised on the pillow like a mask. When he closes his eyes it is as though she were still there but he is far above her, rising with a sickening dizziness, while below him she remains motionless, about to disappear, drop away from him too, and he wakes with his heart thudding. Only a minute, a second must have passed, and when he turns his head to the side the mask is still there.

He reaches for her thigh. She scrapes across the sheets. Hastily they press, lick, push. His mouth drags down her length; she holds on tight. Their faces stay rigid and set and neither speaks even to moan and their breath barely rises before coming, which happens first to her, then him, and hits them like quick senseless charges of electricity. Then, though they hold each other and kiss bare flesh, they still do not look at each other's face. When he opens his eyes, he can see only skin, stretched like some synthetic fiber over the body, giving off a brown scent.

I just don't want her to die.

Her body tenses. What do you mean? she whispers back.

I told you things with the spic and this guy Oliver didn't work out? he says. That was because the spic's wife and Oliver both got killed the first encounter we had. And I don't want it to happen again. I don't want another client to die on me.

He begins to shake. She presses his head down against the tops of her breasts, his body shaking against hers. Both feel at last they have found each other again. The news evokes in her the spectre of her own terror, released like plutonium gas, moving toward her and those she loves; for him, more literally, it means someone is after him, making him fail at his job. Still, they are together in a way, holding each other; and in these positions, fall asleep

Mel's face is clenched into a red knot. You could *skip* the important clients, Joe, he is saying. Run a quick sort on who you've got right now, I mean you've got to have *some* clients who don't have clout—

Joe shifts forward, makes his fingers a tent: Mel, I think you're mistaking the nature of our enterprise at NASA. We don't cater to consumers. They don't know about us. We take *pains* that they won't. So the people we take on do have clout. And they feel they're getting a special service from us because of it.

He unfolds his hands, lays them flat as if about to rise. And I'm not going to jeopardize the prestige of this division by pushing junk to NASA clients!

All right, Mel, Joe, says the man at the head of the table languidly, staring off. I think Joe's got a point. Now, who's got a better idea?

His ass feels hot in the chair for so long, but his brain thrills in a pleasant current as he looks at their tense faces in the two rows, in rows . . .

He clicks his eyes into focus, flashes them at two men sitting halfway down, idly scratches his long jaw: Don't we have anyone from marketing here today?

Yes, one of the men says, jolting forward, tugging at his tie: Well, what I was just about to say, is, uhm—well, if we want to give this thing a good float before rollout—

Yes, Jack? says the man at the head of the table, smiling. Come on, Jack. Out with it.

Helena Fort's front room is a windowless octagon, two of whose facing sides are doors. The other six are eight-foot wall-to-ceiling mirrors, which both reconfirm and confuse whatever is in the room; so that now their glazed surfaces convert the four people on the cushions and seats to eight, reflecting their reflections back to themselves.

The double image talking now is of a young man with a broad generous mouth, hard merry eyes, a green frowsy wig on his head: And *I* maintain we shouldn't argue with a plan that's going perfectly, he whines.

Watching his images with blank interest are two Helena Forts lounging in customfit black urethane slouchcouches near the room's centers: I'm not arguing, Brother Bobbie. I just question what our purpose is in doing all this.

Purpose? snort the heavy lanternjawed women in red enameled suits with yellow capes across the room.

That's right, say the Helenas coolly. What do we need him for? He's not one of us, he doesn't know anything. Why *buy* a member of the organization? Why implicate the poor schmuck?

May I remind Sister, say the Brother Bobbies, teeth baring suddenly, that she is herself a member of this organization, and as such has pledged her powers, loyalty, and obedience toward the freedom through destruction she supposedly desires along with the rest of us?

The Helenas, meanwhile, have unpinned their stacks of hair which fall now, flowing red, over their shoulders, down to midback: I don't see why I can't ask questions when things don't make any sense. What do we want him for? Why did Brother Bobbie have to cut him on the trans?

The Bobbies grin dreamy, wide: Sure was fun, though.

Why can't Sister Helena follow orders with her mouth shut or get fucking out? say the large red women, with jutting heads.

Now now now, issues the calm voice of the fourth person in the room, to whom they all turn. He is a lithe tall man in his early forties, black hair to his shoulders, streaked with grey, a saturnine cast to his face. In shiny silver overalls and an oldfashioned limegreen shirt, he half sits, half stands, in the white strands of webbing draped from floor to ceiling by the door.

Sister Helena knows the organization's requirements, he says. I don't really think that's the issue here. His iceblue eyes, undistracted by mirrors, fix on Helena Fort: My guess is that you feel some sympathy for Goodman. Am I right?

Her eyes flash to him, then away: I can't see what we're setting him up for, that's all. Why can't we leave him alone?

No one has said anything to me about setting him up, Sister Helena, says the man softly. Do you have other instructions from some independent source?

The smirks exchanged between the heavy woman in red and Brother Bobbie travel around mirrors.

But before we continue, says the man in the netting, I think perhaps we should check the premises? He reaches in the chest of his silver overalls, draws out a small black box with a metered front. Helena?

Her face is suddenly slack. I checked it myself yesterday, she says. Really I did, Brother Don.

No one's accusing you, says Brother Don. I just want to make sure. He holds out the box to her: Please use mine.

It is a leak detector, powered by radium crystal. She crosses the room, passing yet constant from mirror to mirror, takes it from his hand. She strikes a button by the door that makes the mirrors swivel, revealing screens as their backs.

I never will understand why anybody needs so many screens, sneers the woman in red.

I used to like a lot of input, Helena says, her back to them, scanning the edges of the first screen.

The woman in red walks to the couch, tests her fit, scowls as she spills over its fitted sides, sits up. The three of them silently watch Helena's progress across the room until, at its far door, she turns to Brother Don with a slight question in her eyes.

The rest of the apartment too, he says. Can't be too careful, can we?

Once she is gone he throws his long arms back, catching them in the nets, smiling without humor at the other two. Sister Helena seems to be displayings signs of disloyalty, he says. What if any action should we take?

Brother Bobbie giggles: Snuff her out.

Sister Jeanine? Brother Don says, lifting his neutral face.

The woman in red, mouth gaping, jaw thrust out, nods her head heavily.

Perhaps that is our only alternative, Brother Don says, swinging a little harder back and forth.

Each night as Billy sleeps there is that much more raw material for dreams, those places where the voices, surfaces, shifts of light he knows from out in the world turn into a single being which has never changed, which you either fit yourself into or run from so it will not hurt you, keep you outside itself, swallow you up. Tonight some parts of that single being, that unchanging law, are a tape of his, soft male tapevoice singing I like you, I love you, let's spend time you and I; the boy Roger he used to run with down the block, who has gone now, his parents emigrated for a job, the only other child in the neighborhood, for whose loss he feels a certain guilt; the L-shaped laser weapons his toy spacemen carry, their obliterating flash as seen on the screen; three women running ragged through dirty green water to get away; his mother handing a glass to him, watching him drink, the sense of the man, Ernest, behind him, his fear of Ernest's valediction, fear of the dark; the darkness under his bed, around the room as he sleeps, yellow patch of light from the streetlight outside; his mother's face displaying all the expressions you can see on the screen. Each one of us lives his first years, distracted or bewildered, as a profound and solitary reality. Here the internalization of the external is an irreducible fact.

Jack, vice-president of domestic marketing, has prominent sweatbeads rolling off his forehead and down his cheeks by the time he is through making up his analysis and suggestions. But he too has done well.

In fact, he has pulled off probably the best maneuver of the meeting so far, by shifting the responsibility to Chuck. Poor Chuck, the old (late fifties) man down near the table's end, who draws back his shoulders as they watch, attempting to show all his hawklike visage one more time; who made the last bid from the considerable position of V.P. Int'l Mark. to unseat him as President, during the brief Volksfodder flap last year; who is now in the pitiful position of V.P. Domestic Services, with nowhere to go but out.

What Jack has done is to propose that the Regroove Centers, OMNI-CO's tax writeoff network of plush quasimedical clinics for the disturbed consumer, be used as marketing sites for heroin. Junk, Jack proposes, can be discreetly suggested to "acclimatized" guests in the serene multicolored softfoam surroundings as a hedge against their manic moodswings and bouts with despair. The results can be gathered, processed statistically, graphed, projected out when the data is in; the corporation will then move according to this truth.

Two assumptions hide in this proposal, one strategic, one a priori. The latter is that there is really little or no difference between the average American consumer and the average Regroove "guest"; the former is that if Chuck should fail—if word should leak out to the media, if the survey is botched—Chuck, whose presence at the table now is token anyway, will be the only one to lose his ass.

Well-thought, Jack, says the man at the head of the table, watching the shiny sweat roll; he'll crack some day or make a move, they all do. That's a fine example of thinking on your feet, he says.

Jack's thick face reddens, chokes out a brief laugh; the rest of them smile at him.

The man at the head of the table turns to Chuck: What about it, Chuck? Can you handle it?

I'm sure we can, Dick, says poor Chuck, still posed.

The man at the head of the table stretches his lips at the use of his first name. His dark eyes turn opaque. All right Chuck, he says. I expect some kind of statement from you in the very near future on the setup. See the whole thing's budgeted under Maintenance or something; for God's sake don't list it as a separate entry anywhere. I'll expect results in six weeks.

He stands, tall slim and stiff, his worsted wool flat black in shadowless light: Well gentlemen, I believe the next item on our docket is a currency report from Howard here. But why don't we break for, say, five minutes, stretch our legs a bit?

They all rise, slowly, relaxing their weight, starting to talk.

Joe? he says. Can I have a word with you?

The conversation ceases for a moment; they watch Joe Merrill glide to his side, nodding his head with its crown of silver, a close match to his natural hair beneath.

Next morning, as planned, Ernest takes an early trans through crisp air to Helena's Bay Street address, a luxury highrise perhaps ten years old, reinforced white concrete in the shape of an old factory smokestack; and finds her pacing back and forth on the street outside, deserted at this hour of all but the blue and yellow guards staring back at the two of them.

His brow furrows. Hey, he says, I got passes. I could've gotten in. You didn't—

Decided to wear something decent for a change, huh? she says, a trifle loudly, and takes his arm and whisks him through the doors.

All right, he says in the lobby's pink glow: What's going on?

She says: Keep moving toward the elevator, don't stop.

Spots of high color emphasize her cheekbones, but the area around her mouth and nose seems white and pinched. On the whole she seems smaller today, and despite commands, less assertive, more vulnerable in her diaphanous green gown: There are some people upstairs, she says quickly, softly. Do me a favor now; keep your mouth shut in front of the guard.

On the way up in the elevator they put on a little skit. He stares doubt-fully at his shinguards: You really think beastery is right for me?

She tosses her head, laughs melodiously: Hopeless. Next thing you'll be telling me you're sorry for the animals. Just so you can get back to your pitiful old unisex suits.

Now hold on, he says, thrusting out his lip: I haven't said anything about this robe, have I? I *like* this robe . . .

From the rear corner of the elevator the slouching guard smiles at them.

The elevator stops, its door opens, they walk into the hall: You've got two seconds to tell me what's going on, Helena, Ernest says.

You'll find out, she hisses. That's what they're here for. It's okay. Now will you please shut up?

They stand beneath the lightbeam by her door, are acknowledged, admitted (GuardAll surveillance throughout the building). Inside, the six mirrors show again; the same three people stand or sit in roughly the same positions, wearing the same clothes—except Brother Bobbie, who has ap-plied sequins to his face along with the green wig, to avoid being recognized.

Ernest, Helena says, these are three friends of mine. Jeanine on the pillows there, Bobbie on the floor, Don—Ernest Goodman.

Ernest's eyes travel up from them, around the room; the mirrors; un-smiling, doubling, the images spin around and in his stomach something cold and wet and loose begins to move. These, he thinks in a crazy flash, these are the ones behind it all, the crazies, they will tell me what they did to Paco's woman, to Oliver, then do it to me—

Glad to meet you, he says seriously.

Please don't be afraid, Ernest, says the one nearest to him, silvertrou-sered in the nets. We're just some friends of Helena's—

Helena brushes past him, wafting her way through the room. Her expression is opaque. So is the fat woman's across from him, notwithstand-ing her chronic scowl. So is the highly embellished young man on the pillows. So is the older man swinging in the nets. What were their names again?

No, he says, with two fingers at his lower lip: You're not friends. She wouldn't need me if you were. Would you, Helena?

Helena, on the couch, has turned her back and does not answer. But he can see in several mirrors her still hard frightened eyes.

The heavy woman spreads her feet apart and swings her hamlike hands. You calling Brother Don a liar?

But I am, Sister, says the man in the nets with an elegant gesture.

Please sit down, Sister Jeanine. We are all quite sufficiently aware of how menacing you are.

From the couch comes the sound of a stifled laugh.

We shouldn't have tried to deceive you on a matter so close to your specialty, says Brother Don, turning his narrow face. What you have wandered into, Mr. Goodman, is one cell of the Liberation Club. Do you know of the Liberation Club, Mr. Goodman?

No, says Ernest, watching Helena's eyes.

Brother Bobbie? says Brother Don. Explain, please.

Brother Bobbie, sequined face flashing, speaks in a rushed monotone: Liberation Club is an organization of men and women dedicated to the restoration of human wholeness and psychic freedom for ourselves in the United States by the commission of acts of random violence against the material world.

Sister Jeanine? says Brother Don.

She heaves to her feet, glowering: The basic unit of the Liberation Club is the cell. Each cell has three or four people, and a leader. The leader is our contact with the next level of cells in the hierarchy. He gets his strike orders from them and gives them to us. Being unable to choose our own targets allows us to destroy with more life-enhancing spontaneity—

Okay, Ernest says. That's enough, I'm incriminated. Now what do you want?

Sister Helena? says Brother Don.

She turns, he watches her turn in all the mirrors, come to a sitting position on the couch, knees tightly together, hands folded in her lap. Sincere.

It's not as bad as it looks, Ernest, she says. You called it right in Bertolino's yesterday. This, the Liberation Club is what I found, what I'm connected with. You're—her eyes shift around the mirrors, at all of them—the one I want to trust. But I had to tell them about you—her eyes shift, the hands writhe in her lap—we've got this loyalty oath, all of us have to know about things like this, any big change in somebody's life, you know . . .

Ernest watches her another second, then turns gimlet-eyed to Brother Don: So, I get three options from you, probably. I can walk away from this job now, in which case I risk getting fingered or trashed. I can join the Liberation Club with you. Or I can implicate myself all the way without actually joining, by helping you trash whatever you've got in mind. That about right?

Oh Mr. Goodman, says Brother Don. You deprive us of our next round of speeches. And Brother Bobbie and Sister Jeanine have practiced so hard too.

I could give a shit, smiles Brother Bobbie up at him with rubbery lips, gold face.

Ernest looks across the room at Helena, who searches his eyes in return. The column of her hair, uncentered, sags toward the right side of her head.

Calm down, he says. Everything's okay.

Slowly, her eyes on him, she nods.

He turns a harder gaze on Brother Don: Option three, the accomplice one. What do I have to do?

Brother Don shrugs, casts a slit of smile back. Go trashing with us. Tomorrow night.

Do I get to know where? Ernest says.

Naw, guffaws Sister Jeanine: Fuck ya, you find *us*. And Brother Bobbie brays along with her.

I don't see why not, Brother Don says, straightening, releasing his hands from the nets: Remember the store yesterday in Union Mall? The one where you got those clothes?

Got good taste anyway, Ernie boy, says Sister Jeanine, lumbering toward him. That robe's almost like mine, you notice? We could practically be twins.

His eyes blur in mirrors; he sidesteps her, strides to Helena on the couch. That's why we went in, isn't it? So I'd know the layout.

She nods again, head bowed; his hand falls on her cone of red hair.

Well, he says, that's all right I guess.

Twins? squeals Brother Bobbie, suddenly gasping. Shit, Sister, you're triplets now!

Rake your eyes out you little shitface, she says and comes after him as he wriggles shrieking across the floor, his face sparkling gold in all the mirrors.

Brothers, sisters! Brother Don holds out his thin white hands, his face hooded and grave: If tomorrow night's spontaneous act is to be a success, we have some minimal planning to do . . .

The nearest section of the inside wall swings out. He and Joe Merrill walk through to a high, spacious room about the size of a judge's chambers, paneled in dark mahogany. The wall closes again.

He reaches for his tie, loosens it with a few deft shakes, sits at the T-shaped alabaster desk. Be a pleasure to take these goddamn things off, huh Joe? he says. Get some decent clothes back on. Goddamn wigs too, drive me crazy sometimes.

Joe firms up his wobbly smile, tries to sound chipper. Well, he says, business is business, I guess.

A series of five data screens, one for each populous continent, are mounted in a line along the back of the desk; he takes some signs and figures from Australia, scribbles on a pad for thirty seconds then looks back up.

About that little matter you've been taking care of for me, he says.

We're coming along quite well on that, sir, says Joe. The screening process is just about over now—quite a rigorous one too, as I'm sure you'll agree, in exact accord with your specifications. In fact, I think I can say with some certainty we could virtually select your man right now.

What's his name? he says.

Goodman, Joe says. Ernest Goodman.

How many'd you test?

Five, Joe says, five besides him. Each with his flaw, the way you said.

You know what I mean there, he says. Nothing dysfunctional. Chinks in the armor, nothing more.

Absolutely sir, of course. No major liabilities whatsoever. Inside, Joe's mind races, flutters, snatches for the list: Like, he says, for example one guy has a thing for nature. Grass, trees, air, you know, that's all. Been with us ten years, steady ratings, very high. We never would have caught it at all in fact if it hadn't been one day his client, turns out he has a thing about explosives, wants to take him out somewhere in northern Maine—

But the other man is waving his hand as if clearing smoke away. I don't need to hear this now, Joe, he says mildly; and rising from his desk, reknots his tie. We've a meeting to get back to, remember?

Yes sir, of course, says Joe; and, hitching his own tie back up over a swallowing throat, reaches the panel first, triggers it open, stands aside.

Yet in the doorway he pauses and looks back with a light smile; so close that even beneath the makeup Joe can see—thinks he can see, anyway—the wrinkles of the forehead, slightly coarsened pores of his shapely nose.

Sometime, though, I really do hope we can sit down and talk more, he says. That's quite an operation you've got going there, NASA. I'm sure I don't know as much about it as I should.

Now Joe can feel the gaze of men in the next room, cessation of all other speech, hot tingling of his cheeks as he responds: I'd certainly welcome that opportunity, sir. Anytime.

He turns, looks up and off ahead of him, moving for his chair. For example, he says, almost dreamily: These men with the single flaws, what happens to them?

Well sir, Joe says, hurrying back down to his own seat, atremble with this private-public conversation's honor and risk: They're out of the company, of course. They're on their own.

Really? he says from the front end of the table, cocking his head bemused. That surprises me somehow. Ordinarily when you know where a man's weakness is, then you have him, haven't you? At least that's how it seems to me.

You want to stay around a while? Helena says when the others are gone. Watch some screen? Eat something? I don't keep much in the place, don't like to hassle timers and stuff. But we could send out.

But what she really wants is a big scene. He makes his eyes flat, with a steely glint.

Cut the timorous glances, he says. You set me up for this. You don't expect me to clap my hands and sing, do you?

She lowers her eyes and walks away, across the pillowed floor. My god, she says, patting her hair, I bet I look a wreck . . .

Ernest steps behind her. How did you get mixed up with them anyway? he says. If you don't mind my asking.

She throws him a weary glance and settles on the floor. About six months ago I met Jeanine in a display room. She had the eyebeams taped in and was burning up a pair of shoes, taking her time and laughing her head off.

She hugs a purple pillow to her face, smiles over the top of it: I ended up helping her. Other people went past, looked in, they didn't give a shit. Half of them laughed too. It was a lot of fun, it was the best I'd felt in years, since I could remember. I met her at a place afterwards, we took a little walk, she told me what was going on. I joined up right away.

Ernest sinks down beside her, fairly close, propped up on a hand; softens his tone somewhat. What were you doing before?

Before, she says. Same as everybody else. Watching screen, smoking dope, taking drugs, going to the store. There were a few lovers in there for a while, too—her eyes scan his, flash away—women mostly. It was dumb either way.

He weighs whether or not to stroke her arm; decides against. And this changed things?

Oh yeah, she says. Changes everything.

She falls on her back and stares off at the ceiling; her chiseled features glow. You can't imagine what it's like, wasting something. When you blow something up, throw it out the trans, smash it hard with the heaviest thing you can find. God, it's just terrific! She rolls her head toward him. You ever torn something apart like that? I mean, just completely down to shit?

No, Ernest says, mouth twisting wry: Now I guess I get my chance.

She grins: You'll love it. You will.

He returns her smile, then flops down beside her, so close he can hear, or feel, her breathing. For a second it makes him think of Charlotte. He lights and passes an Acapulco. Seems like you've escalated your targets a little since back then, he says.

Not so much, she says, toking: Every so often, they have us trash all together. Then it's big.

They'll get you caught eventually, he says, amiably.

Yeah, she says. It's okay. Better than forty years of being bored to death.

They pass the joint back and forth some more.

And you don't mind trashing with them? he says.

Sure, she says, in a slow dreamy voice. They're creeps. But who isn't a creep? I'm a creep. I'm a stupid nothing creep.

She rises on her elbows, giggling: You're a creep, too.

He looks at her happy face hanging above the gauzy green folds tenting them both. I'm your friend, he growls. I don't take creeps for friends. Neither do you.

Granted, she says, almost singing: The only noncreeps in the world.

She lifts a long sleeve, drifts it back and forth across his face. She is smiling, but her green eyes remain sharp. She traces his face with the fingertips of her long hands.

What do you want? Ernest says. You want romance?

She frowns; thinks. Play at it, anyway, she says. No fucking.

No fucking, he says. Fine. Contract forbids it anyway, more or less.

Where's the contract? she says, touching his neck. You bring it with you?

How'd you find out about me? Ernest says.

I heard about you.

He stops her hand. No, you didn't. You couldn't because I don't advertise and I haven't been here long enough to have any other clients.

He lets the hand go again. Now, he says, how'd you find out about me.

Someone recommended you, she says, very low.

He grabs her arm and presses tightly, feeling the flesh under his fingers sink. Who? he says. NASA?

NASA? she says, genuinely surprised. Isn't that some old space thing?

His grip on her arm does not relax: Okay, forget it. But someone referred you to me.

Yes, Helena says, and tries to twist away: Let go of my arm, you fucking goon!

So help me, Helena, Ernest says, if you're setting me up for something, you and the rest of your little bandit clan and NASA and everybody else—

Listen, she says, I checked with them every way I could. Nobody in the Liberation Club is on your ass, okay? I promise you. Really.

He lets go; she grins wide, boyishly: Don't you think it's kind of nice though that you can't trust me?

He reaches over, cups her chin, smiles savvy in her eyes: How's about if you sign this contract I got here right now?

I got it! he says bursting through (once cleared), waving the papers. I got the goddamn thing!

But in the front room, in their bedroom, no one; in the screenroom Billy sits alone, pulling clothes on and off a male doll. Onscreen a quiz show's screams of joy, some man jumping up and down over the black obelisk he has won.

Where's your mother? he says.

Inna kitchen. Without looking up

Honey, he says, bounding in: I got it.

She looks up from the table, turning her head slightly; the intent, removed expression does not alter on her face.

Home early, she says. That's nice. Is everything all right?

All right? he says. I got a contract signed, honey! Six months, a client for sure!

That woman? Charlotte says quietly.

Yes, he says, Helena Fort.

That's very nice, she says. I'm happy for you, dear.

He slips over to the table, rubs her shoulder under the cloth of the russet sari, tries to think of something to say. Already her eyes are back on the book.

Reading, huh, he says.

That's right, she says. I'm trying to get some of it back. It's hard, though.

I bet, he says.

He waits a minute. She turns a page.

What is it? he says.

Play It As It Lays, she says, one of yours. I tried *Couples* last week but it was too much.

Yeah, he says. I remember wading through that for exams. Don't think I ever finished it. This one's pretty good though. You know Didion did *A Star Is Born* too? You know, the movie?

No. I don't like the woman much in this one, she says and turns another page. I don't like any of them much.

He bends over and thrusts the papers before her eyes, in front of the book. Look he says. About halfway down. See what it says? I'll tell you what it says, it says No fucking, okay?

I'm certainly not worried about whether you two fuck or not, Charlotte says in the same tired quiet voice.

What are you worried about then? he says, and keeps his face still, waiting for the anger.

I'm not worried, she says. Everything's all right. I'm not worried about anything at all.

He waits another minute behind her, rubbing her shoulder again. The flesh feels like rubber, moves like dough. Inside it is nothing. She is gone.

Then, on his way back through the screenroom, the audience has stood up, is running around the studio roaring, smashing one another as the host in a suit of black feathers cackles and crows.

Billy, he says, turn that down!

The boy scampers for the dial, to obey. Tonight he will dream a single threat, a single monster looming from the dark: *Turn that down! Turn that down!* Ernest's face will briefly emerge from his mother's, then fall back into it again.

In the dream I was with my lover in an airy white room whose only feature was a large fireplace of scrubbed stone halfway down the wall on our right. We sat on the floor, downstage from it, kneeling before a big unruly scrapbook, a heap of newspapers scattered around. We were clipping articles out of the papers for the scrapbook, sometimes taping them carefully, sometimes tossing them carelessly in. She was dressed in her cotton nightgown, the color of raw milk. We kept laughing at what we were doing, at the impotence of the news, its foolishness flopped in pieces in the sloppy book. It couldn't touch us. We laughed at it.

   In the front room Ernest sits stiffly in a plexiglass chair like an inverted question mark between the couch and Billy's bed, now made up into its sculpture. The cold afternoon sun falls like water, palely, in a vague square by his feet. You should never have told her anything, never tell her anything. It has nothing at all to do with her, with us. Helena Fort and her Liberation Club and the upcoming trash, NASA and T.D.'s hint, Oliver, Paco, Paco's wife, whatever shape they make with him inside, whatever connections there are he will figure out himself, it is his business. She will have to understand that. It has nothing to do with her.

If power is the charge in a gridwork, and we occupy the junctures of the grid; if power passes through us to be redirected, dispersed, passed along; if no one in any position on the grid "holds" power, if power holds us; if this is true then it may be misleading to speak of the inner character, the "soul" of a corporate president. Not only because it is not he himself who is important, his temperament, personality, etc., as opposed to his position on the grid; but because it may be that in that position "his" power—the sheer overcharged aggregate of the entire system directed to his juncture, to him—may have long since burnt away any inner being he might once have had. He will, no doubt, retain his small likes and dislikes: a taste for veal, a predilection for certain body types, a sad fondness at the cry of a mourning dove. He will—always at some risk and expense—have his own private games for restoring some vestigial sense of self. Yet he, more so than the lowliest worker in Brazil or Taiwan, will have no real identity apart from his position on the grid.

The name of the man at the head of the table is Richard (Dick) Devine.

In his living suite atop OMNICO domestic headquarters, Dick Devine sits in a formless orange unit filled with synthetic cartilaginous fiber and a computer the size of a hand, which directs the piece to maximal accommodation of whatever position his body takes. Now, since he is sitting up straight and right-angled, the piece is not allowed to show its genius; it has simply become a straight chair.

A holosette transmitter rests in his lap, flat black disc with two buttons, loaded with its cartridge and ready to go; he presses a button with his thumb.

The opalescent aqua of the walls fades dark, except for three spots of intensity spaced equally, compressed to laserlight; then the hologram of Joe Merrill stands before him affably smiling a foot away, still in his business uniform.

Here's everything we've got on him, Dick—

Devine's mouth grimaces, remembering those *sirs* at the meeting just last week. Lot easier to use first names when you're a holo, huh Joe, he thinks but does not say out loud.

Of course, a lot of it's not true footage, especially the early stuff, Joe continues: We had to use old photographs, home movie film. But it's as accurate as we could make it, I cross checked it myself against all the data we had.

Let's get on with it, Joe, he thinks. No need to play host.

Of course, Joe says with what must have been an attempt to "look" straight and firm at him, we have done some editing here and there to try and give you the major points—he laughs, nervously—otherwise it'd take you three days to get through it, right?

That's all right Joe. Hurry on you little turd.

So anyway, here it is, Joe Merrill says, edging out of the holograph as if, with some reluctance, leaving the stage: This is what we've got on Goodman. I hope you like it—Dick . . .

Again his lips crease in a sort of smile; he leans his frame back in the chair which folds around him, cushioning. Ahead of him the room has become a panoramic section of a small midwestern farm a la late '90s or before. And none too prosperous either, he notes; the farmhouse and outbuildings all seem in need of paint, the machinery puny and obsolete even for its day. All the same, an attractive picture: Cornfield on undulating hills, chinablue sky . . .

First, our subject's birthplace, Joe Merrill's voice intones—how fucking pretentious, he thinks with mingled disgust and glee—two miles south of Ottumwa, Iowa, in 1992—

Ottumwa, Iowa: while Joe's voice chants, he tries to place it on the map: how badly would they have got it from the K.C. meltdown of '08?

Ernest's father drives a green and gold John Deere to the barn, gets down off of it; also in the middle distance comes his mother out the back door of the house wiping her hands on a terrycloth towel, about ten feet from his chair.

On the way to the island, Helena looks around at the rest of them, shivering, rubbing themselves in their gauzy clothes, coiffures toppling, swayed by the stiff cold wind, and feels her difference with a sharp pride. A year ago she would have been just the same, would never have thought of covering her own robes, smudging her lines with a thick brown coat. But she is liberated now; she is different.

And so is Ernest, beside her on the spongy bench, dressed in a heavy limegreen tunic of loose-woven mohair, somewhat unstylish too. His brown hair streams back, spangling gold flecks, as he turns his windtightened face to hers and they lock hands and press, the only people touching on the boat in the whole skidding 30-second hydro ride from the wharf to Alcatraz.

Likewise, while the others start to chatter as soon as they get off and step on the minitrans to take them up to the prison mall, the two of them stay silent. She can feel their satisfaction, specialness around them like a glowing haze, like the gulls wheeling over the receding fog at the entrance of the bay to the sea.

God! she says finally, halfway up the rock hill: I feel wonderful today!

He squeezes her hand; his serious look, turned again to her, has a softness in it now. But the brown eyes still seem to look deep inside her, and to know what they have found. She understands, too, that he is not one to try and talk of things like this himself.

The trans, built on a small-gauge track, has a slightly archaic feel to it; it must date from the time—ten years ago, fifteen—when she was small anyway, when people liked to visit what they took as history, back when the old prison buildings were first malled. As she looks at it all, the grey walls, iron doors, the little trans gliding back down again, she even feels today a sad and pleasant pathos, standing there hand in hand with Ernest on the steps, in bracing air, thin bright light. Not for the time when there were little trains, of course, or when Alcatraz was a jail, she has no sense of that; but for that old quaint urge to keep things from the past.

Then they are walking inside, crossing the beam. You charged up about tonight? he says suddenly, smiling.

No, she laughs: Not consciously anyway. I'd forgotten all about it, actually.

In the huge duncolored room, the old main cellblock, they walk onto the belts. They travel in more horizontal and orderly patterns here, up to and past the three tiers of cells in the middle and on the sides. The piquancy of shopping in a famous prison is meant to compensate for the higher disorientation/security factor in the mainland malls; that and the far greater noise level, voices ricocheting off the steel walls. But these techniques have not been totally successful; there are fewer than two hundred consumers moving past the cells, through the bars of which the goods are visible.

They pass, on the first level, one cell with an inverted cone of light inside; another with an ochre unisex with epaulettes, the next with a self-regulating moog. The belt is too narrow for them to stand together holding hands. So you can feel it like a surprise tonight, he says: Like you never heard of it before.

They pass an ostrich sculpture, metal-leaved. She answers without turning: That's not the point. The spontaneity comes from not knowing what the next assignment's going to be. It's all just random trashing. Plus once we get started, we get to do anything we like—she smiles straight ahead, her face warm—you'll see. Anything you like here?

Nah, he says. Let's go up.

Shit! she hears him say as they reach the next tier: What the hell is that?

She looks at the first cell to their left and smiles: Come on, step in and see.

Despite the fact that Alcatraz never held women prisoners, the effigy inside on the mattress is female, with crazy glazed eyes, matted black hair, wart nose, wide seamed scar down the side of its face, one arm stretched out to them. Around her bed, the sink and toilet of an old cell are also in place.

What is this? he says, almost as if angry, staring abruptly from the effigy to her: You buy this shit or what?

Her eyes narrow on his face slack and unsure, feet shifting back and forth on the steel floor. Hey, she says. Don't flip out on me now.

Then he is knit together again, lean and knowing, shaded with irony: Just took me off guard. I thought she was real.

That's what they want you to think, she says: They got these things scattered around on all three floors just to give naifs like you a charge.

Don't laugh too hard, babe, he says as they step back on the belt. That's what they'll do to you when they catch up.

She tosses her head backwards toward him: You don't think we hit stores all the time, do you? It's a lot more random than that. Somebody's office, private home, a trans—they'll never dope us out that way, they're too hung up on sense. Like you, maybe?

Yeah, he says. Well, lots of luck.

She feels his hand caress the back of her neck; and leans her head back against it, imagining his hard knowing face as they pass a foam gown, chromium armoire, beastery wristlet . . .

And the next time an effigy passes, he says nothing; she senses not the slightest twinge of his hand.

Some take hotzie, shoot junk, get drunk. Some burn down their homes, kill a stranger on the trans. Some join organizations like the Liberation Club for the faint spice of social solidarity they can add to their random acts, for something reminiscent of work, or for the pleasure of being ordered around. But without a political intention, the actions of these organizations are meaningless; moreover, they are easily infiltrated and used by the power structure itself.

The image of another steaming dish floats on the screen: *Couscous,* the voice says, *tempting . . . lamblike meatstyle in savory semolina stew . . . exotic treat that you deserve . . . Couscous: dial 457-277-2619 . . .*

The image holds for thirty seconds, the order number before it in bright orange. The voice does not mention the countries where these dishes originate. Few people would know where or what Libya is.

Billy stands beside her in a light blue smock, his face guileless in need, his little mouth an *o.* Can I dial, Mommy? he says.

All right, she says, and he runs off to the kitchen phone—but not this one!

Why not? he calls back in a puffy voice: Why not, Mommy? I would like that one.

I don't think you would, sweetheart, she calls gently, and hurries on, to teach him something, give him something to replace the mean: Listen, did you hear them say *exotic?*

Next image: thick red broth: *Manhattan Clam Chowder . . . hearty, reassuring . . . chunks of vegetables in subtle soup with chewy clamlike bits . . . made the way we know you like it best . .*

When they say *exotic,* she calls out to the kitchen, they mean it's got lots of strange smells in it, honey, lots of spices, and you don't usually like things with lots of funny tastes in them like that.

No answer: is he pouting, has he gone out? *Manhattan Clam Chowder,* they say: *dial 442-225-2473 . . .* Is he there?

Honey? she says, an edge of worry tugging at her voice: Honey, do you want to dial this one? It's a nice soup, Billy, you've had it before, you like it—

What's the number?

His shout sounds so much older, more firmvoiced than he usually is: the voice of a command. She smiles as she answers, relieved: I'll give it to you slow now; make sure you get the whole number right or we'll get something we don't want. It's 442 . . .

As her eyes pass slowly from digit to digit, her mind blanks again; the slight relief, slight worry leak out to be replaced, to her surprise, with irritation; an ugly trilling voice that almost seems to say out loud: And where's Ernest? Off fooling around? Where's Daddy? . . and with a sudden twinge like pain she realizes it is the same mocking voice of her own mother, shut up in that old house in Tuscaloosa, drinking away. Her mother, of whom she never thinks, her mother's acid voice that says Don't you get tired of worrying about them, of wondering where they are?

Four . . . seven . . . three, she finishes, just in time, before the next item appears: *Quiche Lorraine*, he says . . . *farmfresh dairytype treat . . . succulent, sure . . .*

A shabby street in the southeast corner of the city near the bay, in the area still occasionally called Hunter's Point. Here the wind is hot somehow, and chafing, as if it crossed a desert on its short trip from the sea; it blows wrappers, papers, crap down the streets, carrying a faint curious smell. The sunlight on all the squat crumbling boxes they live and shop in around here hurts his eyes. His robes are out of place, not to mention Hamilton's. They are out of place, walking side by side down the wide street where he can feel the blacks from behind as clear as he can see them ahead: their eyes curious, tired, frightened, trenched with hate as they step by, coming after them from cracked sidewalks, sleazy storefronts before and behind.

All right, he says, trying to keep his voice from hissing: All right Mr. Hamilton, suppose you tell me what's so important you can't tell me on the phone, I have to meet you down here where we can both get trashed.

Why *Don*, says Charles Hamilton of GuardAll, smiling warmhearted, sparse black hair fluttering in the breeze: Brother Don, I'm surprised at you. You're the head of a Liberation cell, aren't you? You're used to violence.

Violence we start, Don says. And not here. We're spontaneous, Hamilton, not stupid.

Charles Hamilton stops walking, blacks streaming around him in both directions, all ages, sizes, looking after them, holding half-empty bottles, clutching packages, probably all junkies ready to kill and Charles Hamilton stops; looks up, squinting and smiling at the cumuli racing the sky, holds out his small fat hands palms up, as if waiting for something to fall.

Beautiful sky, huh? says Charles Hamilton, cocking his head at him.

Brother Don feels an urge to fold up to a ball and cry, or to hit Hamilton and run, or to plead for mercy from the crowd at large. Deep in his heart he thinks he has nothing against blacks but he *knows* they will kill him if they can: What are you *doing*, Hamilton? he whispers as his voice begins to tear. Let's *go*—

An object lesson, Brother Don, Charles Hamilton says, smiling easily, straight on at him, just standing there: You know we are going to make life a lot sweeter for you and your little organization when you come through tonight. We have some very large things lined up for you to hit. You'll like that, won't you? Won't you, Brother Don?

The blacks keep passing, looking. That same look. All Brother Don can do is nod.

You must have noticed how easily you got into this zone just now, says Hamilton kindly, resting a paternal hand on his shoulder. No pass, nothing. And that's how easy it will be from now on for your little group to have its fun, if you do it right. Because *our* organization, the one I represent has a good many friends both inside regular security channels and out. You understand, don't you?

He nods again, his ferret eyes subsumed in the kind brown depths of the other man's, whose hold on his shoulder tightens.

That's how we can make it safe for the two of us to be on the street right now, Hamilton says softly, patiently. Even here, Don, we've got friends all over this street. And that means we can get almost anywhere, doesn't it? That means if you and your yo-yos fuck up tonight in any way, that we can find your little group and hit you with anything we want, doesn't it?

He nods again.

Charles Hamilton pulls him closer, until their foreheads touch, until he can only feel the blacks, not see them. Charles Hamilton's small brown eyes are all he can see.

Now, says Charles Hamilton, The client I represent is going to be in that store tonight. I want you to do your job and make that delivery and do it just right, okay? Because if you guys go off the deep end and fuck up somehow, that will reflect badly on me; and then you will find yourself down here alone. And there will be other orders on the street—he laughs softly, pleasantly—or maybe no orders at all. Okay?

The hand releases his shoulder; the sun and the crowd, the looks strike again at his eyes.

Okay, he says—then realizes the word has not come out. Okay, he says, okay, okay.

More holos, a 3-D montage: Ernest rides a bike down white gravel roads, helps his father put up fence, sits at his tapedesk in school, earphones clamped on, while Merrill's overvoice drones on: . . . every evidence of a normal childhood, with the exception of a somewhat low socialization quotient—no strong familial bond, no close relationships with peers, high video absorption rate. A not unusual personality profile for future acquaintances. In fact, such social distancing in the formative years often sets the stage for the kind of detachment that will form the core of the befriender's mutability type—

Dick Devine passes a hand wearily over his black brows, blotting out the image of Ernest afloat in the small farm pond. The way they all have to puke it out to you: socialization quotient, absorption rate, mutability types. Showing you their stuff, their pathetic lingoes.

The Goodman farm was part of the lands condemned after the K.C. meltdown—the official voice again—and is presently the site of the South Iowa Breederplex. Goodman pere, however, managed to receive some compensation from Missouri Utilities, and found also a position as warehouse manager for Safeway in Okoboji, a town somewhat further north.

(Holo of medium-sized Iowa town, old brick buildings shrunk under dead-hot snotcolored sky)

We speculate, but cannot verify, that it is this transformation of lifestyle that accounts for our subject's apparently above average S-C factor—that is, his desire to succeed and compete. What we do know is that the Goodman parents began from somewhere near this point in time to save sufficient moneys that their son might go to a top school. Explicit provisions in both wills provide for such expenditures.

(Holo of town fades to holo of the Goodmans, Dad and Mom: the former hollowcheeked, chest and body caved in like a crushed jointbox; latter hairless, puffy bloated face; both lying in coffins with shocked eyes open wide)

Norman and Gladys Goodman died in '08 and '09 respectively, both of systemic cancers, site unknown, Joe's voice intones, now over holo of seventeen-year-old Ernest inside the high oak-paneled walls of a visitation room, crying hard in a black suit.

Dick Devine's long thin lips turn downward as he murmurs the old, empty obscenity: Ch-rist.

As if listening, Merrill's voice quickens nervously: I had this one worked up, Dick, only because it's some of the only authentic stuff we've got. Lots of the older film from the Ottumwa days seems to have taken pretty much damage from the K.C. thing. Rays and that, you know. But don't get the wrong impression here—

The boy is writhing slightly, as if dancing or being slowly hurt, and wadding a handkerchief against his mouth. Behind him other mourners, also in black, pass the coffin.

Dick Devine watches from the corners of his eyes, head turned aside (chair adjusts slightly), mouth set in prim, dry distaste.

Our subject, Merrill says, has been extensively and frequently examined for radioactivity and pollution damage, but has always been found to be well within normal limits of tolerance.

But—Merrill's voice returns to formal tones, the great track of its exposition—the behavior you see here is rife with implication . . .

The boy still cries on, less violently, two feet away.

At this time and this place, Iowa 2009, one was expected to mourn the loss of parents grievously. What we are seeing then—

A middle-aged bald man helping young Ernest down to a chair. Young Ernest, trembling, nods gratitude.

—is a glimpse of our subject's intuitive grasp of social and interpersonal realities and needs.

But Dick Devine is no longer listening; he has shifted his weight to the right, the unit has become a kind of chaise longue. He stares off into the dark; his fatigue and disgust ebb away. Just another stew of razzle dazzle and jargon, another poor excuse for a report.

4 p.m. Jeanine Kreps wallows in her sunken foam tub, flaccid skinfolds trembling from fizzing scented jets of water on all four sides. At the surface of the water her wide face hangs, a sullen pout in the creases of the crooked mouth, a furious opacity in the eyes; though her mind is empty, thinking nothing, watching pictures of explosions behind the eyes, cutting slice of torch into cloth, stone, flesh, as she rolls her fat pale body side to side

catching the spray until her mouth splits in a lazy grin at the image of Helena Fort.

So he misses more holos, random slices from Ernest's typical college years, with Merrill's deadening commentary: Normal screw-off at Yale, straight C in Intro Reading, College Algebra, the rest of the cores, obviously not a business head. A little drug dabbling (more simulated holos): American freeon, Swiss ludes, brief flings with hotzie and smack. He misses what Merrill calls the "significant portent" of Ernest's talent for spotting hooks and essences in the classics, Twilight Zones, Alka-Seltzer commercials, etc.; misses Merrill's self-infatuated musings on Ernest's "career quandaries" of nineteen, over standard ethereal holos of Harkness Quad; misses those first classes in Interpersonal Relations in which Ernest appears suddenly, spectacularly, his talent ablaze.

He misses all this—not enough hard info—falls asleep. The unit soundlessly collapses into a kidneyshaped bed.

4:04. Bob Saunders and another man who calls himself Meat Dreams (rhymes with sweet dreams, he always says) stand along the gold rail of a pipebar called Splendide, near Nob Hill. Meat Dreams wears a full-length garment of synthetic feathers, iridescent green and blue; Bob, a purple balloonsuit. After the second hit of coke, ingested through short glass pipettes, chased with tequila, Bob and Meat Dreams (rhymes with sweet dreams) discuss the possibility of sexual union later tonight, after the trash. Bob puts the proposition; Meat Dreams pats his feathers, unallured. He always feels a little silly afterwards, he says, and it is tedious to have to concentrate on anything so long, and for what? a little dribble at the end and there you are. Bob Saunders says that it is different right after the trash, even if he, Meat Dreams, hasn't been in on it, he can catch the glow off him. Bob Saunders tries to make his eyes glow now into Meat Dreams' as he recounts just sticking Ernest on the trans the other day, tries to get across what a nice little rush that was.

The laserbeams burn on, carving shapes of light. Merrill's voice explains, digresses, speculates. In the center of the ellipsoidal room, Ernest appears in his first inspired role play improvs in IR seminars; in the tapelabs soaking up voices and images of Krishnamurti, Skinner, Berne, Rogers, Erikson, the old masters; becomes the most popular student at Yale.

Then, as Devine sleeps on, a new character shows up, his craggy handsome head hanging in the air like a Greek statue: Renssalaer Hampshire, descendant of a long pure line of New England Brahmins, chairman of Yale's IR departmentt, an acknowledged expert in the field.

Renssalaer Hampshire, having heard the florid recommendations of his junior colleagues, follows the usual course of action and has Ernest followed, watched, and bugged for an observation period of six months. Merrill explains that although obviously a great deal of holable material resulted, none of it need be shown. What is important is that, satisfied with Ernest's behavior and ability, Hampshire formally invites him into his advanced studies field action seminar, a research project covertly funded by NASA (OMNICO), in which each class member is assigned a willing member of nearby New York's business community; their encounters and relationships are recorded and filmed, the results shown and discussed in class.

The holos that follow, as Devine dreams lightly, nervously, show highlights from Ernest's relationship to a fat beef-faced v.p. of Chase Manhattan with strong masochistic tendencies and a taste for coprology, both obvious enough in the footage that Merrill's explanations are redundant. Briefly, movingly, the holos recapitulate the steps from that first strained encounter to a perceived intimacy so strong that when Ernest returns from New York to Yale at the semester's close, his friend buys up two blocks of ghetto in New Haven as an excuse to continue the relationship there; then Ernest's final work of disentangling himself with no more than the mildest, most pleasant regrets on the fat banker's part.

As a result of this extraordinary performance, when Dick Devine wakes from his own light flitting dreams he is staring straight at Renssalaer Hampshire's office as it was on a bright day in late May, 2013. Hampshire— whom Dick, of course, does not recognize—sits at his desk of solid oak. His rough austere profile, aristocratic nose and mouth, rise solemnly above his white academic gown, his pukka necklace. The sunlight through the window at his left throws a corona around his curly hair and beard.

I didn't ask you to come by today just to congratulate you on your work in this course, he says, and, smiling, holds up a pack of Acapulcos: Joint?

Devine rolls on his back, stretches, groans. Who's this guy, what course, where, what's going on now?

The young man Ernest holds up a demurring hand: No thanks.

4:13. Helena and Ernest, still together, stroll the beach by the sea at the west edge of the city, pausing to touch each other's faces every now and then. The same still wind that slapped at them earlier, in the Bay, here is much larger and more powerful; so much so that their words, when they do speak, seem to each other like directly transmitted thoughts.

Between the shore and the fogbank's thick white heap a mile or so out, the sky is clear. Gold light splashes off the water, terns walk ahead of them with a brisk waddle, gulls dip, soar, screech, all like an old commercial from her youth, and slowly she has become convinced: never mind you first contacted him on orders, this is what you want.

And Brother Don did say nothing would happen, nothing would happen to him.

She looks over at his eyes, bluegreen now with flecks of gold, the colors of the sea: Maybe I do trust you.

His bronzed face turns to hers. No reason why you shouldn't, he says. Then looks off, shading his eyes, and points: Someone down there, in the surf. Look . . .

A tiny pillar, black in the sparkle; they walk toward it. It gathers light as it grows larger, becomes an old man in red flannel shirt, brown spotted vest and trousers, hiphigh black rubber boots. In his hand a thin stick as tall as he is, tip flicking back and forth. When they get closer they can see a string gliding out as he snaps the stick forward and landing out on the waves.

Suddenly, on a crazy impulse, she calls out: Hello!

The old man turns, waves, and walks out of the glaring waters, the stick tipped forward in his hand. Howdy, he says once he is close enough to speak without raising his voice.

Beside her Ernest nods, unsmiling. She looks at the old man's round sunchapped face, the grizzle of white whiskers. And those clothes: stinking, ugly, old. Try shouting out to strangers again sometime.

So, she says without much troubling to squeeze the distaste from her voice: What are you up to today?

The old man's milky blue eyes fix hers. What's the matter? he says. You never seen anybody fish before?

Heat rises in her cheeks: You get fish with that—stick?

What'd you think you get em with, a magnet? The old man makes a sour face, shakes his head. I was doing this, catching fish when you was still a twinkle—listen, where'd you get that thing there? Can you just tell me where that comes from?

He is pointing a gnarled stub at the belt of catpaws around her waist. Ernest steps close to him, his face set hard. Alcatraz Mall, he says. From me. Not that it's any business of yours.

Just what I thought, the old man's voice growing louder, more high-pitched, ruddy face growing redder yet. You don't even know where it comes from any more, what they have to do so little shits, damn kids like you—want me to tell you?

Listen old man, Ernest says, let me fill you in on just exactly who you're talking to here. He taps his own chest lightly, twice: Assistant Security Chief, S.F.—and I may be off duty now, but that doesn't mean you won't find yourself in a state reprogramming unit by tomorrow afternoon even if your passes are all in order, which I sincerely doubt, if you don't shove off *now*, dried-up croaker. Go crawl off somewhere and die.

For a second the old man stares back; eyes bulge, mouth clamps shut, red worn hands clasp and unclasp the stick with the line. Then he turns and walks back into the sea.

Grinning, Ernest looks over at her: I don't have to be honest with everybody, do I? Just you, isn't that right?

Her arms are around him, she is laughing: You're terrific at that, you know it? You were great! The wind flutters loose strands of her hair, sparkling red, against their close faces; his smooth skin smells to her of sun, air, a light tangy cologne. Opening her eyes again she sees the gulls dive and soar, crashing waves, gold glitter everywhere she looks.

Devine sits up, leans back; the unit converts to a plush easy chair. He runs his tongue around the inside of his mouth and waits for the scene to make sense.

In the holo Hampshire settles back in his leather swivel chair. You know what you're doing next year? Any opportunities open to you?

Not really, says young Ernest, apparently without concern. My old man had some kind of job with Safeway once. I sort of thought I might be able to get something from them—but I really don't know.

Devine recalls the father, mother dying. Nice of Merrill to cut the voiceover, give him a straight scene for once.

Hampshire lights an Acapulco for himself: But you don't want to much, do you?

Young Ernest grins. Fuck no, he says. I like doing this stuff.

How'd you like to go on doing it? Hampshire says quickly; and before the kid can answer, is leaning forward as if trying to cross the desk, narrowing his flinty sharp eyes: Listen. I'm in a position to make you a very confidential offer. Whatever you decide about it, though, before I make it I want your personal assurance it stays confidential. Do I have it?

Devine watches the holo of Ernest's face. The kid's eyebrows have lifted slightly, but the rest of his face is blank: Yes.

There's a company called NASA, Hampshire says in clean rapidfire, eyes steeled: National Acquaintance Society of America. Their people do what you've been doing in the seminar, exactly the same but as a job. They keep a very low profile, make themselves known only to select people. You get only the cream for your clients, so the prestige, pay, etcet, they're pretty much what you'd expect if you're good enough to make the cut.

Young Ernest's eyes are burning in his lean tight face. Dick Devine leans forward himself, bringing the chair up till its back is ramrod straight.

How do I get in? the kid says. What do I do to make the cut?

Hampshire looks off airily toward his tapeshelves along the wall: I recommend you for starters, he says. That's enough to get you into training school. You'll be doing intensive IR for a year—really intensive. If you can't play the roles you're out, and the roles are tough. Want to try?

Devine, leaning forward still more, studies the open look on the kid's face. Smooth as an egg. Yes, Ernest says.

Hampshire smiles through his eyes, a sage worldly smile, joint dangling off his fingers in the bright spring air. You won't be able to tell anybody what you're doing, where you're going. Not even your parents. It's like joining the CIA that way.

Young Ernest returns a full face grin. I don't care, he says. My parents are dead anyway.

As the scene holds, fades, Devine brings his hand up to his mouth, pinches his dry lips, considering.

Then Merrill's voice again: And so six months later our subject found himself in our Silver Springs training center undergoing some of the most rigorous—

Idiot thinks Devine leaning back *why can't you shut up?* as the chair closes round him again.

4:35. Over on Sutter and Sacramento Donald Burchett's small apartment has just been visited by the three Orientals, each with a large black briefcase handcuffed to his wrist. Once again their taciturnity and cold hostile looks have prevented him from asking how in the world they ever get through the city in their shiny black suits of twenty, thirty years ago, with briefcases of weapons right there should any random guard wish to check. Once again they want cash—no billing, no i.d.'s. What can they do with so much cash anyway? All he knows is that late afternoon on the day of a trash, they invariably show up at his door. Whoever it is calls him up, gives him the trashing assignment, must be the one who contacts them; seems like a reasonable assumption, anyway. And Don knows better than to want to know more.

Someone must have told them today, at any rate, how big the upcoming trash is to be; the briefcases practically bulged with highclass stuff. Donald picked .370 torches for everyone, a few oldfashioned semiautomatic 45's for fun, an odd assortment of knives. The Orientals bowed slightly when they received their matching cases of cash, cuffed them to their other hands, and took their leave.

She goes out. She switches off the FoodVend channel and takes Billy up to Lafayette Park, a green square of lawn and spindly shrubs overlooking the marina, bay, and pleasure outposts of Sausalito and Marin beyond. There are perhaps only a dozen other people in the park, all old, come out from God knows where in grey and brown coats. They flop on the grass, blinking, as if they had just fallen down. Their faces are the color of sidewalks. No one much comes to parks any more.

In the center of the park hangs a decrepit set of swings beside a sandbox whose filling has more or less returned to earth. Billy runs there first, insists she swing him. When she does, above the wheezing rasp of rusty chains she hears his steady tuneless happy humming, and is happy herself for a moment; then he wants to get down.

She sits on a green scarred park bench, dully, stupidly, while Billy shoves the muddy sand around. At least he is engrossed; at least no one else knows her here; but then her face—she knows how heavy, bitter, blank it looks—would not seem remarkable to them. Most of them look the same way.

What is it she feels, though, that makes her look like that: anger, sorrow, fear, fatigue? None of these, it seems; or all. Only since Ernest took that woman on, it is as if some possibility had been canceled; as if she had begun herself to get old or sick; as if it will be harder and harder now for things to be all right.

Not just that he will be with the woman as much, more than he will be with her. That the woman will believe he and his care for her are as real as she, Charlotte, believes they are for herself: and really, who's to say who's right?

Or maybe there is no him; maybe there never was. Not since you were a little girl and your father would hold you up against his spicy shoulder. Maybe not even then.

The way our roles define us to ourselves, to each other, how much the definitions depend on the solidity of those roles. When Daddy as autocrat erodes, so does he, to himself and to you. When Ernest feigns intimacy with someone else, when the line starts blurring, is he still your lover, are you his?

But just at that moment, on the verge of seeing it, a sentence slides in to smudge the thought, shunt it away. Life leaks out, she thinks; life leaks out. As if that sentence were a chant, were thinking her; as if that were the simple, rhyming truth: good things drift away, and who's to say? Maybe they were never that good anyway.

So she loses the truth. Life leaks out.

Billy pushes the gritty mud around, meanwhile, till he feels so bad he has to stop. A while now, a whole long time since anybody said anything to him that he can hear. Look at her over there right now, sitting all bunched up just a few steps away, so close you couldn't even run up without crashing up against the bench, smashing into her, falling down. Sitting looking like she doesn't see anything, doesn't see you, doesn't know anything at all. Like there are no sounds left in the world.

Mommy? he calls out. I'm cold, Mommy. I want to go home.

Her grey face softens into a smile as he comes holding out his arms to be picked up, but she still doesn't say a single word. Not even at the park's edge, flipping their passes to the guard; and so all the way down the steep street to their house, silently, to each guard on each block; and he, Billy Partlow, silent too, all the way home: silent, angry, scared.

Three feet away, Ernest applies makeup in a white Training Center room; Ernest shatters the most obdurate silences with perfect gestures of sympathy, makes vicious circles of hostility, latent and overt, into straight lines of love; Ernest learns when and how to flirt. Holomontage of Ernest with his clients from the first vice-president to Paco and Sampson, emphasizing his adroitness with the latter two. And all the while Merrill's anxious cheerful urbane voice points out, stresses, elucidates, talks talks talks.

He watches this last half hour of holos too worn down to resist any longer, with a mind like dust. During the Sampson episode, he leans back like Oliver in the Fat Boy, and the unit becomes a similar recliner for him. In this position, deadened, he finishes the show, Merrill's last snappy entrance into the holo—hope you liked it, Dick; and I hope you like Ernest Goodman even more—his natty figure disintegrating at last into air; and the whole room goes dark.

He presses the time button in his left wrist; numbers flash in his head: 11:43. An hour's wasted time.

Presses another button in his wrist: Yes sir? comes the voice of the woman on call.

Get me Joe Merrill in here on holo, he says.

Yes, sir. Do you want return-pix, sir?

No.

The laserlights burn on again in thirty seconds, and there Merrill stands, looking silly in his sleeping clothes, a dull yellow sheath, casting his eyes around as if to find him. Dick? he says. Dick?

I just went through your report, Joe, Devine says, reclining. I must tell you, I am not pleased.

The flesh of Merrill's face seems to sag visibly. Gosh, Dick, he says, I'm uh, really sorry. I mean, I knew there were some holes in it, but I didn't think it was—

Let me try to explain it to you, Joe, Dick says.

But first he yawns; scratches his neck; runs his fingers lingering through the long black hair of the back of his head.

Joe, he says, you jabbered at me for an hour just now without telling me one thing I couldn't have taken for granted, figured out myself, or found out from a 30-second call to Personnel. And you completely left out the one piece of info I need.

Merrill's silver head trembles; his mouth, fishlike, pops open and shut. What is it, Dick? he says. You just tell me what it is and we'll get the holos right over, I give you my word.

I don't want another show, Joe, says Devine. If I want another show, I'll go home, watch a little vidscreen, okay? You don't have to give me The Ernest Goodman Story any more. What I need is the weakness, Joe, the single flaw, remember? Now's the time to tell me what that is.

Merrill's head nodding so hard up and down it is like the preface to an epileptic fit. Yes of course, he is saying, yes Dick, certainly, of course. We didn't forget, I personally made sure that information was recorded for you in my last memo on the progress of the tests. Of course I see now of course I should have included it in tonight's presentation itself, I just assumed—

That's all right, Joe, he says. Forget it. Just tell me now very simply, in your own words, what the weakness is—and stop calling me Dick.

Yes sir, Mr. Devine, of course, says Joe Merrill; and, after looking down briefly at the folds of his robe, swallowing hard, proceeds to recount with judicious concision the story of that last night at Claudell Westerbrook's, when the weakness first emerged. Now Devine listens attentively, head lowering in concentration, hands plopped fingers tapping on the unit's edges until armrests rise like bread.

Overdefined by the past, unable to become a consumer like the rest. Yet the present sucks the past dry, empties out the concepts of husband, lover, marriage, family she has tried to keep full. And by 2020 there is no movement that would help her see first the corruption in the concepts themselves, then their necessary erosion as the system first uses up love as an advertising ploy, then eliminates the economic dependence that underpins marriage and the family by depriving virtually everyone of a job. Now, within that system's inner circle, everyone (except the few men at the very top) is roughly equal before the neuter desire to get, to buy, to use up. Now, though occasionally a few corporate wives still get together in groups to talk about themselves and their men, Women's Liberation has dribbled away. There is no defense for her against the way the present guts her past, no future she can dream.

At 10:00 p.m. on July 18, 2020, the Webster Street entrance to the Union Mall is guarded by a slumpshouldered man in his late forties. Hooked to the belt of his seablue uniform are an over-and-under torch and an intercom connecting him with the other guards inside and at the other five entrances, and with the GuardAll control center for the complex located on nearby Lombard. Down the block he faces, two security men, both in their early thirties, amble up and down the street, similarly equipped with torches and intercoms.

At 10:07 a trans passes and stops to discharge five passengers. Three of them, two male and one female, walk away from the mall. Another male and female walk toward it. The block security men move toward the threesome; the middle-aged mallguard presses his intercom button to receive, puts a hand on the butt of his torch. It is not normal for five people to get off the trans at one place this late.

As his two approach, a man and a woman, the mallguard asks them to step in his blockhouse of reinforced plasticene, to show their passes and state their business. They nod pleasantly in assent; but hang in the doorway of the tiny shed as the fat woman rummages through the giant leather satchel that apparently serves as her purse. The narrowfaced man watches her fumble with a faintly disgusted look; then he reaches into his purse too.

Jeanine half-turns as she paws through her bag so she can see the other three, Helena, Bobbie, and the other guy. When she sees him, what's-his-name, reel out in the street, acting stoned out of his mind, the two guards watching him and laughing, she grasps her torch inside the bag and shoots a ray through it that slices through the middle-aged guard's skin and ribs over his heart with a high swift whistle, while Bobbie and Helena pull out their torches and trash the two blockguards before they have looked back to them.

Kill the intercom unit, Brother Don says.

As she melts it away, he stands back facing the white dome and starts torching out the icosahedral sections along the dome's bottom edge.

Then Sister Jeanine falls heavily to her knees by the body of the mall-guard. Her eyes are shiny; she breathes hard through her nose. Six inches below his shoulder is the hole burned by the beam, still smoking faintly, not bleeding yet. Around the wound the shredded fibers of the seablue uniform are white.

Sister Jeanine picks up the mallguard's hand, pries the over-and-under away from his fingers, grunting low: Sweet piece. Have some fun with this baby.

That's what we're here for, Brother Don says, tightlipped. He keeps on cutting with the torch trigger locked on. Jesus! What the hell they make these things out of, anyway?

The other three skip up behind them, laughing. Brother Bobbie and Sister Helena hold a torch in each hand. Sister Helena, shaking with laughter, buries her head in the hollow of Ernest's throat. Goddamn, she says, that was *terrific*! You were just incredibly fucked up!

That one guy? Brother Bobbie snuffles, the short one? He was still laughing when we first got him, man! He laughed all the way out!

Ernest laughs too and holds her close, thinking nothing at all.

Sister Jeanine rears to her feet and steps in front of them, waving the mallguard's torch in front of her red puffy face. See this piece? Honey, isn't it? she says in a thick voice. I'm gonna keep this baby, I'm gonna have me some fun before this night is through.

Brother Bobbie falls into a giggle fit; his black djebellah quivers, shines. Helena weeps with laughter, her breath warm against Ernest's chest. Ernest grins, showing all his teeth: Well, goddamn it, let's get in there then!

Brother Don stands and sharply kicks the triangle he has been cutting; another; it falls inside with a resounding brittle smash. His blanched face turns to theirs: All right, get your ass through there, let's go.

Ernest is second, after Brother Bobbie. We must've triggered about five alarms already, he mutters as he bends down.

Brother Don gives him a thin slanted smile: Already taken care of, Mr. Goodman. Don't you worry about a thing.

From the other side comes Brother Bobbie's shaky whisper: C'mon, let's go!

He crawls through, scraping knees and elbows on the concrete ground. On the other side he joins Bobbie squatting low, torch propped on one arm steadied on his knees.

The others follow. There is some trouble getting Sister Jeanine through; Brother Don has to push her from behind; she scrapes her back, tears her robe, yowls.

Christ, Jeanine, says Brother Bobbie: You fucking hog.

Her face is sweatstreaked, bloated, burgundy. Give me a hand, ratsucker, she wheezes. Or so help me, I'll waste your ass.

Brother Bobbie, looking amused, points his torch at her huge emergent head. Then he scurries, still crouching, over to her, takes her arms, tugs in unison with Brother Don to bring her through.

Ernest barely registers any of this. He stays in position, his torch aimed up Union Street. His eyes do not linger on the eerie spectacle of the dark stores and bars bathed in hazy orange, the milky white of the dome over all; he does not hear the scuffles, grunts, curses beside him. He is not thinking of himself and Helena any more. The whole scene is a diagram of lines; if any of them moves, he will shoot.

Finally, with a ripping grating sound, Sister Jeanine pops through, and topples Brother Bobbie. As the two of them pick themselves up, all happy and giggling again, Helena and Brother Don follow.

Brother Don stands; his small sharp teeth shine in the half-light: Okay. Ready to go?

Yes, yes, god yes, they say; Ernest watches the street.

Okay. Straight down the street then. Stop at JM's. You all know which that is, right? and they nod again—First one gets there, start torching that door. Now go!

Then Ernest is running beside Helena, red hair bannerlike flying backwards, head high, wide eyes laughing, laughing, they are all running, fanning out now, past the stores, bars, trees, plants, Brother Bobbie on his right, eyes mad, Brother Don ferretlike scuttling, Sister Jeanine stomping far behind. Running through the diagram. Steps slap off concrete, echo off steel and dome, weapons jiggle scrape in bouncing satchels on Don's and Jeanine's shoulders. Got to be other guards around somewhere.

Then, as if his thought produced it, he sees a blue shape wheel out of a doorway to his left, twenty feet from Helena.

Down! he screams.

She freezes; crumples; falls headlong as the ray passes inches over her back.

He braces his torch on a still left arm and shoots at the source of light: a small high cry; plop; the figure falls into the street and a torch clatters loose from its hand.

He looks over. Helena is alive, tucked behind a bonsai tree in its ornamental wooden box, firing at what? He looks ahead and sees the rays, hers, Brother Bobbie's, Brother Don's, Sister Jeanine's, converge on a motorized guard unit with sidecar that explodes in flames, throwing pieces of two seablue shapes in air. The roaring of the fire sounds like silence. Helena looks back at him, nods, her eyes wet.

Then they are running again.

Then they are at the steel gates of the store, JM's. They have to superimpose torchrays to cut through. Helena's lips are wet. The piece of door falls in. No alarms they can hear. Inside a string of pale electric lights hangs the length of the core of still belts. The storeroom entrances, black holes against grey. Brother Don says All right who wants a gun? passes them out. Brother Bobbie fires a burst of lead into the central computer, which shoots sparks, flames briefly in a few spots, dies.

They are running up the belts. Fifteen minutes! Brother Don yells. Sister Jeanine and Brother Bobbie firing. Each bullet ricochets, echoes, his head hurts, Helena grabs his hand and they duck into a room, shoot toward the center. The sound of breaking glass.

Then another room. Another. Another. Sometimes she has him fire his torch at the back wall so she can see what she is trashing: gametables, knit suits, golden birds on golden limbs that trill when the first bullet strikes, self-moving vacuum cleaners from Italy, carpets of Indian weave . . . Once, after shattering a mirror, she throws herself against him in the doorway, her hips churning. She kisses him, licks his face, openeyed, those strange green eyes. Behind him shouts, bullets, whine of rays, running laughter, echoing forever away.

Isn't it fine? she says wide rich mouth leering slack, kissing him, wet; I just know you'd—so wonderful. Kisses him again, again. Their groins grind; he starts an erection.

That's it! yells Brother Don somewhere behind, above. Let's get out of here!

They walk out to the still belts of the core, the others running down to them: Sister Jeanine, loose hair stuck to her forehead, Brother Bobbie stopping to slice the belts apart, Brother Don's pale grinning face in the rear. Helena's side still squeezes against him as they wait by the ruined computer at the bottom floor.

For the first time since outside the dome he thinks how odd it is they are not dead; how they will probably make it now.

Then the other three, Brother Bobbie, Brother Don, Sister Jeanine stand before them and Brother Don's thin lips smile tight. Which one of you feels the urge?

Me, says Sister Jeanine, lifting the mallguard's over-and-under as Brother Don dives forward, knocks Ernest to the side.

The single "over" ray from Jeanine's torch slices through the bottom of Helena Fort's breastbone; the "under" shot, a spray of laser light, stabs the rest of her torso randomly. Some of the synthetic material of her grey loose suit begins to flame before she reaches the ground, the shock on her face still strangely blended with joy. From the floor where he lies with Brother Don, Ernest hears his voice return from the core, from the steel walls of the store: *Oh no oh no no* no no no no . . .

Then he realizes he is still saying it, and makes himself stop.

Brother Don rises, holds out his hand for Ernest's: Mr. Goodman? We have to deliver you now.

Ernest Goodman stands up. He does not look at Helena. The contract is over. Brother Don is walking him back up the belts, holding a torch on him. From a corner of his eye at one point he can see fire inside one or two of the display rooms. He looks over his shoulder once, down at the figures of Brother Bobbie, Sister Jeanine, very small below, the faintest patch of red hair in the pile beside them.

Brother Don walks him into a room. The room is lit as if the store were open. In its center sits a man wearing a purple robe with gold and silver in the weave. He has black hair, greying and balding slightly in front, a longish jaw, seems to be somewhere in his mid-forties. Helena Fort is dead, with Oliver Sampson and Paco's wife. He finds it somewhat difficult to concentrate on the man.

The man stands up and walks toward him, smiling, holding out his hand. Hello Ernest, he says in a warm quiet voice. I'm Dick Devine.

Brother Don watches Ernest take the man's hand, then walks back out to the belts and back down to Sister Jeanine and Brother Bobbie whose laughter, murmurs, groans of pleasure echo to him; whom he can see, even from this height, rolling around on the bright floor below, beside the grey heap. Brother Don's thin mouth smiles without parting its lips. *Got it done* runs through his head over and over like a line from a tuneless old song.

The tomatoes and other vegetables that, together with the clams, compose the soup grow in squat square windowless buildings, one per crop, about as large as half a square block. Inside, the beds are about four feet wide and run the length of the building. A fairly primitive wrist-thick cord of wires and tubes connects them to a self-regulating process computer which determines the intensity and duration of the Agrolite rays, reddish purple, beamed down from their mounts in the roof, shedding only those wavelengths that assist the plants' growth; the kind, amount, and timing of the chemicals pumped into the soil to optimum nutrient levels, just below toxicity, for each crop; the amount and timing of the "rainfall" which drops from the sprinklers mounted with the lights; cycles of darkness and light; etc.

Four agsheds per engineer is average; aside from his maintenance and upkeep tasks, no human labor is necessary until the crop is grown. Then, for the picking and replanting, a small labor force is temporarily hired. For this reason most agsheds are located on the outskirts of cities in Asia, South America, Africa, where temporary help is both plentifully available (as it would of course be in the United States or Europe) and cheap (as it would not be). Cheap enough, in fact—especially since the engineer is instructed to hire mainly women and children—that it is worth the extra expense of shipping the food by jet back to the States or Europe, to its processing plant.

The women and children hired find tomatoes as large as the children's heads, firm, with skin as tough as hide for easy handling and, under the strange Agrolites, the color of cold blood. The lights give you a headache after an hour or so; unconsciously your eyes have squinted too hard, too long, trying to see clear shapes, find the dimension and depth of this flat, murky place, how far away is that woman working the next row over, and the one beyond her, how many rows are there? It is like being underwater, seeing the way fish see, and it makes your head pulse pain as though miles of water were over it, pressing down, until the dull concussion of the fruit hitting the bucket strikes you too like a blow; and you start to move more slowly, heavily, slowing down.

Sometimes, especially when a shed complex is new, you'd be surprised, they'll stay at 75, 80% efficiency all day when they still want to show you how good, how fast they can work, the line they jabber at you outside the sheds on hiring days. But most of the time once they get inside, they can't live up to it. The productivity of the seeders and croppers drops 50% in four hours; you can actually *see* them slowing down, like the air turns to jello out there. You can talk to them over the P.A., rig the computer to translate if you don't know the language, sympathize then threaten, yell into the mike (in your glass cubicle, in the white clean light). No good. But that's okay, plenty more where they come from, plenty other women and kids waiting right outside the door. You can hire four, five crews a day, what the hell.

The computer, meanwhile, does a scan of who picks or plants how much, makes out a payroll on the spot. The stuff is tossed into crates, the crates transported by truck to jet, by jet flown off to a foodprocessing plant somewhere else, another country maybe, and like the agshed itself not necessarily owned by OMNICO, but perhaps General Mills, General Foods, Westinghouse, Amoco, etc., etc. And the women and children all come back the next day, yelling about how fast they can plant.

Now that they know he will be gone much of the time, they are lovers again, spending as much time together these last days as they can, riding the trans around the city, lying for hours before the screen, wrapped up in each other, hardly watching or listening, wandering the malls, talking, talking even while they make love for time is squeezing out space, only the sound of your voice my voice your voice wherever they are, as if no one can go anywhere, nothing can happen until this conversation stops:

You want to keep the apartment? We can get someplace better now, larger or smaller now, if you want to.

When do you figure you'll be back?

Once a month, my guess is. Probably not less than that anyway. Probably I ought to get it worked out in the contract for sure. Like that canopy?

That what it is? I thought it was just some sort of free-form thing. You remember those things, those cute little cars you used to play golf in, with the little tiny rubber wheels, and you put your clubs in back? My father used to have one, with a green and white canvas canopy on top. And I used to lie back in the back of it with the golf clubs, all squashed up between the two bags, Daddy's and whoever he was playing with, and look up at the sun glowing through that green and white canopy and speckling where we hit some shade. And Daddy and the other man would be up front talking and laughing and he'd say What you doing back there honey? and I'd say Watchin the canopy . . . Do people ever play golf any more?

One of my first clients did. Older man. You can still catch it on the screen sometimes, I think. You going to be all right by yourself?

Yes. Fine. I'll be fine. I love you.

I love you too. I really do. Look, you think that's real skin?

Guillermo Hagen is six two and a half, tall for a European, since his maternal grandfather was an electrical engineer from Las Cruces, brought over to help construct the first small IBM centers in the early fifties lend-lease. The rest of the family background is all European, working class, although his father made the switch from metal worker to process tech-nician just in time to have the family placed in the Tienen compound, twenty miles from Brussels, in the late nineties when things got rough.

Guillermo at twenty-six still lives in the compound with his wife Anna, herself the daughter of a German systems analyst. They make a handsome couple sitting together on the orange plaid couch, watching the halfwall screen: he with his strong tightslung jaw and hawk nose, the curving lines of force running already from eyecorners to chin, legacy of generations writ large on an American frame; she, Anna, smallboned and roundfaced, with light flat blue eyes at once indifferent and lightly, deeply ironic, and straight, streaked blonde hair. The only problem is that they have been watching the screen (flashing all-American viewing, stuff canned in the States not less than two years ago: raid show, quiz shit, snuffers, etc.) for about six hours now, and they are stoned, sunk down out of their minds, glued in place by goofballs even though for some time now, who knows how long, the kid has been crying or making some kind of noise off in the next room, wherever that is.

The problem is for a lot of compound people like Guillermo and Anna that there is not a whole lot to do around these places where you get enough to eat, a place to live, school for kids if you've got them, and that's about it except for Adult Education bullshit nobody takes seriously. (Intermediate Reading: Anna went once, must have been three hundred people in the room, half of them z'd out beyond hearing, teacher up there slurring the words so bad you couldn't tell what was coming out, shaking so it was amazing he could read.) If you're one of the steady workers you can center on that, build out from it; for the rest of them, waiting around in the pastel box apartments for some action, any kind of action, to come down, there is nothing to do but nothing, no malls around and no one could afford them anyway. But the pills are everywhere and very cheap.

Which is why now, when the phone rings on the fake maple stand next to the couch, its shrilling reaches them only after quite a while as a kind of constant gurgling noise which, Anna slowly realizes, Guillermo is trying to answer with a similar noise of his own she can hear with her head against his ribs. Then she realizes that it is the phone; and that G's noise is not going to make it stop; and that, given the possibility that there is only enough collectible energy around for her to say one single thing, she probably ought to say it to the phone instead of to G (something like, say, *The phone's ringing*, you know), since you still don't know if you say your one thing to him if he (since he's the one that's *grunting* at it now) is going to be able to do anything about it anyway.

Right?

Right; and by the time Anna has managed to think all that, the phone is still ringing and so more than ever deserves some kind of award. So she picks it up and waits a second or so for the voice on the other end to stop talking. Then realizes the voice on the other end is not talking after all. Then hears her own strange voice say Hello?

In spite of the way it takes the strange metal voice so *long* to answer, it talks so *fast* she cannot tell what it is saying or believe she has already answered it with her name churning up from who knows where man, plus something else with the sound of Guillermo's name all so fast she cannot believe she has said Yes I'll tell him and the phone call is finally over so fast she is wondering how she did. *What* she did. So see if you can say it right now, before it is *too late*.

Anna trains her eyes on his large head in profile to her, his swollen eyes all but shut on the screen. Guillermo, she says, G baby, hey listen they want you to get in to do some stuff for them like right now.

Then she leans back, down, relaxes watching where these women seem to be in some kind of strange silver suits, laughing and jumping up and down, up and down, for a long enough time that she remembers not just the phone call but the kid crying about something some huge time ago too, did anybody get up?

But before she can answer G's face is in front of her talking, pretty loud: *Did you tell them I was here?*

Anna feels the question swimming back through the air, through her, wandering over the strange paths and byways of her brain inside, and coming back out with the message, with that *incredibly* heavy load—

Hey, she says. You know, I really don't know.

He still has to go every day to the office. To find out, through T.D. and his contacts, where and how to get in to a place where business suits are made. To get what he can through NASA's terminals on Devine, which is not much: a mass of p.r. copy dancing across the computer screens (But when we found this globehopping, mysterious, powerful man, so often characterized by his associates as a man of ruthless efficiency, he was sitting with his sleeves rolled comfortably back and a glass of Cointreau in his hand, beside his attractive thirty-ish wife in the brand new beach house in Redondo. "Call me Dick," he said, smiling, when we. . .), standard birdsongs of power. Plus the predictable career notes: school at Stanford and MIT, early rise to and through vice-presidencies, after ten years overseas management; two marriages, one kid of each sex (the boy in his first year now at Harvard); OMNICO president since 2012, during which seven years OMNICO's growth has jumped from 5 to 7% per annum. To draw up the contract with the lawyer, who meets with him for one-half hour per day, and to sit staring at the TransAm, trying to figure out how to play things.

Somewhere in the back of his mind, of course, are the dead. Paco's wife, Oliver, Helena Fort; close your eyes and see the bodies, watch the killing bright as day.

But for starters the connection between them and Devine is so crudely obvious even bringing it up to yourself now seems a kind of gaucherie. Then there's the matter of hard proof, what would happen to you for that matter if you had some and took the trans down to Security Central to lay it all out for them. Just guess what would happen if you did.

And one more thing too: You knew there was something going on, you were part of some plan. You saw there was a logic, chose to let it work itself out. You consented to the test.

So it is more than a matter of getting the info on the client to suggest behavior and personality patterns which will prove attractive to him. Ernest must withdraw from conscious knowledge, refuse to acknowledge what he has known and seen. He must sit there watching the TransAm and willing those things to sink to the back of his mind and vanish there before he goes home; for of course he must not breathe a word of it to Charlotte; she would just be that much more upset.

The clams are cultivated in special beds left relatively uncontaminated by the thermal and radioactive pollution of the Seabrook and Hudson nuclear plants through the nineties, when they were closed down; but not more than one-eighth of the clamlike bits in the chowder will be clams. The rest of the chewy beige morsels are "textured protein"; a by-product of oil, drawn off and processed during the making of gasoline, using a set of procedures first developed by Amoco in the early eighties. At that time the product appeared only in powder form, and was marketed primarily (and surreptitiously) to fast-food chains who mixed it with their burgers to boost them to compliance with minimal nutritional standards. Thus, it took on its inside names, "blackedge" and "healthdust," as well as the standard TOP (textured oil protein). Then, as the day of fast foods peaked and passed with the decline of the passenger automobile in the U.S., the next widespread use of TOP was as human feed, particularly valuable in Africa, India, South America, and the Philippines, where large colonies of workers must eat every day (Just add water to the dry mixture in a proportion of roughly five to one to ensure a thoroughly nourishing gruel . . .). It was not until the mid-'90s that, thanks to the multinationals' early success in cultivating new bourgeoisie in the Third World with an appetite for cars, oil production surged again, and new applications of TOP technology had to be found; so that by the time the actions of this book take place, and in spite of its carcinogenic qualities, TOP can be used to simulate virtually any meat or fish product in virtually any mass-marketed food item. You can hardly tell the difference, even if you're looking for it. And besides, given the contamination of the clambeds, you could never, not even on top government assistance *with* a job, afford to eat a bowl of clam chowder if all the clams had to be real.

You nervous about it?
Some, I guess. Though when I think just about the guy himself, I can't see how it's going to be that hard. So far from what I can tell he seems pretty clear, pretty straightforward stuff.

Well, she says—at least you're out of that other anyway. You won't have to—you know—take any more of those chances like you were.

No, he says. No, that's true. And pauses before picking it up again, maintaining the flow: It's just that it's different, that's all. Like having the lawyer come in to handle the contract. I mean, it's okay, it's fine, but I never had to deal with a lawyer before. It was always my contract the client signed with NASA, I was the one who hauled it out, you know, when the time was right. Your whole effort was to make it a nice personal thing, a good experience. Now it's a straight-up deal with the corporation, not with him; I'm negotiating with their lawyer—one of their lawyers—about things like retirement, hospitalization. I'm a salaried employee.

So—she keeps on moving, rolling it along—that means you have to sit and look tough back at this lawyer? Like some guy from the—oh what did they call them?—from the unions or something?

Yeah. And stop in time too, you know? I mean, yesterday I was arguing with him on a *house* option, trying to get it three years instead of five. I didn't even know what I was saying, I'm just not used to being up there. I keep thinking, though, the one thing—I do this one right, even if it doesn't last the rest of our lives, it ought to lead to something else that will.

You're going to do fine, love. Come on, I know you will. She leans over; she holds his face in her hands. Listen—they wouldn't have picked you if you weren't the best, you know? Isn't that right?

The film *Persona* begins with what seems to be a rush of raw film through the projector, followed by the undifferentiated image of strong light, a match maybe, brought close to the film. After some time such substanceless images give way to a "fleshed out" one: a genderless "boy" with thick glasses and lips and the dull sullen repulsiveness of a child genius lies on a flat bed, or examining table. He reaches a hand out to the flat white wall as if caressing and/or supplicating it, and the surface—in answer?—momentarily almost resolves itself into another image, this one of a woman's face.

Then what most people, including me when I first saw it, will remember as "the movie," i.e. the narrative portion of the film, begins. Yet this narrative sequence will itself be interrupted about halfway through by a series of images apparently unconnected to the narrative, though some of them (light on raw film again, I think) seem to refer to the beginning of the film again, or at least to produce the same effects. The chief result of these effects is something like a blown-up version of the complicated sensation and understanding that comes when, in a fully narrative movie, the projectionist switches from one reel to the next too quickly, so the action jerks ahead, or else too slowly, so the action runs temporarily into black space. In either case, there you are, left suddenly in the bare presence of the medium itself, before its shocking artifice; and for an instant there is nothing else to do but acknowledge one's complicity in that artifice, one's understanding and agreement with it, or to leave the theatre immediately. But then the action starts again.

Come here. Put your hand here.
Yes. Soft. Your skin always feels so thin and soft.
Yours is so firm. Sometimes I wish I could push through it, that it would break open, it seems so thick.
When it's like this, with you, sometimes I think it does break open.
Oh my love.
It does break open.

Some time in New York, Benson is saying. Not much. More in Brussels, Buenos, other places here and there.
He is a man of about forty, with a square grizzled head, flat face. However, he says, my understanding is that you will in good faith accompany Mr. Devine wherever and whenever he wishes to go, at his request.
Ernest smiles, aiming his expression just off Benson's left shoulder: Kuala Lumpur, he says: Marseilles, Vladivostock, Singapore—
Yes, Benson says. That is correct. It is then your understanding also that you will in good faith accompany my client wherever and whenever he wishes to go, at his request?
Yes, says Ernest.
Very good, says Benson, and makes a mark on the piece of paper on the small table separating them. And Ernest knows, without a word or gesture on the subject from Benson, that he should not try to see what is on that piece of paper, that he should act as though it is not there.
Very good, Benson says again, as his eyes settle back on Ernest's. Now: about the matter of maximum contact hours. We are, as you know, prepared to forego a stated minimum?
And stops, awaiting the next reply.

Within an hour Guillermo is, thanks to the ingestion of some different

```
                                          Date:  8/5/20

Name:  Fort, Helena Jeanne          S.S.#  165-38-3513
       Last    First   Middle

Sex:  M (F)   Race:  Caucasian      Date of Birth:  2/10/88

Date of death:  8/4/20        Age (in years) at time of death:  32

Date received:  8/5/20

Most recent address:   1704 Bay, #438  San Francisco, CA 94123
                     Apt., St., and No.      City        State

Permanent address:  Same as above
                     Apt., St., and No.      City        State

Cause of death: Heart failure
       _____

       _____

Coroner's inquest:     Yes    (No)
```

pills, more or less leveled out and on the road into Brussels in his little Chevrolet under an overcast sky. The end of an ugly day, light slumping back to the horizon, and the square concrete apartment buildings of the compound smear together in a blur. It's been so long since the last job— three weeks, four?—that they had to turn the goddamn apartment upside down to find the goddamn i.d. For a few minutes before locating it under a bunch of tapes on the bedroom floor, he had started to think he was going to have to call them up and tell them he had lost the goddamn thing and try to get them to work something else out at the checkpoints, knowing full well they wouldn't. What do you do, you got a security man, surveillance tech, you call him in he calls back telling you he's lost his i.d.? You're going to get somebody else for sure; maybe get the guy out of the compound while you're at it, plenty more where he comes from that's for sure.

And thinking that was why he hit her, for moving so goddamn slow. So when he left she was crying and yelling and the kid was crying and yelling, and he feels bad about it now but what are you going to do? Think about what you're doing now, that's first priority: you can get her something nice maybe when this one's over, when you get back.

Ahead of him now a checkpoint, and an area of rain. Guillermo switches on his wipers as he slows to a stop, fumbles in his lab coat beneath his jacket for the i.d. Then, when the car stops, he feeds the goddamn card in upside down to the verifier, twice, and thinks Shit let there be nobody watching, sweat damping his palms before he gets it in right, the gate lifts, and he goes on to the guardhouse.

Now he does better. Out of the car before the guards are halfway there, before their torches are out, stating his name in a clear, unfucked-up voice: Hagen, Guillermo A. You got notified I was coming?

The older guard grunts; the young one, on his way to pat him down, stops short. Oh yeah, he says: Your name's been flashing off and on priority line a good while now. They want you right away, mister.

They want him *checked*, man, says the older guard, no matter how fast they want him. His dry tired eyes catch the flashes of pure rage from Guillermo's and casually flick them back. He wets his lips: Check him, Leon.

As the young one passes his hands over him and the old one switches on the overhead scanner for the car, Guillermo looks off past the checkpoint, his car, the guardstand completely, off to the single stunted bluish shrub in front of the nearest apartment building across the road. Just looking at it, getting detached, so as not to think what a bunch of shit it is, all he could plant in the car or on him no dumb fucking guard or scanner would *ever* pick up, enough to blow them fucking apart *nail their ass—*

Then, suddenly, he realizes the scan is over; the guards are walking away, back to their stand. What you do now is, get back in your car and take something else, man, you have overcompensated for the downers, there are three more checkpoints to go, and you have *got* to be cool when you arrive.

When he is gone, she walks around the house slowly, in distraction, as if in a trance or a dream. She tries to think of things to do: puts clothes through the washer, dryer, press machine; runs the vacuwand over the floors and walls; even, one morning, washes the windows by hand, dragging a chair outside to stand on, ignoring the smiles and stares of the glossy passing by. She cannot bear to continue the reading work any more, cannot sit and watch the screen at all. When she runs out of things to do around the house she takes Billy and goes out somewhere, no longer to a park where she would have to sit and think and watch him play, but somewhere where they will keep moving: walking the sidewalks, taking the trans, riding the slow belts in the kiddy arcades of the malls where for children the goods are still heaped in piles of bright junk like ice cream sundaes, like the bright disorder of a child's joy. When he tugs at her hand she always buys what he wants—a gun, a doll, a phallic lightwand, malleable, edible clay made from oil.

But though she smiles down at him when he pulls, loops the basket of junk through her arm and ruffles his hair as she flips the i.d. to the computer, she is, for once, hardly given over to him. Hardly even aware that he is there.

She must think about Ernest all the time. She must be with him now as a lover, lost in that, defined by it, in order to keep back as much and as long as possible this new weariness; the awful restful sense of great distance; the purls and eddies of the growing silence inside her skull, as if something had drifted apart into gaps and blanks, contentless messages. Maybe time; maybe the pressure of the faint knowledge of the dead clients; or the faint, sure sense that this new job and his departure change everything including her whole idea of being with him and Billy whole and safe, so that once again now that idea seems to have always been wrong, emptiness, bitter lie. The sound of her mother's voice in her ears. And not even clean polished windows or the tug of her child's hand can make it stop.

Back in their bedroom the kid is still squalling hard, harder than ever, starting to choke. So she goes in and picks it up and sets it in the crook of her arm. Her own crying has stopped, except for an occasional rippling in her stomach, a shuddering of breath.

Quiet now, she says to the kid. Mellow, mellow . . . everything's cool . . .

When the kid does not stop crying she takes it to the kitchen, throws a thermos of formula in the radar, zaps it and holds it to the kid's mouth. That does the trick; as soon as it is finished it conks out, and Anna puts it back in the bedroom again. On her way back out to the front room to dial down the screen her foot catches on one of the mags on the floor. She looks down, picks it up and sits a while on the edge of the bed looking at the snaps of some guy named Sabre big and mean with a huge belt of cartridges across his chest, putting it to some lady with big tits and a tail then going out and wiping out a bunch of mean dirty-faced frogs. When she gets done with that she sits a while longer, then remembers and goes in and dials down the screen. This big lizard, yellow with slanted half-closed eyes, has broken out of the jungle and stomped into the city and smashed it all up so they have to drop a little nukey on it and wipe it out. When it is blown to shit she gets up and gets out the vacuum cleaner and runs it around the floor in the front room and back in the kitchen for a while. Once when she looks out the window it is dark; the security vans are going up and down the streets. She takes a thing of "sausage and biscuits" out of the freezer, throws it in the radar and zaps it, takes it out and eats it. She drinks a "beer." She goes in the bathroom and urinates, thinks about taking pills, looks at herself in the makeup mirror without remembering earlier, when he hit her. She goes in and picks some stuff off the bedroom floor for a while. At one point she stops and looks at the kid, still sleeping, and thinks about what to call it and realizes the shit has worn completely off and wonders how she got straight so fast. Then it comes back, him hitting her. That was what did it, what brought her down. She puts her hand on the place on her face where he hit her. Nothing. She goes back into the bathroom to the makeup mirror to see if there is anything there.

As Ernest signs, he notes the penmanship of Richard Devine on the

---

Date: 7/16/20

Name: Sampson Oliver Arnold   S.S.# 224-47-3118
       Last   First   Middle

Sex: (M) F   Race: Caucasian   Date of Birth: 11/2/68

Date of death: 7/15/20   Age (in years) at time of death: 51

Date received: 7/16/20

Most recent address: 22583 Irving   San Francisco, CA 04129
                     Apt., St., and No.   City   State

Permanent address: same as above
                   Apt., St., and No.   City   State

Cause of death: Heart failure

_____

_____

Coroner's inquest: Yes   (No)

line above: high peaks, tight scrawl, t's slashed two-thirds of the way up
the stem, i's dotted directly over target. Most salient characteristic the heavy
impression of the signature on the page, the pressing-down. As you would
have expected.

I had thought perhaps Mr. Devine would be on hand personally to sign
this, he says, glancing up.

Mr. Devine is very involved just now in the preparation for the Brussels
conference, Benson says. I'm sure he too regrets the relative absence of
contact between you. He slides the paper round and adds his signature:
Witness. Then folds the document and replaces it in the briefcase, snaps
the case shut, rises to his feet and extends his hand.

On behalf of OMNICO and Mr. Devine, Mr. Goodman, welcome to
the organization.

Thank you, says Ernest as they shake.

You will receive your own notarized copy of the contract shortly, Benson says. We ask only that you surrender at this time all tapes and other
reproductions of our negotiation on the subject of the contract. He raises
a finger and looks around, as if testing the wind, then levels it slowly at
the desk: There, I believe?

Ernest smiles stiffly, formally: Very good, Mr. Benson.

Not at all, Benson says. The customary place, after all.

Yes, I suppose it is, Ernest says, moving toward the desk, where he
removes the cartridges and passes them across the desktop. Then I presume
you understand equally well the customary use of such devices in my
profession.

Understand, says Benson, placing the cartridges in the pocket of his
houndstooth coat: and sympathize.

Sympathize, thinks Ernest, watching the dead grey eyes, the closed
thinlipped mouth as the man turns toward the door. Mr. Benson? he says.

Yes, Mr. Goodman?

Ernest places his hands together at the fingertips. I'm curious, he says.
Would you mind if I asked you what it was that made you confident enough
there would be no last minute qualifications or reservations on my part
that you could draw the document up in advance of today's meeting? So
confident that you could interrupt Mr. Devine for his personal signature?

Benson lifts a hand to his face, strokes his chin and upper lip; then the
strong mouth opens in the only smile Ernest has ever seen on it.

Admittedly in your profession you're a specialist, Mr. Goodman, Benson says. Still—and perhaps especially in matters like the ones we have

discussed—you certainly don't think yourself the only one with an ability to read character?

Of course not, says Ernest smiling back. My thanks again, Mr. Benson.

My pleasure, Mr. Goodman, says Benson. Goodbye.

Goodbye.

Once Benson is gone, he looks as if by reflex out the window again. The sky behind the TransAm is low and grey, the fog is still all around. Three months ago, that lunch at Watergate; four months, and you were still in NASA, just having met Claudell. What happens now is less like thinking back over the rest of it, the time since then, than feeling it all at once: its porousness, senselessness, the way it has had of sliding over him. And now, stopped, over; this new thing about to begin: against which once again, like a sudden wound he feels his need for Charlotte, the dull sad growing ache of balls and groin he carries with him out the door, out to the street and the trans, the other passengers in their robes and jewelry on the pink foam seats.

So that the next time he allows himself to hear, see, think again is in the hallway of the apartment, with her face upturned to his, the muffled sound of explosions coming through the ceiling from whoever it is has the goddamn screen on twenty-four hours a day up there . . .

Hello honey.

Sweet . . . They cling.

You still want to have this, uh, talk with Billy? she says after their kiss.

It takes him a few seconds to remember her wish of this morning. Oh yeah, he says, right. Sure I do.

If you want to do it right now, she says, he's just down the hall screening cartoons.

Good. He walks half behind her, half at her side, his hand feeling the smoothness of her back beneath the robe as he thinks how to play the scene. In the screenroom Billy is lying on his side on the floor, knees drawn up slightly, watching in more or less dusk a dark cartoon, white rabbitlike characters capering with their knives against a background of dark green, almost black.

Billy? Charlotte says sitting down beside the kid: Can we talk to you a minute?

Uh-huh, Billy says.

Billy, she says, placing her hand on his small shoulder: you know Ernest is going away very soon now, don't you?

Billy's legs straighten on the carpet; his eyes shift from the screen to hers. Ye-e-e-s-s, he says.

And Ernest has the cue. He comes down to his knees beside Billy's head, next to Charlotte. I'll be going a long way away, he says, feeling the soft warmth of her eyes on his face. That'll leave you and your mother to take care of each other.

Billy nods. Take care, he says vaguely, trying the phrase on, when the screen suddenly whites and there's a bright blue bowl of candy and the sound of screaming laughing kids, an excited announcer shouting a name; and his eyes snap back to the screen.

Billy, Charlotte says gently. Ernest is talking to you, darling.

I know, Billy says.

You think you'll be able to take good care of your mother? Ernest says, rubbing her shoulders, allowing the ache to return.

Uh-huh, Billy says.

Ernest ruffles his red hair: That's fine, buddy. That's just fine.

Billy smiles back a little and looks back at the screen again. Ernest and Charlotte look at one another. A moment later, wordlessly, they rise, and guide each other into the bedroom, where she places her palms on his chest and presses, her face glowing to his.

How was that? he says. All right?

Wonderful, she says; and they kiss; and move, for their reasons, out of their needs, for the bed. Out of his worries, anxiety, fear, premonitions of humiliation; against her growing knowledge, silence, dread; together they make and pass through one more time that safe space, that world: here now you you in . . .

Afterwards, before she gets up to check on Billy, she hugs him suddenly: Anyway, I'm still glad you turned that woman down for this new job— that was it, wasn't it? I wouldn't want to think you turned her down for my sake . . .

Reminded of his lie about Helena Fort, Ernest turns his face away in the darkness. There is something wrong with lying to your love; he draws the line there, ordinarily. No, he says softly, in his nicest voice. It really wasn't for you, love.

Then you must imagine a number of mediations and exchanges, which, like the chain of messages and interactions regarding Ernest, are so various and interlocking their full extent can only be suggested here. Each crop—

including a synthetic "crop" like TOP—can be sold and resold many times before it reaches the foodprocessing plant and becomes part of the soup. It may be sold to transporters, commodity buyers and firms, who will resell at a higher price. More commonly, however, it will be sold within the conglomerate, from one branch or holding company within it to another, as a way of generating large cash revenues or paper deficits and—when the crop, say, is sold to General Foods Brazil by GF Canada—of exploiting currency inequities and instabilities for the greatest long-term profit.

Imagine, then, many phones ringing; long ribbons of telex; men smiling at each other on the phonescreens saying Listen we've got to get together sometime you know?; millions of sheets of paper, millions of microcircuits generating from the figures of one account "book" the strange synthetic transactions to be recorded in another "official" version; and the crop, whatever it is, remaining almost always wherever it was when the buying and selling first began. It is, after all, only a commodity now; a pretext for profit, for money changing hands.

In 2020, the three largest soup processors are the old Campbell's facility in Paris, Texas; a comparatively new ITT plant in Santiago, Chile; and the Dow soupmill in Singapore. Human labor in each of these facilities is confined almost entirely to occasional monitoring of the systems which themselves administer and monitor the production processes, a small front office to handle receipts and billing, and a skeletal maintenance and jan- itorial crew—these last still usually nonwhite, often women. In the case of the Paris facility, where the components of Charlotte's and Billy's soup are processed, those components are received in Houston by jet and trans- ported northward overland by semis to the plant; then, in their quickfrozen form, with various chemical stabilizers, transported to Campbell's whole- salers in various metropolitan areas by trucks averaging 90 miles an hour, clocking 20 hours a day.

Perhaps the only two additional distinctive or interesting features of the Paris complex and the soupmaking process are (1) the curiously enhancing effect of the K.C. meltdown on the Paris facility, where, thanks to regional climactic changes throughout northeast Texas brought about by the melt- down, machinery life in general has been considerably prolonged; and (2) the fact that by 2020, Campbell's too is a subsidiary of OMNICO.

Hagen, Guillermo A., he says, standing stiffly at the counter.

Ah, yes, says the pretty young man on the other side. Rather late, aren't you?

Fuck yourself, he mutters; and is frightened, amazed; but the receptionist has already turned away—This way please—and is walking down the corridor.

Watch it, boy, he thinks; you are still not right. Look at the fact that it does not seem to have taken three seconds for you to get in this wooden chair—that's right, real wood—across from someone at a desk in a suit whose name, he is telling you, is Roche.

Hear you're a pretty good survtech, this Roche says, opening a wooden box on the wooden desk. Cigarette?

Thanks. As he reaches, Guillermo takes the opportunity to lower his head, try to knit his features together into seriousness, since this is clearly some big fucking deal.

I know my job, he says as Roche lights him up.

Roche nods, lights his own. You ever done scans on residentials? he says.

Dumb fuck; he almost says *Oh yeah, yeah, sure.* They *always* have your file, idiot.

No, he says: Industrial only. He blinks, pauses, thinks fast: But there shouldn't be any difference you know? I mean I can find an extra transmit circuit in a twelve-hundred, I ought to be able to find one in a couch, right?

Roche's answering smile lasts just about one second. Okay. Just don't fool with me now. You mess up and I'm out too, but not before I make sure you don't ever work again. Got what you need with you?

Out in my car.

All right, Roche says and begins rummaging in the desk. I'm writing you a pass that will get you to Crown Center suite in the Central Complex and back.

Back out in the hallway he lets his face relax, twist around whatever way it wants. Crown Center, Central Complex: yes, this is a first, a big one all right. Do a clean job on this one and who knows? Just the thought of it makes him so hyped, so weirded out, that when he passes the last checkout and sees the round black turret of the executive hotel, the dark supersmoked glass cylinder rising into the night, that just to stabilize his hands and nerves for the time required, keep his senses on track, he reaches in the pocket of his white worker's tunic for another pill.

Perfectly timed: by the time the rush hits he is past the lobby clearance procedure, up the private core pneumatic elevator shaft to the huge suite which he and the scopes from his black bag dive into like a motherfucker, man, discovering would you believe it three microtransmitters, one in an apple in the fruit bowl, dig that, plus an actual oldstyle fragmentation grenade wired up to the bed, how crude, man, enough to make you think if you were speeding just enough that there has *got* to be more (as they say) than meets the eye.

Guillermo stops and thinks about it a while, a few seconds while the rush mellows out. When you're a survtech these weird stories run by you all the time. Word is, some of these big guys up on top, hey they don't mind, they get off on it tapping in on each other blowing each other up, doing the old competition that way too. Which would explain everything but that grenade unless they wanted to go for that nice funky low-tech look to help put whatever comes off on somebody else. On the other hand what the hell, maybe you really got some real live terrorists, who the fuck knows?

Anyway, he goes over it one more time, speeding his brains out, very thorough, never suspecting that of course once you are used even just one time to scan the temporary living quarters of the president you will hardly be called upon to work for the company again. You have become too corruptible, man; too many people might think you had permanent access, too many organizations would try too hard to get you to plant some shit for them, the risk's too great. So so long G. baby, Guillermo man . . .

The jet takes off straight up, using its props to lift off the
V-port slowly, awkwardly, like a grouse before it levels
and shoots forward and away. For Ernest it is like an
accelerated continuation of his movement up through
OMNICO-SF since his arrival one-half hour ago, via
the lime limo that arrived at the door of the apartment
for him this morning: the ride there with a completely
silent young white man in the back seat with him, in a
grey business suit like his own; ascent via the elevator
that seemed to stop on every floor, releasing and taking on more men in
suits; glimpses of long corridors so white they seem luminescent, shot by
a camera through gauze; finally, shockingly, out to the bright sky at the
top, into the jet. Now it has started. On your way.

But when he twists his oddly heavy head to look out the wide paneling
he does not see the city he could recognize, no, not the official city of
malls, trans, financial and residential districts butting up against a few
somewhat more dangerous zones: but that city, all of it, like the edge of
a thumbnail on the tip of the bay, pressed to its edge by the splay of the
thousands of houses, shacks, huts, the patterned maze extending down the
peninsula even now as far as he can see, until the jet reaches the clouds
and the picture is blotted out.

And in that second Ernest has seen the whole city, its invisible part
too: the part of it that used to be working- and middle-class suburbs now
a lush forest of human beings, chicanos and blacks and everyone else who
is allowed to live there, crossing the border zones in broad daylight if they
have to to reach the city, you can't stop them, living in their self-built
shacks or with three, four, five other families in the gutted remains of

suburban tracts now without plumbing, heating, water, electricity. Such areas exist in every major American city in 2020–21; though in the case of San Francisco, the peninsula serves to restrict their growth some-what. But even in the Bay Area they have been a security nightmare ever since the decline of the automobile, the race for the few remaining jobs and the rush to defend the nation's business and financial centers in the panics and riots of the late '90s. The borders must be kept heavily guarded; they must not be allowed in, either to get or to ruin anything; we must not acknowledge their presence at all. And so Ernest is shocked and does not know what to do with the sight any more than we know what to do with the pictures of the packingcase huts next to those highrises in Rio or Manila or Lagos today. The clouds swallow him up and the plane levels out and takes off straight forward; and he turns to talk to his client Dick Devine.

Date: <u>6/25/20</u>

Name: <u>Ramos,(Mrs.Paco</u>   S.S.# <u>Unknown; insuf-</u>
     Last   First   Middle   ficient evidence
                                      to locate

Sex: M F   Race: <u>Hispanic</u>   Date of Birth: <u>Unknown</u>

Date of death: <u>6/21/20(app.)</u> Age (in years) at time of death: <u>25–40?</u>

Date received: <u>6/25/20</u>

Most recent address: <u>3924 Noe   San Francisco, CA 94100</u>
                   Apt., St., and No.   City   State

Permanent address: <u>Same as above</u>
                 Apt., St., and No.   City   State

Cause of death: <u>Unknown. Given multiple contusions of head</u>

<u>and body, presumed accident-related, natural.</u>

Coroner's inquest: Yes   No

Devine himself, surprisingly, is not wearing a suit, but a light jade crepe de chine robe, deep blue scarf loosely tied around the neck, no jewelry. The clothes set off his thinning black hair and pale his complexion so that his face, as he turns it to Ernest just before Ernest can speak, appears stark and bloodless, despite its courteous smile.

We'll be in Brussels in an hour, he says in a voice flattened by the cabin atmosphere. Would you like any breakfast now, in the meantime?

So, yes; it is beginning now. A solid sour chunk inside his stomach break ups, begins to disperse lightly in his chest and head. He raises his eyebrows slightly, does not smile. Why yes; I think I would. And you?

Devine's smile broadens. Right, he says; and presses a button on the seat console, bringing a middle-aged black man in white pants and tunic through the door leading aft.

Yessa, says the black man, bending at the knees and back: What can I do for you today, sa?

Two eggs for me, William, says Devine. Benedict. Bran muffin, buttered, no jam. English breakfast tea, quite strong. And you, Mr. Goodman?

(Mr. Goodman? Reversal of power/authority relationship. Opening gambit, surely, but to what end? Conceivably merely to distinguish me from cook.) Make mine two eggs over very lightly, he says, with a slight smile both conciliatory and contemptuous, finely gauged, sensing Devine's grey eyes neutrally on him. Wheat toast, no jam; orange juice; black coffee.

Yes sa.

When William leaves Ernest puts his hands in his lap, stares musingly ahead for two or three beats without focus at the six other suited men around a low table ahead and to his right pooling their notes and reports, making final notes; at the clean brown diagonal lines of the craft's interior; then tips his head back toward Devine. Long day today? he says.

Devine shakes his head. Preliminary reports for whatever's left of the afternoon once we get there, he says. Pretty holoshows. Real breakdown and comparison don't start until tomorrow.

Breakdown and comparison? he says, with a kind of urbane ingenuousness.

And Devine's face turns quickly, directly to him, drawn in what appears unmistakably to be complete, even weary disgust.

Don't you worry about it, Devine says through that tired loathing mask. You were hardly hired for your business expertise after all, Mr. Goodman, were you? Excuse me, he says, and rises from his seat and moves forward to the six men, who return the smile and shift to make room for him on the semicircular divan.

And when, a few minutes later, breakfast is served, he is still there as

William manages to spill a little coffee, quite hot, in Ernest's lap, murmuring: So sorry, sa . . .

Ernest makes no response; hardly feels it in fact, and barely tastes the food he slowly lifts to his mouth as, employing all his peripheral and oblique visual skills, he watches his client eat in a manner simultaneously hearty and absentminded, forking large mouthfuls without looking at them as he watches the faces of one man or another, listening to the answers each man gives to the questions he has just asked.

By now, ten years since the last riots and terror waves, few of the atomized lumpentechs inside like Guillermo have any knowledge of what's outside at all. You hear sometimes people are living in these self-contained villages and you hear mass starvation sometimes. Somebody says he knows a guy, works in a recon room downtown, says they have to check and recheck their diffusion defense systems all the time, so many smallscale armed aircraft fly by overhead; somebody else says they—the outsiders— have at their disposal squads of light fast tanks with medium-range torches and small fission nukes, that they're coming closer to breaking through all the time. Another guy, a tower guard, said once in Guillermo's hearing that there was nothing whatsoever happening anywhere out there; just a few tramps scratching around the building just beyond the forcewall sometimes is all; he said they have their own factories even, oldtime ones; they started business all over again, they don't need us. Then you get the ones who like to lower their voices, tell you what it is is there's some oldfashioned communism out there; or that there's nothing but plagues and wandering bands.

People inside—especially if they're older—they'll talk about their friends and relatives out there, how they are, what they're doing, if they're still alive, or how they died. But very, very few of those allowed in, fewer still of their kids, ever try to get back out. Whatever life is like out there, it's got to be different. At least in here you know things are taken care of, things will be all right.

At the very end came a confusion that will frequently, meaninglessly return to him for the flash of a second in the weeks ahead. They were standing in the doorway holding one another, looking into one another's face, tears breaking down her cheeks, her eyes fixed on his as if in fury, and when they came together again the ripple down his body of the shudders shaking her; while Billy stood a few feet away on the doorstep, his back to them, staring up and down the road to spot the car on its way, as if it would not come unless he watched for it.

And then the car, the lime limo; and as it pulled up, in that very instant, the phone inside, behind them, starting to ring.

Billy, Charlotte said, lifting her head from his shoulder: honey would you please go answer the phone?

The phone ringing, ringing. They were waiting out in the car. Billy turned around, his round face blank. Why? he said.

Ernest leaned his weight away from her. There they were out there, waiting for him, he could see someone's shoulder, a man in the back seat, a white face on the other side of the smoked glass peering out. Her fingers on his back spasming, pressing him back, then releasing again, the open plea in her voice: Because I want to say goodbye to Ernest, honey, this one last minute, so would you please get the phone *okay*?

The kid runs past them, down the hallway to the phone. Ernest looks after him once, quickly, in case he should look over his shoulder and shout Goodbye or something. No: the phone keeps ringing, screaming, finally cut off. They are still waiting in the car outside. He and she hold each other again, kiss, look. I love you, she says: I love you. I love you. I love you, he says.

They break away; he is moving over the old wooden porch, between her in the doorway and the men who wait in the car outside in the chill morning light. Billy's voice in a keen piercing shout cleaves the air: Mommy? Food's there, down at the store, as the car door opens and he gets in, catching one last fast glimpse of her as she is turning, replying to the kid.

The chowder has arrived, from the Texas facility where its components were combined, processed, and quickfrozen, to the S.F. distributor where one last bank of computer outlets tracks the product to the small neighborhood "store" where goods ordered by screen may be picked up and charged; in this case, at the corner of Laguna and Green.

The kind of structure we will have in 1990, said the General Mills Chairman, depends in good measure upon our ability between now and then to redefine capitalism in a manner which is understood and believed.

No passive-aggressive systems at work here; no secret deeply-buried longing for love and acceptance at the base of the silence, neglect, contempt that flow steadily, evenly from Devine whenever, in early morning or late night, before the meetings or after them, their paths cross; when Devine enters the suite's front living area or the little breakfast nook and finds— as though it is a fresh discovery each time—Ernest sitting there.

Ah, he says: Mr. Goodman.

Hello, Ernest says, smiling shyly. So far the shyness is all he has come up with, a pathetically suppressed desire to please expressed in a soft con- strained tone of voice and a closed body position with occasional lapses (knees and arms opening gradually in Devine's direction, closing tightly again); but shyness doesn't work. He doesn't care if you are suffering; he doesn't notice it. As for the desire to please, everyone around him has that.

After long silence at the table, during which time you have shot him four or five "secret" glances from lowered eyes, pretending once, lifting the teapot, to move it toward his china cup, then halting, pouring some more, sadly, for yourself: Another full-day session today?

Devine's jaws hardly stop working the sausage, his flat grey eyes show no spark of light. That's right. And what will you be doing today, Mr. Goodman?

Ha ha. What he has done the first few days is nothing. Sit around the suite, smoke an Acapulco or two, play around the buttons of the enter- tainment system, screens, holos, musicubes, stay put on the off chance Devine might suddenly for some reason be back. Then, when Devine never shows, he begins to make brief excursions. Still within the confines of the Center, its lobbies, halls and quaint clusterings of small shops—furs, clothes, art, male and female "companions"—staffed by human personnel, the first he's seen in stores in fifteen years; the showrooms staffed with live singers, comedians, dancers, available individually or in ensemble in your suite; and up, one morning, on the chrome elevator which of course stops before it reaches the conference floors, ejects his hotel i.d. from the scan- nerbox, returns him to their suite.

Not that it really matters where he is. Not that he would in his present state pick up anything anyway about any conference of any organization he might happen to walk by in their huge chambers, talking, planning, dividing it up. He is only moving that the motion may help fix his subject in his mind, get it right. So that somehow, eventually, just as in Japanese action painting when you have seen the object/painting surface/means of representation clearly you can in one swift motion create and complete the work, he can make the correct gesture to befriend one whose hostility and contempt are not even yet quite real, to whom he is, finally, superfluity itself, an unnecessary yet required absurd luxury item. This one is going to take everything you've got, all you know and maybe more. So he smokes Acapulcos, more every day to stay cooled out, and moves around, turning this thing over and over in his mind.

Montale does not look much like an Italian. Tall, conspicuously raw-boned even in his dark blue suit, he concludes his report in his customary pretentious nasal voice, broadening its o's and a's: So, given this performance we fully expect that the rest of this year will continue to provide us with results that are—uhm—commensurate with or above the level of the monthly estimations for all Ramsfeel lines, separately and combined. And he nods to the pretty boy behind him, who switches the projection off.

Devine looks for a moment longer at Montale, sorting and stuffing the papers from which he has just read. Montale's eyes seem bright; on his cheeks are small high spots of red. There are forty-four other men in the conference room, general managers, aides, and a few vice-presidents of finance, forty-four excluding the pretty boys, Crown Center employees in white robes who stand behind each executive reporting and control the projections, video, holo; and they are all, depending on their temperaments and fears, watching either Montale or Devine.

Could we have that final summary projection again please? Devine says. Also the monthly unadjusted net for the last six months, and monthly target figures from the '20 budget?

One set under another the figures appear on the wall behind him and to his left. He turns his head, gazes briefly.

Very good. Now may we see perhaps to my right here, with those lefthand figures standing—may we see the graph of actual unadjusted net relative to the targets per month? I'd like to see that in both percentage table and graph form.

The boy behind Montale, a towhead with bright blue eyes, presses the button in his hand. It is a binary circuit, "print" or "project"; the technology is self-contained, fully responsive to voice command, the boys are simply for show. The graph and chart appear behind Devine and to his right. These he stares at more directly, brow furrowed, and for perhaps a full minute.

So, he says without turning back. You are saying that you and your people will continue above or at monthly target in spite of what appears to be this rather consistent, almost geometrical relative decline. Is that right, Mr. Montale?

Montale too is posed; head slightly cocked, hands folded atop his presentation folder, eyes squarely on Devine. Yes sir, he says.

Yet unless my eyes deceive me (a few uncertain pseudolaughs from the others) or the relative decline for some reason halts, it looks as though you will be *under* target by—extending a forefinger, aiming beyond the graph—say, November or December. Do you than have some explanation for this relative decline?

Yes; yes we do have some explanation, says Montale: and we are, I think, taking the appropriate steps: Specifically, we believe this relative decline is basically the result of a temporary state of glut reflected to some extent throughout the international market for our core product line . . .

He goes on; but by this time without being heard by Devine, who has risen from the round white marble table to carry a sheet of the thin vellum placed at his seat to the Exec V.P.s of finance and marketing, also brought over from the States. On it a few words scribbled, underlined: *some explanation*; *I think*; *basically*; *as you know*; beneath them, scrawled: Coverup? + rec. action—back to me.

He stands over the Exec V.P.s watching them read, waiting for their nods; and motions, with a quick wave, for the boy to erase the figures, graph and chart on the wall. And all the while Montale knows he has to go on all the same, in spite of the fact that no one is listening; knows that is the first part of the price he must pay.

And who's next? Devine says smiling when Montale is done: RITRA, I believe?

A thin sallow man in a black suit and wig rises and opens his portfolio; another pretty little boy, behind the man, presses the button in his palm when the man motions for it with a wave of his hand.

Charlotte wakes sprawled in the bed; wakes as if she had not slept, with the same whirling in her head, things spinning too fast to be thoughts. And so grabs out for anything, some one resolve, something to do. Say shopping, go shopping, get out.

Quickly she dresses, an old lace-trimmed French blue robe, throws down a cup of WakeUp, wakes Billy. Honey? We're going on a trip. You want go on a trip with me?

The boy catches her excitement. Soon he is running between kitchen, bathroom, and his foldup bed, trying to keep up his stream of chatter—can we go down to the water, can I get any three things I want—with a breakfast square crammed in his mouth and his cotton stretch tunic half-on.

It is one of the rare summer days in S.F. when the morning fog has been replaced by a still blue sky not far from the color of her robe; the coincidence, when she notes it, gives her a slight wild pleasure, as if it were a collusion in which she were, for once, involved. Later, out on the street, she and Billy play a crude game of dodge and touch, laughing and crowing while they wait for the trans; the guard on the corner stares at them disapprovingly. It is already quite hot, sweat popping on her forehead, breaking down her face, stomach turning loose and weightless until when the boy grabs her around the knees and pulls backwards, shrieking joy, the sense of being clung to, crippled, plus the heat makes her say quite sharply *All right now that's enough.*

Billy releases, falls backwards on the pavement, lies with his head in the shadow cast by her frame; the guard turns; both of them appraise her now with narrowed eyes.

She and the boy wait silently then. The trans takes a long time to arrive. Heat soaks up through her shoes, the sweat keeps rolling down her face, she cannot remember ever sweating so much, not even in Alabama, back when you were a child running dry cool through heat ever so much worse than this before there was ever a child with his own strange hot hand in yours, or a lover, any of this life around you now, rising up at you like heatwaves from the street.

So—that was not so difficult, was it? says one of the six men gathered in the stone basement of the chateau in Bruges, an old town once noted for its linen, now for its executive enclave.

The other men shake their hooded heads and mumble: No, guess not; okay; yeah, not this time.

Too damn easy is what it is, mutters the guy next to Guillermo, shifting his feet and turning his mask up as he speaks, creating a strange effect. I don't know about the rest of you guys, maybe you're used to doing this stuff. All I'm saying is, for me, I know I couldn't have gotten through that forcewall and into this place without a lot of snappy equipment I'm not carrying. Somebody's got to be giving us a considerable amount of help, turning off scanners, jamming transmission so we can get through. The rest of you guys think so?

In the silence they can each sense the damp cold air currents purling around their legs, hear faint creaking and stirring of steps above the massive black beams overhead. The first man speaks again: So what's so mysterious about that? This is a company job, right? All of us here are company employees, aren't we? So why shouldn't they be helping us along? You'd rather they left us to get here by ourselves maybe, with no dry run? You maybe want out of the job?

I never said I wouldn't do it, says the man beside Guillermo who can see without looking directly at all, without even wanting to, the man's round smudged stupid face, his stubby fingers twiddling up and down his gunbarrel as he speaks: I just said I thought it was a little strange.

Any of the rest of you think this is too strange? says the first man. Let me know right now. Don't have to do it if you don't want to, that's for sure.

Another silence. Standing still this long down here lets the old dark cold of the chateau cellar creep from the walls, soak through the brown muslin they have been told to wear, lie along Guillermo's arms and legs like a thin subtle slime. Still, this is the second time this month he has been called in; first the Crown Center scan, now this; things are getting better. If it keeps up there will be a better, bigger apartment waiting for them soon: larger screen, more light, a room for the kid maybe . . .

Guillermo moves half a step away from the man next to him and straightens his back and shoulders. The others too straighten up, stick out their chests, shift their weapons to lowslung firing positions. They have no way of knowing, given the masks, how funny, pathetic really, their little displays are to the first man who, with Barine, the one next to Guillermo, works this same routine every time a job like this comes up, the company sends them over with some fresh write-offs for a terrorscene. He plays hardass, Barine takes the reservations; the write-offs watch him get on Barine's ass and fall into line every time. It's so good, so rich, he often wishes he could talk about it, tell somebody else afterwards how slick it is. But who else is there to tell it to but Barine himself; who else could appreciate it on the one hand without probably getting him into trouble with the company on the other? And as for Barine, the funny thing about him is, he seems so sharp, so good at it when he's on; but all he is afterwards, when the show's over, is this dumb redfaced French juicer so far gone that the one time he came up to him afterwards slapped his back and said Barine? Hey Barine baby, that was great, man, Barine turned slowly around, showing rheumy eyes, thick purple lips, and said Yeah? Hey listen, what you fucking talkin about man?

You there, the first man says now, pointing to Barine, the one with the questions, how about you just stepping back out of this? I believe we can get through this from now on without you.

The man beside Guillermo looks down, steps backward. Guillermo edges a bit further away from him too, and stiffens again.

Okay, the first man says. So, four days from tonight you follow the same procedures at the same times to arrive here together. And once you're here, I want you three—-pointing them out, including Guillermo—to make your run up these steps here at exactly 10:12, with your weapons at the ready; the fourth stays down here with me, makes sure this cellar stays secure while the operation's going on upstairs. All right?

Everyone nods.

Okay then, says the first man. Now, the three of you, when you get up there . . .

The one and only reason Garnett's there's because of this old middle-management guy on the planning session team—the kind of old fart who still always wears suits and leather shoes with dots punched in them. Who always slides in at the very end of the discussion whining how somehow this whole operation still seems to lack that "little extra something," that "personal element." So just to get him to shut up, you end up throwing someone like Garnett in with the rest of the mix.

Not that there's anything wrong with Garnett, of course. An old pro at this business for thirty-five years now, something like that; started out designing equipment, they say, for the government during the Reagan years, got wooed away by private industry shortly thereafter; he still knows how everything works and can use it to get more and better info, audio and visual, than most people could get with the subject's consent. An "old and valued employee," as the old fart might say, and known for his ability to stay on top of a job like this twenty-four hours a day, lying low, making crude fixes on the equipment if need be by hand whenever possible, pretty ingenious ones too, rather than risk discovery if the subject were to notice the circuitry being delivered next door or upstairs, rather than leave the jobsite himself.

Still, the point is you don't really need anyone for a job like this, a simple-shit straight overhead snoop on a couple of non-execs with zero suspicions. You could put all the monitors you needed in an upstairs closet, rent it out to an innocent slug, no one notices, no personnel involved. But as it is, here you've got old Garnett sitting up there day after day, screen going full blast to keep everybody else away, tinkering with a circuit here, filament there to improve the reception, coking himself high enough that even without the system he can hear the drop of a fingernail clipping, so desperate to stay in play he tries to cram each communication with everything he's got, no matter how dumb. (Rate of subject-child exchanges continues low and declining, topics similarly limited: 37% initiated by subject, 63% by child. Topics: Commercial desires, approval, agreement, negation 60% [80% of all conversation child-initiated]; Personal, including all phatic/affection discourse 40% app . . .)

There's no need for this kind of thing; all they want is just to keep a simple eye on her, make sure they know at any given moment where she and the kid are, that's all. But there you go; that's the kind of stupid expense and waste some middle-management geezer will insist on every time, pissing his pants over the possibility that something might be missed, insisting on the necessity for human backup on every job. And it all just ends up costing the company money.

At other times he makes his way to the bathing area to have a swim and rubdown among the plump white bodies of other execs—or their companions? he wonders, dozing off under the skilled hands of the Filipino girl in white assigned to him as she moves, slowly, from top to toe, half-dreaming that the knowledge of what to do with Devine might enter or emerge through one of the clean transparent openings she seems to make in his body with her incredible hands.

Oh that is wonderful, he murmurs, drifting away.

My job to please you sir, she says, as softly as a leaf falls to the ground.

But he does not find any answers there, neither in her fingers nor in his light dreams, the desperate scenarios he runs in his head:

(Tonight when he comes in you say So, how'd it go today? in the bright chipper voice you used last night; and when he grunts and moves away the way he did you say Dick, listen; how can I be your friend if you won't help me? very sincerely, openly. And he says I didn't know I was supposed to help you; I thought it was your job. And he says if you knew how to do your job you wouldn't need help.

Or you come up to him, quiet but firm tread, as he sits with his back to you at the table or the makeup sink and start rubbing his back, not like what's-his-name, Sampson, but a real muscle rub searching for the knots of tension, pushing them out wordlessly, forging the unspoken bond until he says, eyes closed, facing straight ahead, if I wanted this done, I could quite readily find someone far more qualified to do it than you don't you think Mr. Goodman?

You let him come in tonight and find you already in your bedroom, or still out. The next morning over breakfast he says I assume you're aware you broke contract last night. You answer something light, witty, disarming; some piece of rapid repartee that, to his astonishment breaks down his defenses and makes him laugh out loud, something like something like something like—)

The Filipino speaks almost no English; he does not ever find out who the other swimmers are in the giant, springfed pool. And always he is back in the suite by four, just to be on the safe side.

The suite: its front room on three levels six inches apart, jacuzzi, makeup sink and blowers highest, under raked plexiglass roofing; to the right the Tudor breakfast nook and kitchen; then, lowest, plush deep red lounging area, couches and lounges under soft hidden sources of light, surrounded by highgloss cedar walls that turn to screens, fold down to playing areas for any private shows you want. By the fourth day there he has used it all, even the little stage; he has a special scuz act, two men and women, racially mixed, swollen appendages, a black dog, come up and perform while he at one point beats off in the sink, looking off from their pyramids and tableaus to the low overcast sky above the sunroof over his head, thinking of nothing. A dumbshit thing to do, he knows it, the very kind of kinkiness and abuse that can throw off, even kill the instincts; and it scares the hell out of him that he has done it not even for a client, just for and by himself. And what if Charlotte knew you did shit like this?

But no, he thinks, lying on the sunken purple couch after the troupe has left, the sink is cleaned, no this has got nothing to do with all that. This has only got to do with what it takes to get Devine, what part of yourself you have to find. And as it turns out, as he sucks on Perrier and searches his mind, he does indeed find a new angle waiting there.

From the corner across the street the guard watches them drooping in the heat; she keeps her eyes lowered, tries to act as though she does not know he is there. Sweat pours from her, drops trembling on her chin, at the tip of her nose, Billy's head falls against her hip. How silly this is, stop sweating. Across the street the guard drops to a squatting position. She looks to the side, up and down the shimmering street. A few couples perhaps five blocks in the distance, walking away. The guard is crossing the street, coming toward her.

May I see your pass please.

Certainly, Charlotte says—and why should her voice *not* sound cool, untroubled? But she waits until her hand is delivering her cards into his before looking in the helmet, at the square, red face. As if he had spent his life before a fire, red and worn with deep lines, though he is obviously not that old. Against the red his eyes are startling green, the green of his vellon uniform with a fleck of the sky thrown in.

This your kid?

That's right.

You have i.d. on him too?

While she sorts through the bag the guard bends down so his face is level with Billy's, who edges closer to his mother's body, yet still stares directly back.

How you doing today fellow, huh? says the guard, cracking lean lips, reaching out and touching one rough scratchy fingertip to the boy's chin: Pretty hot for a fair creature like you to be out, don't you think? Don't you think you might get burned?

A fearful excitement is streaming through the boy. The face before him, gleaming in its fiberglass case, its thin stretched lips and acrid close smell, are the closest he has come to the reality of what he has been playing with, what the toy spacemen and their lasers conjure up each day: all the power, evil, death, he sees on the screen. This one is not like the funny fat one who used to guard up the street where Ernest got off at night, and they would race. This one is *real*.

I don't know, Billy's mouth says; but no sound comes out. He winds an arm around his mother's leg.

Where's your father? says the guard, his mouth still stretched to show hard brownish teeth.

Here's his i.d., Charlotte says. She holds it out over his head. His smile fades as he stands. She sees dark wet patches on the chest of his uniform. She tries hard to think of how hot he must be in those thick tight clothes, inside the helmet, inside the black boots, poor miserable man. It doesn't work. She does not believe he is there to guard her, to defend her at all.

His father, she says, speaking quickly, his father is a high employee of OMNICO, a big company, he's in Europe with them right now—

That's not my father, Billy says. He releases her leg, steps forward, glares up at the guard's face: That's not my father, that's Ernest.

That's okay fellow, says the guard, making a sound somewhere back in his throat. We don't care.

He keeps a smile on as he hands back the pass: Cute kid.

Thank you, she says. She reaches up to pick a strand of sweatstuck hair from her forehead: that's good now, you see it's nothing, almost over and nothing's wrong, nothing will happen to you, you have behaved perfectly well—

How much do you want for him?

What?

I said, how much would you take for him? His red face is completely impassive; he rests a hand on Billy's fine red hair. Thirty thousand? Fifty? I could maybe even get you sixty, possibly, with hair like this.

Even the heat, even his green, red, helmeted figure is almost gone, evaporated, leaving only his words, soft and grating, oil on the air: What do you say, lady, huh? I can find you a buyer for a kid like this.

That's my *boy*! she shouts, and tears break suddenly from her eyes. You *can't* take him from me, that's *my* boy!

Okay lady, he says, smiling again, already backing, okay. Don't get excited then, it was just a joke, I was just kidding—halfway back across the road now—and if you think you're gonna do something about it just remember it's your word against mine, all right?

That's right; his word against yours, he could have you arrested, taken away from Billy, Ernest, everything, how could you *possibly* have yelled at him?

The tears fall faster, hotter still. When she looks up the street for the trans, it blurs so much, she cannot tell; it might or might not be there.

Come on, honey. We're going home.

Billy holds her hand on the way back down the street, humming tune-lessly; then breaks away. Mommy, he says, that guard, he wanted to take me, didn't he?

He said he did, she says, forcing her voice into light, cool tones. But I really think he was just joking, don't you? You heard him, that's what he said.

You wouldn't let him, would you?

No honey, she says, bending to kiss him in front of their apartment door. I would never let anyone else take you.

And he laughs and wriggles loose from her arms, and goes running off up the street.

Want something cool to drink? his mother calls. Want a Bubbly?

No, the boy shouts back. In a minute she will go inside. He will stand there on their corner, near their door, until then; then take off for the back of the apartment house next door, where there is a crawlspace under the foundation in the back he can get into, there, in the rich, moldy odors and cool air, to savor his excitement over everything he feels. Delicious fright of being wanted by the guard, by power; ecstatic disappointment of escaping, rescued from power by his mother, with her like the bad women chased through the jungle on the screen; and the wonder, too, of getting her back so unexpectedly from Ernest, of winning the battle and sending him away. He will squat under the house, clutch and squeeze handfuls of dank earth thinking of this thing that is now once again only his mother, *his* mother, with the same old contempt and desire, love and hate.

Okay, T.D. says without bothering to suppress the weariness, the near contempt in his voice: Let's see what you can do with this one.

He jiggles the switch in the lectern top; the next holo appears. A man of approximately thirty-five, brown hair thinning in front, down loose and wavy to the shoulderblades behind; barefoot; orange and silver-striped robe, expensive, loud; dull hostile gaze coating the eyes.

Who is he; what is your approach.

A kid in the front of the seminar room, Sanders, Stanford draftee, stirs in his seat and frowns: Not middle-management.

No; that's right, T.D. says. He leans his weight against the lectern, drums the fingers: Come on; be sharp now.

He's in comtech, Catlin blurts from the back.

Without shoes? T.D. points at the revolving figure. With these clothes? Come on, think about what you're saying. You guys, listen: there's not gonna be one time in fifteen out there you're gonna have time to mess around like this; you've got to make a closer stab than that *right now.*

The truth is, he has a headache, he can hardly keep his mind on this bush-league crap himself; and the thought of nicer things—the shade of the oaks in the green fields surrounding the complex outside, a comforting injection of layback, maybe after dinner tonight—only makes more pungent the present bad taste in his mouth. Nobody out there seems to have any instincts, any feel for the work anymore.

It probably is true, too, as far as they're concerned upstairs, that you're too old, too many years away from the last working relationship. All this, he thinks, plus Jewishness: no wonder you're not getting the cream any more, it's a wonder you're still working . . .

Entertainment, says Nash from the third row, middle. He is leaning to the side of his chair to see the turning holo better, pointing his pen at it as he speaks, decisively: Producer or public relations.

All *right*, Mr. Nash, very good, says T.D. sardonically, raising his eyebrows. That only took you sixty seconds—too long by half for any pro, but still much better than your colleagues here, right? *Now*—reaching up to wipe the damp curls off his brow with a forearm, smelling his armpits rotted out with the old constant resentments, the nagging fears, walking up to and around the slowly revolving holo one more time, for one more class—will it substantially affect your basic mode of introduction and acquaintance response if this subject turns out to be a producer rather than a p.r. man, Mr. Nash, or vice versa?

No, says Nash from the third row.

And why not, Mr. Nash? says T.D. with his head throbbing, throbbing, hopeless sour, staring at the clock in the wall, fifteen more minutes to go, my whole fucking life ahead . . .

Europe serves two main functions for multinational enterprise: as a conference center, by custom and tradition, and as a technocenter for telecommunications, information technology, weapons and chemical research. Such industry as is located here—excepting of course the tourist "industry," those portions of the continent (the Alps, the Louvre, Venice, etc.) preserved for the enjoyment of the wealthy of all nations—is therefore mainly capital-intensive rather than labor-intensive: i.e., few people and a lot of machines. Through the rising chaos of the '90s—the terrorism and mass demonstrations, the looting, general strikes, revolutionary bands— many manufacturing processes were farmed out to the Third World. Others were retooled, so as to assure the minimal supply of skilled human hands in the making of this petrochemical, that computer or automobile; accordingly, small groups of faithful workers of fully verified loyalty were admitted to the newly created, fortified compounds. Nearby within the same general zones of control live top-ranked engineers in large plush condos, managers and v.p.'s in mansions small and large; the compounds themselves, though, tend to be grey and khaki buildings not unlike the old "urban renewal" projects of the '50s and '60s, back in the U.S.A.

Ramsfeel looks shaky in spots, says the V.P. marketing softly; then closes the folder and looks dolefully at Montale. Unstable, he says.

Yes; unstable, yes; quite so, says Montale, whose accent and diction, keeping pace with his anxiety throughout this interview, have grown more and more preposterously, nasally Oxonian. Still I believe you can merely by consulting the sales growth chart of this most recent five-year period assure yourself that the fluctuations to which you refer are by no means so very abnormal in the marketing history of this line.

Unit costs are up too, Andrew, says the V.P. finance, staring out the window at the skyline, the quaint outlines of a few old churches and buildings outside the Central Complex, beneath its heights. We ran a backup on your areas, Mr. Montale, which disclosed that the jump for the facilities in—Lyons, I believe?—and Turin has been particularly high. Can you give us any ideas on that, Mr. Montale?

Montale, sitting alone on the black decentered sofa, straightens his tie—he is the only one of them still wearing a suit—and lifts his chin to speak.

Mr. Montale, says the V.P. finance, the older of the two men, quite gently: We can certainly find out for ourselves why unit costs on Ramsfeel are up and product turnover is erratic. We may even know now. That's not the point, is it, Mr. Montale?

The V.P. marketing, swinging back and forth in the basket chair, shakes his head slowly, a sad, abstracted expression on his face.

The V.P. finance turns and leans down so close that his robe brushes Montale's creased suitpants. The point is, he says, that we need to know what *you* can tell us about these two facts and their relationship, Mr. Montale.

Montale is looking down at his hands in his lap; at the long moonshaped nails he has cultivated so carefully. They require a lot of work and care, those nails.

There has been trouble in these facilities you name, he says harshly, his accent gone.

Aaahh, sighs the V.P. finance, sitting next to him, gazing sympathetically, like an old priest with long grey hair, into his face as the V.P. marketing, nodding his own more distant sympathy, produces simultaneously a black handrecorder from a fold in his robe and turns it on.

Internal sabotage, Montale says. A large rise in damaged components. On several occasions this year production figures were below projection. Twice off more than 25 percent. And there have been—he moves his head up and down spasmodically, as though something were caught in his throat—shipping and distribution errors also.

What actions have you taken to put this right? says the V.P. marketing.

I instructed my men to find the personnel responsible and get rid of them. It was a small group first, in Turin. One old programmer, peripheral anyway, three or four from the lab, one distribution engineer—we learned they had been meeting in the compound as a so-called study group for the past three years. Obviously we sent them over the wall immediately, *finito*, the next day. Then the same thing happened the next month in Lyons—we got rid of them too. Then in Turin it happened again. Then again in Lyons. I doubled security, kept the story hushed, rechecked all files thoroughly, assured myself absolutely no outside agitation was involved on the part of United, General Tech, any other enterprise; last month I had one group in Marseilles—things are bad there too now—I had them wasted, publicly. No good.

Mmm, the V.P. finance grunts, thinking. There finally *is* a difference between a white and a latin, no matter how much you try to shove it under the rug; who but a latin would think of public executions? Public executions, indeed.

You have a full report on this, he says.

Yes, says Montale, at this moment—

All reports on property damage, shipping delay, sabotage and espionage must be transmitted to the security and finance divisions of the home office immediately, Mr. Montale, says the V.P. finance wearily, rising again to his feet.

Montale looks quickly at the V.P. marketing, the recorder in his lap. I can have them by Monday, he says. At the latest.

You really going to be able to come up with the quota figures? says the V.P. marketing, smiling at him.

Montale rises too; suddenly frightened laughter bursts from his mouth: Oh sure, sure! No problem there . . .

When he is gone, the two V.P.'s look at each other. The V.P. marketing clicks off the recorder and puts it away. The V.P. finance gathers his papers and sighs deeply through his nose.

That damn zone, he says. We should've had everything we had moved out of there ten years ago. It just gets worse and worse.

This ought to put the capper on it, says the V.P. marketing. Brazil or Argentina or some of them can certainly take a couple of Ramsfeel components plants by now; we can keep the distance between components and assembly down then, too. Plus south zone doesn't even buy Ramsfeel any more. He pauses, shifts his jaw back and forth, looking down at the carpet: You think Montale's right, nobody else is involved?

The V.P. finance rises slowly, heavily. We have no indications of any erosion in the terms of our agreements for this zone, he says. United knows full well what we could do to them here if they were to initiate any sort of sabotage again; so do the rest. On that basis, pending further findings, sure I believe him, for now.

So, says the V.P. marketing: you want to talk to Devine with me? He has by now stepped in front of the older man on the way out the door, and is talking back over his shoulder at him. These young guys, thinks the V.P. finance, age forty-six. For a second, it is enough to make you feel sorry for guys like Montale . . .

Then he braces himself; you're still in there, man, still humping, you got moves for situations this kid has never seen.

So he touches the back of the V.P. marketing's lavender robe, smiles, uses a tone of amused authority: Procedures, Mark: we submit separately, remember? But I'm sure our accounts will back each other up all the way.

It is somewhere around midnight when Ernest walks in. As expected, Devine is already there. In the back corner of the room sitting in the jacuzzi, eating some sort of sandwich as the water swirls. That his wet chest hair is grey strikes Ernest, in his carefully deliberately induced stoned drunkenness, as a potentially significant piece of client information to be stored away for future use, as he crosses toward his room.

You are aware, Mr. Goodman, that you have broken the terms of your contract with OMNICO tonight?

Ernest stops but does not turn around. I know that, Dick, he says.

I could get rid of you for this, Devine says. Have you on a jet out of here in twenty minutes.

Here it is, what the coating of dope and good Russian vodka is meant to smooth the way through. He keeps his back turned; he takes a slight imperceptible breath. I know, he says.

Behind him the water shuts off. In a few seconds he turns to see Devine stand, put the sandwich down, begin to towel himself off. And you know I can have you eliminated too, he is saying. Quickly or painfully. Or quickly *and* painfully. Or I could just see to it that you never work again.

Ernest smirks his mouth, makes it emit a fine dry chuckle. But you could do all that anyway, right Dick? So just go ahead.

They are looking at each other, directly in each other's eyes, across the ruby lounge and a six-inch step up to the level on which the jacuzzi, sink, and small enclosed shower are placed; Devine with his towel around his neck, water still sparkling on his chest and neck; Ernest's body held stockstill against the liquor and weed. But what is most important, more so than any details or setting, is the look itself, when all other expression has been peeled away, the acknowledgement. Yes. That's right. And I know you too. Cold dead bastard. Prick.

Devine nods without smiling: We're done here tomorrow afternoon. There'll be a formal dinner tomorrow night at eight at the home of the general manager of this zone in Bruges. I should be back here by four-thirty tomorrow afternoon. We'll leave at seven.

Ernest, meanwhile, moves toward the kitchen as planned, to make the gesture of getting something to eat. There is the cheddar sitting out on the table, yellow, sweating slightly—like you, he thinks and has to suppress the sudden urge to laugh or cry, he is so drunk, stoned, weak with his success.

Fine, he says, tossing the word back over his shoulder at Devine.

The white-gabled chateau dates from the same period as the first plane trees that bedeck the soft lawn outside: the end of the fifteenth century, when Bruges was an outpost of the Hapsburgs. The sun through the leaded-glass window and the low clouds appears like a white thumbsmudge on an otherwise perfectly light blue field of sky. Gwen Knessen, wife of Cal Knessen, executive vice-president of the northeast zone, lets the drapes fall back into place and wheels around. In her eyes there is a child's bright excitement, on her mouth the thoughtful, efficient frown of a grown woman who has many things to do. She smooths her stunning chestnut hair over her right ear, an old habit when anxious, and calls: Jacques? Camilla!

A middle-aged man, stooped and grave, enters the long room in black livery a la nineteenth century; his wood-soled shoes sound harshly on the floor of inlaid oak. Yes Madame?

Jacques, when did Mr. Knessen say he would be home this afternoon?

The usual time, Madame, Jacques says, bowing his head slightly. He said to tell you when you asked that he knows tonight's party will be all the more perfectly successful if he remains away from home until the last possible minute, and that he knows you will do wonderfully.

Gwen Knessen shakes her head, smiling slightly to herself: Bastard, she whispers. Jacques stands awaiting her bidding, expressionless and still.

You've found the people to clean those chandeliers, she says.

Yes, Madame.

They are at work.

Yes, Madame.

Do you know where Camilla is?

I believe, Madame, she is supervising the delivery of the pheasant breasts downstairs.

That's not her job, says Gwen Knessen. Go tell her to get back up here. I want her to call Mr. Knessen's office until she gets an answer from him.

Yes Madame.

When he is gone Gwen Knessen sits at the end of the long, long walnut table, handhewn centuries ago, where all the men will sit and eat their pheasant breasts and talk tonight; and everything must be nice for them, perfect, everything in place, from the cutglass compote dishes to the harmony between her gown, her husband's managerial robes, and the table furnishings. And this goes on every month, almost; whenever the conference returns and resumes.

And her too, think of her, of who she has to be. The strong classic lines of the face, largeboned elegant body, smooth tapered fingers, those eyes, that chestnut hair; plus the private school education, the years at Mount Holyoke, fling at the Sorbonne; Virginia Woolf her favorite author still, Vermeer her favorite visual artist. She will speak of them tonight to a few of the men at the table. They will enjoy it, without much understanding what she is talking about, but taking it as a gesture of flattery and obeisance. Later, if the night has gone extremely well yet ended quickly, her husband, flushed with his success and power, will make love to her. For all this, she gets to wear the expensive clothes she has, live in this wonderful house, read Virginia Woolf and see original Vermeers, and be the wife of one of the executive vice-presidents of the entire European zone.

Such are the parameters of the deal. Only tonight, she recalls, will be a bit more special yet. Tonight there is to be something quaintly called a waste.

His face—that scraped ruddy skull—was virtually split in a grin when he first told her back on Monday, three days ago now. Because this too will redound to his credit, or because he too thinks it will be such great fun?

All right, she said tightlipped to the screen—he was calling from the office, of course. Where does this gala event take place? Which part of our home will we be so fortunate as to see destroyed?

Can't tell you that, he said. Even then, in the wake of her explicit distaste, some traces of his glee remain on the bony screenface: I don't even know that myself, quite frankly. But really, my dear, you needn't worry—I have firm assurances any and all damage will be made good straightaway. You needn't raise an extra finger before or after, all you need do is simply act natural, the same way you always do.

Madame? calls Camilla from the hallway now. He's on the phone, Madame.

Beautiful Gwen Knessen walks to the next room, to the phone, her face an elegant mask, She picks up the receiver; her husband's image appears on the screen. Over her head, on a ladder in the hallway, a young man with a dull pale complexion and a stupid look on his face slowly polishes the bits of hanging glass. Hello darling, she says, mask breaking into a smile. Just wanted you to know everything on this end is going very well.

The other night, when they first called, for that job in Crown Center? Guillermo says, his blue eyes shining bright at her, through her. I was going crazy trying to level out on those downs we were doing, you remember? Never been in the Crown in my life, and I'm half afraid I'm not gonna remember how to do it anyway. But boy—he shakes his head, extends a hand across the table to Anna, who looks at it as if deciding what it is before letting her own hand go out—boy, you should have seen the job I did on that place. Every inch, man. I swear I got everything out of there but the grain out of the wood.

Anna smiles faintly by way of reply. Her head has started to hurt again, that dull stupid throb, the physical sign of her useless solitude, monstrous boredom; she ought to listen more closely, with more smiles and support for him when he is this way. Who knows when it will happen again? But the back of her mouth tastes metallic; she looks down at the plate before her, at the purplish remnants of tonight's "chili dog" supper, then away, idly fumbling for something to say, when her eye catches sight of the greygreen machine on the floor beside the old radarrange.

What's that thing anyway? she says, tipping her blonde head.

You know what that is? Guillermo says, chewing the last of his bun. That's an oldtime gun, is what. U.S. Army issue semiautomatic M-16, 'bout fifty years old now. Shoots bullets; about five hundred a minute with the trigger locked back. Big deal about fifty years ago I guess.

Anna lights a cigarette from the pack on the counter. You gonna have to use that thing tonight?

Maybe, Guillermo says, smiling. Can't tell you for sure.

She puffs, leans against the fridge, her gaze on the brown wall opposite. You watch you don't get shot yourself, she says. I don't know. This sounds like a shit job to me.

Hey look, he says, it's a good job, all right? They picked us for it, handpicked us for this job. The best people to put in on a job like this one they said was survtechs, because we know what we're up against. Okay? Okay?

Anna looks at his tightening face, the red streaks at his temples. Want to keep him going, see what he'd do? Just smack you again, eventually. You know, she says, crossing to where the kid sleeps in its chair: we really got to get these name forms in on the kid. What do you want to call it?

Shit, I don't care, he says. I got to go. What do *you* want to call it, you're the one that had it for chrissake.

She thinks hard for a long moment, stroking the little soft neck. I don't know, she says at last, quietly, staring wide-eyed over at him: Maybe Sabre?

At one point in the program, the reporter was talking with a member of the board of directors of one of the corporations that sells milk formula in the Third World. He asked her about the doctors; she denied they promoted formula. He asked about the advertising campaign and she denied that one existed. So he asked her to tell him why so many women in these foreign countries were buying formula they could not afford to use correctly, so that their babies, hundreds of thousands of them, sicken and die.

The woman smiled: a well-kept middle-aged white American woman with frosted hair and capped teeth and an expensive, austere suit with a double string of pearls around her neck. Once you had taken all this in, she spoke.

Because these women want to be *independent*, Bill, she said. They know that there's a new *world* out there for women today; and they want to go out, have jobs, live lives of their own . . .

She kept smiling. They have radios, she said, they listen; they know what's going on in the world today, and they want to be *in* on it . . .

Lately she has been staying up too long, sitting in the screenroom with Billy, letting him stay up and watch whatever he wants, no matter how bloody and violent. Sometimes even after he falls asleep she leaves it on a while for the noise, the color and lights, sits there a while before carrying him to bed. Anything to cover the sound of the voices in her head—no, *her* voices, her—yammering away, making her sick. Then, when the next morning comes and she wakes stuck in them she blocks them out as best she can with the constant screensound from upstairs, grateful whoever's up there keeps it on night and day.

But this morning it is the phone that wakes her, pulls her up through her black silent sleep, splits the cold damp morning in the kitchen like an alarm. How many times can it have rung? Hello?

Hey, says Ernest's voice laughing. Hi sweetheart! You're keeping different hours while the old man's gone?

She tries to smile, but her mouth quivers. As if the muscles will not work that way. Oh no, she says. I've been such a lump, I'm ashamed of myself, I just sit around here with the screen on all day. What are *you* doing? she says, quickening to get out, away from herself. How are things going for you?

Oh fine, his voice says, cheerful and placid, just fine. He's pretty busy, you know, there's not much chance for private interpersonalizing yet. But tonight I get to try out social acquaintance. I think everything's going okay.

Silence. Her mind races; she hops from foot to foot on the cold floor. You could say I don't know what's happening. I'm not sure who you are. I don't know if I love you after all.

Well, he says—well, I just wanted to call, before he gets back and we have to get ready for tonight, and find out how you are and if everything's all right. We're leaving tomorrow for someplace else, I don't know, Brazil or Argentina or someplace. . .

Everything's fine here, Charlotte says smiling as her eyes fill with tears, thank god for no screenvue.

Only, she says, only I've been thinking about making a trip home to Alabama, while you're away. With Billy.

When did I stop knowing what I would say next?

Is that right? he says. Well sure, why not! I won't be back for another two weeks anyway. You can just go ahead and put it on my card, okay?

Okay, Charlotte says. Fine. If I decide to do it. I mean, I haven't decided to do it yet.

Another silence. On the other end, in the suite, he finds himself remembering those last moments, the embrace broken, ringing phone, flatness in her eyes . . .

I love you, he says, impulsively, a little frightened. I love you too, sweetheart, she says, crying harder.

I miss you too.

I miss *you* too.

Silence. What flashes now in her head is too quick even to hear.

Well, Ernest says. I'd better get off. He'll be back here any time now. Goodbye love.

Goodbye.

Afterwards, she sits on the cold floor, hugging her bare knees, her eyes round and dazed. Are you really going back home?

Everything starts on schedule. The microjet arrives atop the Complex, delivers Devine and Ernest to the chateau at Bruges in a brief minute, landing on a cleared space among the plane trees. An old GM truck dating from before the workers' riots transports the five hooded men there overland, a journey of several hours. Ernest, in a grey satin floorlength gathered slightly at the elbows, is introduced over drinks and assorted canapes (pate d'anguilles, chiefly, and an amusegeule of cauliflower flowerets with a delicate mayonnaise) by Dick Devine to Gwen Knessen, in a sparkling drape of platinized silk with institched fingernails; to Knessen her husband, Vice-President and General Manager of the European zones, northeast; to Montale and the other executives in charge of individual operations, zones, and product lines. A nod of the head in most cases from these men, plus a firm smile—Mr. Devine—and Devine's smile returns with a variable quotient of condescending warmth: Hello Andrew, he will say: Hello Bruno; Hello James. Then wait for a fraction of a second, an actor's beat, to allow the other party to hold his smile a shade too long, or open his mouth to make the subtle graceful power statement he has worked all day, all week, to devise, after which Devine's smile will broaden, his lip curling slightly, his hand gesturing left: Oh Andrew, have you met my new friend Ernest Goodman yet? Ernest, Andrew; Andrew, Ernest. The men in the back of the truck under its buttoned tarp do not talk much at all. They cannot see each other's faces behind the masks. The way the truck bounces, backfires in midgear, you're too busy squatting, tightening, holding on, to talk, and you have to wind your arms around your chest and bundle tight, there's no heat back here and the wind gets through the tarp. The length of time this is taking, plus the shitty road and all; they have got to be outside the compound, moving through unpatrolled, unsecured territory to this place the chateau. But nobody says anything about that. If you look up you see that one guy, the head guy sitting there by the tailgate looking straight back at you. Dinner is a hearty "peasant" waterzool de Poularde a la Garitoise, followed by the pheasant breasts accompanied by asparagus tartlette with poached eggs and Mousseline sauce, all Flemish dishes except the pheasants, of course, and impeccably served. Gwen Knessen heads the table; Devine sits at her right, Ernest next to Devine. Gwen Knessen, glowing with a rich flush of pleasure from the attention of OMNICO's chief executive, describes in detail at his request the justly acclaimed dining scene of *To the Lighthouse* in which, as she presides over her table, Mrs. Ramsay's powers of sympathy and imagination, and Woolf's own, are at their height. And the flow of the sentences! The speed, the spontaneity of associations, fresh again every time one looks back! The gloved waiters at a vastly greater expense now than in Woolf's time remove the plates, exchange one crystal glass for another, full of wine. The talk flows, carefully away from business. Ernest becomes a smiling audience for the monologue of one James Halberdson, V.P. something, on the difficulties of developing and maintaining a Micronesian island homesite. Then, Halberdson is saying, wouldn't you know as soon as I signed and we started blasting off the mountain to build—all any of them is is an old volcano, you know—why all these *brown* things show up out of nowhere. Whole damn *tribe* of them wearing nothing but leaves. Can you believe it? Leaves! The truck seems to get louder as it slows. All right! the lead man says—his hand on your shoulder, he is looking out the flap. All right! he hisses. Now! The truck does not stop; each comes off the back of it pushed by the lead man, hitting the soft crumbled asphalt hard, off-balance, dropping to his knees. Each stands up panting, as if having run a long way, and scrabbles off the road as fast as he can, stays there in the bushes, ditch, whatever, for as long as it takes to slow down your heart, get your breathing back to normal, a little feeling back in the arms and legs. Remember what the job is, how to get there, stare across the little access road, familiar to you from last time, the dry run, for the place in the forcewall you got through then, the flicker, play of ghostlight in the dark where forcewaves are out of alignment, you can get through. Then grab the M-16 and move out, through the chink in the forcewall, dodging and darting from bush, tree, hedgerow, corner, finally in a burst of pure fear across the floodlit lawn around the huge white building twinkling gold light from its windows through the wooden trap into the cellar where the lead guy waits: still on time. Crepes flambées au Calvados for dessert. After them, and the distribution of liquers, brandy, coffee, tea, Gwen Knessen rises to suggest, with an attractively self-conscious irony, that the company assembled retire to the arboretum. Cups, snifters, cut-glass cordials in hand, the company passes through the long hall in which they first gathered, under its high ceilings, massive beams, sparkling chandeliers, saunters past the lounges, sofas, and stuffed period chairs of the lower, more enclosed room in which we first met Gwen Knessen who now, again employing that smile, that accomplished blend— quite European, really—of ingenuousness and irony, informs those nearest her, chiefly Devine, that they must excuse this little sitting room: as if its ormolu clocks or ancient Bösendorfer grand might be taken as some personal, private admission of herself. Devine smiles back; somewhat vacantly perhaps, Ernest notes, as though he were preoccupied; he and Halberdson, still at his side, exchange phatic smiles, as if to say at most Yes; very well done; very good. A servant awaits them at the frosted glass portieres, whose serpentine handles he grasps and opens. The arboretum: warm moist green earth smells, the stink of fecundity assails their nostrils with a pleasant shock; glutted greens burst forth beneath a sky of glass, a virtual tropical colony captured and preserved. Extraordinary! Ernest breathes out to the hostess, primarily to check in with Devine, remind him of your presence and performance by making contact with her. This is all Cal's work really, Gwen Knessen says, smiling. He became so interested in the flora during our Africa days, he simply couldn't—but I should let him tell you all about it himself. Cal? she says, lifting a little from the toes, as Ernest does too, to parallel his position with hers in relation to Devine; so both see Cal Knessen, palefaced highbrowed man at the still open doorway turn swiftly away from them as though at the sound of an overriding call and the three men in duncolored clothing, masks and brown hoods, stride through the study and into the greenhouse. Hey what is this? Ernest hears one man say and the other, Halberdson beside him: Terrorists, terrorists, shut up. How dare you? says Mr. Knessen whose face is very white now as they shove him aside. Just do the work and get out of there as fast as you can. Remember the face you're supposed to get. You find the tall rawboned guy in the middle of the lump of them in the nice grey pantsuit number, English cut. You look at your partners' masked faces, nod; they nod back; they have found him too. Then fire a bunch of short semi bursts over everybody's heads, shattering glass plates everywhere above into sky, and when everybody scatters drill the tall rawboned one with another burst as he tries to get behind some kind of little jungle tree. Then the tricky part: you walk up slowly with the other two to the older guy standing by the woman, the three of you lower your weapons at him. Ernest without thinking throws his whole weight against Devine and topples them into a clump of dense high greenery at the same time as he hears a scream, his own.

Sound of running feet, clatter of their guns at their sides: silence. From outside he can hear the sound of alarms, sirens. Where are the rest of them? Where has everybody gone? Devine, close by him, raises himself up on one arm. Half his face is covered with wet black dirt. Montale, he says, thickly, to no one. Why does someone want to shoot Montale? I want a full investigation of this incident, right away. Ernest puts a hand on his shoulder, squeezes. You saved my life, Devine says, staring deep into his eyes. Thank you. Good job, you guys, says the lead guy, way to go. Nobody answers. Sirens, alarms, everywhere, they have every system in the area alive, probing for them. And the ride back is cold and bumpy and slow. You try to sleep and almost make it a few times, thinking about the apartment, Anna, lying next to a warm body at the end of this ride. Once after a bad bone-jarring bump, you hear one of the others saying Shit what is the *matter* with this fucking truck anyway? Why don't you just keep your fucking mouth shut? says the lead guy beside the tailgate, looking out from under the edge of the tarp.

Abstract animation: eyes that contain all imaginable flickering colors, cross the screenwall in a line; subdivide; pair; coalesce; explode; all before a backdrop of shifting sand designs. Quite peaceful, very soothing, much better than that stupid NBC thing, the woman smacking the animal, whatever it was, because it wouldn't do something or other, and then the other people broke in and everybody on the screen laughed. But it was stupid anyway, and the layback had started to hit, so you just tuned to PBS where they always have this kind of really pretty sort of artscreen stuff, the kind you can pay attention to if you want or just drift off.

T.D.'s headache is gone; he sags out of his seat, drips gently down the mohair floor, smiling up at the eyes that fill the space he falls out of for the rest of the night.

It is as if—*as if*—there were many sounds in her head all at once, drowning each other out, so that the space inside her skull beginning above the eyes and the tips of the ears, ending at the base of the skull behind, feels full of silence but all jammed up at the same time with signals, each of which she should be responding to right away. So her head feels full in some ways, empty in others, all at the same time; she is always close to being very excited about something, yet never is. Terrible things happen all the time, nothing happens. All she does is sit around all day while the past comes over her like so many stupid ugly cartoon dreams, she can't remember anything no matter how hard she tries. She wants to have Billy with her all the time, squeeze him against her, one hand on his back, one pushing the hard head beneath the fine red hair against her belly so hard he comes back into her again; she hardly knows what she says any more to him, never listens to his chatter, hardly remembers he is there, any more than she remembers the hot urgency, breaking open of being with Ernest in bed. She cannot count on them or build from them, she knows that now whenever she wakes with the memory of her daddy telling stories with his hand in her hair, laughing as she laughs with him and the sun catches on its way down the magnolias, gold and green, and her mother smiles and pours herself another drink, everything safe and neverending with Mommy and Daddy wrapped in the lawn, safe, loved, safe. But she is here, alone, in San Francisco. What to do. Where to go.

Little ceremonial thing at the airport, greetings from the head of the regime, Devine says, slouched back on the couch. They're very big on ceremonies and respect down here.

Does that mean nobody's going to try to kill us? Ernest says. I'd like that.

Now wait a minute, Devine says. Since when has anybody wanted to kill *you*?

They smile at each other dryly, ironically, as the jet breaks under the cloudbank, holds above the brown bloom of smog held in by the mountains, hanging in the sky. The character of the relationship seems determined and described, for the time being, by such little exchanges, in which aggression, wit, and barely affectionate sincerity vie for predominance. It is as much a temporary stalemate as an achieved form. You called his bluff then saved his life; here's your reward; now what else can you do?

They are alone in the jet this leg; the V.P.s dispersed elsewhere. Ernest watches Devine lift a paper from the coffee table, run his eyes down it, yawn and press for William.

Suits, William, Devine says when William, impassive as ever, appears. And do we have a hairpiece that will fit Mr. Goodman?

William's eyes glance briefly at Ernest. Your hat size, sa, is seven and one-eighth?

Yes it is, Ernest says. Very good, William.

With dispatch please, William, says Devine. We're almost down.

Sa.

The two of them watch his rapid decorous steps down the aisle, turn to each other and trade curled lips.

The other officers love it, Devine says. Especially the younger ones. Having some old relic like that cut them down while serving them makes them go all squishy. They feel like they've really arrived.

Ernest nods, purses his lips. Arriving at William, he says. That's just about as much fun as wearing a wig, don't you think?

Just about, says Devine, as William enters with the wigs and two three-piece white silk suits.

But can the great William have made a mistake? Ernest whispers in a stage voice, eyebrows raised; then smiles up at the black man the same malicious sweetness Devine has been using on him. That isn't my suit, William. My suit is black, blue-black actually, two-piece—

Goodman, Devine says in a perfect deadpan: William realizes that. But *you* don't realize that suit is not acceptable down here. They like us to wear these white plantation suits. It's sort of tradition with them. And

William here assumed that you would not be familiar with the custom, and so has had one made up for you, I presume. Right, William?

The black man holds the suits and wigs up shoulder-high. That is correct, sa, yes.

Ernest and Devine exchange glances again, each suppressing the urge to laugh out loud. The jet shudders a second, side to side, as the props go up and catch on, and pure vertical descent commences through the smog to the airfield.

By the time it has settled on the runway, before the long blue arm of the terminal concourse and the shouting, waving crowd, they have donned their wigs and white suits; and Devine's face, turning back to his, is set again in its official mask. Take this, he says handing over his briefcase. You'll look more official. We're going to walk out, be kissed by the senile ruler of this godforsaken state, whom I am probably going to have to get rid of, and stand through a very long and elaborate welcoming speech after which the crowd will go wild on cue. All you have to do is shake hands when someone sticks a paw out, kiss the old man back, wave at the crowds and clap when everyone else does. William can give you a translation plug, Spanish-English if you really want to catch anything more than that. I don't care whether you wear one or not. You want one?

No, Ernest says. Not right now anyway.

All right, Devine says. Ready?

Yes, Ernest says, fine, and follows Devine out the hatch, to the deafening cheers of the crowd he does not look at, generalissimo whose dry pink lips on his cheek he barely feels, speeches rolling out interminably against the sunstruck walls of air. It is Devine he is watching: Devine bowing deeply, shaking hands, sitting straight and stiff then smiling, raising his hands in the air to the screaming crowd; watching Devine while performing roughly the same gestures himself, while wondering how to capitalize on this situation too, how to extend the relationship a little more.

What kind of product Ramsfeel is, what it is supposed to do, whether it is a name for coffins or condoms, synthetic foods or a specially processed steel—such information only matters insofar as factors can be quantified, turned into numbers that can be measured with and against other numbers to determine what the short, middle and long-run profitability of a given action, or product, or situation is. Even the mindless empty shit of standing on a line performing the same single action the same way fifteen thousand times a day can be converted into a set of figures relating to job turnover and productivity. And the final number is the form of capital, the end product, to be reinvested to start the numbers moving again.

Some calculations, however, are quite difficult to make. It takes time, for example, to devise a system by which managers can make a reasonable choice of Third World sites for their next plant. For starters they must graph labor and marketing costs against the possibility of civil disturbance: mass starvation, urban riots, revolutions, etc. In some countries, the risk is so high that the managers must be assured of an annual net profit of forty percent after taxes; in other, safer countries, much less. As a professor at the Harvard Business School has written: The challenge for the manager in the international economy is to find the quantitative equivalents that can reflect measures of this sort [meaning, for example, the possibility of any devastation, upheaval, any suffering] in a return-on-investment calculation. The temptation will be to disregard these factors simply because they are so difficult to quantify. But that is a temptation to be resisted. Otherwise, the investment decision may well be made on false premises.

Investment decision. False premises. Difficult to quantify.

T.D.'s eyes open on the soft fuzzy white of the lighted ceiling, move rapidly back and forth and up and down, as if seeking some difference in focus or intensity, a little patch of darkness, a break in a circuit somewhere. Hello, the screenvoice is saying, welcome to this day in your life, August 30, 2020—

The layback has, as usual, left him with a new headache, a line of pain like a minor fissure in his skull along a line just above the top of his thick eyebrows which, he remembers the nth morning in a row, need depilling soon. But not today. Not after the layback; one slump and you'd take off half a brow.

And the slops are hitting all right; T.D. hits one jag putting his WakeUp in and drops, busts the hell out of a mug. Buckles again down on the floor picking the pieces up.

So he has to stand outside in the cool humid air of Chevy Chase in early morning without his WakeUp, rubbing his cheeks and chin and hoping the job he did on them wasn't too erratic, feeling generally miserable, looking back at the shuttered blinds of the other half of the once-ritzy ranchstyle where the fucking slug is, what's-his-name who never worked a day in his life, thinking how that slug is going to sleep the whole day away. Or get up and trans it to a near mall, buy himself some bit of jewelry he thinks he looks pretty in. While T.D. has to stand up in front of wise young pretty boys all day again today, giving them their moves, no matter how much his goddamn head hurts, how worried he is about the job. Sonsobitches, slugs like that guy living next to him there, behind the blinds, they can eat layback all day every day.

The sun keeps rising. His head hurts more. He looks down the winding suburban street at the few other workers standing waiting for the trans like him. Sure, he is glad to have a job, make his living by himself. But they take advantage of that, they do. They really ought to pay you enough so you don't have to live next to, right in the middle of a bunch of fucking slugs.

And so once again, today, wheezes the generalissimo, we take unto our bosom and the bosom of our most fortunate, beautiful, and well-loved nation these gentlemen, our wise and good and generous friends from the North, with whom, supported by the will of God and the dictates of reason, our country's destiny can only continue to prosper. And so we open our arms to say Our land is your land, our wealth is your wealth. Our future belongs to the new, benign conquistadores: to you we say, Welcome again!

The band below the modest bunting-draped grandstand strikes up You're in the Money, with catchy syncopations and bland "Cuban" harmonies a la Xavier Cugat. The crowd erupts into shouting and wild applause. They are the lucky two thousand whom the government hires for these greeting ceremonies. Their records are clean, their thoughts are pure, things are so desperate for them, good lord, if the government will pay fresh clothes, a polyester shirt and pants plus a day's wage if you will register and show up for the rally, they can get any number of people they need to go through any kind of clearance they put on them, to sign and abide by any rules and procedures they want. Besides, there are those widemouth torches mounted on the airport's blue concourse roofs, triggered from who knows where, leveled on them, waiting for who knows how small an infraction, perhaps merely insufficient enthusiasm would be enough. Besides, almost everyone actually is excited; they will get money for this after all, mailed to them by the government; already they have received their clothes from the guardias, to be worn at the ceremony. And finally, insofar as they are not excited—some have done this so many times, listened to the General's same speech standing hatless in the sun, stomach tightened to a small fist, eyes on the small anonymous figures in white seated at the General's side as often as three, four times a day when there is trouble and the jets from America start coming in—they try very hard to *get* excited, to clap and shout even louder, given their fear and need. Only afterwards, when they are safely back home, will they laugh about it, maybe get drunk, hate themselves a little more.

Rough translation of the General's speech: Here all business practices are permitted. We will let you use all the investment capital we have to finance your plants, your agribusiness, your mines, your complexes and shopping malls, more and more of them, like those you have in America. We will let you have the money at especially low rates. In the few cases, very rare now, in which we ask you to supply "matching funds," those funds need not be money at all; they can be secondhand equipment, obsolete junk that will hardly work anywhere else, and is dangerous too; it can be in the form of technical services and assistance, by your people from America or Europe, you set the terms of the exchange. We will tax you at especially low rates; we will never charge you any import or export duties or fees. We can also, of course, ensure a cheap work force, a limitless supply of surplus labor, millions of people need work and money here in the worst way as you can see from the most casual glance at the city, all these unfortunate tin barrios, more every day as you look down from the air. You can pay them virtually as little as you like; there will be no unions, no wildcat strikes or workers' revolts. Finally, you may have first access to our wealth or raw materials, the riches of the alluvial soil on the floodplain, the wealth of the mines under the earth, the wood, the water, all yours. If you need a resource on someone else's land, a tribe's perhaps, you will get it. All our money, all our people, all our resources are yours, the General will take care of everything in the next room for you, please go in and sit down, sign here please, the General will take care of everything in the rooms where his officers punch women in the breasts, pass electricity through men's balls, on the streets at night when the assassination squads are set loose, young excited men who like to kill with the old U.S. weapons supplied them by the government, or their bare hands. We do not necessarily approve of their methods, of course, those of us whose sons and daughters go to the American and European schools to study Borges and Shakespeare, Neruda and Proust, to acquire the newest tastes in goods a la U.S., and bring them back for us to gape, we do not condone the evil these generals and their minions do by any means. Yes, of course it is tragedy that progress costs such pain. But that's human nature, no? Besides, how else do we make our country strong and well?

One morning she tells Billy she has to go somewhere without him, arranges with the screen for a sitter, and takes a random trans without giving a destination. The trans brings her through the business district, where everybody else gets off. A few men and women look at her as if— *as if*—they knew where she was going alone. She gets off on the lower edge of the safe sector, the closely guarded fronts of giant business buildings colored black or grey or beige, and walks away from them, south to Market and the old warehouse district with its crummy tumbledown shops, stuff heaped in piles right out in the street, a place she has never been before where black and brown and some white people mill around, swank up the sidewalk, lounge against buildings of old brick and cracked broken windows with all kinds of cheap bright clothing, dirty orange robes, tunics in loud metallic hues and cuts that went out years ago, even a few thin flimsy dirty business suits. All kinds of expressions too, ones you never or rarely see, and even more rarely remember: brown faces swallowed in wrinkles, tooth-less faces laughing, asian faces locked in rigid furious frowns, a white face yelling relaxed in crazy tranquillity beside a doorway through which spills some kind of half-rotten fruit. People knock and jostle around it, looking at it, picking it up and feeling it, batting the flies away. There is junk coming out of almost every doorway, shoes and cheap jewelry, wigs and clothes and food jumbled up like the goods for kids in the malls uptown. Here people pick them up and feel them, people smelling dirty and rotten of sweat and dust and decayed food and teeth, their lined faces moving, flickering constantly. She steps up to a waist-high bin of clear green glasses and cups outside a warehouse with a sign COSMO'S A UNIVERSE OF BILLIONS OF BARGAINS in English and three or four languages un-derneath it. Two old fat women with grey frizzy hair, huge trembling upper arms, narrow brown eyes, hold the glasses and saucers up to the sun and look through them, talking to each other in a language Charlotte does not know and a huge grin splits her face, she cannot help it, she feels a strange crazy joy at this place, this world so alive, so unlike anywhere else she has ever been.

At the same moment the young guard at the end of the block catches sight of her and her smile and flashes on her strangeness down here, how somebody like her, the way she looks, is not supposed to be down here, is not supposed to know this; and starts moving through the crowd.

Charlotte sees him coming, the familiar helmet, torch, and knife, quick flash of the red face oh no, and without losing her smile holds up her hand, palm out, and shakes her head—No thank you, I'm quite all right—and the guard moves back to his corner again. Such is her power here. When she turns back to the bin the old ladies are gone. She picks up a glass herself, holds it up to the light, puts it back down. Words start running out of her mouth, saying whatever they want to, getting it all out.

Cars, Ernest says, shaking his head at the clogged streets, air blue with hydrocarbons, strings of cars beyond the circle of security vehicles accompanying their limo: Even traffic jams!

The strategy being to modulate by degrees from the uncertain ascerbity of the relationship worked through so far to a smoother and more affable one, with the aggressions and reservations drained away.

Unh, says Devine.

On the other end of the seat from Ernest, the General turns his large liverspotted head and exposes a gleaming panoply of gold teeth, speaking clear English: Yes, here we cannot imagine life without the car.

Devine is leaning his head back against the leather seat; his eyes are shut. Can't imagine death either, he says. How many of our men is it your friendly happy people have blown away in their cars in the past three months?

The General's gold smile stretches; his gnarled hands rub his knees as he leans to Ernest: My friend Señor Devine refers to the tragic automotive incidents which claimed the lives of eight representatives of your beneficent organization, he says. Every effort is being made to investigate these tragedies completely and successfully. I am prepared at this point to show you a list of possible suspects all of whom are in close custody at this time. We are also investigating the possibility that the killers responsible for these acts of senseless violence may be in the employ of perhaps a rival business interest or government, and I think we have—

Yes, General, says Devine, settling further in his seat. Of course only an outside agency could cause your citizens to commit an act of hatred or violence toward the corporation which has done so much for them, and which they therefore love so well. I have no doubt that you will find the criminals responsible to have been secretly in the employ of ITT or Sears. But of course that's hardly the point, is it General? The point is that you're where you are because you can give us security, right General? And it doesn't seem as though you've been doing much more than a halfass job lately, now does it.

To Ernest it is as though Devine is speaking a tape, or out of a dream. It comes out of him automatically, naturally, there is no need for him to put himself in it at all. Where then is his self? Ernest wonders, as the limo reaches the end of the flashy commercial district with its fresh gleaming facades, and plunges directly on to a beltway beyond whose concrete embankments the thousands of huts and shacks are visible again, spreading away like the same sprawl seen above San Francisco the other day. And when he moves his gaze back inside the car, he finds Devine has one grey eye, the right one, wide open regarding him; and he bursts suddenly into the contemptuous laughter Ernest knows, for the time being, he can only join.

Get up.

The figure is dark, enormous, blurred. It stands beyond and above him, so indistinct it could be very close by or far away, big enough to tower over him even so.

Get up, it says again, moving toward him from whatever distance until a spark of pain flares somewhere on his body—knee?—and Guillermo wakes up.

That's right, the guard says and taps his knee again with the electric baton so that this time his whole body snaps. You got it now. Wake up the woman and get your stuff.

Guillermo reaches behind him for Anna's shoulder, shakes it. Anna, baby, something's happening.

Anna rolls to her side, trying to work her puffy eyes open, find words: What's so . . . fucking . . .

Shut up Anna, Guillermo says, wide awake, his long face and body set. He can glimpse the uniformed shoulder and leg of another guard just beyond the bedroom doorway: of course.

You fellows sure you've got the right place? he says. I sure can't think why you'd be here for us. I've been working for the company for eight years, whenever they asked me, whatever they wanted me to do. Just within this last month—

But the guard has reached over him to touch the prod to Anna's hip so that she screams and jumps to her feet, as the kid too starts to scream and cry; then he takes a step back toward the doorway as if to survey his handiwork.

Get your shit ready, he says. You got fifteen minutes.

What *is* this Guillermo, Anna is shrieking, drowning out even the baby's squalls, What the shit is going *on*?

But her voice seems to reach him from far away. It is all still dreamlike, distant because so final: already it has taken less than a second to imagine every conceivable move he could make, insisting there must have been some mistake, showing i.d. and papers and records of past work performed, pleading for mercy, time to clear up this whole thing, whatever I've done wrong . . . Not a chance. They have their orders same as you have; used to have. Working it through that way even breeds in his mind a certain peace.

So Guillermo runs his long strong flattipped fingers back through his black hair and thinks quickly, decisively, one second ahead of his low even voice: All right, Anna. Be cool now. Get what clothes you can together for us, warm things mostly, okay? I'll get the food and something for us to put things in.

He rises, moving toward the doorway, watching the fine mesh grill that covers the guard's face.

Anna is standing against the kid's bed, leaning against the bedrails. Behind her the kid is still screaming. She grips the rails and, standing there in the bright orange bra and underwear they bought together once when they were out shopping all fucked up a month or so ago, stares hard straight ahead of her at the cream yellow wall across the room, so hard her eyes are narrowed almost shut as her knuckles whiten on the rail. Then she turns her gaze to Guillermo; her hands release the rail.

Yeah, okay, she says, returning his gaze. Let's go.

The second day she is down in the district a young man steps into her path and begins talking to her, weaving his shoulders from side to side. His eyes are green and slightly crossed, the bare skin on his waving arms and chest exposed by a deeply cut green knit robe, raveled with dirt and wear, his skin tinged with yellow, and he smiles at her sweetly, showing large brown teeth, a smile she has to return. Hey listen baby, real thing, he is saying, you need a good looking to a good screwing to, that what you down here for? I can do it to you any number of times for hardly a thing, real thing, and nothing like your dinky downtown man or lady either, what you say? And stops still, holding out his longfingered hand.

Charlotte stares back; the bright crowd moves around the two of them. My *lord*, she says. It is an old expression of her mother's, in the lazy fluid drawl she has not used for years: That was just wonderful. Where did you ever learn to talk in that remarkable way?

The crosseyed man takes a step to his right, subdued by the accent, the highclass tone of grace and poise. His expression is troubled and uncertain; he is looking over her shoulder, not at her any more. What you want, lady? he says. What you doing down here?

Oh nothing, she says in the same strange airy voice. I'm just looking, thank you.

The crosseyed man slips away, mumbling something down at his shoes.

But all the rest of the day, eating a piece of damaged mango, fingering cheap fabrics, she thinks of him: the amazing riff, the foreign strange body twisting side to side as he spoke. Thinks of him as she stares at the smeared image of herself in the green weathered window of a used screenvue store (OVER 1000 TO CHOOSE FROM BIG OR SMALL WE GOT THEM ALL), in her oldest tunic suit with the fresh rips and the stains rubbed into it. To think of herself here in this funny crazy place, talking back to that crazy rubber man in her mother's voice, why it's enough to make you laugh all over again. And are you really going back to Alabama, sugar? that voice says to her, she says to herself; which lets a bright fresh stream of giggle loose.

La Rinconada, as it is known, some forty miles from the capital, had been in the hands of the Coitia family for three hundred years when the Porfirios acquired it from them, seventy years ago now in the days of "land reform" that placed the estates of the ancient decayed aristocracy into the hands of an ambitious mixed-blood bourgeoisie. Even before the reforms the Coitia fortunes had declined steadily, in the traditional way: too great a dependence on land, cattle, and crops for a steady income, too little interest in mining, railroads, and other foreign-owned industries, in investment generally; too much Catholic piety, especially among the women, and too few male heirs. So Pablo Porfirio, sprung from who knows what scummy bed in what sordid quarter of the capital city, oliveskinned mestizo with coarse thick black hair, a scraping laugh and his hands full of cash and stock certificates, had no real trouble when the time came convincing the last cadaverous Coitia patriarch to relinquish the family holdings in accordance with the reform laws, allow the last fragments of the noble line to retire with their final bag of money to a corner of Europe or a convent perhaps, and gracefully, decisively disappear.

Pablo and the brief line of Porfirios that have so far followed him are wiser. While retaining the latifundia as it is, as it always was—the deep burgundy, splashed with white, of the herds against the tawny gold of the slight rounded hills in late afternoon, the simplicity, courtesy, and wrinkled classicism evident in an ancient tenant farmer's face, etc.—they have always understood it as, primarily, a sort of fantasyland in which they can pursue the nature of nobility, a work of art to live in, not a serious commercial enterprise by any means. So much is evident from the conversation after dinner between the three—Ernest, Devine, and Ramon Porfirio, son of Pablo—the General having departed by helo, asleep, back to the old viceroy's palace in the capital for the night.

They sit in wicker furniture on the tiled patio sipping brandy by candlelight to the strumming of an invisible guitar, tapes perhaps, somewhere offstage.

Lovely night, is it not, gentlemen? We are approaching the end of the rains now. There will be more and more clear brilliant weather like that of today. Personally it is my favorite time of year.

Ramon's English, like the General's, is vaguely quaint and hyperformal, uttered as impeccably as the black hair, short as a business wig's, is swept back from his short, sloped brow. Ernest, with Devine on the wicker loveseat across from the formica table, notes not only the arch style of speech but the stiffness with which the young man holds himself in his chair, and so checks the impulse to reply. Beside him Devine too is silent. Without a glance over, Ernest can sense him holding himself ready for the real thing, whatever that will turn out to be.

Soon the moon will be up, Ramon is saying. This time of year the illumination it casts is so pale that it is often called la luz del espiritu triste, light of the sad soul. Would either of you gentlemen care for a cigar?

And again everyone is still. It is a ritual, an art form, a part to be played out. This silence hangs a long while on the air.

Very well then, says Ramon, leaning back in his chair, showing a little teeth.

The pale moon rises over the clay rooftiles, as he said it would, and completes his imitation of a Spanish aristocrat; Ernest sees the previously dark face now as a luminous pallor set off sharply against the flat black of the cabellero suit; sees the teeth bared now in eagerness for hard talk, high stakes.

So, says Devine softly, almost soothingly: what will the General and I have to say to each other tomorrow, Ramon?

Ramon's lips twist in a harsh swift smile. The General believes you are worried about security. He is afraid that you and some of the others—he waves a hand in the evening air, as if summoning them up—are considering or will consider cutting back your operations here soon. Tomorrow he will show you a new plan for stricter security he has drawn up, and give you his personal assurance it will be carried out. His minister of security will be on hand if you have any further questions.

Huh, says Devine. How serious is it?

Ramon frowns, tenting his fingers before his face. Hard to tell, he says. Our people in the plant swear nothing's wrong on the inside. So it must be riots in the barrios or something bigger. If the General and his men know, they're not saying what. But security's doubled everywhere in the capital; and, interestingly enough, our people have some evidence that that old databank we put in for them a few years back has been running overtime for the last month or so.

Devine lifts his snifter and sips, his face in the moonlight apparently still relaxed and detached, floating free. Yet Ernest senses that actually he is at this moment most completely alive. Surely, Ernest thinks, it is no accident that he has been given access to such a moment; surely there has been progress; just as surely he must stay quiet and watch.

What are you thinking? Devine says. Uprising? Coup?

We just can't tell, Porfirio says. Seventy-five hundred a day coming into those barrios, no addresses, no jobs; we can't keep a true tab on it.

Ramon, Devine says, leaning forward smiling, with his elbows on the knees of the white suit. I'm not going to cut off your hands if you're wrong.

Ramon nods, smiles, and reaches for the brandy decanter, speaking as he pours and the guitar continues unabated. Okay, he says. What I keep coming back to is this thing about the databank.

Ernest watches the way Devine's eyes follow Porfirio's, watching the moves.

They're not running pure counterinsurgency games on that thing, Ramon is saying. C-I doesn't take up that much terminal time. They aren't looking at the barrios, cause the barrios got nothing that registers, no jobs, no credit rating, nothing. If they're spending that much time, day after day, I figure they've got to be running scenarios, researching who's pushing for them and who's against them when the blow comes down. It's got to be a coup.

Ernest watches Devine's head swivel sideways, regarding Porfirio from aslant narrowed eyes: And you know nothing about it? No advance work whatsoever?

A rush of breath, both laugh and sigh, from Ramon. Hey, he says. We get all the advance work anybody could want. Only never on the same officer, hardly ever on the same group.

The guitar stops; from somewhere behind them, Ernest can hear the white noise of a speaker humming, between the distant lowings of the cattle herd. So yes, it was canned after all.

All of them against him? Devine says.

Sure, Ramon says. You know how it goes. The regime starts jugging and wasting too many people's cousins and nephews, crime rates edge up in the suburbs, price of cars and iceberg lettuce shoots up too fast, not enough young officers get promoted high enough; and it's all over. Trouble is, we don't know when or where. Everybody's got equipment squirreled away, secret people's armies on somebody's payroll getting soup every day. So far the General's still got the biggest piece of it all. But if the old bastard's calling a public conference on security and his computer room's running overtime, he's scared.

Devine stands and walks to the edge of the round garden of succulents, dully sheened in the moonlight, and speaks with his back to both of them. Rural areas looking clean too?

Ramon Porfirio's hands are neatly folded as a schoolboy's in his lap. That's right, he says. Nothing out here but the same scattered crazies in the mountains. Old foco shit. Infiltrate them twice a year, bust them up with a few Indian spies, they never learn. No problem there.

Okay then. Devine turns back, begins to pace up and down behind the loveseat where Ernest still sits. In the absence of such activity, and the presence of counterproductively dispersed antigovernment activity throughout the Army's highest ranks, the General calls his American supporters to tell them publicly he is going to crack down. He stops, slaps his fingers against the seatback so suddenly, sharply Ernest starts: And how old is our General?

(The challenge for the manager in the international economy is to find the quantitative equivalents that can reflect measures of this sort in a return-on-investment calculation.)

Seventy-seven in April, Porfirio says. April twenty-third, a national holiday. We have to shut everything down for it every year.

Ernest feels two fingers on his shoulder, tapping. Once, twice. He does a slow turnaround take, composing his face spontaneously, professionally into a look of pure blank innocence and expectancy, open to Devine's luminous brow, sharp nose, and jutting cheekbones, the eyes sunken in darkness, the mouth moving, speaking as if out of some trance:

The old bastard. They'll start coming after him one by one. They'll take one thing—the radio station, the airport, the palace—and wait for the rest to fall in. And he'll be able to beat them easily at first. Bomb them out, waste them all, even ignore the stupidest ones, let them go right ahead for a while. But every time it happens no matter how fast he stomps it out the thing will cause three other ones, four other ones; then the folks down in the barrios in Shitville start really stirring around. Pretty soon nothing works; you got Commies walking the streets in the middle of the day, you can't pump enough money in to keep things moving, your whole capital investment goes down the tubes. And the old bastard knows it's coming, and is going to try to reassure us before it breaks.

A three-beat silence. Devine's hand grips Ernest's shoulder hard. Ernest stays still, his eyes off Devine, away from any acknowledgment (of the fear, the projection) which would only be repulsed.

Then the grip releases, the hand slips away; the voice resumes its neutral tones: And where are the others in all this?

They have what we have, says Ramon, as far as information goes. We've seen no top-level meetings here lately, but there's clearly concern. Our people inside say American Telecom's been having some unruly squabbles with their chip assembly people—same thing, I gather, with Unifoods. We've also been picking up some heavy levels of communication traffic between their bases here and the home offices. That's all I know.

It's enough, says Devine. Enough to tell us they're moving. Absorbed, he slowly recrosses the patio; sits down; pours himself another brandy. They come up with anyone yet, separately or in combination?

Not that we know of, says Ramon softly. It's hard to be sure.

Devine frowns, rubs his forehead; looks up into the deep blue sky. Maybe there's still time then, he says. Just possible, if we move. Swiftly he leans forward, aiming toward Ramon. Okay, we play this one fast. Pledge the General what he asks tomorrow, verbal commitments only; in the meantime, get on the line to our other friends from the North. Tell them we're backing our own man, we want it over with clean and fast and they'd better get on board. Tomorrow morning I want to see full dossiers on your top three choices with ratings and evaluations attached.

You shall have them, says Ramon Porfirio.

Devine nods his head and turns back to his brandy. Porfirio lights a cigar and leans back, his black costume sagging into the chair. Ernest concentrates on the hot spreading ache in his left knee from sitting with his legs folded over one another for so long, completely still. You can review the scene later, now just play it through . . .

At a certain point he notices the music back again, plaintive strumming wafting through the cool soft air. After a further, indeterminate stretch of time Porfirio rises crisply, slides his smile into place beneath the neat moustache.

Ah gentlemen, he says, spreading his arms palms out, but such hours of conversation pass only too quickly, and I fear that the night air grows chill and damp. May I show you to your rooms?

The ones who kept on the sticky shiny new shirts and pants and blouses the government hands out get back well before the others who, choosing to save these clothes for future occasions, held their customary rags in their hands during the ceremony, or wore them under the good clothes they removed for the trip back. The guards and patrols stop the ragged ones more often and detain them longer than the ones with the cheap new clothes. The ragged ones get beaten around sometimes, laughed at; they scrape dogshit off the guard's boots, do the chickenwalk down the block, on their knees with their hands held on top of their heads until they are out of sight. This way they save their clothes a little longer than the others, even though they get back later to their homes (in the best parts of the barrios, shacks with actual street addresses, made of tin or real packingcase wood), when the rest of the family is asleep and the fire in the brazier is out. The government clothes go under the blankets they sleep on. If they have a can of food, they open it. They squat in the darkness on the packed earth, hearing the rest of them sleeping around them, the shouts and sometimes shots outside, their fingers picking the chunks out of the can and putting them in their mouths, thinking of the long day, the journey, the clapping of hands at the right places, the heat rising off the tarmac burning their feet through the government shoes.

The third day he twists away from her when she bends down to kiss him goodbye and when she grabs his arm to catch and pull him to her, tries to scratch her cheek open with his little nails. Don't do that, she says, laughing a bright strange laugh that means to him that his power is too slight to hurt her, he is nothing and she is hardly listening, hardly there for him. When she has gone he sits and sulks again for a while, though without much heart; again he says nothing to the ashenfaced woman she and the screen have brought in to take care of him. He brings his paintbox in and begins to make a picture of bright reds and yellows with a big black patch in the corner, a design, until his attention is caught up by the screen, a time adventure, a bunch of guards and scientists send themselves back to an old time in some hot place where they sweat a lot and give the other white men who are already there in their brown and green suits the big deathray they need to kill from high up in the air the little gooks who killed their good buddies, who fly out of their little dumb houses yelling, getting killed. After that he goes into the kitchen, finds and eats some banana flavored "pudding" she bought the week before; sits at the table spooning it in with his eyes wide open but blank as any little feeding animal's, turned in upon themselves.

When he re-enters the screenroom the ugly woman is putting a pill in her mouth. I'm going out, he says. That's fine, says the woman. Be careful and have a good time.

So he spends the rest of the afternoon until she comes back running up and down the street, pretending that the other little boy, Roger, who used to live on this street with him is still here, telling him No no you can't go down there Mommy says that guard's bad, no you can't come in you have to wait out here on this porch while I shut the door on you and then just fool around inside for a while, past the grey woman asleep with the screen on, making you be all by yourself out there then bringing you out something to eat, no when you drop the candy on the step and smash and grind the chocolate and sweet center into the flaking paint and wood.

When she comes back he will show her. Look what that stupid Roger did, he will say, he's pretty stupid isn't he, he's pretty bad. And will she just laugh?

The grey woman is still asleep when he goes in again. He does not want to look at her, the way she is. He goes into his mother's room and sits on the bed with his arms around his knees drawn up to his chest, all alone in the world against whose roaring emptiness he can no longer put up anything, no toy, no screenshow, no pretend friend, no mother. Once he goes into the bathroom and gets up on his knees on the sink to look at his pale features, red hair, green eyes in the mirror: that makes the roaring calm down a little bit. When he goes back to his mother's bedroom all he can hear is the sound of their screenroom and the one always on upstairs. After a while his body slumps to the side, then down on the bed in a deep exhausted sleep.

The General too is still up at this late hour, refreshed by a postprandial nap, lounging in the rec room of the palace with a lifelong associate, General Antonio Rodriguez, watching tonight's lateshow, the one they ordered, *The Missouri Breaks*, and reflecting on the events of the day.

Does he think I enjoy it? the General is saying. Standing in the goddamn sun where any crazy fool could shoot me down? Does he think I do this for myself?

General Rodriguez, Minister of Finance, a tall stout man with a fleshy pearshaped head, pats the General's arm. I'm sure he understands, Jorge. I'm sure he meant to thank you. Probably he has lots to think of too, you know, plenty of things on his mind.

And I don't? The General's withered head snaps around like a bird's, black eyes deepset in the skull. They forget that this country would go up like *that* if it were not for men like you and me. He points a crooked index finger with a long yellow nail: We hold their pants up for them every day. We keep their fat white asses covered up for them.

General Rodriguez giggles a short high peal, rocking. Did you see, he says, heaving himself up in his chair, did you see—

Shut up, says the General. Here's a good part.

It is the scene where Brando, the psychotic bounty hunter, puts an arrow from his crossbow into the back of one of the grizzled horsethieves, a scene that entertains the General hugely every time, satisfying his desires for both order and violence, raw justice and swift bizarre death. The same desires anyone in his position on the power grid would feel. Also he likes the way the singing arrow thunks into the flesh, the solid sound it makes. Once, back during their days in the guardia, he and Rodriguez, drunk one night, found an old crossbow and took it in to the examination rooms in the basement of the old detention center and tried to reproduce that sound. But the results were inconclusive; either it doesn't sound like that at all, or else they were too drunk to do it right.

Touched by the memory, the General smiles fondly at his friend: And so, what was it you were saying, Tonio?

Oh yes, says General Rodriguez, blinking to rouse himself: You see that other one with him today? The cuteypie with light brown hair?

Holding his briefcase, you mean? the General says. Light brown wig, very fine?

Right, says General Rodriguez. What position do you imagine he holds in Senor Devine's master plan?

The General's laughter rattles his withered frame, tears tremble out from the corners of his rheumy eyes. I imagine, he wheezes . . . down on his knees holding the . . . little rooster of our friend Mr. Devine!

Oh yes, General Rodriguez says, shaking his head and daubing at his own eyes. They all must have their little cuteypies.

They are nothing more than fairies, all of them, says the General with sudden seriousness. I have known this a long time. But wait, here—

It is the scene where Brando has his throat cut. You get to watch his face close up; the shock first, then the growing comprehension, then the light beginning to leak out from behind the eyes. One night years ago, when they were young . . .

She sets down the foodsacks she carries, cold against her arms and chest with the chill of the quickfreeze goods. Beside her Guillermo kneels and spreads jackets and blankets for the baby he cradles in the other arm.

No G., she says. We better hold him.

Yeah, okay.

The two of them sit propped against each other, leaning against the side of the unmarked van, their stuff heaped around them and the baby in Guillermo's lap. The front of the van, with its guards and drivers, is sealed off; but it is one of their voices, distorted by both facemask and microphone, that speaks to them as the van's engine fires up.

Okay, it says. Now we got you monitored here. We've got video on you from three sides and you're miked for sound. So don't think you can plan any cute tricks without us catching it up here. You couldn't get out of here anyway without a torch, okay?

Anna and Guillermo exchange a brief hard look.

Touching, says the metal voice, but not enough. We've got to hear it up here. So okay?

Okay you fuckers, says Guillermo.

Okay, the voice says; and the van begins to move.

Boy, Guillermo says after a while. Boy they fucked me over good.

It'll be all right, Anna says. We can make it.

I bet every single one of us on that damn operation is getting tossed out, Guillermo says. He lifts his head and shouts to the roof: Real good, didn't you? We don't know shit, we come in and pull a few triggers for you, you throw us all over the wall. We don't even know each other, who the hell we are. That's it isn't it? *Isn't it?*

Hagen, says the voice. Nobody up here knows what you're talking about. So why don't you just shut the fuck up, okay? Otherwise you won't even make the wall.

Anna takes hold of his arm near the wrist and squeezes it. He looks at her, his face locked, straining.

Come on baby, she says. Cool down.

They ride the rest of the way in silence. The baby sleeps. Gradually the road gets rougher; once they hear something scream in low from overhead. A few times the van stops for a moment; checkpoints. Finally the van's back door slides open, exposing stars, pale moon, a gravel road lying before them white as a bone.

Okay, the voice says. Get your ass out.

So they do, silently, the two of them with the kid, and move toward whatever kind of place it is out here, outside the compound and the forcewall, as the van moves away from them, back down the gravel road, toward the lighted walls of what must have been the place they used to live.

He calls you Dick, Ernest says.

Uh-huh, Devine says from the edge of the nearest single bed, beneath the gauzy crepe canopy that arches over both. Yeah. Ramon's a good boy.

Ernest pretends to be watching himself remove the wig at last in th makeup mirror—Ah yes, he sighs, so fine—while his real attention remains on the bent immobile figure of the man on the edge of the bed.

And how long were you down here, he says, casually.

Devine looks quickly up, back at him in the mirror. A second later he smiles. Good, he says. Very good.

Nothing spectacular, Ernest says. Obviously you must have had to move around to get where you are. Then the way you said *good boy*—

Devine has risen from the bed, is undressing quickly, three-quarter turned away from the mirror: I'll have to be more careful in the future.

No need, Ernest says. He raises his eyebrows, smooths the rest of his face, turns his head in ingenuous openness over his left shoulder: Honestly. There's nothing wrong with letting me know who you are, Dick. I'm supposed to be your friend, remember?

Devine turns around, his black tie draped across his open palm, its ends dangling. I was here for five years, between ten and fifteen years ago, he says in a voice bereft of all but the tone of a report, as his eyes stare past Ernest to the stucco wall. We were putting in a new facility. Ramon's father got us some cheap credit that was supposed to be all tied up for GM. So when the time came there was a job here waiting for Ramon. I was here then; I broke him in myself.

He's turned out well, Ernest says, lowering his head to unbutton his shirt, waiting for the reversion, the How the hell would you know?

But Devine merely frowns and peers upward. It is still not quite as if he were really talking to anyone; yet once you get him to incorporate you in this way . . .

He's all right, Devine is saying. He could be better. His old man was better. He chuckles softly, to himself. His father's the one who sold us all on the General we've got now, twelve years ago, last time things got out of control. They were, too—his smile broadens, softens—I never hope to see anything like that again. They had production shut down, they were smashing cars on the streets, hauling our people out and throwing gasoline on them and lighting it. We didn't know; we didn't think anybody here was going to be able to handle it, it looked like we were going to have to start talking to government people back in the States about coming in, which at the time nobody very much felt like doing. And Porfirio kept telling us No, there was this one officer he and his guys knew who could handle it, some guy with ten years in security. Ice water in his veins, he told us, integrity in his heart, and brass balls . . .

Brass balls, Devine repeats and laughs again; then his face darkens and lowers toward the coarse wool rug. Never checked back to see what Porfirio got out of the deal. Plenty probably. Land, cash privileges. Deserved them, anyway. But it was a good deal for us. His men had this place clean in a month, you never saw so many guardias in your life. To this day I don't know where he got them, if they'd been standing by the whole time or what. Fully armed too.

Now Devine is smiling, smiling at him, the clear intelligent smile of a relaxed friendly man sharing his knowledge of power and control: And that's the difference between Ramon and the old man. If the old man had been on that patio tonight, he would have told us who the successor to the poor old bastard has to be; he would have convinced us; and he would have made a heap of money out of the deal.

Ernest, of course, smiles back—warm broad smile with the lips closed—and holds a second, standing facing Devine, perhaps five feet away from him in front of the beds. Okay, fine, don't push for any more for now.

So he twists the smile back to the familiar wry grin: White suits and wigs again tomorrow then?

Not for you, Devine says, stepping out of his pants and tossing them out the door for the servant. You wouldn't be too welcome at this bullshit conference with General. Anyway, we'll be taking off right afterwards for Luzon. I'm going out to take a look at a new installation we're putting in there. His grey eyes glitter: You want to call your woman.

Mmm, says Ernest, holding the wry amusement: You're pretty good yourself, Mr. Devine.

It's my business too, Mr. Goodman, Devine says flashing his teeth: Go on. Make your call.

Nude, he steps into the adjoining bathroom, from which the hissing of the waterjets soon comes.

Ernest removes the rest of his clothes, punches the buttons and puts the call through in a state of exultation that fades only a little when there is no answer on the other end, in the kitchen of the apartment on Green Street. Where is she? Gone already to Alabama, and for what, who's still there? How good it would be now to be able to go home to her flushed with this success and lie down with her and move slowly, without urgency, into that space, over and over, now that things are at last really on track. What time would it be there anyway now?

But it's all right though. It'll wait. So, smiling at the stucco wall, he hangs up the phone.

Though there is no name for the spreading glow inside him it seems not unlike the tingling spray of the tiny jets along the shower's ceiling and three stippled walls. Not unlike the feeling just as some waste scene begins. The way the body gives in to the water's teasing stings, the way when the shooting first begins at Bruges or tomorrow for at least one second it feels like you truly might be killed. At such moments the skin of the world tears open into pure possibility, true risk against which no barriers can be mounted, no defense can avail. That moment of weakness out on the patio; your hand on his shoulder. *No need* he said just now. The thought of opening up to him, cracking open letting go—

Devine twists the dial; the shower cuts off. Standing there in the pale blue shower he feels the water's chill on his body, looks down at the dark hairs stuck wet to his arms and legs and chest. He waits until the cold reaches far into him, until that feeling—whatever it was—has knotted into one small localized ache and he is once again able to think clearly, throw up some safeguards, make a plan. It was, you will remember, against just such an eventuality that you insisted on a flaw; just in case the guy did turn out to be this good.

So it seems, as he towels himself off, that he is back to himself, in full control. Seems that way all through the call on the red line to the home office, GuardAll division, on the bathroom phone. Only after the orders are issued, the call is complete, does he realize the feeling has crept back, it was there quavering in the very orders you just gave, not knowing what would come, what you wanted to come, simply pulling the chain you had set up and letting it go then lifting your fingers to this smile on your face.

Mr. Hamilton, says the low thrilling voice, computer-generated: Hamilton's position being well below the level at which he could own his own secretary: There's a Mr. Garnett on line three for you. He says it's urgent.

Hamilton snorts, shakes his head, alone in his cubicular three-sided office with its three-quarter high walls.

Put him on, he says, sighing. With screen.

Garnett's head appears on the white wallboard to Hamilton's left: gaunt and huge, with balding pale hair, hollow sunken eyes with tiny black pupils really strung far out.

I'm sorry to disturb you sir, says Garnett's head. But I have some information I thought you might want right away. Have you received and processed my last transmissions, sir?

Hamilton's thick fingers fumble through the litter of folders on his desk. Yes, of course, he lies, feeling his pudgy face grow hot, regretting he ever called for screen.

Then you will remember, continues Garnett's head, that our chief subject has formulated, albeit rather vaguely, the notion of returning to her former home in Alabama—Tuscaloosa, Alabama?

Yes? says Hamilton, growling to disguise the fact that he is racing his eyes up and down the last summary, trying to catch up, understand what the hell is going on, these things are hardly his goddamn responsibility, why do they always stick him with this shit with third quarter figures coming up . . .

So? he says.

I believe she is about to make that move, says Garnett. Her anxiety and dissonance indices are rising rapidly. There has also been a pronounced drop in the number and affectivity of her exchanges with the second subject; and then the matter of her aberrant daily excursions in Sector Five, a low-scale and insecure area.

Hamilton curls his thick lip downward, taps his pen on his desk So how does that figure out to her making the move now?

For an instant Garnett's visage loses its frozen intensity; his eyes blink once, twice. On the basis of experience, sir, Garnett says, I believe she will.

Hamilton feels a mild warmth moving in his chest, along the meat of his arms and upper legs. Experience, he says, wrinkling his mouth as though the word left an ugly taste. You believe, he says. Well, thank you very much, Garnett. We will of course process your intuitions immediately. But don't bother me with garbage like this again unless you've got solid figures on it, all right? Is that understood?

Yes sir, says Garnett; and Hamilton punches the call out, leans back in his cracked polyurethane chair with a grin that sours as soon as he realizes what he has to do now, if only just to cover his ass. Call Nickerson and tell him. Hit the right tone on it too.

Breezy, he decides, yet in control. And so, a few minutes later under Nickerson's small shrewd brown eyes he is smiling as amiably as he knows how: I *am* sorry to bother you about this, sir, he is saying, in the absence of any corroborating figures, no real probability scan. I just thought—

Then he notices Nickerson's hard stare and stops short.

Yeah, Nickerson says, obviously more to himself than to Hamilton. Yeah, well I guess we better get moving on it then.

Then Hamilton is facing a blank wallpanel, at which he stares a moment in humiliation rage and fear, thinking *Well fuck you then* until he looks up and sees Banks looking at him again from the cubicle across the way; and so he goes back to work.

He sits in her lap in the trans. He leans against her shoulder, watches her bright eyes. They get off and walk down the streets in a hurry, as though she were looking for somebody, something. But when he asks where they are going she laughs and says just around, no place special, just walking around. And everybody moves fast down here and they are all talking fast in ways he can't understand, sounds he does not know, and there are all kinds of kids, the most he has ever seen staring at him from the corners of the big dark buildings with all the stuff out front. Does she have another boy down here, will she leave him and take the other one back with her? He holds her hand tighter, brushes his head against her dirty robe, against her hip. Could that boy Roger be down here somewhere, safe or a prisoner?

They stop at this one pile of stuff outside this one place and she has a big brown man there with a red cloth around his head take his big flat knife like he saw once on the screen and chop a chunk of this green thing, then chop again and hand it to him, so big he has to pick it up with both hands and push the cool red stuff into his mouth and suck it until it falls apart in his mouth, leaving a taste of sweet water. She smiles down at him, down over her piece: Look, she says. You just spit out those black things the seeds. Right on the sidewalk she does it; so he laughs and does it too.

Like it? she says. It's watermelon. We used to have it all the time when I was a little girl. Daddy used to come home with one practically every night. Would you like to go back down there with me and eat watermelon someday? and slowly he nods Yes. Do you like it down here? and softly frightened, he nods Yes again. Do you know if you take one of those black things and put it in the ground and water it we'd get more watermelon? and he shakes his head No. She talks almost as fast as all the others here, and in a strange slidey way. Well it's true, she says and laughs. It's a seed, honey, a watermelon seed but you don't even know what a seed is, do you now, poor baby, she laughs and he shakes his head No. Well we'll sure enough show you when we get to Alabama, she says and laughs.

And they walk around some more. Strong spicy dirty smells going past.

They go inside the dark hot buildings. There is stuff, clothes or dishes or slabs of some kind of greasy stuff all thrown together like kid's stuff in real stores. But everything is going too fast, smelling too much, not like in the real stores with their cool lights and no smells. Not like here where smelly people bump and rub against them and from under the tables with the stuff the eyes of little kids flash back at him. Is that how they are brown, like the ones sometimes on the screen? From being in these dark places, eating watermelon and the strange greasy other things, not washing off and wearing dirty clothes? He wishes, hard, he were in a real store. Is she going to make him stay down here with the rest of them until he smells like them and has their skin and can never get back any more? Is that Alabama really, where she comes from?

Flies buzz around the greasy stuff. She is laughing and bending over and filling her hands with it. Look honey, she says in that soft fast voice that slides everything together. This is sausage, real sausage, lord only knows where they get it, smell honey, oh we've just got to get some, smell it honey, oh and we'll have to figure out some way of really frying it, can we do it with the radar, oh it comes out so nice and brown and hot I just know you're going to love it sweetheart, we'll have plenty of this too in Alabama, here now honey won't you smell it for Mommy just once?

And he turns. Turns into the tangle of legs, the dark, the smells, out the open door into the light and everybody walking around outside. Runs up the street past them before they look down and catch him in their smelly brown hands. Knowing she is flying wild behind him, her face large dark swollen bad Mommy, hands like claws out to catch him, rip him up. So that as soon as he sees the silver uniform with its torches strapped on the belt, he runs up to it and wraps himself around the guard's leg as the tears spill down his face.

I don't like it down here! I don't want to go to Alabama! I want to go home!

The silver fabric his face presses into has no smell. A hand descends on his head. And he hears the guard's hard voice: Now what's the trouble here? You this boy's mother?

Why yes officer, she says still in that strange fast voice, I surely am.

May I see your passes and i.d., the guard says; and he can hear the edge in the guard's voice. He is going to get her now. When he peers up he sees how the rest of the people, the dark smelly ones have moved away from the three of them and are moving much more slowly, watching them as they go. He still does not look at her, though.

Haven't I seen you down here before? says the guard.

Yes officer, she says and laughs, oh you know I just sort of like to nose around. You probably know this is the only place you can get—

Look lady, says the guard. I can't prevent you with a pass like this from coming down here and getting whatever kind of kicks you get, fucking with bloods and spics or shooting shit or whatever, it's okay with me. But I catch you down here with your kid again, I'll have him taken away and removed to custody. That clear?

You and that other one, his mother says, her voice high and trembling, her hands digging his shoulders, grappling him loose from the guard. You *can't* take him away! This boy's grandfather is an Alabama state senator and his father is the close personal friend of some very big man, and if you think you can—she has pulled him against her now, she is shaking all over, making him shake too and start to cry again, without knowing why: If you think you can—

But the sentence has no end; she cannot finish; so then she is running suddenly back into the crowd, crying, dragging him along by the hand.

He waits for the guard, the planes to shoot at them, to shoot them down. But no one shoots.

She keeps on crying even after he has stopped, making little rhythmic noises all the way back as if still in laughter, down the streets, back in the trans, past the tall shining towers and rows of real stores.

We're getting out of here, she says every so often. We're getting out of here right now.

Billy, frightened, slides over against her, curling his body to her side, watching the buildings glide past. Will they have them too in Alabama? Will there be only dark people there? Bad Mommy, Mommy love . . .

Oh jesus, she says, drawing a final sight dabbing her eyes with her robe: And that man still has all our *papers*, honey. Oh, we've got to get out right *away* . . .

Breakfast is in the cool dusky dining room at the center of the hacienda, with its thick rough-plastered walls, giant table of dark heavy wood, small grotto chipped out of the north wall holding its ancient statues of the Virgin, whose stylized elongated face Ernest rises to pretend to contemplate, maté in hand, as Devine looks over the file set beside his plate.

Thirty-two, Devine says after a few moments. That's pretty young, isn't it?

Perhaps, says Ramon from across the table. He is dressed this morning in a black suit to whose narrow lapel a single red rose is pinned. Yet there are certain advantages, too, we think, he says. A younger man right now will be more popular for a time, no matter what he does. Marketing says thanks to the General's long tenure, people associate repression with age.

He reaches across the table, taps the snapshot in the file. The other big marketing plus, they say, is the name. Pantucho is peasant, mestizo. People are far more likely to believe in and go along with a coup and some urban renewal and security drive if it comes out of lips like those.

Yeah, Devine says. Yeah, well, it's the lips and the age that worry me. You sure he's our man?

His parents are both fully employed, Porfirio says. VW. Father's a foreman. They believe in economic progress, he believes in the miracle of growth and in his own success as one. Our tests reveal no significant trace of low ethnic or class cathexis. Nothing but upward-projected indi-vidualist. He s all ours.

Devine turns a page, runs his finger down a column of figures: I presume you've had the appropriate people making inquiries, he says. What's the rundown so far?

Ramon answers with his suavely handsome head leaned far back, as though reading from the rough massive beams overhead. AmTel won't say yes, won't say no, he says. Unifood's also playing it coy. My reading is there's a real disappointment, even anger in both quarters that they won't be carrying the ball. I'd look to see some heads roll within the next few days and weeks for letting themselves get outjumped again, but they won't put up a fight.

And who else, says Devine without glancing up from the pages. How about the Japanese?

You can just about guess it, says Ramon. They have to discuss it, neither Sony nor Honda will commit. It's safe to say they'll go along once the rest of us are firm.

GM and GE?

The GE people are the ones that first brought him to our attention, over a year ago. And GM's in.

Nabisco?

In all the way.

Devine closes the folder and stares off at the wall opposite him, his mouth twisted shut. Ernest runs a finger down the graceful curve of the Virgin's robe, his senses all keyed to Devine. But even when he turns, silently, smoothly, to take a look, he detects nothing: neither excitement nor repulsion. Just a calculation going on.

We figure it ought to be good for at least ten years, Ramon says quietly. And he's ours, solidly ours.

Devine nods: If your data are sufficient and correct.

We think they are, says Ramon. We feel pretty sure.

Sure you do, Devine says, smiling thinly: It's your data. And turns his gaze back to the folder, paging back through the figures and charts so long Ernest finally senses it is all right to sit down again, pick up his cup and pretend to drink while keeping his own mind clean. He thinks of the statue he has just been examining; he wonders how old that statue might be.

All right, Devine says at last, wiping his mouth with his linen napkin, rising. Start setting up the account.

Very good, says Ramon.

Oh, and by the way, Devine says, how'd you like to have production on the Ramsfeel line down here?

Very much, Ramon says, slowly smiling. Very very much, sir.

Well, Devine says, you handle this one right and we'll see. Let's say when the stabilization factor hits nine, all right? I'll have Ames get back to you then.

Great, Ramon says. Thanks. We'll do it too. You'll see.

He and Devine smile at each other as Ernest rises now too, stepping noiselessly between them and to the side.

But here you are, he says, about to leave without yet having your situation!

No Ramon, Devine says, looking down and away, his face growing suddenly unmistakably red; knowing Ernest must be looking, looking hard.

There's no time for that this trip, he says in his firm neutral voice. In fact, we should be going right now.

The pilotless minicab heads down the pathway, through the green glittering lawns, past the stands of maple and oak with the sensors encased, lenses mounted overhead, toward the asymmetrical pile of white rectangles that is the NASA complex. Sometimes on his way in T.D. imagines that the tree scanners or the car itself could pick up on the last vestiges of his condition; the final few slump instants, the twisted folds of robe, wrinkles that will not convert to folds; sometimes, as his minicab converges with his colleagues' on the final drive, he wonders how many of the rest of them, the others are feeling and worrying about the same thing. Impossible to say: on the inside, all employees are invariably friendly and winning, of course, to one another; outside, except on official business, double-teaming or something special like that, they never meet. Sometimes, especially when he is loaded or strung out, T.D. imagines briefly that they all, colleagues and students alike, really *are* that nice at bottom, really do feel that constant sympathy; and that they all can spot him at a glance for what he is, no matter how nicely he smiles as he exits the minicab, hops briskly up the steps; can smell the sourness in his stomach, touch the greasy sweat along his spine; and even disregarding the whole Jewish thing, it is only a question of time.

But this morning, once again, the door recognizes, admits him again. There are the long white corridors, stretching off inside. There is the clock overhead, saying 7:47 a.m. So yes, once again, he must be at least minimally all right; able, that is, at least to make it through the day.

My lover dreamed she was part of a group standing outside the longhouse they lived in, hearing a low bestial roar. They looked up to a man in a business suit with a bull's head and a monster's body, on a platform in the air which began to drop rapidly, straight down. Everyone broke for the longhouse, behind which a car door slammed, and a car roared around to the front with him inside. Meanwhile they were inside the longhouse, scattering in confusion to their rooms, listening at their doorways: Don't you know how dangerous he is, what he'll do to us? my lover said and the woman in the doorway next to hers looked back suspiciously. What makes you think that? she said.

On the way back in the trans it occurs to her that there must be cameras hidden on these things. She can see them, the men watching her on some screen, somewhere in a large room banked with screens and lights, torches and guns. Will they be waiting for her down here? How far will they let her get?

But when she and Billy get off at the corner of Folsom and Mission, the usual place, without being stopped, the dull throbbing eases in her head. The neighborhood is different now, at night. The storefronts are dark, locked up with their heaps of goods gathered inside, the grey streets lit only by archaic lightbulbs in entrances to stairways leading up to god knows what. Apartments? Is that where they all live, where they are now in those bright colors, strange voices in which she could lose herself, find a way out, to Alabama somehow? Where are they all now? Out here there are no guards even, anywhere she looks, only a damp wind blowing cans and papers down the street.

What are we doing? Billy says. I don't like it here. Are you going to do any more bad stuff?

He has stopped without releasing her hand, so fast that it is she who breaks the connection by walking on a few steps. She turns around and he is staring at her with cold eyes. He does not love her either; not even him.

Billy, she says. We're going to Alabama. Everything's all right. You mustn't be afraid. She holds out her hand: Now come on.

Still he hesitates, until from the next doorway, unlit, a few yards away, a short stocky figure emerges, speaking softly.

Thees ees not the way to Alabama, lady, the man says, moving toward them as Billy's hand finds hers. Thees a dangerous neighborhood, you don know that? Why don you go home, see eff you can make a nice reservation on a plane or sometheeng, eh?

His round face above the dark coveralls is smiling, as he speaks she can see white teeth flash. I can't do that, she says, trying to make the voice and words right, steady, not babble. I have reason to think there are people looking for me. This afternoon I had to leave my i.d. with a guard. I was hoping I could find someone down here who could help me find another way out, I had no idea everything was shut up like this.

Everybody goes eenside, the man says, smiling, because eet ees so dangerous out here. He has his arms crossed on his chest, his squat legs spread. So how much money you got?

How much? she says, and realizes nothing came out and if you turned and ran he would have the two of you in ten steps. Money? she says.

You don have no credit left, he says. Ain't nobody take eet down here anyway. He takes a step closer, so short he has to raise his head to show her the fading of his grin: Come on, lady. Just tell me the truth.

I have a little over a thousand dollars, she says and suddenly, absurdly feels herself blushing. We always kept some cash in the house for emergencies, as far back as I remember, it's just an old habit—

The man holds up his hand, palm out, to silence her; frowns and rubs his fingers over his moustache. Okay, he says. I theenk I con help you, come weeth me.

They walk block after block of unlit unguarded streets, turning often. The storefronts give way to clumps of old apartment houses, candlelit inside, stretches of rubble leading to a brightlit district of low flat buildings they approach from the rear. Billy keeps up well, though occasionally stumbling; his face, when she looks, always stares straight ahead. Inside her head feels light and giddy now: she knows it is that district they are moving toward, almost there, and she will pay him and get away, everything will work out right and she will never see this man, this sweet short man again.

What is your name? she whispers, just at the edge of the warehouse lights. I'm Charlotte.

Paco, he says; and feels the pounding starting in his brain. If she remembers, if she ever knew, if she makes the connection you're dead. So all the rest of the way there he is sneaking looks at her, watching her face; but all it does is smile.

The limo, police cars in front and behind, proceeds back down the freeway toward the capital. Ernest gazes out the smoked glass at the brown grassland, its slight silvering in the fresh, delicate morning light. On the other end of the wide seat sits Devine, eyes fixed on the seatback ahead of him as if in a mild trance, hands clasped on the folder in his lap. It does not seem to Ernest to be an exclusionary posture or moment; his sense of it is quite the opposite. It is—it feels—curiously *intimate,* this time of preparation, the collection and binding of all Devine's powers for the business of the day, a process so palpable that he can feel it even with his face turned to the window, like the rush of the car through the bright air. Being privy to it, trusted with it, seems to confirm and consolidate the progress of the night before.

Yet moments later, as the first scatterings of shacks appear, the farthest outskirts of the city, and he turns his head away, he sees new signs on his client's face: a tightening of flesh along cheeks and chin, a faint frown at the corner of his lips. Because of the conference? Some other business matter? Something more traditionally personal than that? It feels somehow more personal than that—

As he is working to parse this out and hit on a response, the limousine is entering the city proper, the barrios spring up fullblown on each side, new ones at first then older barrios whose windowless buildings are of clay, set well back from the highway and separated from it by a high steel fence through which comes suddenly an old Chevy panel truck with a steel wedge like a cowcatcher welded to its front fender ripping through at an insane speed while the people in the back put out a spray of gas and bullets which first immobilizes then kills the driver and all three guards in the front car before they can get their torches out. The driver's body slumps against the wheel; the car goes left. Their driver in the limo tries to swerve hard right but it is too late. The limo hooks into the front lefthand door of the guard car and swings around broadside against the back. Devine and Ernest are thrown left hard, then right, Ernest against the door, Devine down on the seat then off to the floor. Ernest gets down on the floor too. Devine hands him, from his jacket, a small handtorch like the one he used the night Helena was killed. Devine is staring at him from inches away, his square face quiet, his grey eyes feverish, a faint flush above his cheeks. What is he looking for, what does he want you to do, say, feel? Then, at the sound of the screams outside the car as the police in the back car torch the people in the truck, Devine smiles at him with his lips shut; to which his response, of course, is to raise his eyebrows, give a wry twisted smile back.

The firing stops. Devine cocks his head, listening. Ernest watches the luster in his client's eyes fade. Devine puts his hand out for the minitorch, reinserts it in the coatpocket of his white suit. Cautiously they sit up, Devine gathers his papers, they ease out Ernest's side of the car, and discover their driver standing by the truck alongside two guardias running laserstreams over the bodies, five men and six women in drab green rags, to make sure they are all dead. Ahead and behind them stand uniformed police, knees bent, weapons ready, in case anyone in the ragged dirty crowd on either side of the freeway dares to make a funny move. He and Devine step briskly to the other guard car, empty now but for the other driver. Room for two more? Devine says, laughing as they get in back; and this time when he glances at Ernest, Ernest takes a risk: he smiles slightly but shows a few thoughtlines on his brow and keeps his eyes flat, letting Devine see he is now starting to know a little better what is really going on here.

In his apartment on Divisadero and Sutter, three rooms on the second floor with dust and damp and ancient cooking smells, Hamilton is having yet another fight with his roommate Carberry, a young sallow man with little wisps of facial hair too meager, he says, to depil. Tonight Carberry has started up again, arguing in his perpetual ridiculous whine that the least Hamilton could do in view of the services he has rendered him is to finesse him into a niche in GuardAll somewhere, away from his part-time street guarding, which he hates.

And I really *don't* think it's fair, he is saying. Not after everything I've done for you, to turn right around . . .

While he slinks around the room in his atrocious spotted robe, collapses in an old Sears module then stands again, triggering the yellowed screenwall by crossing it, waving his hands, Hamilton settles his pudgy body further into the couch, feeling tired and dirty and hot, and presses his fingers to his closed, burning eyes. When he opens them again Carberry is standing in the middle of the floor before a blurred gigantic image of Wheat Thins. *Well*, he is saying. So what do you intend to do about *that*?

What makes you think, says Hamilton, unable to keep his hate out of his voice, his little eyes, that I owe anything to a pathetic little whore who answers an ad to split the rent and fucks me a few times a month for his share?

He heaves himself up, watching the cracker box. His head feels about to split apart. I am terribly sorry you can't find a decent job, Carberry, he says as smoothly as possible. But it really doesn't have a damn thing to do with me. Now, if you'll excuse me, I'd like to wash up and eat. I've still got a whole report to finish up tonight.

He walks out of the room wondering if he has made a mistake. Could Carberry possibly be smart enough to know how much trouble he would be in if they found out he was taking work home? Even medium sensitive stuff like this Garnett report?

He can feel the day's acid office sweat breaking out again along his arms. No, he thinks, no, no way. The thing is, if Carberry is stupid enough to believe that he is in any position to get anybody a job in GuardAll even emptying wastebaskets, he is too stupid to know the first thing about corporate rules.

Charlotte watches them talking at the side of the warehouse, the edge of the floodlights' reach. The trucker's sandy hair, shoulder length, shakes as he nods to what Paco says. She watches them, watches the money change hands. Then they walk back into the lights again, over to her and Billy, standing by the truck. From ten feet away the trucker's eyes look like two blue steel points. Paco laughs and pops his fingers. Fuck off greaseball, says the sandy-haired trucker in a dull raspy voice.

It will take this, this is the price of getting back home, being safe again, you will have to pass through this test, this zone, these men. Behind her she can hear Billy starting to snuffle and cry. The trucker comes around close to them, close to her, at the front of the truck. There are red blown veins in the trucker's face, at the edges of his eyes.

That kid gonna cry, it's gonna make me very irritable, he says. I'm a very irritable person anyway, you know? So tell your kid to shut up and get in, we gotta get going.

He turns on his heel, strides over to his side of the cab as she squats down. Billy? she says softly. Honey?

But though his lips are twitching and his eyes are still wet, he has already ceased to cry. He allows himself to be lifted up into the cab. Blue, all blue inside. Through the blue floor under his feet, in the rounded blue seat he crawls into he can feel the engines shaking, trembling and strong. When she is in too he curls against her side, holding himself rigid, turned away from the man behind the wheel he does not even want to see again but holding himself stiff against her, smelling her smell, thinking how she ran from the guard, brought him down to the dark dirty places, here to this man. When the truck begins to move the shaking turns into a roar louder than anything, than even his fear.

Charlotte slowly strokes the fine red hair at the back of the boy's head, stares straight ahead with a fixed smile on her face, holds it steadily yet vaguely in her mind: back, home, safe. Keep it held there yet not think any more about it than just that. The truck moves over the gravel, out of the yard, mazes through the streets and neighborhoods she dully realizes she has never seen before, crumpling buildings with windows boarded up, one block surging with ragged people, the next deserted, fewer and fewer streetlights, occasional fires by the side of the road where young men and women stand drinking, passing the bottles to each other, shouting after the truck. Surely this is not the main route, turning and turning through these streets. Does this way evade some checkpoints, is he doing this for her? When she glances over he is bent over the wheel glowering, moving his lips incessantly, forming sounds or words she cannot hear. In her head there is very little, nothing but this pleasant glow, warm hole where the words used to be. She does not really care where they are, why they are going through the city this way. She is going home, going home.

Only the trucker keeps thinking, keeps talking to himself. To get out this way they must finally pass through a few miles of rockbottom slum, potholed crumbling asphalt of abandoned access roads beside shattered bungalows and ranchstyles, children playing, adults wandering down the middle of the street, the sort of shithole you can't tell what the fuck might happen, they could blow out your tires, raid the truck beat your face in out of nowhere give them half a chance. But it's okay, the speed hits good and smooth and he has no problem taking the stretch between seventy-five and eighty, laughing his ass off watching them scatter and break for the sides of the road, poor stupid bastards anyway kill your ass in a minute if they could. Hey you, lady, he says as they break free up the old ramp tottering on its cracked concrete supports, so close to collapse they never bothered to block it off only a crazy fucker like yourself would ever have the balls to get on the interstate this crazy halfass way. Hey, he says, you want a little something keep you going, greenies on the console there just help yourself, and jacks it up to ninety now ninety-five up and away. But when he looks over grinning like a bastard she and the kid are both fucking asleep.

With all due respect, says the General in the bunkerlike conference room in the basement of the capitol building, formerly seat of the National Assembly and, before that, the viceroy's palace, we believe that the threat to internal security has been greatly exaggerated. Nevertheless, as you gentlemen know, our government takes any and all such threats to the efficient functioning of your industries as a violation of the utmost seriousness.

Out in front of the capitol dome, in the new limo supplied him for the morning the air conditioning is up so high Ernest has to wrap his cold hands in the folds of his robe. Where to? says the driver in rough English, pulling out. I don't care, he says: Just take me around, give me a tour. And is pleased to hear the way his tone now automatically can reproduce Devine's suave, fatigued contempt. Though now there is far more to think about, to take on, to be.

These are in any case isolated groups of demented, irresponsible in-dividuals, the General says. Yet they are pitted not merely against your industry or this government but against the very notions of the State and of Social Progress themselves! He thumps his hand on the table, once for *State*, three times for *Social Progress*. We must wipe such degenerate ver-min out before it spreads! the General says; and Devine, sitting against the back wall of the room like a bystander—Ramon and the other division heads are mixed in with the other generals, the old man's cronies, at the table in front of him—does not fail to notice this departure from accus-tomed rhetoric. Usually they have been agents of other corporations, na-tions, of the Communists. Now the bad guys are just nuts. The old fellow must be scared all right, must be working up to hitting them up for some-thing big.

The driver heads south, down white, palmlined boulevards. Ernest runs back over it and it all checks out again. The odd tail-end of Devine's conversation with Ramon, that posture of expectancy in the car, plus some-thing else, a certain—detachment perhaps?—in the event itself, an order and efficiency even in the chaos. That attack was a put-up job. A fake. So, perhaps, probably, was the one the other night in the greenhouse, which has so many structural similarities to the earlier trials with Helena, Oliver, Ramon, he has to figure it too was a test. And what would have happened if he had run away, had not thrown himself against Devine, hurled them back into the plants? Would they have killed him? No, surely not; more likely, you.

Ernest stops a minute with this thought; the limo is stopped at a light. They are in a central district, beneath towers of glass and steel. The pedestrians on the crosswalk before him move swiftly with their smooth olive faces, dark suits, bright robes. The thought of being killed by those men, by Devine, slips into place, disappears in the back of his mind. Yet this morning's—what was Ramon's word?—"situation" was too cut-and-dried and fast for any element of a test, a make-or-break instant in which to save Devine's life. So maybe it was that much more to charge against the regime, embarrass the General with? What for, if they're getting rid of the old bastard anyway?

With your help, the General is saying, we could have these camps in place in six months. The only expenses would be the materials themselves and the extra expenses for security. Labor will be volunteered free of charge by the community. And these installations, gentlemen, once erected, with a capacity for holding up to five hundred thousand potential enemies, will have an immediate yet lasting impact on the structure of peace and progress in our land.

Several generals at the table make slight nodding motions. Devine furrows his brow, narrows his own eyes, nods along with them. From the corner of his eye he can see Ramon watching him from the table, picking up on the move: Good boy.

He's got to do it because he likes it; gets off on it in a big way. But off on what? Being in danger, seeing people killed, the system momentarily jeopardized? Yes, all of that; but something more, something else too. What? The limo is rolling through a long green park, heavily guarded by handsome young men in bright blue uniforms with frogs on their chests, sabers at their left sides, machineguns in their right hands. Ernest stares blankly at the lawns, strollers, guards as though waiting for them to answer his questions, as though he were dealing from an old deck in front of him, waiting for the right card to come up. Why would anyone in Devine's position derive enjoyment from having death and chaos visited about him at random moments but more or less regular intervals? Because he has so much power, because everything is under control. Why create this risk of death, expose himself to it? Because there is nothing so exciting, so exotic for a man in his position, no commodity so rare and valuable as a soupçon of authentic fear. Because for lack of it he must be terribly, terminally bored.

So, the General says, to recapitulate. He turns over the diagram of the model camp, exposing the next page of the flipboard. A new, strong security program in three steps. A reinforced, invigorated counterinsurgency program with greater numbers of personnel and sophisticated American-made firepower; increased technology for a more inclusive surveillance system extending throughout the problem sectors of the city; and the camps for political re-education. The camps would be under the supervision of my old and able friend General Rodriguez; surveillance, of General Avillo; counterinsurgency, of General Vasquez.

The generals nod again with formal serious faces as their names are called. Devine nods and smiles slightly, formally at them. We will now entertain questions and comments on these proposals, says the General, showing his yellow teeth, shakily sitting down.

The beige background was agreed upon almost at the start, with little testing, as a color which, while suggesting a certain intimacy and likeness to skin, therefore humanness, nonetheless excluded the natural/organic associations still triggered all too often by greens or deeper browns. The point being that the product has to be perceived as being likely, "realistic," without being natural: this last an unfruitful association, particularly so here. So, a beige background. Then the problem became one of what angle for the field of view—purely horizontal? infinite plane?—and, inextricably, of how the product would be shown against it. As a white heap, mounded and viewed from the side? Or more roughly, a scatter of white crystals stretching back toward the top or bottom of the picture from a more concentrated area? As various pilots were made to explore these options it was even suggested that perhaps the product might be shown in its prepared form as a liquid (without syringes, of course). What could be more neutral, so the argument went, more unobjectionable, yet more real than a clear colorless drop? This point of view, however, was quickly rejected when a few tentative simulations indicated that a product viewed in this way, although indeed neutrally perceived, seems in fact too substanceless to register at all; so it was back to the powder again.

Claudell Westerbrook, senator's son, throws down his picturemag, slides out of the small bed, walks from the back of the truck into the cab.

The sunlight strikes through the windshield so harshly he turns his head aside and shuts his eyes. When he opens them again, he finds the cab empty. When he opens the truck door the heat hits like a full body blow, the sweat pops out like some loathsome disease. A few yards up the road the driver is just sitting there, hardly off the gravel at the edge of the ditch. Claudell moves toward him. This heat is really like some incredibly, impossibly awful nightmare, already the sweat is coursing all over his body, staining the mauve robe that is all he brought to wear. And this man, this truck driver with his squashed nose and short brow, staring off at nothing, grotesque ape. How in the world could you ever have let Daddy rope you into this? he thinks now for the hundredth time; then for the hundredth time remembers the tall rumpled figure in the doorway, in the flesh, flanked by two other younger white men whose lack of expression seemed stamped permanently on. How long since the last real-life visit from Daddy—six, nine months? May ah come in, mah son? said the Senator and did, the two men following after. It was mainly those two, though, who did the talking while Claudell watched his father's eyes, yellow with fear, sliding back and forth, side to side as they talked. You take the jet there, they said; get on the truck, pick up the woman and the kid, take them back to the jet and shoot her up while taking off for somewhere else where you will receive further orders for what next, they said; simple as that.

What in the world are you eating? says Claudell. The ape grins, extracts the long green stem or plant or whatever, exhibits it to him. Ooo, he says stepping back quickly: You got that out here and put it in your mouth? The apeman merely turns his head forward again. Claudell follows his gaze through the glaze of sunlight, out to the gigantic machines moving over the fields. What is that? he says. Farming, says the apeman without moving even his lips. Oh really? he says, feeling the heat drive out every thought, all aspects of himself. Mah son, said Daddy softly, finally, when the men were done: Ah owe these men much more than ah cud say. The suppuht of thyuh awgunuzashun has been instrumentuhl to me ovah thuh yeahs. Thuh withdrawl of that suppuht would be disastrus. It is yuh suppuht ah must ask, then, with awl mah huht. Fuh thuh love of uh fathuh, boy, say yes.

And what is your name? Claudell says, making his mouth push the word out against the heavy air. Larry, says the apeman, finally turning his head to squint back: And I don't like niggers. Maybe you and your dress ought to get back in the cab fore you get mussed up.

Somehow in this heat it does not sound as horrible as it would in

Washington; it is so all of a piece. He has stood there so long, sweated so
much there is nothing left of Claudell Westerbrook, only this spot in the
heat. As he turns back he can discern a gleam off to his right. That the
jet? Where are we anyway? he hears his voice say aloud. Kansas, says
Larry's voice somewhere behind him. Ralston plantation. Those there are
Ralston machines anyway. How much longer does this go on? Claudell
says. Shit I don't know, Larry says. Few hours. Half a day. All right; I'm
going back, Claudell says but does not move. When, after another endless
moment of raw heat he looks back over his shoulder, Larry too is still in
the same place and position, squatting watching the machines, a fresh stem
in his thin hard mouth. On their way out—only yesterday?—a sudden
crooked crack in the face of one of the white men as he turned to you and
Daddy back in the middle of the room, arm in arm. Hey, don't worry, he
said: We won't ask you to do anything you don't want to do.

    In the middle of the review, taking them through the personality im-
plications of the powerflows of inneroffices, projecting various layouts on
the board, T.D. turns from a schematic of pillows, chairs, and desk to find
the class watching the door, where some young guy he has never seen
before is waiting for him to stop.
    Excuse me? says the young guy softly, almost apologetically. Mr. Mer-
rill would like to see you upstairs?
    He nods briskly, as though he knew exactly what was going on. Run
the rest of these yourselves, he tells them on the way out, ignoring the
curiosity burning in their eyes. I'll look at them when I get back. And he
keeps his face firm and knowing all the way down the corridors, up the
stairs; keeps telling himself this is not it, not what you have been waiting
for, what you knew was coming all along.
    Ahh, Mr. Duberman, says Merrill with a smile from some purple throw
pillows across the room from his desk.
    Mr. Merrill, he says, feeling the muscles in his lower abdomen release
as he lowers himself to the gold stack beside Merrill's and shakes hands.
Nobody cans you from pillows surely, not even here.
    How long have you been with this company, Duberman? Merrill says.
    Twelve years now, sir, says T.D., fighting to drive the rush of resurging
panic back down from his chest.
    Long time, says Merrill. You probably remember when I first came.
    That's right, T.D. says, twitching out a smile. I was still in the field

then, of course. You called me in the next year, for a consultation on the Crocker account. I just somehow never went back out.

Yes—Merrill pats his fingertips—I knew we'd met before. Remember the, uh, name. Yes, we managed to save that relationship too, didn't we?

Went on another two years, says T.D.; and keeps his eyebrows raised, his gaze square but unthreatening, his body bent forward, demonstrating his awareness of, receptivity to, the business at hand.

But Merrill's smile is slightly askew, his eyes wavering. Whatever is coming, he doesn't quite know how to do it, how to make the pitch. T.D. lets his knees and elbows splay outward, opens up his posture to him.

Twelve years, Merrill says dreamily. That's quite an accomplishment in itself. Then licks his lips and lunges: How'd you like to get out again? We need a job done, and we feel for various reasons you're the best one to take charge of it. A sensitive and ultradiscreet job—not acquaintance work, exactly—whose successful, uh, execution will, I guarantee you, earn some lasting gratitude, not only here but higher up as well. However, Merrill says, raising his brows, it does involve some heavy s-m, you should know that right now—

T.D. leans back more, assumes almost a full-body sprawl; only his face stays appropriately taut. So? he says: I'm listening. . .

Ernest has the driver stop the car, and opens the door himself.

Sir, the driver says, perhaps it would not be wise—

No, says Ernest, it's all right, I'll be fine.

But the driver gets out anyway and stares around, his torch in open view. And for a second Ernest stiffens at the image of the driver blowing him too away, as ordered. But the man's eyes continue to sweep the crowds, the torch stays aimed their way. Besides, what sense would it make for them to kill you now? What pleasure could Devine get out of that?

He moves away from the car. The driver hustles around to catch up to him. No, he says, stay there; and is surprised at his own sudden vehemence: Goddammit, let me alone.

The fact is, he has to admit it, he is sick of it all. The guns, the craziness, the nasty lines, the fear. The idea of going through another "situation," and another, and another, the bodies shot or torched or knifed or blown up makes him tired in advance, puts the metal taste of a particular weariness in his mouth. Is this the taste that accompanies Devine's dry malice in between attacks, his efficiency detached to the point of indifference? Now he too, Ernest, will come to share that ennui with him. Is that what Devine wants the core of the relationship to be? What other choice is there, what other evidence has he seen?

He stands now in an old cathedral square: the crowds of suited businessmen, latino and white, move across and over the stream of picturesque beggars and cripples in their bright rags and hideous infirmities, scuffling toward the baroque spires babbling their prayers. Perhaps this is their job too, why not? How do you know what these cries are that burst from their lips, tangle with one another, float over the air to reach you? And even if those prayers, those sores are real, they can be paid for, easily. Perhaps they are paid and freed to go out the back door, once they get inside. Perhaps one of these beggars, or the driver, or the businessmen moving five deep up the streets, any one of them any minute now can pull something out of his suit or rags and blow you away as assigned. Nothing is quite real, but anything could kill you. That is the way it is, the way it will continue to be. For of course it is still the best acquaintance job you could ever hope to get.

There is an old fountain in front of you now. From level to level the water spills, over the old stone. You step over the unreal crawling supplicants on their way to the unreal church. You sit at the fountain's cold lip and raise your eyes above cathedrals and skyscrapers and the haze level of the smog to the bright and empty blue of the sky, and then, finally, permit yourself to think of her and the space you share with her, where everything has to be real.

Meanwhile the driver, his torch still out, advances to a position some twenty feet away, and stands in the middle of the businessmen and beggars in mortal fear of losing his job, should somehow something happen to you out here.

Charlotte wakes to dull heavy slaps thudding over the engine noise, grey panels lifting off the windshield of the truck, folding back to roof and hood. What is that? she says before knowing where she is, who she is talking to. What's going on? Are we all right?

That's lead, says Billy. Those are the lead shields. Cause we been where the air can hurt you if you let it get in.

In his voice a curious mixture of pride at his knowledge, contempt for her. Sometime during the night he must have wriggled from her lap; he is curled up on the blue console now, arms wrapped around his knees, his head almost into the trucker's lap.

The blond longhaired trucker grins down on the boy, over at her; a few hours ago, when the sun was coming up he took a smoothie along with the greenie and it has him feeling just fine.

That's right, he says. See you pretty much gotta do that any more in Nevada, Colorado, keep the rays out. We're about through it now. Old Billy here, he knows where we are, don't you Billy?

Billy nods, his small lips primly set. Almost in Kansas, he says.

Kansas! she says. Oh, that's wonderful. She stares out at the straight road before them, brown flat earth on either side, the other trucks miles ahead like giant insects moving both ways, toward them and away; and she smiles so widely in her terror and joy that her cheeks ache, it is all, everything, so much like some wonderful awful dream.

The use of physiological tests to evaluate advertising started back in the 1940s, when some adventurous marketers started experimenting with galvanic skin response, often called the "sweaty palms" test. GSR, as it's formally known, works much like the polygraph machine in lie detection.

First, subjects are linked by electrodes to a monitor. When an ad's aspects draw response, the subject's nervous system reacts, his sweat glands open, and it's all recorded on the monitor.

Lately, Erisco Inc. of Los Angeles has taken the GSR method a step further. It sells advertisers its so-called Emotional Response Index System, which is a computer databank containing the responses of 7,000 consumers to a variety of stimuli. The responses were measured by a psychogalvanometer, or GSR machine.

Erisco takes a print ad and identifies elements that draw emotional response—things like money, status, and affection. Then the computer analyzes the ad, by telling how the 7,000 consumers reacted to the selected elements. "This way we don't even have to talk to people," says Kirby G. Andrews, an Erisco vice-president.

Actually, Merrill says, it's not even all that unusual. He reaches in the folds of his robe, extracts a leather jointcase: I've often thought of it as a kind of compensatory mechanism—you know, to have one solid commitment, something authentic that is all theirs. Or perhaps simply one source of simple pleasure, a gratification that can't be faked and doesn't need to be paid back. Your friend Goodman is only exceptional in the intensity of his devotion, which goes hand in glove with his extraordinary professional instincts and skills. Joint? he says, lighting up.

No thanks, says T.D. No use letting him know you use anything at all, ever. Asshole's probably got a theory about that too. He keeps his posture open, his face interested and serious, his hand pensively rubbing his chin. I never thought about it, actually, he says. You may have a point. Though I was never much for lovers myself, not even when I was out in the field.

Right, says Merrill, giggling smoke. You see?

T.D. manages to grin briefly, crookedly back. Still, he says, what I was talking about earlier were the personal factors for me.

Ah *yes*, says Merrill ecstatically, wide-eyed, already so stoned T.D. realizes it must be quality import stuff, almost wishes he had taken some anyway, fuck the risk. Of *course*, says Merrill. So what do you want?

A contract, says T.D. A long-term one. No more year by year.

That's the way we work, says Merrill, raising a hand in the air. You know that. We can't risk getting stuck with someone who has suddenly lost his competence. And it happens, you know it does. You've been around here long enough to see it happen even to quite good ones, I should think.

You've kept me on here long enough to know I have long-term effectiveness, says T.D. holding his tone even, holding the sweat behind his brow. You want me to do this special, I want a five-year contract with my duties guaranteed. Otherwise you can let me go. But you won't find anyone else as close to Goodman to do the job.

Merrill looks at him with narrowed, sullen, stoned eyes; then down at the joint in his hand, which he drops and crushes on the floor. All right, he says. I'll have it drawn up so you can sign it before you leave.

When am I leaving? says T.D.

This afternoon, says Merrill. You should be in Palm Springs this evening at the latest.

Palm Springs, says T.D., standing, feeling giddy as the blood starts to move in his body again. And my classes?

Merrill, still seated, stares blankly across the room. I think we'll be able to cover your classes, he says, after a long pause.

For the minicams and holobeams, on the steps of the capitol, Devine shakes the dry yellow hand once more: You have my personal assurance that OMNICO will give your proposals very careful and thorough consideration in the days and weeks ahead.

And the rest, grins Ramon when he joins him, is silence, as the man says.

They are still near others, at the base of the line of black limos flanked by a squad of guards. Oh yeah? says Devine. And who's the man?

Shakespeare, says Ramon, holding the door open, eyebrows raised in self-mockery. Read him every night.

You're all alike, you foreign managers, Devine says cheerfully as the limo takes off: What you all really want is to be some goddamn professor in the States. But all the while he is pointing at the driver, around the car, staring questioningly at Ramon.

Who, leaning back, removes from his suitcoat a thin green cigar. It's clean, he says. At this point, the scanner on the General's survboard shows us heading west, while whoever's listening gets to hear a conversation on the merits and demerits of the new security plan. And the men the General thinks he has following us know what to say too.

Well done, says Devine. So where are we going for real?

Pantucho's headquartered in the back of an old hotel, says Ramon, relic of turista days. Close enough to the barrios so nobody notices the uniforms going in and out, far enough out so no one watches it too close.

He has a communications setup in there? says Devine.

Ramon nods.

GM, IBM, Gulf-Western, they aren't going to want to make their move through us, says Devine. They'll be jangling the phones off the hooks for fresh deals with him. Is our peasant friend quite clear on the fact that OMNICO has been the prime initiator here?

So far he has been, says Ramon.

I want you to stay on him, says Devine, up to and after the time it blows. Give him as much firepower as he needs but keep the quality a good notch under our best. Make sure he knows if he tries to screw us we'll break his ass. All right?

Ramon taps the first of his ash into the tray in front of him. All right, he says. Fine. Yes, just as you say.

It takes fifteen minutes to negotiate the choking traffic of the central district, past the office buildings, department stores, cathedral square to the outer edge, the old city with its faded stucco apartments, progressively decaying grandeur, streets lined with sickly, wilted palms. The Embarcadero Hotel is on the end of a block of boarded pink stone homes, a creamcolored albatross from perhaps as far back as the 1940s, all heavy scarred darkwood in the lobby, native carpets worn down so far their patterns are all but invisible, glittering haze of dustmotes trapped in sunlight falling through long transverse windows that once must have had drapes.

They stride past the front desk and its weasely acned clerk without speaking, take an elevator soaked in the pungent sweetness of insecticide up to a dark hall sick with its own stale heat, the urinous impacted stench of sweat and dirt, of those about to slip away, down into the barrios or below, to a door on which Ramon raps sharply first three times, then four more.

The door opens; they are frisked by a tall hawknosed man in a flowered shirt and khaki pants, and waved on in. The suite has been cleared of all furniture but a few stuffed chairs, these occupied by four young men also in civilian pants and shirts, but with unmistakable shortcropped military haircuts. Their brown faces do not move from the scanners they are watching, the tape their dresser-size computer feeds out. Devine sees no weapons anywhere; notes the soundproof ceiling insulation they must have installed, the presence of a hidden noiseless filtration system issuing clean scentless air, as a short cleanshaven man with wide lips and the barrelchest of a mountain Indian comes foward with his thick hand held out.

Captain Manuel Garcia Pantucho, he says. It is a great honor to meet you, sir.

My pleasure, says Devine. The young man's eyes are small, with tiny pupils. Already he can see those eyes as they will be in five years' time. The General lost weight, shriveled as his power grew; this one will bloat, those wily eyes will be encased in folds of fat.

You want to take over this country, Captain, Devine says smiling thin-lipped, you're going to need a larger system than that. Unless your computer's bigger than their computer, you don't win these things any more. Ramon here can put you in touch with some people who'll set you up with a terminal into our system downtown, all right?

Here, I'll show you how now, says the trucker, and places the boy's small hand on the trigger: Now see, like you got some crazy asswipes with guns jumping up out of the ditch to mess you up and take your rig or something, or like if some rig rolls up and starts giving you shit, fucking with you and trying to push you off the road and shit cause the other driver's all messed up, you know, you just aim this motherfucker over at them like this—he wraps his rough red hand over the boy's, directs the trigger handle so the machinegun mounted on the cab points left—and let it go. Here now, go ahead, squeeze.

The end of the gun spouts red, he can see them stinging curving through the air, as the trigger throbs against his hand like something living. Why do the bullets go in curves? He would like to ask the man next to him with the hot sour smell on him, rough gold hair all over like no one else he has ever seen, he would like to see where the bullets hit, what they look like then, but they go by too fast and the man is still shaking his hair and howling, pressing the button to make his voice so it sounds outside the truck, over the noise of air, engine, bullets spitting out, and he does not want this moment to stop, not ever to take away his hand.

Then his mother opens her eyes and looks around. What is it? she says. Is everything all right?

And the man stops his yell and takes Billy's hand away from the trigger-grip. The bullets stop and the gun is just sitting there again, out on the hood.

Everything's fine lady, says the trucker, his face tightening. We were just fooling around a little, is all.

Oh, says Charlotte, already shutting her eyes again as her fingers reach out for, vaguely touch Billy's shoulder and back.

Billy turns and glares at her, but she is already back out. The man beside is not smiling or looking at him any more, he is looking bad the way he first did and looking straight ahead; once again she has spoiled it, messed it all up. He moves away from her limp hand, leans down on the console against the man's hip, against the good smell. In a little while he is nodding in and out. After a while the driver puts his arm around him, takes another greenie, begins mumbling again to himself.

Later, when the boy wakes, there are giant moving things in the fields, big and tall and long as a big building, a mall, but all shiny yellow, moving toward the road and away. But when he asks the man what they are, the man says Can't he see what, use his own fucking eyes, what's the matter ain't you ever seen a fucking farm before? He tries not to cry, tries to do like the golden man says, looking behind the big things where it is shorter and dark green cut down. Where do they put what they cut down, in the big long yellow bellies they have? Are there people inside them like him and the golden man? But they go by so fast he cannot tell anything, cannot keep the tears back any more.

Shit, says the gold man, the truck driver, full of guilty speeding rage, what the fuck's the matter with you now? as the boy cries, Charlotte sleeps on, the agribusiness machines, Ralston Purina, General Foods, ITT, etc., etc., keep moving over the green fields.

Fifteen minutes later, the amenities over, they are back in the limo heading downtown. Ramon is smoking another cigar, staring in apparent placidity out the window. So, he says, what'd you think of him?

Devine's long lean head is back against the seat; his eyes are shut. I don't know, he sighs. The way I learned when I was here, you never give a damn thing to a breed, they make you pay out the ass then fuck you just for fun. But to tell you the truth, I don't know the situation any more. When I was here it was just a few of us—Sears, GM, IBM, ITT, Ford, and OMNICO. Now everybody's in on it, even the Japs, I can hardly recognize our building any more in all the other ones. And then you got all these fucking peasants to keep penned up. Hell, I don't know. You think he's the best, fine, we got him. I just hope you're right, he's really ours.

A long silence. Devine remains in the same position, his eyes still closed. The burning in Ramon's stomach increases, sends a flash of sour bitterness up to his mouth. He turns the cigar in his fingers a moment, watching the burnline move down the leaves, then stubs it out. And how's your friend there, Ernest working out? he says.

Pretty well, says the mouth, barely moving. He's a hell of a lot sharper than the last one they sent anyway. Then, slowly, under Ramon's eyes the thin mouth forms a grin: Were you picking up on the way he was reacting last night? It was very good, very interesting. He's a hell of a lot of fun to watch.

And his grey eyes open on Ramon as if they had been on him the whole time. You going to get us to the airport now with no more surprises?

Come on, says Ramon grinning back. You knew I wasn't going to let you get away without a little something.

Well, says Devine, opening the bar in the back of the driver's seat, if there's nothing else coming up I think I'll just relax a bit. How about you?

No thanks, Ramon says, screwing up his mouth in feigned displeasure. Some of us still have work to do today.

Devine laughs, snuffs a line of fresh white powder up his nose, and pours himself a dollop of Courvoisier.

By now, 2:30, Merrill has had his assistant Blanchard signal Davidson's consent, bring lunch, then get the contract worked out: What the hell? he figures, that's enough for me. So what he elects to do is get just a little more stoned, few tokes off a fresh one from the case, can't work anyway, and sit back just for fun and dig on where the whole, this whole project began.

He has to fumble around the damn desk a while to find the tape—they only got tape that night, no holo, something about not enough advance word—and so while rummaging he tries to picture what the place must have been like. Lots of people crowded around with drinks and joints, of course, very dressy, freeform dancing to the music you hear in the background, yes, and all in what must have been given Westerbrook's high nasal voice and stupid accents a pretty fey space. Maybe frilled walls in salmon pink, sort of round and cornerless, something like that. All these people crowded around, very chi-chi. Goodman in something modest and tasteful, a beige robe say, no jewelry; Claudell in an orange and blue print, encrusted with beastery and stones. And there they are, dancing in the frilled room. Okay.

Merrill punches the tape on, leans back in his plush semicircular desk-chair, lets his eyes fall shut. The first voice is Ernest's:

Awfully quiet tonight.

Mmmm—really? Claudell's tone soft and blurry here; in Merrill's mind the image is of him raising his head from Ernest's shoulders, slowly opening his eyes.

Very quiet indeed. Sure you're all right?

Oh yes, says Claudell hurriedly: quite sure. But the next noise on the tape is a distinct sigh. A genuine sigh, as Merrill imagines it, involuntarily produced as the arms wrap again around Ernest's waist, the head seeks to settle back down, the fluttering eyes to close. He has gone over the tape so often by now, played it back so many times that now thanks also to his own stoned condition when he closes his own eyes Merrill feels himself practically there in that poor poor black man's skin feeling what he must have felt: that gliding contentment blending with that gnawing sense of lack. That need to truly have him, have him all.

Tell me, says Ernest softly, firmly.

Claudell's voice high, almost whining: Oh Ernest. It's just so—nebulous, somehow.

All right then, let's try articulating it together. It'll help.

The pause that follows is on the tape the opposite of a silence; finding no speech forthcoming from either of the principals for the next minute fifteen, minute twenty, the boys at Acoustic have left the stretch unedited, so the whole undifferentiated blast of music laughter talk comes roaring through, the raw sound of party in the midst of which stoned Merrill has to work, frowning, to stay tuned to the pulse of the moment, the two of them still dancing, the dreamy troubled pout, no doubt, on Claudell's face.

It's just, says Claudell at last—oh it's so hard to explain. And I certainly *don't* mean to suggest I'm not satisfied or that anything's wrong. In fact what I feel comes precisely *from* this sense of having everything I want, you and everything else. Oh Ernest, can you possibly understand what I mean?

I understand, says Ernest Goodman, gentle and soothing, that you want something more or different in our relationship yet for some reason hesitate to tell me what that something is. And I feel very bad about that, because I don't know what signals I can have been putting out that have made you feel as though you can't or shouldn't tell me what you want. I guess it makes me feel as though I've failed to be the kind of friend to you I want to be.

No Ernest, Claudell rushes in quickly, urgently, you must never think that, no no no—

All right, then, says Ernest Goodman. Then you must tell me what you want.

The following pause is short enough Acoustics must have decided to clean straight through; but a good thirty seconds even so. Merrill, still in his chair listening, eyes still shut, takes a deep breath himself, cups his chin thoughtfully in his hand. Here it comes; here amid the smoke and the salmoncolored frills, the festooned guests, speckled patterns of party sounds and lights—

I found out, Claudell says—please don't be mad—I found out you have a lover. Completely by accident I found it out, only because it turns out her family used to also be in politics and so knew families that know ours so when I mentioned your name as my own friend to this other family that's what I heard. A false nervous chuckle: Anyway, you know what it's like to try to keep a secret in this town.

A small and voluble world, Washington, murmurs Ernest, still affably. Please go on, dear.

You know I've asked her here tonight? says Claudell. You know she's here? And somehow he is simultaneously gulping hard and going on: And I thought—

And you thought, repeats Ernest's toneless voice.

I thought, says Claudell rushing headlong in excitement, barely audible even in the Acoustics-rendered hush, I thought—well you know I don't go with women ordinarily. But if the three of us got together afterwards?

Yes?

And you and I on her? whispers Claudell. Especially if we, if you and I could get perhaps a little rough—

And there, where the tape ends, just before the blow, Merrill realizes both that his own heart is racing and that someone has been knocking on the door. Come in! he shouts and reluctantly opens his eyes to see Blanchard, of course, standing tall and straight as a reproach: Mr. Duberman, says Blanchard, has signed his contract and is off.

Fine, says Merrill, suddenly tired. Perhaps it is just that his end of this whole project is at last complete; perhaps, finally, he is starting to come down. But the white noise of the blank tape still running through the machine fills his head, feels like a wind he speaks against with some difficulty: I think, Blanchard, he says, that will be all for today.

He watches them come through the glass doors, past the security cordon, across the polished floor in which the OMNICO insignia is inset. Ramon's mouth, he notices, is somewhat pinched, his gaze abstracted, as though already focused on some other work ahead. But Devine's eyes are shiny, his walk less precise, clearly he has taken something to loosen up, let down. Does that mean no situation on the way to the airport? Yes, probably so. Might Devine not be just a little tense or shaken at the General's impending fall, might there not be some slight identification there?

But Ernest wonders these things only idly. He knows what the core of the relationship is. He has the right expression on his face.

So, you ready to go? says Devine, sending a whiff of brandy to him.

Anytime, says Ernest.

You have a good time this morning? Devine asks.

Great time, says Ernest. And you?

Oh fine, just fine, says Devine.

Good, says Ernest with another slight smile which he turns to Ramon: A pleasure to meet you. I trust we'll be seeing each other again.

I hope so, says Ramon, flashing teeth, yes, I'm sure we will.

So long Ramon, says Devine and shakes hands; then Ernest and Ramon shake hands; then Ernest and Devine walk out past security, through the glass doors to the car and get in. And the whole time Ernest has looked and sounded the same. There has been no irony in anything he says or does, no more than there ever was, finally, in Devine's behavior; that was a misreading he has corrected now.

You settled down from this morning's little incident? says Devine when they are back on the freeway, heading out.

Ernest glances back at him: the same complete weary knowledge, the same cold bored death. Oh sure, he says.

Once we're up and out of here, Devine says, his eyes still shining, I think I'll have some material to show you that you might be interested in. Ever seen live holos before?

No, Ernest says. I look forward to it. That'll be great.

Something swipes against his shoulder: Larry's paw. Claudell's first impulse is to scream at him, Don't you dare touch my robe you animal; but then his eyes open and freeze on Larry's twisting mouth, the twitches spasming his cheeks and large guns strapped on his chest.

That was them, shouts Larry, ramming the truck in gear, pulling off the berm, flooring it. Son of a bitch just went by doing a hundred easy. Wonder I could even catch the number on the goddamn thing.

Claudell casts around for something to say, if only to appear to have some knowledge and to disguise being scared out of his wits. Oh well, he says at last in a voice somewhat higher than he would have liked: Surely you know how to drive these things as well as he does. I'm sure we'll catch right up.

Let you in on a little secret, nig, Larry shouts over the engine's full roar, I ain't no fucking trucker. I'm just your basic garden variety goon on assignment. Which is why I'm gonna have some trouble catching the asshole; which is why if you don't want me to take your cute little dress there and stuff it up your ass I'd appreciate it if you would from now on just keep your fucking mouth shut.

In the following perhaps twenty minutes of pursuit, as the truck reaches 95, 100, 105 and begins to pass the other rigs, as he smooths the wrinkles this escapade has already wreaked on his robe, Claudell finds himself trying to cope with his abject fear in the only way he can think how, trying to imagine it as pleasure instead. No one, after all, has ever spoken to him before so cruelly and aggressively, with so little pause for breath. Now why can't Daddy buy someone like Larry to have around? No real imagination, that's why, thinks Claudell; although as soon as he himself even begins to imagine them together under any circumstances, what if Larry and you, his mind first shrieks then grows quite numb, and he falls instead to looking down his own front at his lap and legs and knees, idly fingering the eyepin on his chest.

There they are, Larry finally yells. Ahead. You can see the woman in the mirrors.

Claudell looks up snd squints and at that moment realizes truly, viscerally, that they are moving incredibly right up against the back of the truck before them, and Larry has pressed something to carry his voice outside the cab: PULL OFF THE ROAD, MORON, he shouts.

The woman screams from the truck in front of them, followed by an answering voice: GET OFF MY ASS, FUCKFACE, AND MAYBE I WILL.

Larry edges their rig closer, frowning at the back doors of the truck before them as if trying to read something, some secret message there. Larry's mouth is working, saying something Claudell cannot hear. He leans his head over, tries to raise his own voice without shouting: What?

You drive like a fucking pussy? says Larry.

Claudell nods, excited. In fact, the statement does not make much sense to him, but he is delighted to have been consulted nonetheless.

Larry pushes the speaker button again: YOU DRIVE LIKE A FUCK-ING PUSSY!

OH YEAH?

Claudell sneaks a peek at the speedometer. It looks as though they are traveling at a rate of 115.

YEAH MOTHERFUCKER, Larry shouts. YOU MOTHERFUCK-ING SLIT-TAIL PUSSY! YOU THINK I'M LYING, JUST PULL YOUR SHITHEAP OFF THE HIGHWAY AND I'LL SHOW YOU WHAT YOU ARE!

OKAY, OKAY, ALL RIGHT SCUMFUCK, YOU'RE ON!

Then Larry is braking hard enough to jerk him up and forward off his seat, swerving the truck off toward the lefthand side, still yelling but with the loudspeaker off: Okay, as soon as we get these motherfuckers stopped I'm gonna be out of here moving for this dork driver up there, to put him out of commission. So you don't worry about him. You just get your ass out of the cab and get over and start doing whatever your thing is with the other two, all right?

Fine, shouts Claudell. He is so excited, his heart is beating so hard and fast it is as though he can see it throbbing through the robe, as the truck ahead of them is jolting off the shoulder, brakelights flashing, brakes screaming, screaming, other trucks whip past them, honking, yelling things he cannot hear, Larry still mumbling with his mouth stretched upwards like your own now as both trucks more or less simultaneously screech to a halt: everything happening slowly, magically, as in a terrifying dream.

Preliminary GSR's indicated subjects demonstrated a marked preference for the heap over the rough scatter, and a somewhat less emphatic one for a semi-infinite angle: the beige plane on which the crystals rest shot at an angle of app. 60°, thus extending the plane to a "horizon" two-thirds of the way up the screen. When analyzed, these results suggested a further possible enhancement, when it was suggested that a white heap viewed against a semi-infinite domain connotes not merely *purity* but also *challenge,* and a quality of dramatic risk of great potential correlatability with that of taking heroin in the consuming mind. It was, therefore, proposed that this dramatic fact could be strengthened, the slight preference increased and capitalized on by a limited amount of camera movement—limited to minimize adverse reaction to "manipulation," "phoniness," "inauthenticity"—tracking a scatter of crystals across the raked beige becoming more and more consolidated, a white chain as it were suggesting both a rising range of hills or a benignly white yet equally thrilling counterpart to the ancient image (cf. Disney's *Davy Crockett*) of a trail of gunpowder leading to a bomb: in any case, an imagistically *narrative* sense of boldness, climax, risk. GSR to this prototype turned out to be extremely gratifying; at which point it was agreed that all that was left were the words.

I don't know, says the man Paco calls Control. I don't know what the hell we're gonna do with you, man. We give you something simple shit like this and you fuck up.

She deent make me, Paco says. I know, I could tell she deent know who I am.

So, okay, says Control, so that's your dumb luck. I mean, if she'd made you, man, you wouldn't be talking to me right now, you understand? See Ramos—and his phonevoice softens—you just don't understand what's going on here. Like I don't even give you a *fake* name for me, right? You never noticed that?

Yeah, sure, says Paco, I noteece but—

But shit, says Control. Now I got a tape here off your buttonmike I got to report on to somebody else where you give your real name to a subject whose squeeze knows who the hell you are. What do you think the people I report to gonna think about that? How you think that's gonna make me look, huh? Listen. I don't know if I can use you any more. I mean it, man.

Hey, Paco says, you listen, man. His hands are prickling, hot tears have sprung to his eyes, he is aware of these things in the same way he knows he has dropped the stupid accent they like too, but what the shit.

I'm sorry for what I did. But you guys come in my house and you kill my wife; you kill my kids; you don't tell me you gonna do that either, man, you just say you're sorry after and you give me some more work.

All right, all right, come on, says Control. I understand, I feel for you, man. But I got my own ass to think of, too, I got my own guy listening to this tape if he wants to; and I'm telling you I can't carry you any longer man, you're through.

When the phoneline goes dead Paco can hear again the voices of the others in the bar he is in, talking and laughing, and behind them the music of a song. But still they sound a long way away, far on the other side of the silence in him. He walks away from the phone, back among them, and orders a beer and sits down at the table with it, but nothing comes any closer. That nice crazy lady, he thinks, and she probably dies too.

Over on Green Street, Garnett has turned off the screen, finished packing his stuff, the clothes and personal articles, probes and wires, in his cracked leather tote. He opens and closes the door of the apartment and walks down the stairway noiselessly, by habit, knowing no one is there to hear him any more. Then, obeying a sudden impulse—an old pro, he can feel when he is being watched, knows now he isn't—he reaches quickly for the old set of blades and thin l-wrenches inside the bag from way back in the Reagan days.

The lock is ancient, kid stuff; in a second he is inside, moving around in the dark. He goes straight back to the kitchen and works his way forward, not particularly straining his eyes to make anything out, bothering to note anything. As he steps quickly, lightly for a man of his age and size, through the screenroom the wall bursts to image, box of Wheat Thins on an infinite white plane, fades out. He pauses once to stare at the bed where first the two of them slept, then the woman alone; in the front room, at first, he cannot find the kid's bed. Was it just on the couch? No, there is one of those Jap foldout things, over in the corner. These are the spaces the voices inhabited, the presences his instruments measured and judged.

He checks the street from the front window, lets himself back out. Damn, Garnett, he thinks, smiling on the wooden porch steps, but you're getting sentimental in your old age. Then he walks to the corner to wait for a trans to take him home to his wife.

Devine, grinning, passes the joint to Ernest, beside him on the couch. I'll take you around once we get there, he says. Biggest production facility in Southeast Asia, it's going to be.

Ernest inhales, exhales. Is that right? he says. That will be very inter-esting then, won't it.

Devine's grin broadens. He reaches for the brandy, on the table beside the silver tray of cocaine lines and more joints. William? he calls.

Sa? comes the voice aft in the jet.

We have transmission on those holos yet?

The golden man's face is deep red, almost purple. Stay in here, he says. I'm gonna beat this dipshit's ass for him and be right back.

I want to come with you, Billy says.

No, says the trucker in the same motion with which he hurls himself, blond hair streaming, out the door.

No Billy, she says, grabbing the boy by the back of the collar as he slides down the seat after him. No, you stay here now and be quiet.

And there is something in her tone of voice so drifting, so devoid of any interest or urgency, that Billy obeys it for that reason alone, as if convinced that what is about to happen does not really matter after all. And it is true that none of this has mattered or made any sense to her. She sits quietly as she has sat through the taunts and truck duel, the crazy anger of the trucker screaming, smashing his hands against the wheel. Now the sound of gunbursts hardly registers; it is all just more of the strange things men always seem to have to do. Like Ernest's going away on the job instead of staying with her, like that sweet boy Randall going to the Regroove then away, Daddy always flying around on his business all over the state instead of loving her, staying next to her, staying home. You sit quietly and let them do whatever it is they think they have to so you can get home, where they love you; sit and let your eyes track the paths of the huge incomprehensive machines through the fields. So when the face of the black man appears at the window she is likewise neither surprised nor alarmed.

Hello there! he says with a British accent, tossing his head. Remember me?

She returns a smile, makes a polite effort to recall but nothing comes. And the door is open, he is standing still smiling on the side of the cab. He has a somewhat soiled robe on, one of those eye things on a chain around his neck. We met one night in Washington not too long ago? he says. I used to be a friend of Ernest's?

Oh, she says, Ernest. He's away on business now.

I understand that, says the black man after another semi has blasted past, whipping the hem of his robe. Actually I came for you.

Oh really? says Charlotte, gazing on his dark face. But how does this man come from home yet know Ernest? When did they meet in Washington? Why is the air spilling in on her so hot?

We're going to my parents' home in Tuscaloosa, she offers, my home too, actually. Did you already know that too?

Yes, of course, says Claudell. That's precisely what I'm here to help you do. Do you hear the little jet we have overhead? It will come down in a minute, we'll get on it and just whisk you right down there, okay?

Oh fine, she breathes, wonderful! Come on then, Billy honey.

Claudell offers his hand down from the cab and keeps her arm in his as they walk around the side of the truck in the steaming air. On the other side of the truck, at the edge of the ditch, the blond trucker's body spasms as though still in rage. Billy wants to stop and look at it, she has to pull him along as they cross the ditch and enter the freshmowed field where the sleek silver plane awaits.

This will be so nice, she says, leaning against his arm. You're really so sweet to do this. You people have always been so wonderful to my family and me.

Billy too is excited about getting on the plane and flying away, even if it does mean he doesn't get to look at the first dead guy he has ever seen offscreen. But he wonders: Does that mean the trucker was a bad guy now that he is dead? Even though he let you shoot? Because he wouldn't answer the questions you asked?

He tugs at his mother's hand, looks up at her. But she will not answer either, will not even look down at him, she doesn't know anything. But he asks anyway, in case maybe the black guy will talk. Can black guys be good guys? he wonders but keeps to the question, the last one he had for the bad dead guy: Mommy, what's a pussy? he says as they step on the steel ladder up into the plane.

Ernest Goodman keeps his lower back rounded and relaxed, his shoulders slumped, and does not fail to pluck the joint from Devine's hand when it is passed. He watches the three of them, Charlotte, Billy, and Claudell, step into the jet; watches the jet take off from the green fields into the  sky. His sharpest awareness throughout is of the efficiency with which the instincts take over, unaided by will. Almost as though there were two holos, this one plus another of some man walking through a large house, closing and bolting every window, locking every door: that abstract, that real. The holo fades; the house, dark and shut. He slants his head toward Devine and makes a single nod of acknowledgment, with eyebrows raised.

Another line? Devine says, lifting the tray of coke.

Oh, I guess so, he says.

Devine continues to hold the tray between them, as Ernest places the delicately embellished wooden straw in his left nostril, bends over the white lines and begins to snuff, sensing a rush of blood out of his face and hands, a crackling of nerve endings everywhere which he must suppress.

Ah, he says, leaning his head back again, closing his eyes yet still aware of the fixity of Devine's smile, of the shining eyes on his: Ah yes. Though in fact the dope does not seem to be touching him at all.

They say it's live, says Devine, but I think they must do some editing and retouching, don't you?

Yes, he says. I'm sure.

His eyes are open now. He watches Devine rub his nose with forefinger and thumb, watches Devine's long hand rub itself along his mouth.

I don't know how the hell they do it, says Devine. Never had all that much to do with GuardAll, all that survtech stuff, tell you the truth. Just have to keep my finger on things, the whole thing. See it all together. Move around. Keep in touch.

In another moment, with its mouth still open, Devine's head slides the last few inches to land against Ernest's upper arm; and from the back of the cabin the white-coated William appears: Everything satisfactory, sah?

Fine, Ernest mouths, nodding. Everything is fine. After this test, after she is dead you will have this job locked in.

When William vanishes, Ernest turns his head, looks down at Devine's wavey greystreaked hair with its scent of scalp beneath the shampoo rich as chocolate or warm earth. Not unlike what your face buried in Charlotte's hair could have discerned. This for that. Simple exchange. He turns his face forward again, gazes across the cabin, past table and chairs, briefcase and drugs and Devine's humming handdigital terminal, beyond the space the holo filled with Charlotte and Billy crossing the field, out the cabin window to the same bright blank blue that took his gaze at the fountain before the cathedral earlier, already so long ago today; and keeps a close watch on, tight control over rate of breathing, heartbeat, the trickles of energy leaking through his system, threatening to gush. For Devine's head is resting on his shoulder, Devine's body is against his; and even in sleep, he might be able to sense any change, any quickening or breaking open, were Ernest to allow it to occur.

For four hundred years virtually without interruption, the 7,100 islands called the Philippines have been the property of some foreign power: first the Spanish, then the United States, now the multinationals themselves. At the time I was there, fall of 1974, near the end of the Viet Nam War, I stayed in Olongapo, a town of about 100,000 attached to a U.S. naval base where a Spanish fort had previously stood. To get to town from base, you crossed over the Po River bridge—the Shit River, the sailors called it, for carrying all the sewage from the town. On the bridge, at one of its dark stands, you could buy some grilled monkey meat for a joke. Or you could throw some pesos over the side and watch the ragged barebreasted women leap off the boats they live on, go into the shit for the coin they come up with, grinning, holding it in their mouths. And on the other side of the bridge are the hookers in the bars.

The men I was with motioned me into a stairway on the first block of dingy buildings and bright crazy lights. At the top of the stairs we went through a door on our left into a dark vault of a room under black light, with a dance floor and rock band at one end, a bar at the other. One of the sailors asked the Mama-san who greeted us and took our orders for the hooker he had last time through; the rest of us had our own before our beers arrived.

Mine said her name was Mary Jane. Her hands and fingers played in my lap. You stay how long? she said. You stay with me tonight? You buy me drink? You like dance?

I bought her a drink and danced with her, mechanically; what I really wanted was to talk. How long have you been here? I asked on the dance floor, and then back at the table again. Where did you come from? Is Mary Jane your real name? When do you come to work? What do you do when you're not working?

At first she slapped and tickled me, laughing, telling me what a silly man I was. Then, when I kept it up, she took her hands out of my crotch and stopped looking back at me. She told me she was from Manila. She had been in town since August 1. Her name really was Mary Jane. She would not tell me what she did when she was not at work.

By this time, too, she had stopped smiling. I no tell, she said. I no wanna tell about my true life. You don't ask me about these things. She had to have her own zone, a space where no conqueror could go.

Palm Springs: the name calls up for T.D. a vague skein of associations from perhaps his tv-watching childhood in the '70s and '80s, long ago, of glamour, beauty, wealth. But the town through which he limos now is dead. Sand lies in serpentine circles, obscuring the road along which he and the suited, silent driver are the only travelers. On either side sit cubes and rectangles of concrete, plastic, and steel, ex-franchises, motels with toppled signs, their former gaudy oranges and greens bleached to pastels; and the palms overhead, stretching off, look lacerated and whipped. T.D. wonders, idly, to pass the time, what happened here, what the place is a casualty of. Winddrift from a hot wastespill in Nevada, decline of the passenger car, a simple, inexplicable change in fashion? Whatever—this landscape is certainly a *drag*. He peers upward through the limo's closed window, trying to catch sight instead of the jet that brought him, flashing through the pure sky.

The Palm Springs Regroove is from the outside front a dark stone block with slim tall apertures for windows, like one of those old IBM cards with keypunched holes. In the dim lobby, he blinks and wavers, blinded by the swift transition from the blaze outside; then makes out a sort of giant epergne of padded surfaces to his right, on his left a large languid circular whirlpool, nude bodies of men and women draped over the blond seats, cushions, and couches everywhere, the only figures in motion a few people, obviously attendants, with bald depilled skulls and long aqua robes, proffering something from silver trays; and hears, in the same instant, the sound of his name being spoken, quite close by.

Mr. Duberman? Ky Blencher, Mr. Duberman. A short man with a pug nose and small close eyes. His voice has an unexpectedly dry, sneaking irony around the edges. The memory of someone else, from tv, an old newscaster—Cronkite, Brinkley?— slides across T.D.'s mind as he shakes hands.

Our guest has not yet arrived, says Blencher as one hand waves near a pocket of his robe. Would you like a joint? a down? Or an up if you like, though those are back in the office, we don't stock them out here.

I think I'll pass, he says, looking again at the slow lolling of the bodies on either side, hearing, over his words, the faint presence of a muzak whose every note and gesture are resolved: I'd just like to go to my room.

It is the second time that day that he has turned down dope, he realizes, as Blencher leads him behind the lounging tower down a corridor lined with ferns and vines nurtured by inset sunlamps, at one point stepping over a thin woman with broad cheekbones, shriveled breasts, eyes floating up to her forehead as she rocks along the floor, murmuring Oh wow man, over and over: *Oh wow.*

The room itself is almost starkly simple, in sepia and russet tints. There is a rippling mattressed floor with scoops for sitting, a sink and waste dispenser recessed in one wall, the other three of which, explains Blencher, are screens customarily kept on all the time with programming preselected to smooth out the individual's hostilities, anxieties, what have you, Blencher says. In your case, of course, we have programmed nothing special. If you want normal network fare you can get it simply by hitting this switch we have attached here beside the sink. We weren't able to do anything about the omtrack, though, of course.

Omtrack? says T.D. looking around.

But Blencher, smiling openly, is already back at the door. One more thing, Mr. Duberman, he says, cocking his blond head back. It is very important for our clients to perceive all others not actually serving them as helpless and well-cared-for and equal as they are themselves, among themselves. So should you go outside your room from now on, would you please remember to be naked?

T.D. grimaces but nods;. Blencher flutters his fingers and leaves. T.D. removes his robe, throws it in a corner, lies down on the stippled floor. The plan is to be the pro you always were, don't get stuck in how much this place creeps you out. Empty out your experience, your history, your fears completely, prepare for the action that lies ahead. Only thus, with his mind blank and ready, his body relaxed and alert, does he notice the deep bass vibrating the floor, the entire room; and realize, distantly, this must be the omtrack of which Blencher spoke.

Claudell's faint flush of triumph at getting this far pales at the sight of the two ancient tubular chairs connected and separated by a metal snaptop ashtray, the cracking brown couch and dun carpeting. With the three of them in it, the cabin of this jet will be even skimpier and more cramped than on the flight out from Washington. What must she think of such seediness, such a slap in the face?

Nothing, apparently; no more than she seemed to notice your filthy robe. Now, in the same fog she seems to have been in so far, she strolls over to one of the chairs, sits down, and folds her hands in her lap like a good child at table, waiting to be served. *You people have always been so wonderful to me.* Yes, Claudell thinks, it will be only too wonderful, my dear.

Might be bumpy, he says off-the-wall. Better have a shot of this.

He bends over, scrabbles in his bag, almost loses his balance as the jet begins to rise. When he comes up with the syringe a smile trembles on her lips, her eyes are misty. Is this going to be all right? she says. For even now she is still yielding to a man, giving herself up to him; even he, Claudell, is unable to resist. As he rolls up her sleeve and slips the needle in, nervously, wondering how the bloody hell he is expected to know if he is hitting the vein or not, he hears his voice answer with a simple quiet directness it has rarely, if ever, possessed.

Yes Charlotte, he says. Yes dear. It is going to be all right.

Then Charlotte's mouth moves, soundlessly, and her head flops back against the chair. Claudell, panicked, looks up in time to see her pupils dilate and for a horrible instant imagines he must have hit some huge vein by accident, spiked her so hard the black pupils will somehow spread all over the eyes; watching her for that horrible moment he stops breathing himself.

Then the jet is up and leveled off; and Billy turns back from the cabin window he has been peering out, and steps in front of his mother on whose sightless face a smile has begun to grow, and looks from her to Claudell. What's wrong with Mommy? he says quietly, carefully.

Your mother? Claudell says, wiping the cold sweat from his brow. Oh she's just resting, that's all. He stands, hesitates, feeling the boy's opaque gaze, now what in the world are you supposed to do with him? Is the woman going to die or what? What happens to you and Daddy if she does?

Aaaaah, groans Charlotte's face with a full loose smile on it now. Everything is all right. At last some man has taken her home.

See? Claudell says, smiling so hard his face aches, see your mother's all right now. Clumsily he reaches out, pats the boy's hair. The boy neither stops looking back at him nor smiles. You still want to know what a pussy is? says Claudell.

Slowly, gravely, Billy nods.

Well, says Claudell, guiding him away toward the window again, actually all a pussy *really* is is just a little cat. You've seen cats, haven't you?

The function of the copy is to underscore the visual content, not to supplement or counterpoint it. The main consideration is, as always, to keep the words few and simple, let the images do their work. In this instance, the two content elements to be equally if not simultaneously reinforced are the dramatic (adventure, risk, achievement of successful product use) and the certain (product's well-nigh luminous concreteness as shown, its potent comforting reality). So, as the image first appears and the camera begins its tracking movement, a calm deep soft male voice says simply, *It's here.*

Five-second pause. The camera continues to track; the white heap comes into view, looming purely against the horizon.

For you, says the voice. Dramatic closeup of mountainous heap. *Safe*, says the voice, *when taken as directed*.

Camera begins slow zoom away from mountain, as if ascending into sky. *The best it's ever been*, says the voice. *The best it could ever be*.

Then the camera freezes on the mountain, the scatter, the beige plane stretching away; and only then, in the advertisement's final second does the voice utter the product's name, as though it were itself a complete assertion: *Heroin*. Followed, in a second, by the number you can call in your zone.

This time the holo forms for him alone—programmed in, perhaps, by Devine's handdigital—and viewing it by himself seems to be somewhat more difficult than it was the first time with Devine awake, watching him. Or perhaps it was that this scene—Claudell and her smiling at one another, the needle going in, watching your lover get shot up by a former client who has expressed the desire to hurt her—is worse than the last one in itself.

And there are other questions on his mind as well. What has happened to her between the day he left and now to bring her here, like this, her head lolled gaping on a chair apparently not ten feet away. How long this has been set up with Claudell, what he is getting for it, over and above the kicks. What she was shot up with. What was that dreamlike state she moved in even before, back at the truck. What she is—was—really like, his love. Whether he ever knew. If, when they are done with her, they will kill Billy too. He allows himself to think these questions, acknowledges them and puts them aside, he knows if any one of these questions were at the moment to be followed up, something would happen to his heartbeat, his breathing, his control; that now, above all, he must not think about what he wants or wanted, would like or would have liked to do.

Then there is something about images, about taking them in. You see an officer of the South Vietnamese Army put a pistol to the head of a Viet Cong suspect and blow his brains out on screen. Behind his podium the president declares nuclear energy the safest in the world. Blacks come up out of the mines in South Africa, get hauled into the precinct stations of the United States holding their hats over their faces, a Pakistani woman holds up her baby dead from malnutrition thanks to Nestle's third world milk formula campaign. Then two housewives talk gaily over a hedge, a dapper foreign gentleman drums his fingers on the hood of an expensive car in front of a chateau. Only that which narrates can make us understand.

For the moment the holo from the other plane has become a virtually static image. The boy and the black man staring out the window, side by side. The woman, Charlotte, flopped in the chair no more than six feet away from him. Those questions—he had them a minute ago but he cannot recall them now. Now there is only Charlotte in the chair with her eyes filmed over and her mouth slightly ajar like a stupid child. When her right hand slips off the chrome arm of the chair and dangles there in that other space it is so real he wants to push away from the sleeping man resting his weight against him, breathing soft against his shoulder, step forward and pick it up and put it back and kiss it and her, walk into that space and not come back. But he controls himself, swallows back down what is so thick and hot like vomit rising, scalding, bursting the barriers of his stomach and lungs and heart to reach his mouth, brain, eyes. In the holospace Claudell turns from the window, leaving the boy to look out, and comes to sit at the worn brown couch, looking across at her. The holo fades, dematerializes. *My love, my love.* Ernest does not move.

Sometime later William is before him again in his impeccable white livery, bowing deeper than usual to sneak a glance at Devine's slack sleeping face. Then, back up, speaking to him in a strange, barely audible voice:

How you doing? You all right?

Ernest looks back into the black man's steady eyes without attempting to read them, or his tone; this one, after all, is not his client. Fine William he says. Why? Is there something *you'd* like?

No sah, he says, pivoting stiffly, disappearing aft again just as Devine begins to stir.

Damn, he says, blinking as though trying to focus, rubbing the red spot on his cheekbone where his head has rested against Ernest's shoulder: These time zones really sneak up on you. I guess I lost it there for a while.

Ernest's smile deepens, with its tinge of irony. He understands perfectly; they have arrived at a familiar, not to say classic scenario of full acquaintanceship. The client yields to you his official personality and allows himself to regress, to depend, to fall apart into his own heretofore suppressed chunks of simple desire and need. The trick now is to know, moment by moment, how to respond to the regressive behavior without dropping the official personality that is now your own. You missed another show, he says.

Still dulleyed, stroking his face, Devine stands and moves for the windows. So fill me in, he says.

They're in a jet, Ernest says. The black guy hit her up.

Heroin? says Devine, looking back over his shoulder.

Ernest nods; Devine grunts assent—Uh huh—and looks back to the window. We've started our descent, he says: Come here, take a look at this.

Rising, it is as if something had gone wrong with both space or time, he had not until now even noticed their nearly vertical descent yet now everything's speeded up so much it almost hurtles him across the cabin, against Devine and through the airplane wall out through the air to my love. Then, equally swiftly, the sensation's gone. He is beside Devine, looking down at the wide brown jaw of land rising to meet them, on which he sees massive earthmovers and giant cranes shifting pipes and girders to the grey outlines of buildings, masses of people moving in block formations here and there, black groups of specks. To the right of the construction site, at the southwest edge of the land, he sees rows of long tin rooftops gleaming, surrounded by some sort of wall or fence, beyond which rises the dense black smoke of a huge fire, burning the jungle back.

The Olongapo works, says Devine, smiling. Biggest chemical facility in the world when we get done. Put out enough synthetics to cover Asia. When this thing goes on line we'll be able to flood out the whole world market if we want. Dow, Du Pont, everybody. What do you think of that?

It is a real question, a real desire for approval. You have won. Ernest nods with his eyes one-quarter closed, with Devine's own former bored languor on his face. Nice, he says. Very nice.

Well, says Devine as the jet settles on the tarmac, one good thing here is, we don't have to do any high-level stuff. We'll just bunk up overnight, check the scene out, relax and enjoy ourselves and take off for the San Fran office again tomorrow. All right?

Sure, he says. Fine with me. And risks—from somewhere else, far from her face sunk back against the seat, her mouth, her hand, Mommy, Daddy in a box—sending Devine the trace of a generous, affectionate look, which is returned full force.

Duberman, the floor and walls are cooing. Time to wake up, Duberman. Your friends will meet you in the lobby lounge area. Don't forget to take off your clothes.

Fuck you Blencher, T.D. thinks; though, whoever may have drafted the message, its delivery is too soft and sweet for Blencher's dry voice. The truth is, he is irritated both at having fallen asleep to the goddamned omtrack and at having to go to work at all, the damn thing works so well, the pressure to just lie back is so strong. My clothes, he says loudly, are already off; and slams the door to his room, feeling like a raw bitchy fool.

Blencher is waiting for him out in the lobby, in his aqua robe. Well Mr. Duberman, he says, looking him over from top to toe, with little crinkles at the corners of his eyes: Now you look a little more like one of us.

T.D. glances from side to side at the loungers—no one seems to have left, or come, or moved but the attendants—and feels his vexation curdling into a slow, deep malevolence. Really? he says through a clenched smile. And how so?

Oh, says Blencher blithely, just the nakedness, I suppose. Then his eyes cut sharply to T.D.'s: They ought to be here any minute. Pilot signaled us about five minutes past now. We'll be at your service, you fellows just feel free to go right ahead with whatever you need to do. I only ask that you be as quiet and discreet as you can; keep in mind that this is, after all, a haven for some fairly anxious people. He spreads his hands, vaguely indicating the draped white bodies on either side. A paying establishment, he adds, with a certain—well—*reputation*—

Then his eyes go over T.D.'s shoulder, his thin mouth clicks into a grin: And there they are, he says. Hello there!

T.D. turns in time to see the slim black man shove the woman Ernest Goodman loves in the small of the back, so she stumbles unsteadily forward, up to them. He takes in her slight figure, broad flattish nose, the brown ringlets stuck to her brow with dirt or sweat; and trailing behind her and the Senator's son, the boy, a pouting redhead maybe four, five years old. The woman, Charlotte, is somehow not how he would have expected Goodman's lover to be; but then all three of them look fairly tousled in their wrinkled robes. He can half-see, half-sense the curious stares of those patients nearest them still aware enough to notice things, or turn their heads, as he puts out his hand. Duberman, he says.

Claudell Westerbrook, replies the black man, offering a wet limp palm. Delighted, I'm sure.

Blencher, perhaps also picking up on his clientele's discomfort, has taken Charlotte's arm, is leading her off toward the vinestrewn corridors, his jaw nervously set: Right this way, gentlemen, right this way . . . The woman Charlotte smiles as she scuffles along, opening and closing her mouth every so often as if engrossed in some strange exercise.

You shot her up already? T.D. asks.

My impression was that that was what I was supposed to do, Claudell says. They did more or less explicitly tell me that I would be administering drugs to her at some point. But they gave me so little guidance or instruction on what to do and how to do it. I certainly hope you have a better sense than I do of what to do now. It's been rather stressful so far for me.

It's very simple, T.D. says. Remember a night at your place in Washington a while back when you were with an acquaintance of yours, Ernest Goodman, and you suggested something to him and he decked you out?

Claudell's pink tongue flickers, wetting dry lips. Yes? he says.

That's what we're going to do here, more or less, says T.D. Pick up
on your suggestion and take it all the way. Just follow my lead, okay?

Yes, Claudell says, all right, but his plucked brows are knit on the
disheveled figure before him, stumbling forward on Blencher's arm. Then
his eyes, open wide, pupils large, dart to T.D.'s face, his hands lift waist-
high, palms up, trembling. All the way, he repeats: I never meant—what
you don't understand is that—that was a specific set of circumstances, that
night, I mean I couldn't just—you know—not just like that—

Sure you could, says T.D. You've got it in you; just a question of
getting in touch with yourself and letting it out. Blencher? he calls.

Blencher looks back over his shoulder without either halting or bothering to disguise the irritation all bunched up around his mouth. What is
it?

Think we're gonna need some beenies, my friend. Something good for
a sharp short rush—say an hour and a half, two hours on the outside. A
little mean around the edges, all the better. Better make it injectable, so
we can get moving here. What do you say, can you scare something up?

I was told, Blencher says gently, sighing, his passive-aggressive down
pat, my understanding was that aside from making these premises available
to you my only responsibility from here on in was the boy.

Blencher, my friend, says T.D.: I don't have time to fool around with
you. So let's cut the little authority games, okay? Can you get me and my
friend here what we need or not?

But at this point Charlotte stops—stops so suddenly Claudell collides
softly with her, Blencher's guiding arm falls away. She leans back against
the vines, grabbing them to right herself, raising her head as though with
a huge effort. In the following moment of confusion T.D. notices her eyes
do have an interesting greenish cast to them, even in her present state.
Was that what did it for Ernest? Who knows.

You have, she is saying to Blencher, thickly. You have to take good
care of him.

Of course I will, says Blencher firmly, pulling her off the wall. Your
boy will be just fine, Ms. Partlow. You have my word on that. And you,
Mr. Duberman, will get your drugs, he says to T.D. who finds himself
looking down now at the boy's small pinched face and tight mouth, eyes
darting around like a little hunted rat's.

Obviously, the class structure of this country is deeply confused. How

can there be all these people getting great wads of money from the government to consume while people like Hamilton, with low-level managerial jobs, have so much less? Why does Carberry the part-time guard
even want a job, why don't he and Hamilton both simply go on the dole?

One answer is that people want to work, to have something to do;
another is that the corporate state can't pay for everyone. Initially i.d./
credit cards were issued not only to maintain necessary levels of consumption, but to preserve enough of the middle and upper-middle classes
to keep them from making common cause with the poor. Accordingly,
such cards were never issued to storekeepers like Hamilton's father, a drug-
gist, or Carberry's, a legal aide, members of a petite bourgeoisie too small
and moribund to make any difference anyway; and the upshot in the early
'20s is that the sons and daughters of that vanished class have to fend for
themselves. The cost of the present program is already staggering, there is
no chance of extending it, every new application that comes in to the
Welfare Office has a harder time. Already in certain corporate circles it is
argued that the cost of American consumption has become far too great,
that the companies should concentrate instead on developing large healthy
middle classes, full consumers, in other countries where the industries
themselves are truly based. Certain far-thinking corporate leaders go so far
as to speak of this move as part of business's global mission, and to point
out to those unmoved by such rhetoric that certainly things cannot go on
much longer this way here in the U.S.A. It's too expensive; just look at
the rise in control costs alone, merely to keep the urban cores safe, with
suburban shanty towns growing larger all the time. Eventually all the
corporate offices will have to be moved, at least to Europe. This country's
had it, it's all gutted out.

Mistah Merrill, comes the subdued boom of the voice as the rotund
face appears: Senatuh Westuhbrook hyuh.

Merrill, more or less down at last, straightens slightly on his sunken
mauve bed. Ah yes, he deadpans, blinking in lieu of a smile. The distin-
guished Senator. To what do I owe the honor of this call?

Mistah Merrill, the Senator deeply sighs. Ahm rallah tahbly sorrah tuh
bothah yuh aftuh hours lak this. Ah *trahd* tuh reach yuh uhliuh this
aftuhnoon, without success.

That's right, Merrill says. I was busy.

Yass, says the Senator, actually slightly bowing his grizzled head. So
ah wuz tuhld. Then he raises his face slowly, with intense drama, as though

he had just caught sight of Merrill some distance away and was quite moved by the experience; and clears his throat, producing an appropriately impressive sound. Ah wuz mehly curious, Mistah Merrill, as tuh whethuh uh not theh wuz any wuhd cunsuhnin thuh small pruhject un which mah boy Claudell is embahked?

Merrill raises his eyebrows, opens his face to an innocent, candid width. No Senator, I'm sorry I can't tell you anything. I believe at this point the entire matter is out of our hands. In fact, I really couldn't tell you who else *is* in charge of it.

The luster visibly fades from the tumid eyes: Uh cuhse, Mistah Merrill, yuh must unduhstan mah uttah and cuhmplete willinness tuh suhve thuh awgunuzashun yuh repruhsent tuh thuh full extent uh mah resources an uhbiluhties, he says, includin mah son.

I understand that very well Senator, Merrill says, smiling thinly, examining his nails.

Ah honestluh buhleeved, says the Senator, that piece uh legislashuhn needed uh little mahw seasuhnin time tuh get thuh votes fuh passuhge. Ah had absuhluteluh no intenshuhn in the wahld, he says, of draggin mah feet on that thing—

Senator, says Merrill, standing and stretching, looking away, I'm afraid I have no idea what you're talking about. Nor can I give you any information at this time on the project or your son's part in it. Now I'm very sorry but if you don't mind? For me this has already been a very long day . . .

The Senator's face collapses in a mass of jowls. Suhtenluh, suhtenluh, he says. Ahm vurrah uhpreshuhtive uh yuh genurawsuhtah as it is. G'naht, suh—an if thah shud be ennythan ah cuhn evah do, fuh eithuh you puhsuhnully uh yuh awgunuzashun—

Merrill softly places his hands over the loungeside phone, cutting him off in midstream; and shakes his head, emitting a little dry chuckling sound.

The shots from the little sealed vials hand-delivered to their room hit in something under five minutes, very clean hard liftoff just like that. One minute you are looking down at the woman wondering how to get started, what the hell to do, the next angels scream in your head. Ernest Goodman's lover Charlotte lying on the floor, five-year contract for one job, those eyes of hers, the way they go down into her as though they might as well be black. He raises his head, looks over at Claudell who is grinning wide, uncontrollably. So, he says, you all ready to go?

Claudell's hands flutter patting over his thin body, smoothing himself down. Ready as I'll ever be, he says, right-o.

Come on over then, says T.D. Bring her stuff. And he rises from his scoop in the soft floor, steps over, squats down to her right. The whole thing from now on is to channel this energy, you don't have to keep it moving keep it clear.

Ms. Partlow, he says softly to the sprawled figure, the bottomless eyes: You don't know me, do you?

Slowly, without focusing on him she shakes her head.

My name is Thomas Duberman, he says. I know your lover Ernest Goodman rather well. You may have heard him speak sometimes of a friend and former teacher of his named T.D.?

In a second she nods again. But it is not as if she really were listening to him so much as to something else, quieter even than the omtrack; and as though she were only making her replies to prevent his voice or presence from impinging any further on the position, the sound, in and on which all her real attention rests.

What do you think of Ernest Goodman? he says.

For an instant, just before it can be seen, something flees behind the eyes. I don't believe I know what you mean, she says; and turns to Claudell, crouched to her left, turning the needle over and over in his hand. I would like that shot now, please, she says. I would be able to answer your questions far better if I could have that little shot.

T.D. runs his index finger over the russet floor, onto her bare knee. The warmth of her skin, another slight surprise. I'm afraid you will have to answer our questions and perhaps do a few other things before we can let you have that shot, Ms. Partlow, he says.

That's right, bitch, says Claudell, stepping in front of her and bending to his knees: You gon let us do any fuckin thin we want to do fore we shoot you up and get you off, you hear?

That fake spade accent, horrendous clichéd lines, classic trite badass black dude rubbing the needle back and forth in his sinister hands—it makes T.D. want to laugh out loud though he knows if you start you will not stop. *See what you know?* he would like to shout out straight in his face. See what you can do?

Do you understand, Ms. Partlow? says T.D. turning his calm gaze back to her, keeping hold of the omtrack, almost inaudible around them in the padded room, keeping time with the pulsing screenwalls.

No wonder, then, he likes to stop off here for a day on his trips around the world: to a place where for him and his company, just as for the Navy and its sailors before him, everything is permitted. In my time the cold beer in your mouth, the blowjob under the table, the beautiful women faking their orgasms to your real ones for just a few dollars U.S. per night. In OMNICO and Devine's, the work crews of fifty, one hundred, two hundred men walking silently under one white supervisor's control to their position for the day or night, the buildings rising in the open mocha earth against the jungle's green, and smokestacks rearing up to spew exhaust into the stifling air, and conduits forming underneath to spill their wastes into the Olongapo River, on top of all the human shit.

And it is exciting too, the rough raw element of it. Here he does not need to invent a situation. There is something still primitive, dangerous in the fetid weight of the air; something classic about getting off the plane to no reception, no speeches or bands, just the hot tarmac still uncongealed and sticking to your shoes, the jeep waiting some twenty, twenty-five yards away, and Esser's fat, tough ham of a hand in yours.

And just before this, that one final moment on the plane, as the two of them were moving toward the open door where William stood attendant: a moment when the holos formed again practically at their feet. In the room at the Regroove, wherever it is, the other two get down to business with the woman, the action transmitted in the greatest detail. Up that close, only inches away it seemed, the image quality so precise you could see the tiny brownish-gold hairs on her outstretched arms. Mainly, though, he watched Ernest watch, without making any attempt to disguise that fact, watching him closely, directly enough no single twitch or extra eyeblink could have possibly escaped his gaze. What would have been the result had Ernest broken down in a fit of rage or weeping, had his frame begun to quiver, if his eyes had shut, his body locked tense? You will never know, never have to know. He simply looked on; it might as well have been the gridwork of Olongapo, seen from the air; so watching him just now on the jet, standing by him on the airstrip now, facing Esser, it is all he, Devine, can do to contain the tingling in his own legs and hands, that wild giddy urge to touch, to shout out for joy, and instead hold the same exact expression on his face even though all he is thinking is *Good Good Good* like some giant flashing sign.

He keeps on looking straight at, into it. Yet it feels as though he is not

quite seeing it. Or as though he were looking beyond it, past the room
where Claudell slaps her backhanded now across her face, her breasts,
toward wherever it is T.D., kneeling beside them, looks off toward too.
For a while it is as if he and T.D. both are watching something somewhere
else. Then even when Claudell sticks himself in her and then T.D. goes
to work too his own eyes keep on going past what's there. He cannot keep
them on it and he cannot seem to hear what they are shouting at her,
calling her, or what sounds she makes in reply. In his ears a loud rushing.
A tremor passes up his leg and trickles out. His eyes burn so he blinks.
You never heard her make sounds like these sounds before. He stops the
thought; he holds the pose. When the holo fades, he turns his head and
lifts an eyebrow at Devine as if to say Okay so let's go. As they move toward
the door again a very strong wave moves up through his body so hard he
has to stop still and hold onto every muscle but Devine is outside the hatch
and only William in the doorway is watching him now. It takes him maybe
five, ten seconds to start moving again and as he goes out the hatch and
down the stepladder it feels all right again. Then those sounds come together with the pictures, in waves, and it is all you can do to, to

Hey Mister Devine, Esser is growling, eyes slits in the round red head,
how you doing, how you doing, glad you could come.

Me too, he says, feeling how helplessly the smile cracks his face; and
turns to where Ernest stands staring off ahead through the hot haze at the
men and the machines. So, he says again, knowing he is repeating himself,
so what do you think?

Ernest's mouth is set in a closelipped frown: It's amazing, he says.

Vernie, says Devine, this is my friend Ernest Goodman. Ernest, Verne
Esser, head of construction and security for the Olongapo works.

Devine watches Esser's eyes slide away from Ernest's as they shake:
Hey, Esser says, nice to meet you.

Pleased to meet you, Ernest says.

Esser looks away, off to the slow flames burning off the greenchoked
hilltops to the east. Well, Esser says, you guys been traveling all night,
you probably need to get some rest. Anything you want before you go to
your, uh, quarters?

How about if you take a turn around the place on our way there? says
Devine. Show Ernest here what we're up to.

Oh sure, fine, says Esser with brittle false enthusiasm, turning and
taking off for the jeep so fast that stepping after him Devine can feel the

burnish of the day's first real sweat forming on his skin beneath the robe. That Verne is disturbed by the way he is acting and/or the strange presence of Ernest doesn't bother him, he is that happy. Now, as Verne Esser wheels the jeep over the rutted gluey earth, past the workers, shouting across to Ernest, back to him, what he sees and desires in Ernest's cold stiff face is his usual self, the one separating him from who he is now released to be.

In the Olongapo ruled by OMNICO and Esser, the bars and hooker-shacks are gone, long bulldozed away. Yet the workers' women and children still get in to the new workers' compounds, though their presence is strictly forbidden. At night they sleep on the concrete floor by the men's hammocks until a few minutes before the guard comes through; then rise, roll up the bedding, sneak away; pressed further, they slip somehow back across the forcewall and electric fence to the jungle, children and mothers alike. God only knows how they stay alive, what they eat, for the TOP human feed is served only in one vaulted steelbeamed feedbarn, and every worker searched on the way back out. But the thing is, these people—with their broad flat highboned faces, their dull black eyes—they can smile at you one minute, slip a knife in you the next. And should you be so lucky as to catch one of the women, a few of the kids, and kill them—knowing damn well that if you put them in a jeep, drive them out of the compound and drop them off, they'll be back the next night—if they find out it was you your life isn't worth two farts. They'll find you on the compound's northwest edge where the garbage gets dumped, hacked in chunks by machetes which, like the women and children, are strictly prohibited and almost never found or seen.

But Esser is not, of course, about to tell them any of this. And over here, he shouts above the grinding of the jeep, we've got your stearates, vinyl chlorides, all that stuff. Line machinery and tooling pulled from Puerto Rico last, originally from Michigan, Illinois, chemical plants up around there. Illegal as shit to make this stuff any more in the States.

The smell of her. Warm rich brown. A hint of bitterness, acridity, next to the skin as though too pungent to be sweet, as if she were the most real, endless thing in which you had to move, touch, leave and find again, again the dusty fungoid smell of Mom and Dad, splotches of hairless skin beating of red light behind your eyes my love my love the dustsmell on your limbs dry smile stretched on your face

Course we won't be putting you up in anything quite like this, yells Esser as the jeep jolts past the last of the blocklong stone barracks, five stories high, leprous grey. Thousand laborers per unit, he shouts. And I mean laborers. Know the meaning of a day's work. Scramble all over each other, get these jobs, live in a place like this, get out of what filth they came from.

Next time worse still. She will be bleeding, hurting, She will have started to die. And he will watch you watching, watch that distant contemptuous halfsmile on your face. They will be taking her too away, again watching you. Killing your love. Watching your face. Giving you the job, the job for good—

Course we got a little different accommodations for you, Verne says over the sighing of the engine and the settling of the mud at the edge of the strip of lawn at the southwest edge of the building site.

Ernest turns his head and stares up the banyan-lined path, up to the porticoes and columns at the head of the emerald yard. Crazy pops, he says with his smirk still on; and hears Devine's snort of laughter from the back of the jeep, in the shade of the striped parasol held aloft by the armed native guard. *No no no no not lost not my love*

You got holo set up in there now? says Devine. Body leaning back relaxed; brown eyes wide; smile half-formed.

Yes sir, says sweating Verne Esser, we sure do.

Don't you want to look at the pretty pictures? Blencher says, gesturing at the four screenwalls displaying four landscapes in a coordinated pan: coastal water splashing soft against the shore; winding forest path through the still pines; deep green heath, with outcroppings of rock; and gold sunset behind soft brown foothills.

But Billy, in the chair across from the desk, shakes his lowered head No.

Blencher slides open a side drawer of the desk, looks down at the bright capsules scattered there. Been a long day for you I bet, he says, smiling. Aren't you getting tired? Wouldn't you like to go lie down someplace?

Again, in the same way, Billy shakes his head.

Here, says Blencher, holding up a twotone brown spansule, using his most jocular voice, here, why don't you just take one of these? Relax you; calm you down; help you sleep—

Again; over and over, still without glancing up.

Blencher stands in place a moment, pill still upheld. The woods, fields, beach slide by. The boy stops shaking his head; slowly, back and forth, his legs begin to swing. When Blencher realizes that is what they are both doing, watching the legs move, he crosses the room quickly and fills a plastic cup with imported Norwegian water out of his own personal cooler, and brings it over and holds it with the pill under the little boy's chin.

Here, he says. Take this and drink up.

Billy takes pill and cup from the man's hand and swallows the pill without looking up from the swinging of his legs.

You stay right here, all right? Blencher says, moving back to the desk, scooping a handful of spansules into the pocket of his robe. I'm going off on rounds, be back in a minute, all right?

All these people, everybody always talking about everything being all right. The boy keeps watching his feet.

Blencher slams the office door behind him when he leaves, and does his rounds—counting the amount and expense of the food and drugs consumed by each client, sharing a few tokes with the most well-heeled of the not-yet-cooled-out, watching selected holo from clients' rooms, receiving the reports of the aqua staff—in an abstract fury he permits to surface only on his return, when he finds the boy has slid down the chair into a sort of broken doll position, his head flopped over the left arm of the chair, his mouth open as if in stupid surprise. Then Blencher reaches in the other pocket of his robe, extracts a slip of paper, self-dials the number written there, with the screen off.

Hamilton? he says. Hamilton of GuardAll? Blencher here.   Yeah okay I know.   *I wouldn't* have called if I didn't think it was important.   So okay, report it, go ahead. And I'll let a few people know what kind of shitty plan we got to go on from you guys as well.   Okay, like for example, so what am I supposed to do with the kid? Goddamn thing— you know I had to stone him out to cool him down.   Yeah, he's here, crashed out in the office right now, creeping me out.   Yeah, he says. Well, you get back to me pretty fucking fast, you hear?

A shock of airconditioned cold as they walk into the hallway opening directly onto a sweeping staircase and, to the left, an oldfashioned living room: overstuffed flowered sofas grouped around a low hardwood table, standing brass lamps, old books stacked high in the far brick walls. As soon as Esser shuts the door Devine steps into the room, starts unbuttoning his robe. Ernest follows but keeps his on. Devine throws his clothes across the back of the couch. Well, what do you think? Devine says.

His brows lift but the line of his lips remains straight. Great, he says.

Well, says Devine: well, good. Then looks down at himself, his round-ing, softening body with a frown, as if only now realizing he is nude. Devine is feeling shy; he can see, he can understand that. He watches Devine look up again, avoiding his eyes, turning his head to peer at the ceiling. So where's those holos? he says. There ought to be more holos here. I specifically said the living room as well as the upstairs.

They'll be here, says Ernest. Just wait.

Then for what must be a full minute they are standing alone together, one clothed, the other nude, at the two corners of the couch like strangers waiting for the same something—maybe a trans. Devine, humming faintly, looks off toward the bookshelves, while Ernest's gaze is aimed down toward the nearby coffeetable which he does not really see, cannot seem to keep his attention on, as though the table, the room were about to dissolve or were themselves like a part of a holo, far away from the roaring where he really is in spite of knowing that his expression is still all right, holding steady though he can no longer feel his face.

Then, behind the sofa and a few feet beyond them, the next holos form; and for him it is as if since the last set on the plane nothing has happened, he has been here watching, being watched the whole time while she is lying on her stomach with her puffy bruised face turned grimacing on its side while a gurgling comes up from Claudell's throat and he shoves down with both hands at once, while beside them T.D. takes a drag off a fresh joint from a tray at his side and says, You want to think about the answer we want to hear, and taps his ash over one of the cuts nails have raked on her back and says, You still want a shot?

Yes, she says. Yes please.

Then you better start thinking about giving us the right answers back, T.D. says. Now: you used to do this stuff with Ernest? Fuck around with him like this?

There is no answer.

You love Ernest Goodman? T.D. says.

A few more seconds. Then Claudell turns her over and sits down on her again, spits on the hand that was moving up her ass, wipes it in a slant across her face and moves down to claw more at her breasts so her body locks rigid but her eyes stay dead and Yes she says through clenched teeth and Claudell rolls partway off then rests his whole weight into his sharp thin knees, into her abdomen below the ribs and this time a cry does burst out of her, but quickly fades into the background noise and Claudell falls back panting on the floor. That's not the right answer, T.D. says, holding his joint over her upturned face, above her greygreen left eye which quickly shuts. Keep it open, he says.

She opens her eyes. You want a nice shot sometime, T.D. says, you want to keep this joint out of your eyes, you'll give me the answers I want. You love Ernest Goodman?

More humming seconds. No, she says.

You love your first husband?

No.

Behind them you can see the green of the screens coming around to lavender again and Love your father and mother? T.D. says.

No.

Claudell, with his chest rising, falling more normally, sits up and looks at the two of them with feverish eyes, a foolish half-embarrassed smile and T.D. scowls over at him, then back down at Charlotte and Love your kid? he says.

No.

A long moment now, you see her and T.D. look upon each other the same way, neutrally, even softly, and she lifts one hand to scratch at the dried blood on her nose.

Now can I have my shot please?

Nah, says T.D. in that same gentle voice, Not just yet, as he straddles her now with that same deliberateness, with Claudell now behind them and off to the side tossing back his gleaming head cracking up laughing hooting *Fuck you bitch*! as the holo fades out. And you realize you have no idea any more what look is on your face, no idea, it is like terror like indifference, as though they are killing your love and you don't even care.

Devine, naked, is smiling softly, shyly at you. Want to come on upstairs? Devine says.

You put in so many years in this business, he is saying, laughing, it's inevitable I guess. You spend all this time learning to make the right moves at the right time around the conference table and in the office and marrying the right sort of woman and having the right kids and all the rest of it, and after a while, when you're my age I guess, you just get tired of doing it by the book. Know what I mean?

He is lying again against Ernest, both naked under the bed's cream canopy, upstairs in the brick house. He has slid down and turned so his head rests on Ernest's chest, his arms wind around Ernest's waist. You can feel this weight, this pressure of touch. Sure, says Ernest and you can hear yourself murmur it, watch yourself stroking his hair.

I mean, you can't do it right all the time, Devine says. There has to be a place where you can't worry about it. Or where you don't know what the right thing is. That's how I got started with these waste situations—you know, those attacks?

Um-hmm, hums Ernest whom you watch now, Ernest this part of you that feels Devine's skin sticking hot against his, whose eyes move to the old print of happy negroes putting cotton boles in kneehigh baskets on the wall across the room, who wonders in dull dumbness Currier and Ives? as Devine's head shifts against his ribs, who feels the brush of lips against his skin.

First it was just a sort of fun way to get rid of assholes, Devine says. The kick was using the organization without anyone knowing quite enough about what was happening or where it was coming from to trace it back to me. Sort of using the system against itself, you know what I mean?

It is nothing unusual, thinks the Ernest that watches the Ernest that still thinks, sees, acts: Once a relationship of this kind is established the client's repressed need for approval typically surfaces in such strong, semi-obsessional forms, accompanied by an equally powerful craving for affection, often physical, everything is right on course . . .

Then, Devine is saying, when you advance to the point where you have the wasters coming at you the problem becomes how to keep that same control, so that nobody would be able to *really* get me one way or another through it; but without losing the excitement, either, the whole risk thing. Sort of like playing chess with yourself, you know?

You know. You know. That same part that knows you, Ernest, knows Devine; how in this ensuing silence Devine feels, as though they had been moving all along without his notice, the smooth light touch of fingertips along the upper edge of his resting penis. How he tenses, unsure of what Ernest is up to, how to respond; feeling how strictly taboo this is for a man anywhere near his position on the grid. He must be straight, marry and have children, all of which he has done. But how sweet it feels to let go and give yourself up to the caresses, the back of Ernest's hand circling, touching you faintly, steadily to hardness he looks down to see as though he were separate from the pleasure he feels.

Ernest, you hear Devine say with his mouth too thick with feeling to form the words and no idea of what will follow, what protest, shame, delight, Ernest I don't—Ernest I can't—

Shhh, you say. Be quiet now. Let me.

So Dick Devine closes his eyes and feels his weight falling away like a stone down a well, as the slow silk of Ernest slides over him. Then, for a long shocking instant, no touch at all; until just when you know his eyes would have opened, and time begun again.

Ernest's mouth—your mouth—closes over his cock.

It is so exciting and forbidden that in terrified joy he pulls away and you have to make your hand press down on his chest.

Lie down, you whisper. Let me.

And then he lies there motionless as the opening closes over him again and again, taking him, sucking him in, against what you know must be the countersensation of the cool air from the vents across his skin, against the grain of his thought, the tape you know he realizes goes on even now.

For such a moment cannot last, you know that; it it too difficult for Devine, for anyone in his position, too rare and strange. Already he will be beginning to notice the coverlet's scratchiness against his back, to think of the work waiting for him back in San Fran. He will sense the approach of his orgasm, still some distance away, with the same mixture of boredom and urgency as with his wife in their proper home leading no doubt to the same predictable closure, the pinch before the seconds start again. At the same instant in which he is most pleased by being served, Ernest blowing him off, he is already past it, thinking how to keep word of this from ever getting out when it could be used against him someday. Briefly his mind brushes up against the possibility Ernest and all this are part of something, some other plot. No, he thinks; not likely; surely not. Now he simply wishes it would hurry up and end. Then you know his thin pressed mouth is cracking wide, releasing scraped breath. His eyes open flat on the canopy, a hot sick swelling edge of pain rolls up from his crotch through abdomen and ribs, crests and buckles there, this man Ernest Goodman has *bitten* him, *hard*, and he cannot tell if it is bleeding or even still there, there is no time, no time to look down at it or up at Ernest's face to find what expression there, figure what the hell is going on, what is the move before your thumbs are at his throat pressing the windpipe soundless down so fast and hard you can see his sight fade as one hand scrabbles on the mahogany nightstand for the handsize minidigital, knocks it to the floor. And then you know that he feels nothing at all.

Two hundred odd yards east of the house and downhill from it, they are placing the blocks for the core insulation of plant one. There are three

piles of blocks, stacked like cordwood, five hundred to a pile, made of
pressed asbestos and fiberglass, slivers of which glint in the still, heavy air
like small gold needles as they pass them from hand to hand over the dirt
and up on the iron scaffolds to be placed in the steel frame of the core.
The workcrew is split into three lines of some sixty each, passing these
lightweight blocks the size of a man's trunk, breathing in the sprays of
needles that pin and kill their lungs and prickle skin past fire with the slow
slide of their sweat over the needles in the flesh of their bare arms, chests,
faces blank and opaque under the glare of the even sun in the thick air,
under the even contempt, boredom, and irritation of the white supervisor
looking on from within his fringed jeep, in the silence broken only by the
grinding of some engines in a distant area of the site. And in a soundproof
room in the United States a woman is being killed. And you can imagine
this.

The primary word *I-Thou* can be spoken only with the whole being.
Concentration and fusion into the whole being can never take place
through my agency, nor can it ever take place without me. I become
through my relation to the *Thou*; as I become *I*, I say *Thou*.
    All real living is meeting.

It was so easy, finally, to say she did not love them, any of them, easier
and more natural than you could ever have guessed. The shot they gave
her once she finally gave them what they wanted comes together finally
with the webbing of pain from down there where one or both of them is
doing something again to make finally something soft you are inside looking
back out at the men coming at her again and again to crack her, open her
up against the screenwall, pulsing, but they cannot do that any more. This
is not so bad, at least you're where you belong. Where you knew, always,
it would be like this once you got back far enough, that they would not
be able to do that at all any more once you were home.

Oh god, Claudell is saying, jesus man will you please stop?
    Yelling, actually. T.D. suspends motion in midstroke, looks back over
his shoulder to find Claudell behind him now rocking on his knees, weeping, shaking his head.
    I didn't do that, he is babbling like some goddamn little kid. You did
it. You're the one who put her out.

Hey, T.D. says, just hold on a second, all right? Though what he would most like to do at this moment, with this new steelbar ache in his head, is step over and beat his wet black chickenshit face quiet as well.

But he keeps a lid on it; he takes himself out of her, wipes his penis on the floor. She does not move. He shakes his head to get out some of the sudden heaviness, and reaches his fingertips in along her throat, pressing down. He rolls her over belly up; one arm flops out to the side; a slight filminess already forming over the green of the eyes. He puts his head on her left breast, listens: nothing. He wipes off his ear, wipes the side of his head, bends over the face and pinches the scalp next to the hairline: no response. Okay, it's over. Five-year contract. Fine.

He looks back at Claudell, still whimpering away. Again it takes some work to control his revulsion at such blatant fucking unbelievable hypocrisy, to keep from hitting him with all you got left.

Now listen, my friend, he says to Claudell. I know you're agitated. You're starting to come back down from a pretty high lifter; so am I. The thing to remember here is we had a job to do, we got it done. It's over now, Claudell. Let's just go home.

Editing of this final holo at GuardAll studios in San Fran is under the personal supervision of Hamilton's boss Nickerson, who remains at the office to watch the final cut in a basement screening area guarded by laserstreams, passbeams, and even a few aged armed men; and leaves a taped message directed to Hamilton's office telling him to complete ASAP the file on his end of the operation and await further instructions on its disposal.

The shapes form in the brick house at the foot of the bed as Ernest is picking up his robe. She is tortured and killed by Claudell Westerbrook and T.D. Soon he is crying so hard he has to sit back down on the edge of the bed, the crying tearing itself out of you because they have killed your love again. At the foot of the bed T.D. bends over the face, pinches the scalp next to the hairline: no response. Ernest Goodman weeps on his side with his knees drawn up close to his chest. Ernest Goodman cries and whimpers and rocks back and forth as the holo fades at the foot of the bed.

Later, still rocking, he is gradually aware of something touching his feet. Something cool and soft. He sits up and is staring into Devine's face. The head tilted far back. Skin darkening red. Eyes bulged: you could do this to me, to me?

Yes, Ernest Goodman says to it.

Then the door to the bedroom opens and he turns to see who will be there to kill him. It is William, in his white uniform.

Come on, William says. We got to get out of here.

When he does not respond, William moves quickly across the room, grabs his shoulder, slaps his face, hauls him up. Hey listen, William says. We got some people stalling on the survsystem, but that's only gonna work so long. I'm sorry man, I'm really sorry but you hear what I'm telling you?

Ernest looks over at the place at the foot of the bed where she was killed. The black man picks the robe up off the floor, holds it out to him. Come on, friend, William says softly. Get your clothes on, let's go.

The next thing he knows William is half walking, half carrying him down the curved sweeping staircase, under the chandelier he vaguely re-members, past a silver tray of round white objects on the phone table in the hallway at the foot of the stairs.

What's that? he says, pointing.

William's mouth breaks into a wide smile. Biscuits, he says. My ticket here, once I got the word. I mean, you know—who's to say the man didn't order biscuits?

He steps ahead, moves away from Ernest's side in the hallway, cracks the front door open. Now I'm gonna drop behind you here, he says. Be your servant. Just get in the jeep and be quiet. You're close enough to him nobody's gonna wonder what's going on as long as we can hold it up on the screens.

Slowly Ernest's head turns to him from the direction of the living room, where it has been looking. What the shit is this? he says, speaking harshly, slowly, staring blindeyed. What is this *we* shit? Some new kind of Violence Club? What happened to your fucking accent?

William lifts his free arm up and away from the outdoor sightlines, puts his hand around the back of Ernest's neck, squeezes and smooths.

Look man, he says. Devine is dead. You killed him. I can fill you in on all the rest later. Now if we gonna get outta here intact we gotta move, all right?

The same flat stare for another long moment, coming back at him. Then Ernest turns and walks past him, out of the cool brick house into the light and heat and noise from the construction site; and William deftly slides the door shut and follows behind.

Helping Claudell snap his little eyepiece clasp in back, rubbing his drooping arms and shoulders, keeping the soothing patter up. There now you look just fine, fresh as a new day, not a bit rumpled, well shall we be off? Back out in the corridor, murmuring more pleasantries, maintaining one hand spread on the small of his back, gently pushing him along, keeping the pace. In the lobby, now deserted, all its chairs and cushions empty, even the muzak stopped overhead, the whirlpool's lapping the only noise, shaking hands with Blencher again, congratulations thank you best of luck to you too. Then out to the waiting limos, desert night's startling chill, one last smile for the Senator's son whose eyes still stare off dully, whose voice is low and drawn. Who's to say how much to mark down to the comedown from the lifter, how much comes from something else? Anything but lack of pleasure, thinks T.D.: Just don't give me that line, my friend.

You've been very kind, says Claudell with just a trace of the old phoney accent. I'm sorry we had to meet in such—circumstances. But I hope we'll see one another someday again.

Really, says T.D. past a pounding head, issuing somehow his last bona fide full smile: By all means let's.

And then is in the limo, following Claudell's past Palm Springs rubble rendered ghostly by the moon, in silent wondering thanks to whoever made the decision to give them separate limos to the airfield and their jets, for whatever reason. Then, sagging back into the soft plush, thinking how for somebody thirty-five years old, out of the trade for years, to come back in on a special job like this on zero notice, play off Claudell, get your dick to stand up on demand, you got through it all pretty well . . .

Caught in such thoughts, T.D. does not notice the limo slowing until it is almost stopped. Hey, he says rapping on the window between seats, what the hell's going on? Then looks where the driver is pointing at the guard in the middle of the road, waving them down with his torch; and beyond him, the taillights of Claudell's limo speeding away.

His name Duberman? the guard calls out. T.D. sees the driver up front nod. You want to follow me then? calls the guard.

Maybe I forgot something back there, he thinks on the way back. Maybe they got another assignment for me. Maybe I'm just supposed to stay to-night, and go back in the morning fresh. But he can pretty well guess by now what the deal is going to be.

Back in the room in the Regroove Center, there are more guards, fully dressed and booted, stepping over the soft floor, at the center of which stands Blencher bent over the crumpled bleeding sprawl with his pig face squinched in a simulacrum of horror. When he catches sight of T.D. he straightens and speaks into the microphone held out by the guard at his side.

Yes, that's him. He came with this woman this afternoon. They came well recommended by business acquaintances and friends, like all our clientele. Nobody had any idea there was this sort of thing going on. We do not tolerate abuse in any form in any Regroove Center, I want to make that clear right—

You talked to Merrill, T.D. says, working very hard to stay, sound calm: This is some kind of weird fix to screw me out of that contract. Isn't it. *Isn't it.*

He starts to move across the floor to Blencher. Someone has an arm in his way, a torchbarrel at the side of his neck. Blencher across the room, over the body, sends him a look of artificial, abstracted pity.

In spite of everything, you know, Blencher says, I still wish we at Regroove could do something for you, Mr. Duberman. But I'm afraid you're really out of our hands. He pauses for a second, three beats, then cocks his head at the guard next to him: But do you gentlemen need anything now before taking him away? Some downs, smoothies, anything at all? I'm sure all this must be somewhat upsetting for you too . . .

Still, of course, the grid is undisturbed. Each year a vote of the board of directors, including the present president, is retaken on the question of who the next president shall be. The result of this vote is then stored in the bubble memory of the central system for future use if necessary to assure an immediate and orderly succession if ever and whenever things go wrong. Thus it is that in the early morning of September 12, 2020, a stone mansion on an estate in Carmel, California, resounds to the ringing of a phone; and OMNICO's v.p. finance throws off the eiderdown which has been making him too hot anyway, giving him bad, turbulent dreams, and answers it.

It is my duty to inform you, says the neutral expressionless voice, that on receipt of this communication you may consider yourself the president and chief executive officer of all enterprises designated under the title OMNICO Industries, Incorporated, with all rights and duties pertaining thereto. By the authority vested in me by the Board of—

The computervoice goes on, screenlessly of course. The new president strokes his fingers over and over through his grey hair. The family will have to be convened from wherever the hell they are. The kids no doubt in school somewhere, maybe even college by now; Evelyn, last you knew, in Venice or some tourist trap like that. There will be pictures, interviews, film and holo of you together, eating meals and other family things, smiling, smiling . . .

Please record on all hand and local terminals these access numbers to central storage and memory, says the computer. Then, when he has read the numbers back to it for verification, it wishes him every success and signs off.

The new president picks his hand model off the nightstand, feeds the new access codes in, and sets about finding out what happened to Devine. His handdigital begins to throw words up on the screen. At first he can hardly believe them. Within a few seconds the new president knows that his predecessor was killed by his professional friend, Ernest Goodman—whom he distantly recalls, now he thinks of it, from the last Brussels conference, a night at Bruges marked by one of the old man's raids. That Goodman was aided in his escape by William, the black servant on the presidential plane, now revealed to have been a member of yet another terrorist group. Scant data currently available indicate no previous ties between Goodman and this group, nor any ties direct or indirect between either Goodman or this particular group and any rival business enterprise. Recommended course of action is to reprogram the death to natural causes, e.g. heart attack, meanwhile placing all present information in a new and separate confidential file in which additional data may from here on in be collected and summarized: obviously the true story's too provocatively looney to get out. Once the new president has approved these suggestions, he sits back in bed and takes a few hits off an opiated Acapulco left in the nighttable ashtray to help him get a few more hours rest before the whole thing starts. At least, he thinks, at any rate he will know enough to stay away from, never need a professional friend. But the grid being what it is, he will sooner or later almost certainly change his mind. Right now as he slides back down in bed it occurs to him how funny it is that he is no more excited than this about being president of the whole works, the whole shooting match. The moment you've waited and worked for all these long years; and you hardly feel a thing.

Days later, on an overcast yet humid afternoon, Ramon Porfirio, head of OMNICO industries in his country, including the Ramsfeel line, issues his colleagues in to a first-floor screenroom simply furnished with a long couch down the left side of the room, two armchairs to the right against the wall. The men, dressed like him in conservative dark suits and shoes, move in silence past his outstretched hand to sit along the couch. This way they will all have to crane their heads around each other to see; still, no one would have presumed to take an armchair, in which only Ramon finally, crisply sits down.

Such awkwardness and stiff decorum are not entirely the result of the ordinary power relations in a corporate-colonial office of a multinational, but rather symptoms of the strain they have all been under for the last forty-eight hours, even though everything has gone according to plan: the early morning seizure of the airport, the tv, radio, and newspaper outlets, followed by a few swift assassinations by men in peasant mufti of those radical leaders most likely to foment any real revolution and most capable of doing so; then, beginning at noon, the heavily televised daylong "assault" on the capitol building Pantucho's men—by this time most of the Army and the National Guard—could have easily taken in less than an hour from the sprinkling of palace guards taking potshots at them from the windows, directed by hysterical aged generals, tears streaking down their flaccid cheeks; finally, this morning's occupation of the factories, hours before the staged capitulation of the old General and his last supporters, marching out into the sun, before the cameras, their soft hands clasped atop bald heads for all to see. And now the screen is filled with Pantucho's round face before the red green and white stripes of the national flag behind him on the wall of the tv studio, beginning his victory speech.

For too long, says Pantucho, our land and its resources have been the property of foreigners. For too long we have stripped the skins from our backs and the years from our lives to give to strangers with the power of the dollar over us: the power to stunt us that they may prosper, to kill us that they may grow.

Pantucho pauses and nods on the last phrase, his jaw set, just as the OMNICO-hired director instructed him to do; picks up a glass of water by his hand and takes a good strong swig. The men on the couch sit quietly, looking thoughtful. Ramon fidgets, stretches out his legs.

Up until now, Pantucho resumes, these foreign forces have been given the full support of the regimes they erected in the people's name. But the government that begins this day will be different. I am of you; I will be for you. You can depend on it.

During this pause they can hear a muffled roaring sound, like waves breaking some distance away, carrying all the way in to the screenroom: the response of the crowd to Pantucho's words reaching them via sound-trucks sent out to every neighborhood, owned and rigged by OMNICO.

That is why, Pantucho says, my first action as the head of the new Provisional Government has been to order the armed forces of our country to occupy every foreign-owned industrial site in this capital; because we have worked too long for others, my friends. It is time that we worked for ourselves.

Someone grunts over on the couch. Ramon darts a sharp glance over. The palms of his own hands, in fact, are wet resting on his knees.

The camera begins a slow zoom. So I come before you tonight, says Pantucho, to convey to you my eternal and lifelong gratitude for your support in the struggle of the last two days, and to tell you that we the people have won. The revolution is over. The country is ours. You may go back to your homes. Regularly scheduled programming will return to this station tomorrow, and you may return to your jobs. For tonight, peace—in extreme closeup now, so that they can see Pantucho's smile, the fleshy lips, the bristles above the capped white teeth—and goodnight.

Again, even louder, the roar from outside the screenroom, as the national anthem plays from soundtruck and screen. Ramon looks over at the couch to see one pair of narrow brown eyes trained on his. Guturriez, of course.

Well, I hope he's on the level with us, Guturriez says. I hope we know what the hell we're doing here.

We know exactly what we're doing, Ramon says. We're protecting our holdings with government troops until all danger of a rebellion is past. Production will continue on schedule. A small percentage of those funds which have until now gone into the General's defense and weaponry coffers will now be used to produce some highly visible urban development and job training programs. Pantucho will continue to tell them he has broken our backs, we are finally paying our share. Everyone is going to be happy for a while now, Guturriez, don't you see?

The others swiftly reproduce Ramon's light ironic smile; all but Guturriez, who scowls back: And what if he doesn't give the factories back? says Guturriez. What if the son of a bitch is for real?

Ramon Porfirio stands, slowly, and opens his mouth in a wide, relaxed smile. Hey Guturriez, he says, what if ITT decides it wants to take us over? What if your mother comes back to life?

And while the rest of them too stand and laugh, even Guturriez himself finally, Ramon laughs with them, with his stomach coiling and burning, knowing what Guturriez is doing, covering his own ass in case anything goes wrong, the production figures drop, as might well happen anyway in the short run. And no Devine on top any more to push for you; Guturriez in fact might well be in touch with this new guy Olsen himself, which could be why he feels so free to criticize these days. Have to check it out, wait a few days and see. If not, then fire the bastard, get him out of there. Have Pantucho waste him as an imperialist pig. Yeah, that would be good, that would be just right—

Just thinking of it makes him start to laugh again, this time chuckling out loud for real. All the rest of them, even Guturriez, cock their heads at him with wide expectant grins.

But Ramon merely waves his hand at them. I'm sorry, he says. Excuse me. It's really just a private joke.

EPI
LOG

They gave him this room with a flat standup bed, a chair and toilet and sink, and its own screenwall too. There was only one channel on the wall but they were good programs, cartoons and hunting people and shooting stuff, so that was all right. When he first got there he didn't like it very much and was afraid a lot, thinking there were bad people around who were going to hurt him, and he cried a lot and hid in the corner or yelled at the white doorway for somebody to let him out of there. But whenever they did open the door it was just to take him down to walk around outside with the other kids, around the circle on the sidewalk in the open space in the middle of the building he was staying in somewhere. And he didn't like that either very much.

They didn't like you to talk when you were out there walking around the circle with the other kids, but he didn't really know that at first, and so one day, when he was still not liking it he said to this one kid who had walked close to him a couple of times already and looked back at him something about this one thing he saw on the screen that was neat, a bunch of guys up in space living together and flying around with their space guns, a cartoon. They were going really fast, *whoosh*, he said to the kid and spread his arms out to show him and the other kid was saying Yeah and then, when this lady's hands came down hard on his arms, this lady who was one of the ones who stood out there watching while they walked around, and he started crying right away.

You keep your mouth shut out here, the woman said, holding him still, pinching his arms with her hands while the rest of them went by all looking at him. You hear me, she said.

I want my mommy, he said. How loud he yelled surprised him and made him yell louder. You better show me where she is! You better give her back!

Then a bunch of things happened at once. A whole lot of other kids slowed down and stopped to look and some of them started to cry too, he could hear them, and this woman's face down real close to him, with little black hairs on her chin and lips and the smell of her breathing all over him: I don't know nothing about no mothers and neither does anybody else around here so you just keep quiet about it now or you ain't never coming out here anymore. You hear me now?

And he had to answer right back to her, right into her face whether she was a bad woman or not. Yes, he said, he heard. Then she let him go and didn't do any more to him. But he could see her with her eyes on him just the same.

Sometimes at first he would have these dreams about her too, his mommy, that they were back together walking somewhere or snuggling with his head in her lap, and he would wake up and want her to come back and take him out of there and everything be all right, back like it was. But then after he was crying for a while it got so he just lay there watching it, into it the whole time. He didn't want to go outside and walk around and miss everything that was happening. He wanted to talk to it, be into it all the time. They had to lift him up, make him get off the bed and go walk around and she would be watching him and he would have to try not to cry again.

Then one time they came and made him get up and go down the way out to the circle but then up another way, into a room with a bunch of people in it, standing, the first time he ever saw men there not on the screen, and one of them smiled and talked to him and gave him something to drink in a glass.

When he woke up again he was inside something, moving. The sun was all hot, burning on his face, and the thing he was in was all bumpy, banging up and down. He looked out the open window by him and there was a bunch of houses with people in the windows, everywhere, sitting in front of the houses out in the sun doing things, and big kids ran across the road in front of them, and sometimes threw rocks. There were a lot of kids, everywhere, and some of them didn't have any clothes on, and some of them yelled things he could hear or figure out, but he starts to remember her again, Mommy, Charlotte, and to wonder where they are, if she didn't maybe come here with him once sometime before.

Then, when he turns to the brown man driving like they do on the screen he knows he has seen him too sometime. The brown man looks back at him real quick, then back to the road. He has a big gun with him hooked up to the side of his pants. Maybe they are inside a program, on the screen, on all the screenwalls in the building, with everybody inside watching them. Maybe the ones out there in the funny houses, looking at them, sitting and walking and running around out there are the ones they have to beat.

Keep your head down, shouts the brown man over the noise of them bumping, moving along, and be quiet, or I knock you out again.

So he stays down and listens from there to the bumping, sometimes yelling outside, rocks hitting them sometimes. All there is to see from down here is the brown man. He watches the sweat coming down all over the brown man's face, and the one hand not on the wheel pat the gun hooked up to the side of his pants.

Then all of a sudden they stop. The brown man takes the gun out and points it down at him. At his head, so he is looking straight inside it at the real round dark.

Now you get out very slow, he says. Then you wait for me to come around to you.

So he gets out, stands and waits. They are in front of another house like the ones they were going past before, a white house with green stuff growing up all over in front of it. It has windows too, but empty, without anything in them, nobody and no glass either, and it smells funny. The brown man comes over and presses the gunbarrel into the back of his head. He sees high mountains up over the side of the white house. Inside him saying *Mommy Mommy Mommy* over and over and he starts to cry.

Okay, says the brown man behind him. Now we go inside.

They walk through the green stuff up to the porch. Some of it is as high as him, but if he ran away the brown man would find him and shoot him, dead.

One fonny move, Goodman, yells the brown man, and thees keed gets eet.

There is no door at all. They move in out of the hot sun, into the dark house. He can feel the brown man's hand on his shoulder keeping him against the gun. He goes the way the gun and hand move him, and tries not to let his crying make his head shake back against it. Everything smells strong, dirty. He gags, blinks, starts to try to stop crying to keep from getting any more sick. He sees a chair beside a table, someone in it in torn spotted dirty robe.

Hello, Billy.

It is Ernest, dirty, with hair all over his face.

Hello, Billy says.

How are you? says Ernest. Are you all right?

The crying makes a noise in his throat. He swallows and nods. How are you? he says.

I'm fine, says Ernest, smiling.

He swallows again, hard, and can tell he is not crying any more. Is Mommy here? he says.

Ernest shakes his head. No, she's gone, he says. He opens his mouth like he is going to say something else, but then looks up behind him at the brown man instead.

Hey Paco, he says. How you doing?

Okay, okay, says the brown man behind him. How you, Meester Goodman?

So let me guess what you're here for, Ernest says. They sent you down here with Billy to show they're still in control. They know where I am and they have the boy, and they can get either one or both of us if I don't cooperate. Now, what do I have to do to cooperate?

The barrel shifts to the side of his head, the fingers clamp his shoulder down tight. They send me down here to tell you they con have you any time they won to, lake thees, jes lake—

But Ernest has started to laugh: tossing his head back, laughing, rubbing his hand over his whiskers as the laughter hangs in the still dark air until he speaks again.

Paco my friend, he says, you'll let them fuck you any way, with anything they want, won't you? Don't you think those assholes back there damn well *know* you won't get out of this place alive if you do what you're supposed to do now? As soon as you pull the trigger on that kid you're going to get blown away from two directions at once, thanks to my friends behind you against the wall.

The brown man's fingers dig in harder, he twists to get away, the gun shoves hard against his skull, and he starts to cry again.

Lies, the brown man hisses behind him. Ther ees no one behind me.

Then the hand on his shoulder goes loose, he can hardly feel the gun against his head, he starts moving to the side, away from the gun, from the brown man. Nobody else says or does anything, Ernest and the brown man just stand there looking at each other while he turns and sees the other two against the walls with their guns. The woman looks back at him, smiles and raises her finger up to her lips. Not Mommy, someone else.

You think they need you? Ernest says. You think they give a shit whether you die or not? Any more than they gave a shit about your wife and kids? Any more than—

I don nid to leesten to you! says the brown man, waving the gun now at Ernest. I con keel you right here, right now!

Did you know, Paco, says Ernest, I got away with killing the president of the company? That a bunch of people got me out of there and out of their reach? And helped me get visible again now, to see if I couldn't draw the kid back out? Did you know that, Paco?

The woman has long light hair down all over her shoulders and the back of her old dirty robe. When he is over beside her she reaches down and touches his face. It feels so nice he starts shaking, he almost starts crying again.

Oh Betsy, says Ernest, looking over from the brown man and smiling. I see you've already met Billy. You want to say hello to my friend Paco Ramos here too?

Hi Paco, says the woman he stands beside.

Hello Paco, says the man down the wall, on the other side of the doorway.

The brown man's head jerks from side to side.

You want to go back, you can still go back, says Ernest. You want to spend the rest of your life running stinky little jobs, putting on that sleaze-ball bandito accent, go right ahead. Only you have to see my point, my friend, which is this: out here, out of bounds, they *can't* keep track of us, there's never going to be enough guards or computers for that. Back there, if they don't kill you right away, you still know you're garbage they can throw out whenever they want.

Beside the woman he watches Ernest stand, step forward smiling with his hand held out for the hand with the gun.

So what's it going to be, my friend? Ernest says. Do you go back; or come with us?

Everybody watches, all of them around the room. When Paco puts his gun down on the floor and he and Ernest hug right there, in the middle of the floor, Billy can feel the woman Betsy's long fingers twining in his hair, like a talking he can answer leaning his head rubbing his face against her thigh.

Then, after Paco gave Ernest the gun, they all left right away, and went walking a long time in back of the houses, or right through them sometimes, talking to people, saying Hello, how you doing, and the people just let them go right through, in these houses with no programs and no screens. When he said something about it to Betsy, she laughed and told him, no they weren't on a program either, and later that night when he asked Ernest about Mommy, Ernest told him that Charlotte was dead. And he started crying again because she was dead and the food the people cooked with fire tasted funny and dirty, the way everything smelled, and there were no screens or trans or malls any more and he missed her, he was scared of all those other kids in the houses looking at him when they went through and they had walked too far, he was tired. He kept crying like that off and on all the way there, and they would hold him all of them, Ernest Betsy Steven and even Paco after a while, pick him up on their shoulders as they went and sing him songs or tell him stories sometimes. And at nights, when they stopped, he could stay with Betsy, he could sleep against her side.

Finally, when they got where they were going, it was already better. But Ernest stayed around for a while with him anyway before going away again with his friend William, and with Steven and Betsy and Paco too. But by then he knew a whole lot of different people there, Gary and Tito, Alexis and Zora and Claude, and a whole bunch of grown-ups and kids. Because in those days, by that time, more and more people were coming to stay, everything was really, suddenly changing so much it would be almost impossible to tell you now what it was starting to be like.

Palo Alto, California
Columbia, Missouri
Corvallis, Oregon

Spring 1976 – Spring 1980

Several quotations are given without acknowledgment in this book:

p. 13—"really, strictly speaking, relations stop nowhere" is taken from Henry
James's "Preface" to *Roderick Hudson*.

p. 53—"Each one of us lives his first years . . ." to end of passage, is from *Search
for a Method* by Jean-Paul Sartre, translated by Hazel Barnes.

p. 109—The General Mills Chairman's remark is quoted in *Global Reach* by Richard Barnet and Ronald Muller.

p. 137—"The challenge for the manager . . ." to end of paragraph, excluding the
bracketed phrase, is a quote from *The Manager in the Multinational
Economy*, a graduate-level business textbook by Raymond Vernon,
a Harvard Business School professor.

p. 176—The passage which begins "The use of physiological tests . . ." is quoted
from "In Their Quest for Sure-Fire Ads, Marketers Use Physiological
Tests to Find Out what Grabs You," an article written by John E.
Cooney in *The Wall Street Journal*, April 12, 1979.

p. 197—"Only that which narrates can make us understand" is quoted from Susan
Sontag's *On Photography*.

p. 214—The passage which begins "The primary word *I-Thou* . . ." is quoted from
I and Thou, by Martin Buber. The translation is by Ronald Gregor
Smith.

In somewhat altered form, chapters 2 and 3 appeared originally in *The Missouri
Review*, Vol. VII, no. 2 (Spring 1984).

Editor: Nancy Ann Miller
Book Designer: Matt Williamson
Jacket Designer: Matt Williamson
Typeface: Electra and Serifa
Typesetter: J. Jarrett Engineering, Inc.
Printer: Haddon Craftsmen, Inc.
Binder: Haddon Craftsmen, Inc.

FRED PFEIL is Assistant Professor of English at
Trinity College in Hartford, Connecticut. His
short fiction has appeared in *Ploughshares, The
Sewanee Review, Prize Stories 1979: The O.
Henry Awards,* and elsewhere.